"I know we still have a great deal to discuss"

Phoebe had said while she loosened the knot of her cravat.

"But I think that we'll be able to think more clearly after a short intermission."

Either that, David thought, or we'll be too besotted to be able to think at all.

Swiftly, she unwound the long strip of linen from around her throat.

The cloth slithered down her shirtfront to lie in a heap upon the Persian carpet at her feet. She kicked it to the side, leaned against the door, and settled back for the instant it took him to reach her.

For a moment he merely savored his body's closeness to hers. Only an inch away—he could see the pulse beating in her neck. Gently he dipped his head toward her, tracing the curves and hollows of her flesh with his lips and tongue. He took tiny kisses, nuzzling her throat, licking the long lines of her neck, breatheing her smell until it began to make him giddy.

Also by Pam Rosenthal

THE BOOKSELLER'S DAUGHTER

A HOUSE EAST OF REGENT STREET
(appeared in the anthology
Strangers in the Night)

ALMOST A GENTLEMAN

PAM ROSENTHAL

KENSINGTON PUBLISHING CORP.
http://www.kensingtonbooks.com

BRAVA BOOKS are published by

Kensington Publishing Corp.
850 Third Avenue
New York, NY 10022

All Kensington titles, imprints and distributed lines are available at special quantity discounts for bulk purchases for sales promotion, premiums, fund-raising, and educational or institutional use.

Special book excerpts or customized printings can also be created to fit specific needs. For details, write or phone the office of the Kensington Special Sales Manager: Kensington Publishing Corp., 850 Third Avenue, New York, NY 10022. Attn. Special Sales Department. Phone: 1-800-221-2647.

ISBN-13: 978-0-7582-0444-8
ISBN-10: 0-7582-0444-2

First Trade Paperback Printing: May 2003
First Mass Market Paperback Printing: December 2007
10 9 8 7 6 5 4 3 2 1

Printed in the United States of America

For my mother, Anne Ritterman

Acknowledgments

No one is born a romance writer, but I got a good start: just before I was born, my mother, a lifelong book lover, was wheeled into the delivery room reading *Forever Amber*. Thanks, Mom, for sharing your love of reading with me from the very beginning, and for introducing me along the way to Jo March, the first scribbling woman of my acquaintance.

It's been a long time since then, and almost five years since I first thought I might write a romance novel. During those five years, I've received lots of generous and enthusiastic help. Ellie Ely encouraged me when I wasn't sure whether to continue, read numerous drafts of two novels, and caught countless errors, obscurities, and infelicities both large and small. Thanks to Robin Levine-Ritterman, Barb Levine-Ritterman, Ellen Jacobson, Barbara Schaffer, Jeff Weinstein, Ron Silliman, Krishna Evans, Anne Bard and Amy Bard for ongoing sympathy and encouragement. And to Dr. Jeff Ritterman for information about wounds and dislocations.

My son, Jesse Rosenthal, asked difficult, provocative questions about the romance genre and what I'm doing here; someday I hope to have some definitive answers for him. My husband, Michael Rosenthal, simply did what he always does. As a brilliant bookseller, he finds historical and literary resources I need and have overlooked; with his customary critical energy, he helps me understand and strengthen the structures underlying what I've written. He'll always be my most astute reader—and not just of the words I put to paper.

Romance Writers of America is a treasured resource for anyone who takes it into her head to write a romance novel and needs to learn how. I'm particularly grateful to my local San Francisco Area Chapter for hosting a presentation by Helen Breitwieser, who later became my agent. My debt to Helen is inestimable: not only for her unfailing confidence in me, but for the combination of intelligence, enthusiasm, and hardheadedness with which she expresses it. Thanks also to Kate Duffy and Lisa Filippatos of Kensington for their input to the manuscript.

The first thing a fledgling romance writer learns is that her book must derive its energy from the "conflicts" between its protagonists. In *Almost a Gentleman*, I found my lovers' conflicts in studies by three extraordinary cultural critics. For how a nineteenth century outsider could also be an insider, Ellen Moers's *The Dandy: Brummell to Beerbohm*. For far-from-trivial matters of dress and style, Anne Hollander's *Sex and Suits*. And for the discontinuities between a culture's shining self-image and its darker realities, Raymond Williams's magisterial *The Country and the City*.

Prologue

London, 1819

"Kate?"

The eyes fluttered open in a very white face, surrounded by wild, shining tangles of hair.

Her cheeks are so pale, thought the woman sitting beside the bedstead. *They're whiter than the lace pillow she's resting on. And her eyes are huge against the dark shadows around them.*

She squeezed the hand she'd held for hours while her friend had writhed in tormented sleep. She tightened her grasp, willing a lifetime of love, gratitude, and sympathy to pass through her warm flesh into the slender, icy fingers that clung to hers.

"I'm here, Phoebe. Don't try to talk, darling."

But the white face was composed, the gray eyes focused, the lips wrought so finely they seemed to have been etched with acid.

"I remember all of it, Kate."

"Hush, not now."

The cold fingers squeezed back tightly.

She's strong, Lady Kate Beverredge thought. *Even*

after the horrors of this week. And even after those four dreadful years of marriage.

Phoebe's voice was a bit louder now. Louder and strangely matter-of-fact, as if she were choosing a new fall wardrobe or instructing the gardener to plant zinnias instead of dahlias.

"It doesn't matter, Kate, whether I say it or not. It's true, it all happened, it's not some terrible dream."

"Your brother will be here soon."

"He knows?"

"Not all of it. I wrote to him as soon as I arrived, to tell him there'd been an . . . accident."

The phaeton overturned, the two handsome grays panicked and tangled in their traces. Bryan was thrown from his mother's arms onto the gravel path. One of the horses had reared back . . .

"What date is it today, Kate?"

"September twenty-second, dear."

"I must have slept through Bryan's birthday, the day he would have been three years old."

Kate nodded. *You slept, thank God, with the aid of a powerful dose of laudanum.*

"I sent the cakes to a foundling home." Tears began to trace wavering paths down Kate's pockmarked cheeks. But Phoebe's eyes were disconcertingly dry. She raised dark eyebrows, plucked into a fashionable arch.

"And the baby I lost. It was a girl, wasn't it?"

Kate tried to say *yes*, but no sound came through her lips.

"I would have liked a daughter. But I would have been afraid—ashamed, you know—to let her see how weak I've been, how easily dominated by her silly father. Still, how lovely to have a little girl . . . what a pleasure for me, and what an irritation for Henry. He'd have felt obliged to get me with child again as soon as possible . . ."

"Shhh, darling."

The noise that came from the bluish lips might have been a laugh. But it sounded dreadful, mechanical.

"Oh, he wouldn't have minded. It wasn't his *preferred* . . . mode of gratification, but he could schedule an evening now and again for it. Anything, after all, for the requisite heir and a spare."

Kate shook her head helplessly. "Don't, Phoebe."

"Just this once, Kate."

"All right, dear."

"No, what would really anger Henry would be seeing me all swollen and bloated. Wasted months when he couldn't parade me about during the Season, tricked out like a show pony in satin and kid gloves with twenty vicious little pearl buttons up my arms, diamond bracelets like manacles on my wrists, and that stupid family tiara threatening to topple off my head without so much as a by-your-leave."

Kate nodded slowly, forcing herself to suppress a smile at Phoebe's jaundiced view of life at the center of London's most exclusive circles. Rarely going out into society herself, Kate followed the notices in the newspapers, especially about the *ton's* most celebrated couple. Tall and elegant, young and effervescent, Lord and Lady Claringworth had been the crown jewels of many a glittering dinner party. Kate could well understand how entering a room with a stunningly gowned Phoebe on his arm would have stoked the fires of her husband's vanity.

"He was terribly drunk, Kate. He'd been drunk for days, since he'd lost all that money on a racehorse. They'd laughed at him at his club, his mistress had made eyes at Lord Blassingham—all excellent reasons to torment his wife and child, don't you think? So he went round and got the phaeton, ordered us into it, and drove to Hyde Park.

"I should have refused to go. Or insisted, at any rate, that we leave Bryan at home. But, but . . ." her lower lip trembled, "Bryan was so happy to go anywhere with the papa he so rarely got to see."

She hesitated before continuing. "He drove like a madman. He wanted to make us scream, you see. But Bryan and I were too frightened to scream. So he drove even faster, until he lost control."

Kate thought the tears would come now. But Phoebe's contralto voice—always a surprise how low it was—seemed almost tranquil, as though she'd found some bleak comfort in the word *control*.

"He'll never control us again, Kate. He was a weak, spoiled, arrogant cad. A *little* man really, for all his long legs and fine looks. He was a cur and a coward and he's dead and I'm glad of it. And I'm going to sit up now and you're going to brush the tangles out of my hair."

This time Kate allowed herself to smile, even to rejoice at Phoebe's commanding tone of voice. And to respond, as readily as she'd done for the past twenty years, since she'd been eight years old, shyly returning to school after nearly dying of smallpox.

The other girls had quietly shunned her, frightened, probably, by the ugly pitted skin on her cheeks. But a nasty little clique had taken to taunting her, until Phoebe had boxed the ringleader's ears and proclaimed that henceforth she'd be playing and sharing treats with nobody but Kate—Kate and anybody else, she'd added as a casual afterthought, whom Kate might like to play with.

And because games were no fun without Phoebe, who was taller, faster, and more daring than any of the village boys, Kate had regained her place within the circle of schoolgirls and Phoebe would reign in Kate's heart forever.

"You have such beautiful hair," she murmured, drawing the soft brush through its thick waves. A little long to be quite *à la mode,* it rippled down Phoebe's back, pale chestnut with shivery highlights of champagne.

Phoebe looked thoughtful. "Lately it's seemed to have a mind of its own; sometimes it wants to stand straight up, like a person demanding the respect she's due. If you fetch a pair of scissors from the drawer in that table, we can trim it back a little."

"Right now?" Kate felt a chill as she pulled the drawer open.

"Right now, Kate."

They were heavy shears. "The draper used them," Phoebe explained, "when he recovered the damask chairs."

And while Kate hesitated, Phoebe took the shears from her hand. "Don't worry, dear. I'm not going to plunge them into my breast."

"Of course not. But do let me help you."

"That won't be necessary."

It only took four swift cuts. The thick, shining hair fell to the coverlet like the curtain dropping after a tragedy.

"So simple," Phoebe murmured, "to effect the death of that sham creature, an elegant lady of the *ton.*"

With her hair chopped to an inch below her ears, one could see a resolute jawline. And the shadow of Phoebe's old, mischievous smile. A few golden sparks danced in her gray eyes.

She ran a hand through her cropped hair. A mass of willful curls sprang up in its wake.

"So simple," Phoebe repeated, "and yet so satisfying. Rest in peace, Lady Claringworth."

Chapter 1

London, three years later

"Phizz" Marston wasn't the richest or most notorious of London's dandies. His house, though exquisite, was small and compact as a jewel box, and his *bon mots* didn't take to public recital. His sharp wit was perhaps a bit too pointed to be cherished and repeated throughout the city's salons and clubs.

But Phizz had something else: a cold, unerring eye for style, a deadly instinct for exclusivity. If Phizz proclaimed that something wouldn't do, then it wouldn't, whether that something were the tilt of a hatbrim, a turn of phrase, or the newest aspirant to London's select circles.

Reed-slim and elegant, dressed only in the deepest of blues and blacks, his narrow trousers the palest of fawns, his boots or dancing pumps glowing like flawless tropical ebony, he hovered at the fringes of the most exclusive balls and dinners like a ghost at an ancient abbey.

When he was at his club, White's in St. James's Street, he sat in its most coveted venue: the bow window overlooking the street, where an Olympian race of dandies hurled verbal thunderbolts at the everyday run of humanity passing below.

"I say, did you *see* that coat?"

"And his lady friend's hat?"

"A hat, did you call it? I took it for a slumbering owl."

Luckily, most ordinary mortals were blissfully unaware of the amusement they afforded the languid demigods in their deep leather armchairs. But a few unhappy souls walked by quickly, and only when urgent business made the route imperative. These gentlemen had had the great embarrassment to be blackballed from this most discriminating of clubs. Most often by Marston.

"But why, old fellow?" one or another fellow club member would ask. "After all, he's got manners, horses, money. Well connected, too: dined with His Majesty at Carlton House only last week."

"Because he relies upon his valet to knot his cravat. And deuced ugly and unpleasant knots they are too."

"Oh well then. Doesn't tie his own knots? Truly? But however do you know?"

He'd smile slightly, shake his head, and seal his lips. They trusted him all the more because he never revealed his sources. For once you looked at a gentleman through Marston's lorgnette, so to speak, you began to see subtle flaws in what had hitherto seemed a perfectly fine and acceptable specimen of *ton*. And now that you thought about it, the duke of thus-and-such *did* have a commonness, a boring, striving quality about him, the cut of his trousers or the turn of his cravat not really up to the standard required for a member of White's.

"I've heard that Baron Bunbury is *furious* at you, Phizz. Threatens to absolutely *undo* you. Holds you entirely responsible for his application having been refused."

The two young gentlemen were tracing their way through a particularly unpleasant yellow fog on a chilly Wednesday evening in late autumn. Mr. Marston was in black, Mr. FitzWallace in blue. The Almack Assembly Rooms, "seventh heaven of the fashionable world," were close by in King Street.

"Undo me? Really. But that's rather good, isn't it, Wally? However might he undo me, when I've never been *done* at all? And isn't that just like Bunbury—to think that being a gentleman is a matter of *doing*—rather than of merely, perfectly, and exquisitely, *being*."

No one knew Philip Marston's origins. He'd burst quite suddenly upon the social scene a few years before, and in an instant, it seemed, began to be invited everywhere. When asked about his parentage, he managed to be both scathingly honest and charmingly evasive.

"Oh, frightfully common. Horribly boring. My father the most earnest of vicars, summoned at all hours to minister to the fat local squire in his squat little castle, my mother doing endless good works among the multitudes under their thatched roofs . . .

"Luckily, I was spirited away from all of that quite early, snatched from my cradle by a good faerie of exceedingly discriminating taste."

London had accepted him easily, on his own terms. He conferred an undeniable *je ne sais quoi* on a dinner party or a lady's Thursday at home. His own infrequent parties were small, highly select affairs, limited mostly to his own inner circle: fellow dandies and a few ladies ancient enough to tell a dirty story with finesse. His finances were mysterious: one wouldn't want him courting one's daughter. But he showed little interest in marrying. Or—except for his perfect manners and skill on the dance floor—in women in general. There were occasional rumors of other preferences. But London shrugged and pretended not to notice.

Messrs. Marston and FitzWallace were readily admitted to Almack's. Their subscription tickets to the Wednesday Night Ball—harder to secure than a peerage, it was said, even during the less selective "little" Season of autumn—were snug in their pockets. But nobody asked to see these vouchers; Marston would have been profoundly chagrined to have to prove his right of entry.

He nodded to the ladies of the Almack Assembly committee—Lady Castlereagh, Lady Jersey, Princess Esterhazy, and the cold, officious Dowager Lady Fanny Claringworth, who walked stiffly, with a cane—before leading Mr. FitzWallace on a stroll about the room's perimeter, scanning the crowd with a savage, practiced eye.

"*That* one's just up from the country. Look, her mother's incompetent modiste has concocted just the wrong sort of sleeves for her. They're not only graceless—they pinch, dammit—but they went entirely out of date the second week of last Season. And she knows it: she's got the wit to be embarrassed by her silly gown, and no doubt by her mother's crudeness as well. Ah yes, there's the mother, sniffing up to Lady Castlereagh like a nasty little pug dog. Well, I'll dance with the daughter; she's a bit plain but clearly not stupid. She looks like a decent dancer at any rate. And she deserves a pleasant turn about the floor to fortify her for the rigors of the marriage mart . . .

"Just an hour, Wally. They'll play a waltz soon; I need a bit of exercise. I'll know when it's time to go when I'm so thirsty even the lemonade they serve here will begin to tempt me."

But Marston never touched the bad Almack lemonade, and he shuddered at its worse bohea tea. His nickname—since the heyday of "Beau" Brummell all the London dandies had had nicknames—came from the fact that no one had ever seen him drink anything but the best champagne. It never made him tipsy; he claimed that it ran in his veins.

The orchestra struck up a waltz.

David Arthur Saint George Hervey, eighth Earl of Linseley, groaned as the tinny strains of music wafted across the ballroom.

"Not only," he said to his companion, "have I been obliged to make more polite conversation this evening than I have made in the past six years, but now they play this confounded dance that I could no sooner do than fly."

Admiral Wolfe laughed. "It does seem quite the rage. And very amusing to watch. Perhaps we should learn it, Linseley, if we're serious about this marriage business. The young ladies do seem to like it.

"We could hire a French dancing master, I suppose," Wolfe continued. "Split the cost between us, you know. Try not to laugh as he twirls each of us old duffers about your front hall."

"I should overturn tables and send vases crashing," the Earl of Linseley replied. "Best to bring him out to Lincolnshire into a very large open field, with only the cows to witness my shame."

Wolfe nodded. "I expect one picks it up eventually. Like cricket."

Lord Linseley shrugged. "At forty-one doesn't pick up anything easily. Nor does one adjust to new companionship."

He sighed. "I hadn't supposed that it would be a romantic venue, but I hadn't thought I'd find this ball so reminiscent of a livestock auction. The young ladies are fairly obliged to open their mouths and show their teeth to the bidders. And one has the disconcerting feeling that their mammas have memorized the stud-book—*Debrett's Peerage,* you know."

"Well then," Wolfe said, "*you're* all right, man." The earl's family lineage reached back to within three generations of William the Conqueror.

"While for you they must consult a far more important authority: the accounts of a young officer's heroism at Trafalgar, and a noble naval career ever since. Well, if this is how one shops for a wife nowadays, so be it. I suppose that at our advanced age one would be a fool to expect a bit of inspiration. But I confess that I had."

He peered out onto the floor at the dancers twirling by. Wolfe was right. One probably *could* pick up the rudiments of the waltz with relative ease, certainly with more finesse than some of the gentlemen bobbing about like corks out there.

The steps didn't look so difficult as all that. After all, he was hardly the most decrepit specimen in attendance. At least he still had all his hair, even if its thick black waves were a little grizzled at the sides. He ran a quick exploratory hand down the front of his neat waistcoat, as though expecting a paunch to have settled there since he'd entered the ballroom. No, not yet. Not for some years, perhaps. His belly was flat and hard and he could still feel a satisfying ache in his wide shoulders from last week's planting.

Too bad he'd had to interrupt the farm work he loved in order to come up to London. Voting in the House of Lords was a tedious, infuriating business but a necessary one. Still, he trusted his steward to supervise the remainder of the job. The winter wheat would be planted by an excellent crew of farmhands: honest fellows and their wives, who demanded a decent wage but did at least a decent day's work in return. And who might be robbed of land their families had tilled for generations, if the vote in Parliament went as Lord Linseley feared it would.

He roused himself from his reverie to watch a particularly graceful couple glide by. *Yes, that's how it should be done,* he thought. There was a purity, a concentration to the young man's swift steps, a perfection to the set of his hips and shoulders, joy of movement elevated to art through intense control and mastery. The lady held herself very upright, but one could feel a tiny shudder of surrender in her posture, a willingness to be led. One could see it in the arch at the small of her back, the confidence with which she entrusted her balance to her partner's gloved hand at her waist.

Of course that's how it's done, Linseley thought. It was how all the important things in life were done—from the body's center. It was how you guided a horse over a gate, heaved a forkful of hay onto a wagon, took a woman to bed. This new dance led one's thoughts to lovemaking: no wonder there had been such consternation in fashionable circles when the waltz had been introduced. The couple whirled back into the crowd; losing sight of them, Lord Linseley stared at the space they'd occupied, astonished and rather shaken by the feelings that had seized him.

"Perhaps," Admiral Wolfe observed slowly, "you should ask that young lady to dance."

"Young lady?"

"The one you've been staring at, man. Rather intently—as though you'd found . . . inspiration."

"Ah. Yes. The lady. Perhaps I should. When next they play something I *can* dance."

It would be impossible, Lord Linseley thought, to confess that he'd be hard pressed to distinguish that particular young lady from all the others whirling or promenading about the room in white and pastels. But it wouldn't hurt, he supposed, to invite her to the next quadrille.

If only he could fix her with his eye, get a sense of what she actually looked like. He searched the crowd for the couple who had so moved him.

Suddenly, abruptly, there they were. A quick turn. A flash of exquisitely polished pumps followed by a flutter of gauzy white ruffled skirt. Linseley raised his eyes: the black-clad young man was looking at him over the lady's shoulder. The earl found himself staring back into gray eyes flecked with gold, under straight, rather heavy black brows.

Thank God they'd whirled away again.

Lord Linseley took two glasses of lemonade from the waiter standing at his elbow.

He supposed he'd recognize the lady now: she had reddish hair in curls and a gown that bunched rather oddly at the shoulders. He'd offer her a lemonade, he resolved as he drained the other glass in one unconscious gulp. Lord, he thought, but it's hot in here. He nodded to Wolfe, in silent apology for his abstracted behavior. But Wolfe merely seemed amused, pleased that his friend seemed drawn to someone in this impersonal crowd.

Ridiculous, Linseley thought helplessly. Impossible. He wasn't the sort of man for an exotic passion. But there was no denying that he'd felt something—a bolt of strange cold lightning had flashed through him when he'd returned the young man's gaze. He'd shared his bed for years with one woman, raised a child with her, and helplessly held her hand when she'd died. He'd been prey to romantic infatuation in his youth and energetic libertinism these last few lonely years. But never had he felt anything like the unspeakable emotions that had seized him just now.

He directed a sidelong glance at Wolfe. He'd never asked him, of course, but everyone wondered about sailors, all those months with only men about.

Stop it, David, he commanded himself. *Stop this idiocy at once.* For he would certainly lose his oldest friend if John Wolfe caught the merest whiff of suspicion that David hadn't been in any way drawn to the young lady. He winced, imagining how shocked Wolfe would be to learn that what had roused decent, solid Lord Linseley's attention so profoundly had been the elegant posture and extraordinary eyes of a young man in black.

Nonsense. It must be a trick of the light or the unaccustomed lateness of the hour. Or perhaps that deuced waltz was *simply too erotic for polite society.*

He'd be home in Lincolnshire in a week, to deal with the consequences of the vote in Parliament, back working his fields beneath an innocent wide country sky. He'd be safe, far from this clouded, cynical capital, wreathed in smoke and fog, mired in greed and vanity.

He took a calming breath. The lemonade had cooled his flushed cheeks. The little orchestra was striking up what sounded like a finale. He stood, holding the lemonade glasses in strong farmer's hands that strained the seams of his fine kid gloves. The music crescendoed, crested and stopped.

The waltzing couple stood right before him.

He blinked, recovered his manners if not his senses, and offered the young lady a glass of lemonade.

The young man smiled. "I think you've made a conquest, Miss Armbruster. You've captured the attention of the best dressed gentleman in the room."

And here, sailing into view like a clipper ship, was Lady Castlereagh to make introductions all around. The young lady smiled in pleased amazement (perhaps, she thought, this gown isn't so hideous after all) while David felt as though he were in some odd, unpleasant dream in which everyone including himself was speaking an incomprehensible language.

"You waltz beautifully, Miss Armbruster," he heard himself say. The next thing he knew, she was offering to guide him through the steps when they played another. And he seemed to be assenting, on the condition that they take it slowly and that he be permitted to stop if he felt too much the buffoon.

Mr. Marston remained silent, his eyes slightly veiled, his lips in an ambiguous curve that might, David thought, be a smile. But then again it might not.

Abruptly, David turned toward the young man, only to realize that he'd interrupted Miss Armbruster in mid-sentence.

From the corner of his eye he saw a slightly bewildered Admiral Wolfe move forward to fill the gap in the conversation. Ah well, he told himself, what's done is done.

"Mr. Marston."

"Lord Linseley?"

"I thank you for your compliment a few minutes ago, if compliment it was. But I confess to finding it quite mysterious. I'm a country farmer, you know, and quite out of touch with what a gentleman wears in Town these days."

"And yet, my lord, I called you the best dressed gentleman in the room."

"You did sir, but why?"

Marston knit his heavy black brows before answering slowly.

"I suppose, Lord Linseley, my assessment was inspired by the *fit* of your jacket—its drape about your shoulders—rather than its newness. And of course by the sublime knot in your cravat."

The young man had allowed himself a bit of a smile. How cleanly shaven his cheeks were, David thought. He'd heard that these London dandies spent hours shaving and then tweezing what was left. And that they used the finest soaps and oils. It must be true, for this Marston—this *boy* really—had the most exquisite ivory skin.

But the boy was saying something else now, that David had quite missed.

"Excuse me, Mr. Marston?"

"I asked you, Lord Linseley, how long it took you to knot your cravat this evening."

David laughed and shrugged his powerful shoulders, which were, in fact, quite perfectly encased in his jacket. "How long? I haven't any idea. In fact, I hardly remember doing it at all. My father taught me how to do it years ago, and I haven't given it a moment's thought since."

Marston nodded solemnly. "As I suspected. A *natural,* a spontaneous gentleman. The only one left in England, perhaps. And certainly the only one under the roof of *this* benighted pleasure dome."

Lord Linseley wondered if he were being mocked.

Marston lowered his eyes and bowed slightly from his slender hips.

"A pleasure, Miss Armbruster. And a pleasant evening to you, gentlemen. But I have another engagement this evening. And if I'm not mistaken, that's the opening phrase of another waltz."

He faded into the crowd, while David tried without success to see where he was going, to follow his slender silhouette, the tilt of his dark head above his dazzling high cravat.

Gone.

The Earl of Linseley shrugged, smiled a bit grimly, and held out his hand to the obliging Miss Armbruster.

Chapter

2

Mr. Marston and Mr. FitzWallace dined at their club on turbot and champagne. They made it a leisurely meal; Marston believed that food and drink should always be savored. Luckily, they were able to find a cab with relative ease, and so they entered the opera house just as the curtain rose on the fifth act.

The next venue on their night's prowl was Vivien's, a club devoted to gambling. One *could,* if possessed of enough style, frequent that establishment without sitting down at the tables. And in fact a few prudent gentlemen *did* drift about, sniffing the sulfurous odor of lives being ruined and families destroyed, as old fortunes were lost to clever upstarts. These timid voyeurs were expected, however, to toss a ten pound note onto the center of a table before leaving, in tacit acknowledgment of a good night's vicarious excitement.

What gave Vivien's its particular cachet was the house's custom of bringing out a new deck of cards for every hand. Thousands, perhaps tens of thousands of cards were discarded in the course of an evening, the used bits of pasteboard tossed onto the floor, kings, queens, twos and tens trampled beneath the polished Hessian boots of the knaves who strode through the room.

Marston was a player and not a voyeur, and had been known to remain at the tables until the cards on the floor had piled to the level of his well-tailored knees. He played with calm concentration and just a hint of recklessness, and he usually won enough to put to rest any question about how a vicar's son could afford to live as expensively as he did.

Of course, there were those who wondered whether he was a vicar's son at all. At least one bitter bankrupted gentleman, who had been physically threatened by a moneylender's thugs, suggested that Marston's shadowy origins be investigated: "For all we truly know of him, he might even be a Jew." But nothing had come of it. London continued to be amused and entertained by the young man, if occasionally inconvenienced by his skill at the tables.

Tonight, however, he was barely staying ahead, even as he continued to fortify himself with his preferred refreshment. And so it was a mere two-thirty in the morning when he rose to bid his surprised adversaries a good night and collect his sparse winnings.

At the entryway, he bowed to the two gentlemen just coming inside.

"Mr. Raikes. Mr. Smythe-Cochrane," he murmured. The pair nodded stiffly, almost cutting him but not daring to do so. *Cowards,* he thought as he turned the corner. The gas-lights accentuated his pallor as he made his way back to his house in Brunswick Square.

A ragged beggar called out to him from the shadows.

"'Ere, guv'nor, got ha'penny for a man down on his luck?"

Marston pulled a coin from his pocket.

"Not a ha'penny, old fellow. Too small a thing to hold my wandering attention, don't you know. But here, take this. And better luck to both of us after this night."

It was a golden sovereign.

The beggar gaped. The smell from the few rotting teeth left in his mouth was overpowering. Marston nodded politely and strolled off.

Guv'nor. Marston allowed himself a small, private grin as he savored the word. *I haven't lost my touch,* he thought, *I'm still as good as ever after three years of playacting the gentleman.* London's poor had sharp eyes, and yet this specimen of that beleaguered class had been absolutely taken in.

It was invigorating, enlivening, this power to do and say anything he liked. And best of all was the risk and danger of the late-night gaslit streets.

Marston never worried about whether he'd gulled society people. *That* benighted class couldn't see anything but glamour and social position, style and confident bearing. Glittering gowns and an unsteady tiara were all they'd ever really known of young Lady Claringworth. And after three years they'd grasped nothing of Phizz Marston except for his immaculate dress, style, and bearing. Their shortsightedness made him fearless. For whatever else he might be lacking as a gentleman, Marston knew he had quite enough *ton* to overwhelm any member of the Polite World.

Almost as much, he thought suddenly, as the gentleman he'd met earlier this evening. Lord Linseley, wasn't it? Yes, Lord Linseley, the earl with the perfectly knotted cravat. A formidable man: no matter how he might play the simple country squire, there was nothing simple about his inborn grace, lit by the stubborn glint of intelligence Marston had discerned in his blue eyes.

Beautiful eyes, Marston thought reluctantly. Dark and dangerously beautiful eyes in a strong and chiseled face.

Marston's own face softened for just a moment as something threatened to reveal the identity hidden behind his features. Not yet, he told himself as he let himself in at his front door, I'm not ready to think about Lord Linseley yet. He composed his expression. The two gas lamps flanking the entryway illuminated his face: eyes glittering and opaque, mouth falling back into its accustomed cynical curve; no one watching this personage would have taken him for anything but a fashionable young gentleman.

The butler had gone to sleep, but Marston's valet was waiting up for him, discreetly omniscient, a quiet, steely, gray-haired presence in the evening dimness. Nothing happened in the house in Brunswick Square without Simms's consent.

"There's a . . . guest waiting in the small sitting room upstairs, sir."

Marston raised his heavy brows.

"Thank you, Simms, I'd quite forgotten I'd made that engagement. Arranged things with Mr. Talbot, you know, so that Billy visits twice a week now. I'm becoming quite the domestic animal, don't you think?"

Simms nodded somberly, and Marston immediately regretted his little joke.

Callous of me, I suppose. It's impossible, though, to read his expression. Impossible, even now, to know Mr. Simms's opinion of my late night assignations.

"Shall I send Billy to your bedchamber, sir?" Simms asked.

"In twenty minutes, Simms. I'll ring when I'm ready."

"And you'll want a well-iced bottle of champagne as usual, sir?"

Marston almost nodded. But he stopped suddenly.

"No, Simms, not tonight. A nice pot of tea is what I think I'll be wanting tonight, if it's not too much trouble at this hour."

Simms hid his astonishment smoothly.

But he's been well trained for this job, Marston thought. *All those years of reining in that wild hoyden, Phoebe Vaughan. All his loving patience with her when she*—when I—*insisted upon learning Latin alongside my brother*. Marston grinned, thinking of the minor deceits, the narrow escapes, when dear, trusted Mr. Simms, the very soul of honesty, hid the Latin lessons from Phoebe's mother. For Mrs. Vaughan had been certain that girls would lose what she called their "feminine essence" if they were given anything moderately challenging to think about.

Marston sighed. *Poor Mother. I suppose she was right after all.*

The transformation from Phizz to Phoebe proceeded in well-ordered, practiced phases. First a rose-scented cleansing cream dissolved the dye that darkened the fuzz at her upper lip. Next, the eyebrows: soap and water worked best here. When left unplucked, her brows were quite thick for a lady in any case, but every morning Phoebe made them heavier with pencil.

She began to look quite feminine as she brushed the dyed black hair out of the studied Byronic disarray she produced every morning by dint of repeated struggles with comb, brush, and curling iron. How maddening it was to force every wave and spit curl to appear an act of spontaneous nature. Women's poufs and chignons were far easier to do well, she thought idly; after a day as Marston it was a relief simply to tuck her hair back behind her ears and be done with it.

She'd taken especial pains, when dressing for Almack's this evening, to conceal her small, pretty, shell-pink ears among those poetic torrents of short curls; it seemed to her that she looked a great deal more like a woman with her ears visible. They were startlingly bare and vulnerable now, a fitting complement to the lines her face had begun to relax into, a set of expressions that belonged to Phoebe and not to Phizz.

She'd already draped her black jacket—padded just a bit in the shoulders and around the waist—carefully over a chair back. Mr. Simms (in her mind she still called him *Mr.* Simms) would brush and hang it tomorrow. She peeled her breeches and stockings down her long legs, after stepping out of her pumps regretfully. How wonderfully comfortable men's footwear was: she never tired of the embrace of strong leather about one's feet and legs—so much more civilized than flimsy women's half boots that could cause one to slip and perhaps sprain an ankle on uneven cobblestones.

The waistcoat had a bit of padding too: she was fortunate that Mr. Simms's brother-in-law, Mr. Andrewes, was such a gifted tailor. Mr. Andrewes had prospered under Phizz Marston's patronage—half the dandies in London took their custom to him now.

The cravat and shirt were still a dazzling white, but they bore the faint odor of an evening's exertions and would be sent to the country for laundering tomorrow. As would the muslin bands she now unwound from her small breasts and the slyly designed bit of cushioning she unstrapped from her crotch.

A strikingly beautiful woman, broad shouldered and narrow hipped, stared out at her from the pier glass, naked except for black velvet slippers on long, white, high-arched feet. She'd be thirty on her next birthday—the age when a merely pretty girl begins to fade but real beauty begins to find itself. Many attractive women spend anxious hours in front of the mirror at thirty, but Phoebe barely glanced at her reflection most nights. It took too much effort to create Marston every day: life was too short to spend every minute preoccupied with one's face and body.

And anyway, what good had her graceful woman's body and extravagantly molded features ever done her?

For much of her youth, she hadn't been in the least bit pretty. Until her teens, she'd been gawky, coltish, and far too tall: funny-looking, really, with her heavy eyebrows, square jaw, and too-thick hair that wouldn't be bound by pins or ribbons. Her brother Jonathan had been the handsome one in the family, which was quite all right with Phoebe. It meant that no one expected much from her; she was free to read or ride or climb trees as she chose.

And when, at sixteen, it became time to attend the modest parties that constituted the social season in their remote corner of Devonshire, she'd been sure that no one would want to dance with her. She'd counted that as a blessing, for she and Kate would be left alone to whisper and giggle on the sidelines, blissfully unencumbered by the attentions of clumsy local swains.

It hadn't worked out that way. Astonishingly, the young men had flocked to dance with her, and Phoebe could only glance helplessly at Kate, sitting alone against the wall with a brave, wan smile on her pockmarked face.

She did love to dance, though. And she was good at the reels, quadrilles, and schottisches the little orchestra played. In those years no one had waltzed in their quiet, provincial part of England. Phoebe had heard of the shocking new dance, but she had to wait to try it until she'd arrived in London at twenty-two. For her mother, having belatedly realized that her hoyden daughter had mysteriously become a beauty, had somehow wangled a Season subscription to the Almack Assemblies.

She'd learned the new dance quickly enough; handsome Lord Claringworth had waltzed divinely. Far richer and more worldly than any man she'd known at home, he'd courted her aggressively, deciding that he must have this most exotically beautiful girl of the Season despite the modest dowry she brought with her. Of course, it hadn't hurt that her looks had set off his own so perfectly.

He'd taken her riding in Hyde Park, brought her magnificent bouquets from his family's hothouse, overwhelmed her with compliments and with his knowledge of Town and *ton*. She'd never met anyone like him: surely, she thought, there must be a very grand and substantial person beneath the glamorous exterior. Quietly, she smiled at his jokes and gossip; London was *his* world, after all, and she would have thought it presumptuous to speak out until she'd learned a little more about the Byzantine rules that governed life in exclusive society. Sadly (as it turned out), Henry mistook her prudence for admiration. Misinterpreting her quiet curiosity as humble complaisance, he congratulated himself that she was not only beautiful but awed by his social superiority and quite properly overwhelmed by his attentions.

They were married in a ceremony that the gossip sheets seemed incapable of describing without reference to the tale of Cinderella. The Prince Regent gave the bride away, with all the *ton* crowded respectfully into the grand, marble-pillared atrium of Henry's mother's house in Grosvenor Square. It was the Season's dream wedding, and in just a few short months it transmuted into a nightmare marriage.

Which is quite enough to remember for one evening, thank you, Phoebe cautioned herself as she wrapped her dressing gown about herself. The heavy, unlined silk was cut very simply. Its style and color were ambiguous: the pale pink might be too delicate even for the exquisite Marston, but there was nothing feminine in its austere detailing, gray satin piping outlining graceful lapels that met in a deep V at the apex of her breasts. The dressing gown didn't need to signal femininity: the body and face of its wearer were clearly those of a woman, even if her cropped hair created a provocative, slightly ambiguous effect.

But why am I gawking at myself in the mirror, Phoebe wondered, like a silly young girl in her first ball gown?

She knew the answer all too well. It was simply a matter of admitting it to herself. She gazed ruefully at her dressing gown, at the hard, erect nipples grazing their sensitive points against the silk's underside. Absently, she ran her hands over the smooth fabric while her mind struggled to understand what her body had grasped with infuriating readiness.

That gentleman tonight. The one with the dark blue eyes and lovely shoulders. The first man since Henry . . . no, not Henry—I was too young and foolish truly to feel anything when I met Henry. No, better to be completely honest and then to forget this nonsense. Tonight I met the first gentleman ever . . . to make me feel, to make me want *to feel like a woman.*

Abruptly, she dropped her hands from her bosom, clenching them until her fingernails bit into her palms. She welcomed the pain, grateful to be distracted from the waves of erotic sensation that had threatened to overpower her.

There will be no more of *that*, she cautioned herself.

Because in *that* direction lay disaster. The success of this past three years' masquerade lay precisely in the fact that she *didn't* feel like a woman. She didn't stand or sit or act like a woman because she didn't *want* to feel like a woman. Not ever again.

Oh, her disguise was clever enough; she'd done a good job of turning her unusual looks into those of an exquisitely well-realized dandy. But the icy heart of Phizz Marston pumped champagne instead of blood because its possessor refused to feel what was buried deep within it—the humiliation of having submitted to a spoiled, stupid husband, the agony of losing a beloved child.

She was so convincing as a man because she didn't ever want to be a woman again. And no handsome sunburned earl just up from the country would stop her from living the daring, eccentric life she'd chosen.

She rang the bell. Poor Billy, I've kept him waiting too long already.

Lord Linseley had left the ball early. The waltz lesson had gone rather better than he'd feared; he supposed that he could negotiate his way about the floor if ever called to do so at a cousin's wedding or some similar festivity.

He didn't know if he'd be returning to Almack's, though. Lonely as he was, and in need of female companionship, David doubted that the London marriage mart was the way to find it.

He'd had a drink with Wolfe at their club, fixing himself another, back at his town house.

And another. The hours had ticked by, the fire had almost burned itself out, but David made no move to rouse himself from his armchair and take himself to bed.

The trouble, he told himself, was that life with

Margery had been all too comfortable. It had been the perfect life, perhaps, for a man who wanted sex, companionship, and understanding—but who had been oddly wary of love.

She'd been an innkeeper, a pretty young widow when they'd first met. There'd been a storm, he hadn't been able to get home to Linseley Manor that night. He'd never stayed at the Red Boar Inn before, but he was impressed by its cleanliness and by the quality of the kidney pie she served him on short notice; all the other diners had been abed when he'd arrived.

Her cook had gone to bed as well; she'd been too kind and fair an employer to wake him. She'd heated up the kidney pie herself, serving it up with some good ale. She'd been blond and buxom and freckled, pretty in a country way, still ripe and desirable at twenty-five. And as lonely as he was, for all her energy and good cheer. Her husband had died the year before, she told him when he'd invited her to join him in a second mug of ale. She'd been running the inn by herself. It was a good business and kept her too occupied to feel sorry for herself. Except sometimes, late at night.

Yes, I know what you mean, David had responded. He'd been busy too, fairly overwhelmed by work and responsibility since he'd come into his property. He liked farming—he was lucky to have wonderful lands, a good steward and excellent tenants. But sometimes he wondered if he were up to it. He was only twenty-one, after all. Sometimes, during the lonely late nights, wrestling with the accounts and wondering whether to plant or leave a certain field fallow, he feared that he'd make terrible mistakes, go into debt or disgrace his family in some horrible way.

Well, you'll marry soon, she'd told him. No problem there anyway, a rich, handsome boy like you. All the local gentry must be after you for a son-in-law.

He'd shrugged and sighed. He'd had a shattering youthful romance a few months before and was still cherishing his early heartbreak and passionate vow never to marry. He didn't say any of that, though—perhaps, he thought now, because she would have laughed at his childishness.

What he did do was make love to her until dawn, in her own large warm feather bed. He'd returned a few days later. And a few days after that. She had to caution him not to make so much noise in bed—she ran a decent inn, after all, and not a bawdy house. So sometimes in warm weather they went out into the fields; she'd pack a magnificent basket of food, they'd spread a blanket, he'd make all the noise he wanted and so would she.

It was on one of those summer excursions, David was sure, that Alec had been conceived.

He'd proposed marriage when she told him she was carrying his child, but she refused him gently. Thank you dear, she said, but I'm happy with my own business, you know, and I wasn't really raised to be a countess after all. And as for the child, well, I know you'll help if we ever need anything, not that I'm worried about providing.

He'd been chagrined; rejection is hard for any young person, particularly one who believes in doing the decent thing. He persisted, though, making his fair and logical case until he wore her down. The laws of inheritance brooked no compromise: if she delivered a son, that son must be a legitimate one in order to inherit the peerage. And didn't she want the best for their child? he asked. Not simply wealth, but a chance to help decide the affairs of the country.

Finally, she capitulated. They were married in a secret ceremony several parishes away, less than a week before Alec's birth. David's family—he'd confided in a few old uncles—had been furious.

And yet it had all worked out quite well. Margery had continued as innkeeper, and Alec had been a cheerful, loving, extremely intelligent child who'd understood very early that his parents came from different worlds. His large, greenish eyes—Margery's eyes—seemed to consider this fact judiciously, and to conclude that it was, on the whole, a good and interesting thing. And as he came to reasoning consciousness, it appeared that he'd accepted his situation quite happily.

Both Mummy's and Papa's different houses were fun in their own ways, Alec had remarked when he was about three years old. Papa's house was bigger, of course, and full of funny old suits of armor. But you never knew who'd come visiting at Mummy's house. And, he'd added (with a quick glance at David to assure himself that he wasn't hurting his feelings), the food was better at Mummy's. By which time it seemed clear to David that Alec knew that—each in their own ways—both Mummy and Papa loved their little boy quite delightedly and unreservedly.

They agreed on most things having to do with his upbringing. Though Alec lived with his mother until he was ten, Margery had consulted David about all the important decisions. They agreed that Alec's welfare was more important than either of their desires or prejudices. And so, tearfully, Margery agreed to send him to Eton, where he'd suffered a rough first month from some beastly little snobs before becoming generally accepted, partially through the use of his fists—David had taught him to box—and partially through his own sunny self-confidence.

Margery wanted him to have every advantage David could afford to give him, and she feared that Alec might find her common some day, or be ashamed of his lower-class origins. Happily, he never did. He'd been devoted to his mother until she'd died five years ago from pneumonia.

He was at Cambridge now, wrestling enthusiastically with natural philosophy. David regretted not having more children, but if you had to have only one, Alec was an excellent one to have. Lately, though, he'd begun to feel awfully old when thinking about this son, suddenly almost an adult and a scholar as well. Alec used his own title now; the young Viscount Granthorpe was beginning to be invited to balls and house parties. Young ladies paid attention to him, for he'd inherited David's rugged looks along with Margery's large light eyes. He'd gotten David's height, too, and even a bit more: on his last visit home he'd measured an inch taller than his father.

David missed Margery terribly, though he knew that they'd never been passionately in love. Two lonely people in need of companionship, they'd bonded together to help each other through life's challenges. Two sexual beings in need of pleasure, they'd always enjoyed each other's bodies. Two well-ordered, highly responsible people, they'd met regularly for twenty years, to hold each other through the night, refreshing themselves for their daily responsibilities: hers to her business, him to his lands and the people of his district.

It had never really been a marriage, David thought, except in a strictly legal sense. But it had been better than a great many marriages he knew, for it had been based upon mutual respect and admiration—and upon a shared love for a beautiful child. Margery's death had left a huge gap in his life, but David was wise enough to know that you couldn't easily replace such an arrangement,

For a while, a few years ago, he'd tried buying sex.

Not back home, for he couldn't rid himself of a stiff-necked notion that to do such a thing in his beloved Lincolnshire would be to wreak some obscure violence upon Margery's memory. No, he'd come up to London for it, during a winter when the vile weather would have kept him inside anyway.

It had seemed the sensible thing. London was the world's center for buying and selling: stocks and bonds, securities and futures (what odd, homely names the money men gave to the abstractions they traded in!). Brokers and solicitors prospered and grew fat on other people's greed, aspirations, and desires. You could buy anything if you knew where to find it.

At first, innocently, he'd tried the streets, where youth and beauty could often be gotten cheaply. But the streets were dangerous. Better to stick to the network of procurers who catered to the needs of the Polite World, cold-eyed men and women who made it safe and easy for you, while pocketing most of the money that passed from hand to hand.

He'd spent a few uncharacteristically wild months indulging himself in the pleasures these transactions had brought him. A veritable harem of girls had passed through his hands—each very nice in her way, he thought, and some, the more expensive of them, offering quite interesting specialties. All in all, he'd quite enjoyed the interlude. The girls had been good at what they did and of course he'd tried to make things agreeable for them in return. Perhaps he'd been naïve, but it seemed to him they'd rather liked him.

But after a while he'd grown bored with it, coming, on the whole, to prefer the challenge of connecting a likely girl with better, less damaging work. The procurers had come to hate him; many refused his custom after he'd convinced one of the highest-priced girls in London to leave the business and accept a situation at an inn between Lincoln and London. A brilliant cook and hostess, Alison had not only made the inn's fortune, but had wound up marrying its proprietor. David had given the bride away, at about the same time that he'd concluded that he was more reformer than roué and had ceased going to London for sex.

No, he had to marry. Marry and perhaps even father some more children. Why not? He wasn't too old for it. It would be agreeable to fill the echoing halls and bedrooms of Linseley Manor with noisy, busy new life. Although he sometimes still dreamed of a romantic love—he'd never quite outgrown the misty chivalric fancies of his adolescence—he doubted that such a thing would come to him: somehow it seemed too late for that. But he thought he could offer some likely lady a good enough life. Devotion, decency, fidelity, and a measure of physical pleasure ought to be enough to promise a future countess of Linseley.

He'd intended to begin searching for the lady this evening. The Almack Assemblies were certainly the most practical way to meet prospective brides: the *Beau Monde*'s trade in marriageable flesh was as efficiently and heartlessly managed as the traffic in less respectable flesh conducted at its fringes. The only trouble was . . .

But here he stopped, yawned, and glanced at the clock. Absurd, it was after three in the morning. In the country he often woke at four.

Confess it, David. You've spent hours avoiding the crux of the matter.

The *only trouble* was that if he attended the next Almack ball he might encounter that young man again.

Marston.

He stared into the low fire, but what he saw among the brilliant reds and yellows, the dead-white embers and tiny hot slivers of blue flame, was the proud set of a young man's torso, the energy rising from his hips and waist. And a pair of hungry gray eyes with strange golden lights in them.

I think he wanted me as much as I wanted—as I want—*him. And we could both burn in hell for it.*

Of course, such liaisons happened all the time, at least in London. David had heard the rumors about Lord Crashaw, who would be his chief rival in Parliament later this week. Too bad you couldn't discredit a gentleman's political arguments on the basis of his sexual preferences. Well maybe it's not so bad after all, he thought with a wry turn to his mouth, if it turns out that I share the same sinful desires.

But desire was one thing. Action was quite another. And David knew that he'd never act upon whatever it was he'd felt for the young gentleman—even if he'd quite understood what one actually *did* under the circumstances. After all, he thought, life presents opportunities for many different sorts of desire. One simply learns to control one's feelings and move on, as he had when he'd ceased using prostitutes.

And it wasn't as though he'd be running into Marston every day in London. Those dandies had their own haunts, their own paths through Town. Fascinating ones, perhaps, but not David's. They certainly weren't interested in debating the future of British agriculture, for example.

And now it *was* time to go to bed. He'd sleep until noon, he told himself, and then he'd spend the entire afternoon on his speech. Crashaw was a decent orator: a fat, slow-moving gentleman, he used his bulk to put force and presence behind his orotund rhetoric. Somebody needed to make the opposing arguments with clarity, and with all the eloquence and persuasiveness that this critical issue required.

And if, next time he came to Town, he wished to attend another of those assemblies at Almack's, he'd certainly go. He'd go wherever he pleased, dammit.

Because it would be craven, silly, and an insult to his own self-respect to let a strangely attractive young gentleman stop him.

Chapter 3

Phoebe had been as gentle as she could when she told Billy that she wouldn't be requiring his services this evening. But his pretty face fell nonetheless, his sunny blue eyes wide and stricken.

Quietly, he asked her if he hadn't pleased her on his last visit.

"Of course you did, dear," she protested. "Oh bless me no, it's not on *your* account that I'm refusing." Hardly. Billy was tall and well built, with a seraph's face atop a strong, column-like neck and plowman's torso. And he was obedient as well: skillful, compliant, and eager to please.

A gentleman need only send a note to Mr. Talbot's discreet establishment and Billy—or someone equally lovely—would be delivered to his doorstep like a well-wrapped Christmas present.

Phoebe had learned about Mr. Talbot from cronies at White's. As such topics were discussed largely through hints, winks, and innuendo, it had taken her a while to master this private coded language. She bent her skills to it, though, and had finally come into possession of one of Talbot's pasteboard business cards, along with an assurance that the boys were clean and healthy.

"And I take it he's to be trusted with one's silly secrets—those absurd tastes and habits, don't you know, that make life bearable," she'd murmured, flipping the card through her long fingers. Her voice sounded offhanded enough, she thought, if a bit distracted.

"Make life bearable, that's a good one, Phizz. Oh, yes, he's most trustworthy, entirely discreet. Well, he wouldn't have any custom if he couldn't keep a secret, would he?"

Still, it had taken her some months to summon the courage to visit the address listed on the card. The venue proved unexceptional; most of the building's occupants seemed to be solicitors. And Talbot did seem trustworthy, if unpleasant. He'd reacted to Phoebe's terse disclosure of her sex with only the faintest of nods, letting heavy lids fall over colorless, reptilian eyes, and then quoting her a price that she suspected was approximately double what he'd charge a "normal" client.

She'd been terribly nervous as the night of Billy's first visit approached. Receiving him in her bedchamber, she adopted a coldness of demeanor that should have intimidated him, but to which he responded with exquisite sweetness and docility. Still costumed as Marston, she'd told him to undress for her. She'd sat in her big armchair, feet resting on the ottoman, directing commands at him: "Slowly, slowly, that's better. Now bend, turn, a little more to the right, boy. Stop now, and open your legs. Ah, yes, very nice indeed."

She'd felt encouraged that he seemed to enjoy performing for her. Her imperious tone of voice might perhaps have masked her nervousness, but there was no hiding the desire she felt, nor the evident pleasure he took in it.

Finally she'd risen from her chair and instructed him to undress her.

For a moment she'd feared that she might disappoint him. But, after a gasp of astonishment, he grinned so broadly and embraced her so enthusiastically that she let go her fears and simply let things take their own delightful course.

Billy wasn't in his line of work by choice or preference. Mr. Talbot had a standing arrangement with the constabulary to inform him when they'd picked up a likely candidate. And so a pretty young pickpocket or street tough might avoid prison if he were willing to be of regular service to wealthy gentlemen of a certain persuasion.

It wasn't a bad life, Billy had told Phoebe after they'd gotten to know one another better. It wasn't his first choice, of course, but there were worse things than having it off with gentlemen. What rankled was that he and the other boys did all the work while Talbot pocketed the money.

"But when I saw that you *wasn't* no gentleman," Billy had added, "well then, miss, I thought I'd died and 'ad gone directly to heaven."

He did everything Phoebe might want—how extraordinary, she'd thought at first, to have this beautiful young creature completely at her service: hands and mouth and the eager, pulsing member that grew so magically at her touch.

He seemed to have an instinct for pleasing. Which was fortunate, for sad to say, now that she was free to take what she wanted from a man, she'd quickly discovered that she didn't exactly know what that was. *Her* enjoyment, after all, had been the furthest thing from Henry's mind. In fact, the few times that he'd chanced to satisfy her he'd seemed oddly fearful of her response, as though erotic pleasure were somehow spoiled by sharing it.

It wasn't as though he hadn't spent time in her bed, especially during the first year of their marriage. He'd been an energetic, dutiful husband, she supposed, acquitting himself quickly, successfully, and with reasonable frequency. In return, meanwhile, she'd become quite expert in giving him what he wanted. Obscurely troubled by her moments of enjoyment, what he'd truly demanded from her was gratitude. She'd soon enough learned to feign this; a long sigh and a bit of rolling her eyes did the trick nicely.

Poor Henry, she'd surprised herself by thinking one night as she cradled a sweetly sleeping Billy in her arms; it was the first sympathetic thought she'd had for Henry in years. But how sad it had been, she thought. How strange, how *unnatural* his insistence upon segregating satisfaction from affection, copulation from caring. As she learned more about pleasure and desire, she began to wonder if he'd been abnormally lacking in emotional capacity. Had he been dreadfully hurt by someone before she'd met him? Or was he, on the contrary, simply an ordinary exemplar of his type? Perhaps all men were as fearful, as dead to human connection as her husband had been.

Of course *Billy* wasn't that way, but Billy was hardly more than a boy, only recently grown into possession of a man's beautiful body. And Billy had no choice, she thought, but to take what pleasure he could wherever he could. For he was in no position—*ah, but there's your answer,* she told herself. *Position.* Social priority and power. Money, property—the unnatural but perfectly legal freedom to rule and to exploit—perhaps it was these things that numbed a man to the warmth of shared touch.

It was a decent hypothesis anyway, and she hadn't

yet encountered a gentleman among the *ton* who seemed to present a convincing counterexample. Meditating on this alienation from human connection, she'd come increasingly to model Marston's coldness, self-regard, and empty perfection of style upon it.

She'd become quite enthralled by these matters. How interesting the human sexual animal was, she'd thought—until a few weeks ago when Billy had come to her with welts and bruises on his body, and her rather abstract fascination had given way to the most concrete rage and horror.

Absurdly—since it had been he, after all, who'd suffered the pain—she'd burst into tears at the sight of the livid marks on his back and buttocks.

"But that's what lots of 'em wants from us, miss," he'd told her, gently drawing her into his arms. "Them that don't want to be punished themselves. It's just the luck o' the draw, you know, that you ain't seen me this way before."

"But . . . why?"

Stroking her hair and kissing away her tears, he'd patiently explained to her about the vagaries and varieties of human desire. She'd been abashed at how much she still had to learn from a barely-grown, hardly literate ex-pickpocket.

"Well, they enjoy it, you see. Why not, takes all kinds, don't it? Ain't nothing wrong with enjoying a thing, if the other fellow does too. Rather like going to a show, full o' thrills and danger. Only you two is the show."

"Do *you* enjoy it?"

"Ain't my style, miss. No, I hate it. Ain't no thrill to me when somebody takes a whip to my back. But it ain't me wot's doin' the paying, innit?"

Mr. Talbot had laughed when she'd asked how much it would cost to buy out Billy's arrangement with him.

"More than *you've* got, *Mister* Marston. The boy's a gold mine."

Phoebe breathed a long, steady breath. It would demand some strength of character to maintain Marston's sangfroid while that calculating laugh rang gratingly in her ears.

"All right, then, sir. Let's see what I *can* afford."

Finally they'd worked out a new arrangement. Billy would visit twice a week (at even higher rates) and Mr. Talbot would make a serious effort to honor Mr. Marston's delicate sensibilities by keeping the boy's skin unmarked.

"No promises, though. My rule is that they can do anything they like to my boys, short of bruising the face or injuring the working parts, so to speak.

"But if Jamie or Jo is otherwise occupied, Billy goes where he's wanted, no questions asked, and it's the customer's right to make forcemeat of him if that's his pleasure. Business is business, so to speak. And *my* business is your pleasure, eh, Marston? Particularly as it's none of my business what *your* particular pleasure might be. You do follow my logic, don't you, *Mister* Marston?"

She'd followed it precisely, especially the threat to her privacy. But it didn't matter. Nothing mattered except that she'd done what she could for Billy—even if (though she tried not to think about this) it probably meant putting more of a burden on the other boys.

So far it had worked. Billy hadn't been subjected to any more beatings from his other customers, and he'd made it delightfully and abundantly clear how happy he was to be in her bed twice a week instead of once.

The irony of the situation, though, was that she'd come to need him rather less these days. For now that she knew a bit more about what she liked, Billy's visits had lost some of their charm: an element of surprise, perhaps, or of complexity. She still enjoyed taking her pleasure from a skilled and willing provider—England, she thought, would be a far happier place if every woman in the realm were granted one night a month with someone like Billy.

But sometimes she thought there must be something more to this lovemaking business. Something a bit daunting, perhaps—for she suspected that what she wanted would mean giving away a measure of control—but something beautiful as well.

Of course, *she* would never again give up any measure of her inner self to any man. She'd been too deeply hurt, too absolutely emptied of trust and innocence. But she suspected that there were women who'd been luckier. They might be the most ordinary, hard-working, down-at-the-heels women, whose skin had never known the touch of satin, whose heads had never rested on lace pillows. But she was sure that such women existed—sometimes she liked to imagine that she saw one hurrying by in the street, eager to get home to a husband who desired and cherished her.

It made her oddly happy to think that there were women who had what she lacked. Somehow she needed to believe in a city of secret nighttime lives, mysterious and darkly beautiful in ways she couldn't even begin to divine.

She roused herself from these meditations.

"But what I *would* like, Billy," she said, "is for you to rub my feet. Rub them hard. I've been out waltzing tonight."

She poured herself a cup of tea and abandoned herself to Billy's strong, patient hands. He had a lovely touch—sleepily, she considered taking him to bed after all. But when she closed her eyes, taking deep slow breaths as her muscles revived under his pulling and tugging, it wasn't Billy's face or body that filled her inner vision.

" 'Oo's the gen'leman, miss?" Billy asked quietly as he finished up the massage with a few long, gentle strokes.

"What, Billy?"

"None of my business, of course, miss, but in my line of work we get to know that sort of thing. People hire us, sometimes, to pretend we're somebody else entirely. It ain't hard to tell, you see, when they've got somebody else in mind."

"I see. Not very kind of them, is it?"

"They ain't very kind to us most times, as you know, miss. Don't understand it myself, why they think there's got to be something mean and sneaky about it."

"Poor Billy. Have some tea, dear."

"Thank you, miss, I believe I will."

Mean and sneaky. For a moment she thought again of Henry. Both she and Billy had suffered from the same sort of stunted, exploitative sexuality, though she wouldn't tell Billy that; some things were simply too difficult, too intimate to be spoken. She wouldn't know how to give voice to certain truths—for example, that when she'd wept at the sight of Billy's welts and bruises, she'd been weeping for herself and the humiliations of her own marriage.

Or that when she'd closed her eyes this evening, it had been Lord Linseley's face and body that had appeared in her imagination.

Foolish of her, she thought. She knew nothing of him; they'd spoken briefly, trivially. And yet her memory seemed to bear an indelible seal—a profound impression of massive shoulders and thick waves of black hair just beginning to be tipped with gray. Of eyes the color of a warm night sky and a rich laugh rumbling from deep within him.

He'd laughed kindly at her foolish witticism about his cravat. She'd liked the sound, its large-spiritedness, its comfort and sensuality. And then he'd gone unconcernedly on his way. By now he'd doubtless completely forgotten about her.

Might the Earl of Linseley be an exception to Phoebe's hypothesis—did he constitute the one case that would logically disprove her theory about gentlemen and their crabbed emotions? Could he be easy enough with his prerogatives that he wouldn't need to impose power upon those weaker than himself? Might he want more from a woman than servility and gratitude?

Well, *she* would never find out. Never have the opportunity. Just as well, she thought. She intended to forget about him. Utterly and completely. Starting right now.

She raised her eyes to Billy's patient face.

"Have any of your customers been physically cruel to you—or to the other boys—lately?"

"Not to me, miss, though I can't say the other boys have been so lucky. But we've been sharing some new tricks, see. Ways to distract 'em, you know. There's one, Lord Crashaw, used to like to take a riding crop to me—and *hard*, too, damn 'is eyes, made me scream, he did. But then one night I discovered it excited 'im when I blacked 'is boots for 'im. I'm all naked, see, and down on my knees rubbing away and twitching my arse; 'e made me finish up the polishing with my tongue before 'e turned me around to get onto 'is own business with me. Well, it was silly, but I didn't mind. All in a night's work, you know. And it worked last night, good as gold, for Jamie too. 'E didn't get walloped at all, though his tongue ain't a pretty sight, I can tell you."

No wonder Crashaw's boots never had a proper shine to them, Phoebe thought. The sight of Billy or Jamie lapping at his toes must make him too impatient—"to get onto 'is own business," as Billy put it.

She smiled grimly. So Crashaw liked to use the riding crop, did he? And *hard*—hard enough, damn his eyes, to make Billy scream.

Well, Lord Crashaw would scream too, with rage and chagrin—after his recent application for membership in White's was rejected.

"What sort of boot polish did he make you use, Billy?"

Billy shrugged, clearly surprised by the question.

"Think, dear. See if you can remember."

"Well I *think* . . . I think it's Drumblestone's: yeh, it's Drumblestone's Bargain Blacking."

Phoebe's smile widened into a triumphant grin. Drumblestone's indeed. Well, you couldn't blackball a gentleman from an exclusive club for cruelty to boy prostitutes. And nobody at White's cared that Crashaw intended to pauperize half the farm hands of Lincolnshire by pushing this next Enclosure Act through the House of Lords later in the week.

But it would be an easy matter to deprive him of the club membership he craved. One need only draw attention to his badly polished boots—and make it generally known that proud, supercilious Lord Crashaw was personally so cheap that he used Drumblestone's Bargain Blacking.

"Thank you, Billy," she repeated.

She took his strong hand and kissed it gently. "And now you must leave me to get some rest. All right, dear?"

He smiled regretfully, for he'd clearly hoped that she'd want a bit of a cuddle at least.

But he could see that her mind was made up, about

the cuddle anyway. A darting look of anxiety flashed through his eyes.

"Good night," she said. "Have sweet happy dreams and take good care of yourself until I see you this coming Saturday. Quite as usual."

His smile of relief was like a benison. "G'night, miss," he said.

He paused at the door of the bedchamber and turned to her. "Begging your pardon, miss, but I 'ope the gen'leman you've been thinking of is a good sort, one what's . . . what's worthy of you."

Phoebe stared at him.

"Yeh well, g'night," he repeated.

He paused once more, his lovely face clouded and thoughtful.

"And do be careful, won't you, miss?"

Chapter 4

"Damn his eyes," Phoebe muttered as she scanned the newspaper at her noontime breakfast a few days later.

Badly polished boots notwithstanding, Crashaw had prevailed in the House of Lords. The special meeting had voted; the common lands in the north of Lincolnshire were to be enclosed—given over to private ownership. The opportunities for quick profit would be stupendous, the newspaper said, with the vast majority of the benefits going to a few large landowners, chiefly Crashaw himself.

And the small farmers of the region? The newspaper was noncommittal as to their fates, mentioning only that they'd have to depend more heavily on the employment of the large property-owners, since they wouldn't be permitted to grow their crops or graze their few animals on the former commons.

And some of them will have to leave their homes altogether, Phoebe thought bitterly, to seek employment in the textile mills. Indeed, the newspaper commented that many of Crashaw's supporters had financial interests in that industry and hoped the surplus of cheap new labor would drive down wages.

She took an uncharacteristically messy, ungentlemanly sip of coffee.

"And damn these Enclosure Acts as well."

She was only glad that thus far these baleful developments hadn't spread to Devonshire.

Not that her own family would have been directly affected. Like Phizz Marston's mythical progenitor, Phoebe's late father had been a country clergyman; her brother Jonathan had inherited the position and its slender living. Jonathan took his duties seriously and he and Phoebe had had long discussions about the economic livelihoods of his parishioners.

Phoebe had been following the progress of the Enclosure Acts for years; the newspapers had been reviewing them since she'd come to London. Her mouth took a wry turn now as she remembered the first time she'd tried to discuss the subject with Henry.

It had been at breakfast, early in their marriage, before she'd learned to discern the signs of one of his violent hangovers.

That morning she'd been too involved in her reading to notice his red eyes and the slight puffiness distorting his aristocratic features. She'd been far too infuriated by the newspaper's account of a recent parliamentary debate.

What selfishness, she'd thought. What shortsightedness on the part of the gentlemen who ran the nation's affairs. And she'd been amazed that Henry didn't seem to understand how important this matter was to the health and welfare of the countryside.

Innocently, she'd tried to explain it to him.

"And so you see, Henry, some of these big farmers think they'll make more money if they take over those tracts of land the common people have been using for so many generations. They want to turn their farm-hands into nothing but wage laborers, with no property, no resources of their own, no independence.

"They're absentee landlords, for the most part, the gentlemen who are voting for these stupid laws. They spend nearly all their time in London and know nothing of the land or the people who actually do the farming.

"And they don't understand that the best worker is a proud, independent one, rather like a woman who has her own independent intellect . . ."

It had been then, as she remembered it, that Henry had slapped her. Then and there, under the chief footman's bland, respectful gaze. In fact, as she remembered it, Trimble—one of the servants Henry had brought with him from his mother's home—had looked on with a certain quiet approbation, as though a slap from the master were long overdue and no more than what his upstart of a wife deserved. And—or had she imagined this?—he'd sneered when she'd lifted her hand to her cheek. Yes, she was sure of it: it had happened very quickly, but it had, nonetheless, happened. Her servant—no, her *husband's* servant—had bared long grayish teeth at her, taking his moment of pleasure from the spectacle of her powerlessness.

Of course Henry had apologized. And that afternoon she'd found her boudoir full of splendid pink roses, with a diamond and ruby bracelet wrapped around the tallest stem.

She'd worn the bracelet to the opera that night, and had arranged some of the roses in her hair.

The slap hadn't left a mark. The pink roses were lovely against her ivory skin. She'd looked young, gay, innocent.

Well, it's nothing, she'd told herself. *He simply needs a bit of quiet, the morning after a late night out. And after all, I* can *be a bit of a bluestocking at times. Hasn't mother always told me that? Men hate it, she says, and I guess she's right.*

And so she'd given up newspapers and political conversation at breakfast. Henry purchased subscriptions to several fashionable lady's magazines: it was terribly important to him that she be elegantly dressed. She owed it to herself and her beauty, he told her. And to him and his position as well, he'd add in a slightly frosty voice, mornings when Trimble would bow respectfully and hand her the latest installment of *Ackermann's Repository* or *The Lady's Monthly Museum*.

Phoebe spent many weary breakfast hours poring over fashion plates while Henry monopolized the newspaper, sometimes reading aloud to her from the gossip pages. He always opened to that section first, to find out who had been invited to the most exclusive events—and more importantly, who had not. It didn't take Phoebe long to realize that he hated politics, found it boring, intimidating, and far less important than the latest society news and horseracing results.

And that nothing in the world was more loathsome or frightening to him than "a woman with her own independent intellect."

It had taken her a bit longer to understand that her handsome, sociable husband had the worst absentee voting record in the House of Lords. And that when he did vote, he did so frivolously, or to gain points with gentlemen who were richer than he was.

It had been a year later, after her confinement with Bryan, that she'd learned there was only one matter upon which he was sure to vote a consistent *yea:* that of enclosing common farmlands.

She and Henry had been to a brilliant reception at his mother's. She hadn't wanted to be there: her mother-in-law was always cold and rude to her. And as this had been Phoebe's first evening out since Bryan's birth, she'd been bored and sleepy, wishing almost from the outset that she could be back home with the baby. *Just allow me a moment's respite before I have to make any more polite conversation,* she'd implored Henry. *I'll sit behind those ferns where nobody can see me.*

And it seemed that nobody *had* seen her—at least not the two gentlemen on the other side of the ferns, who were clearly discussing Henry and his voting record.

"A bit of unusually astute thinking for him," one of them commented. "Somebody must have taken him aside and explained the principle of Enclosure; typically he's too lazy to follow the simplest debate. But last week he even made a little speech in favor of this latest bill. What old maxim did he quote? Something about how 'the workman, like the willow, sprouts more readily for being cropped,' was it?"

"Sprouts quicker profits for an investor, I'd say," the other had returned.

"Well," the first had added, "you know he made a nice little pile investing in that new textile mill."

"Needs it, I expect, in order to support the handsome establishment he keeps. Wife and new baby, you know . . ."

"Not to speak of that mistress with the big . . ."

When just then Henry had returned from the refreshment table with the lemonade she'd asked for, and the gentlemen's conversation had ceased abruptly.

But it had never really ceased for Phoebe. It still echoed hollowly in Phizz Marston's austere pale blue breakfast room six years later.

She drained her cup and forced herself to relax as the coffee's warmth seeped through her. The tragedy of her marriage was over and there was no point reliving it.

And even, she thought now, if her present life were in truth a bit of a farce, at least it was a farce of her own authoring and control. Phizz Marston moved about as he liked: no more riding sidesaddle or following a man's lead on the dance floor. He was master in his own house: no more sneers from cold-eyed footmen. He set styles rather than copied them: no more anxious perusal of an endless stream of fashion magazines.

And no more anxious wondering whether she'd offended some pretentious dowager or stuffy old lord by speaking too directly or arguing a point too well. Phizz always won his arguments, making mincemeat of the stupid, stuffy, and pretentious alike. Phoebe had always needed to be on the lookout for one of her husband's rages, but Phizz had only Phizz to please.

Best of all perhaps, Phizz Marston had the newspaper to himself at breakfast.

Her eye fell to the bottom of the page, where a brief but respectful article described the minority position in Parliament. For it seemed that even though this latest Enclosure Act had passed, it had done so by a surprisingly narrow margin. The reporter attributed the close vote to "the quiet, reasoned eloquence of David Hervey, eighth Earl of Linseley, who spoke modestly and masterfully of 'a decent, traditional England that pledged all due reverence to its commons and its community.' "

The article quoted a few more phrases—*nicely turned as well,* Phoebe thought—and then gave its attention to the gentleman's elegant bearing and style of address: ". . . a tall, powerful man, who seems to bring the countryside into the hall with him. At courteous ease with his noble peers, one imagines him more truly at home in his bounteous fields and among the yeomen whose rights he seeks to protect."

One imagines him . . .

For a moment Phoebe didn't look anything like

Phizz Marston. For a moment only, before she caught herself and rearranged her features into their accustomed mask.

"A bit preciously wrought, that bit of reportage," she said aloud. There was no one in the room to hear her, but it wouldn't hurt to rehearse. Even though none of the dandies at White's cared about agricultural policy, they would all have noted that Lord Linseley possessed an original and dramatic style and bearing. Which Phizz would be called to pass judgement upon.

"Oh, quite elegant." Her icy dandy's voice echoed in the empty breakfast room. "Spent an hour endeavoring to tie my cravat like his this morning, without quite achieving his miraculous fluidity and simplicity of line."

And the hell of it, she thought, was that this was quite nearly the truth. For all her resolve to forget about him, it had been Lord Linseley whom she'd seen in the pier glass this morning, during a particularly long and challenging session of disguising herself as a man.

Crossing a brilliantly polished boot over a well-tailored knee, she wiped a miniscule bit of dust from the toe of her boot with her napkin. Not that it mattered—she'd be tramping through mud this afternoon anyway and would have to return home for a change of clothing before setting out to White's. Tramping through the mud . . . the thought brought an involuntary smile to her lips. For after three years, she still reveled in having a man's freedom of the London streets.

She had an important and delightful errand to do, in fact—one that ought to take her mind off this troublesome man. Reluctantly, she corrected herself. *This* good *and decent man,* she thought, *damn his beautiful dark blue eyes.*

* * *

"Well, you fought the good fight and that's what matters in the end." Admiral Wolfe tried to sound bluff and hearty over luncheon.

Lord Linseley put down his coffee cup and allowed himself a short, dry laugh.

"And if England had fought the good fight but lost the battle at Trafalgar?"

"Not the same thing, man, not the same at all. You'll live to fight another day. And you gained adherents to your cause. The newspapers . . ."

"The newspapers seemed more interested in my 'elegant bearing' than in my cause. As though I'd made that speech in order to advance myself in the marriage mart."

He was exhausted, numbed by the futility of his endeavor, and furious at the shallow senselessness of the whole event. But after all, he thought, what could he have reasonably expected from gentlemen so ignorant of the land and the people who worked it?

It was time to get back to the country and do the best he could to repair the damages. Time to leave this corrupt city that cared for nothing but style, wealth, and pleasure, and had forgotten its roots. Time to turn his back on Lord Crashaw. And to forget about Phizz Marston.

But before he could leave London he had an errand to do.

The house at Three Fountain Court was shabby, the street itself rutted and muddy, without the raised wooden walkways that made walking easier in London's better districts. The tired-looking old lady who answered Lord Linseley's knock at the door smiled sweetly through wrinkles that years of care had etched on her face.

She'd read the morning newspapers too, and commended him for his "angelic" words in the "vicious" Parliament.

Unfortunately, though, her husband was currently entertaining another guest. But if Lord Linseley would be so good as to return in an hour, Mr. Blake would be happy to see him, and to show him the latest of his prophetic words and engravings.

The tavern just up the street, she added rather vaguely, was comfortable enough.

David had bowed and shaken her hand, bidding Mrs. Blake tell her husband that he'd return in an hour, and smiling to himself at the old lady's serene assurance that a peer of the realm would be happy to wait attendance upon her husband, a simple engraver.

Still, she was right, he thought, sipping watered ale at the Coal Hole Tavern a bit later. He'd wait all day if asked. He supposed the tavern was "comfortable enough," if one applied a very liberal definition to the notion of comfort. No matter. He'd endure considerably more discomfort than hard bench and bad ale, for the opportunity to buy a hand-colored book or manuscript by one of the most gifted and eccentric artists that England—or the world—had yet produced.

Hardly a student of the arts, David nonetheless found himself enthralled by Mr. Blake's strange poems and illustrations—of angels and biblical patriarchs, mystical beasts and meek, frightened orphans and urchins. A world unto itself and yet a familiar one, rendered in assured line and glowing color: muddy, filthy, corrupt London somehow reshaping itself and arising from Mr. Blake's imagination as a new Jerusalem.

He consulted his pocket watch. Yes, an hour had passed. He gazed out the window at the house where the Blakes rented their poor two rooms. And indeed, the door of Number Three swung open to reveal a gentleman taking his leave. David gazed intently at the man's gracefully crooked arm, a precious package carefully tucked beneath it. It seemed a book by the size and shape of it. He reached into his pocket for some coins to pay for his drink as he watched the man bid Mrs. Blake good-bye at the front door.

At first he felt only envy and resentment. What marvel had this gentleman purchased that he, David, might have taken home to admire and contemplate during his solitary evenings at Linseley Manor? Mr. Blake couldn't afford to have his work widely published. He created very small editions: some pieces were unique.

But on second thought, David knew that his initial response had simply been a cover for a far more distressing recognition—that the slender, simply dressed gentleman striding energetically and exuberantly through the muddy street was none other than Mr. Marston.

Energy, Mr. Blake had written, *is Eternal Delight.*

And *Exuberance is Beauty.*

There was no doubt about it and no other word for it. Marston was beautiful.

David stared in a sort of trance: the pure perception overwhelmed him with shamed rapture. So these were the pleasures of vice, he thought. But the uninhibited moment soon passed, to be followed by his sure regret that he'd never abandon himself to such desires.

What was it Mr. Blake had once told him about vice?

What are called vices in the natural world are the highest sublimities in the spiritual world.

Which is all very well, David told himself, for some cracked genius. But my world *is* the natural world, dammit, and not some mad, impossible artist's paradise. And in *my* world we don't do things like that.

He paid for his ale and stood uncertainly at the doorway of the tavern.

Marston was strolling easily down the street. In another moment he'd reach the tavern. It would be easy, David thought, simply to turn his back as the young man passed. No need, after all, to greet him outside of Polite Society. Of course, it might be a trifle ignoble. *Ignoble?* Bloody hell, it would be gutless, unmanly, and entirely unworthy of himself to avoid saluting a gentleman of his acquaintance.

It would also be admitting that his passions were stronger than he was.

And anyway, he found that he couldn't have turned away even if he'd wanted to.

"Mr. Marston."

Was that a hint of a blush on the young man's meticulously shaven cheeks? No, probably just the effect of a brisk wind blowing through the street.

"Lord Linseley. Good afternoon, sir. And what a surprise to find you here. Don't tell me that you've been set to wait in the Blake family anteroom."

A quick, firm handshake. And then the maddening half smile that had haunted the margins of David's thoughts since the night at Almack's.

"Yes, Mrs. Blake sent me here."

"She'd set the Angel Gabriel himself to waiting at the Coal Hole if her husband wasn't quite ready to see him. Oh, but I've forgotten to congratulate you, sir, upon your fine speech in the House of Lords."

"Ah. Yes. Th-thank you, Mr. Marston."

David had had a slight stammer as a child. But he'd lost it completely in early adolescence. He hadn't thought about it for years, hadn't given it a moment's care even as he'd rehearsed his speech.

Absurd, he thought, to be so reduced, and in the eyes of a trivial, if beautiful, youth who lived for nothing but corrupt London style. Still, he found himself unaccountably pleased that Marston had known about the speech.

Even though, he reminded himself, Marston probably cared more for the parliamentary reporter's mannered prose than for the issues involved.

"I wouldn't have thought, Mr. Marston . . ."

"That a dandy would attend to the results of a boring vote on agricultural policy, my lord?"

"Well, yes, actually. Something like that. Seems rather a dull business for someone like you."

The two attractive gentlemen—the older one a well set up forty-year-old, the younger one slimmer and more carefully attired—stared curiously at each other in the midst of the shabby street. A sharp wind off the Thames ruffled their hair and sent bits of ash and urban filth swirling about their legs.

"And I, sir, must confess to a bit of surprise . . ."

David grinned. "That a stuffy country squire would take an interest in so rare a creature as Mr. Blake?"

Their eyes met. And then they both looked quickly away.

"Well, you must agree that he's a bit of a minority taste."

"Perhaps I'm fated always to find myself in the minority." David grimaced. "Still, I always visit Mr. Blake when I'm in Town. I wanted to be sure to see him before I escape back to Lincolnshire, for he's this city's chief attraction for me. I responded to his work immediately when I first saw it, quite by accident one day in a tiny gallery that I'd ducked into to avoid a sudden rainstorm."

Phoebe nodded emphatically, with a lack of irony completely unbefitting Phizz Marston. "I was introduced to him at Lady Caroline Lamb's some months ago. She's taken him up, I'm sure, partly for the amusement of his quaintness. But I don't find him quaint. I think he's a genius, though his view of things is so eccentric that he sometimes takes my breath away."

What in the world am I doing? For it certainly wasn't Mr. Blake who was taking her breath away at the moment.

A cordial nod to Lord Linseley would have been sufficient. A bow more than enough. Shaking his hand and engaging him in enthusiastic conversation was excessive, to say the least.

Mr. Blake, she remembered, had once written that *the road of excess leads to the palace of wisdom.* But Mr. Blake wasn't a woman trying to preserve a perilous deception.

And I'm in deeper danger of dropping my mask entirely, she told herself sternly, every moment I stand here conversing with him.

It was bad enough that she couldn't cease gazing at his fine face and powerful physique. Or how much pleasure she took in his evident appreciation of Mr. Marston's elegant looks.

What was worse was that she was evidently coming to *like* him. Of course, she would probably feel a similar affinity with anyone who admired Mr. Blake's work as she did. But there was also his brave stand in Parliament: she couldn't help but respect him and his beliefs. And she wanted his respect as well.

She wanted to continue this conversation, to tell him more about the astonishing illustrated *Book of Job* she'd just purchased. And to hear more of his thoughts and observations—on anything he might wish to tell her. She wanted to know him.

Perhaps, she thought, he might like to have a drink with her in the tavern. After all, a gentleman *could* invite another gentleman for half an hour of intellectual conversation, even in such raffish surroundings. And this might be her last opportunity before he escaped back to Lincolnshire . . .

"I've heard," Lord Linseley was saying, "that there are new printings of *Songs of Innocence and of Experience* to be had. Did you get a look at those, Mr. Marston?"

Oh dear. She felt her stomach clench. Her eager smile faded immediately.

David watched in amazement as a wave of icy cynicism swept over Marston's features like a cold gale from the north. It froze his face into a haughty mask and almost hid the sudden pain darkening his eyes.

But what did I say? The young man had seemed so pleasant and forthcoming. But here was his sensuous mouth, twisting into a nasty sneer before David's astonished eyes.

"*Songs of Innocence and of Experience,* Lord Linseley? You mean those inferior ditties about *children*?"

"Well, they're about childhood, in any case. And I don't find them inferior at all. I find them haunting."

Marston shrugged. "Each to his own. I try not to look at the nasty little beasts myself. Can't stand children, either in the flesh or on the page. Good day, my lord. I wish you a fine winter in the country."

He performed his graceful little bow and turned sharply away, leaving a confused and vaguely troubled Lord Linseley staring after him.

Phoebe turned the corner onto the Strand, hailed a cab and climbed hurriedly into it, and scolded herself for her rudeness all the way home.

But I couldn't help it, she thought. Truly I couldn't.

For she *wasn't* able to look at children. She couldn't

even think of them without trembling. Not since Bryan and her failure to protect him.

This fear was part of the reason she'd chosen to become Marston and to lead his sort of life. No one would expect a dandy to have anything to do with children. And since Marston never woke until afternoon and rarely went out during the day, she was able to minimize her contact with children in the streets. One did see tiny beggars curled up asleep in doorways, or little street sweepers working late to earn a few extra pennies. But Marston and his cronies would simply walk a bit faster, shuddering genteelly and looking the other way.

Of course, once in a while her gaze would stray to a little procession of shabby charity children being herded to a late church service. There seemed to be more and more of them these days, probably because their parents had been forced out of the countryside. But these humble little wards of the parish were trained to keep their eyes lowered in the streets, as though they didn't deserve a child's natural curiosity about the world around them.

I can bear it so long as I don't have to see their eyes, she thought. But even so, last week a filthy chimney sweep had stared innocently at her as she and Fitz Wallace had shared a joke in the street. The little boy had large eyes in a pinched, sooty face—Bryan's innocent hazel eyes, or so it had seemed to her at the moment. She'd needed half a bottle of champagne to settle herself and for several nights she'd woken, sweaty and shaken, from a hideous dream of Bryan trapped in a sooty, suffocating chimney, screaming helplessly for her to rescue him.

Still, she chided herself, none of that excused her behavior to the Earl of Linseley. Her terror of children was her own problem, and one she'd be ashamed to inflect upon such a good man. Lord Linseley had a grown son, she'd heard, and a wife who'd died, though she couldn't remember the circumstances. In any case, he'd doubtless been a fine father and a worthy protector of his own children. And since he'd appeared at Almack's to survey the marriageable goods, he probably wanted a new wife who'd give him a few more.

She sighed. *Well, good luck to him. Even if it's too late for me.*

David held his new purchase snugly beneath his arm as he strode away from the Blakes' doorstep. What a wonderful possession, he thought, the *Songs of Innocence and of Experience,* newly printed and marvelously colored. Mr. Blake had raised the price from five shillings to three guineas. Absurd. David would have happily paid three hundred. It was priceless, even if Marston has sneered at it.

And what had all that been about, anyway?

Mr. Blake had been enigmatic when David had questioned him about his earlier guest.

"He lives in Hell," was the artist's most coherent reply. "He suffers its torments and writhes within the coils of his secrets in Brunswick Square." The rest had been some claptrap about human sublimity and androgynous beauty.

Still, David thought, it was good to know where the young man made his physical—if not his metaphysical—residence. In case he ever needed some sort of assistance. Because of all the impressions the odd meeting in the street had left him with, the most intense was the flash of pain in Marston's eyes.

Children? I hate the little beasts.

Blake is right, David thought. Marston lives in Hell. The young man's in some sort of trouble.

He paused in front of the tavern, as though he could still feel Marston's presence at the spot where they'd conversed. A wave of protectiveness swept over him. It was almost as strong as the lust he'd almost begun to accept as the price of thinking of the young gentleman.

He hugged the book to himself, as though to protect the children whose pictures adorned its pages. Perhaps another ale at this fine establishment, he thought, while I feast my eyes once more upon the marvel I've purchased.

Chapter 5

She'd relaxed a bit by the time the cab had reached Brunswick Square. After all, she thought with a grimace, her sufferings were hardly those of Job.

And anyway, in a few days she'd be off for a little vacation.

Giving her package to a footman, she bade him unwrap the book and display it among the cherished items in the drawing room.

She fiddled with the pile of letters—invitations, by the look of them—ranged next to the pale porcelain vase on a table in the foyer. She'd attend to them later: most of them would need apologies, since she'd be out of Town—*grouse hunting season, don't you know,* she'd write in her excuses—for a few weeks beginning this Thursday.

First, though, she needed a scalding, steaming bath and perhaps a nap, before dressing for the evening and setting out on Marston's round of engagements.

The staircase curved invitingly before her. But instead of running lightly up the softly-carpeted stairs to her fragrant, rose-colored bathroom, she paced agitatedly, prowling through her downstairs rooms, distractedly picking up this or that pretty bibelot and putting it down again.

It's all right, she told herself, pinching a less than perfect bloom from a tall floral arrangement, *you won't see him again.* He'll be back in Lincolnshire before you know it.

What had the newspaper said of him?

". . . more truly at home in his own bounteous fields and among the yeomen whose rights he seeks to protect."

Fortunate yeomen, she thought.

Anyway, he'd made it abundantly clear that he didn't approve of city life. *And he certainly couldn't approve of me.* Or of Phizz Marston anyway.

There *is* no *me*, she reminded herself. There was only Phizz Marston. For with Kate's clever assistance, Lady Phoebe Claringworth had been buried next to her son and husband, ten days after Henry and Bryan's joint funeral. It had been Kate who, under cover of nursing Phoebe all by herself, had dismissed the disrespectful, inquisitive servants, spirited Phoebe home to the country, found a suitable female corpse to take her place, and bribed the doctor to register Phoebe's death in the parish records.

Only Kate and Phoebe's brother Jonathan knew the truth; everybody else had willingly accepted Kate's story and had deferred to her insistence upon a simple burial service with a closed casket. The official word was that Henry's mother, the older Lady Fanny Claringworth, having suffered a fit of apoplexy upon learning the news of her beloved son's death, was too incapacitated to visit her injured daughter-in-law. But the more knowledgeable among the *ton* whispered that the old lady had always loathed Phoebe anyway—for coming from such an obscure corner of the realm, for maintaining her own opinions, and for being *much* too tall in the bargain. The inner circle smugly agreed that the older Lady Claringworth had been quite satisfied see the younger Lady Claringworth dead and buried.

Not that any of it matters now, Phoebe thought. The only thing that matters three years later is that Phizz Marston is the only thing left of me. *Cold, frivolous, Phizz Marston, who prowls London by night and hates children.*

And takes lovely young men to bed.

Or *had* done so, anyway—at least one of them. For Phoebe knew that episode of her life had come to an end. She'd continue having Billy visit her, but it was clear to her that these would be chaste, familial sorts of evenings, times for him to rub her feet and her to inquire after his welfare. Perhaps she'd even help him work on his reading. He'd be disappointed, of course, but he'd accept it. Their intimacy had been profound enough to lay the basis for friendship.

These meetings were going to cost her a small fortune (she'd have to dip into the fund she saved for emergencies). It would have been a lot of money to pay for sex; no one would believe her, she thought, if she told them she was paying it to keep Billy out of someone else's sexual clutches. Still, Billy deserved to have someone to fuss over how he got on. And anyway, it was pleasant to have someone to fuss over.

Of course, appearances would continue to suggest something a great deal more lascivious. If he hadn't already done so, Lord Linseley would be bound to hear the rumors about Marston's taste for the male sex.

As if he'd need to hear rumors. *For*—she blushed a bit here—*he'd be a fool if he hasn't already noticed how much I admire his looks.*

She shook her head. The Earl of Linseley was clearly no fool.

He's simply too secure in his manliness, to be disturbed by another man's desire.

She might have asked him a bit more about his plans, she thought now, rather than nattering on so incoherently about Mr. Blake and his work. For if she'd asked him exactly when he planned to leave London, she'd know whether she needed to worry about meeting him again before her departure next Thursday morning.

As things stood, though, she might run into him anywhere the *ton* gathered. At the club where she'd agreed to dine tonight, or at the theater afterwards. Or at Vivien's? No, he wasn't a gambler; she wouldn't see him at Vivien's.

But how about the day after tomorrow at Almack's? Yes, surely he'd be there.

For a glorious, forbidden moment she allowed herself a tiny fantasy: Lord Linseley approaching and asking her to dance, her own veiled smile and nod of assent, and then the touch—light yet firm, she could imagine it perfectly—of his hand at the small of her back.

She'd wear a gown of the thinnest silk . . . his hand would be warm through his kid glove . . .

Blast it all! The touch of his hand was the last *thing she should be imagining.*

She slammed her fist down on the foyer table, shaking it so violently that the Chinese vase—made for an emperor five hundred years before—tipped, tumbled, and shattered into a thousand pieces.

"Ah, Simms. No, it's nothing. Well yes, of course it is a shame. A damned shame—it's, it was . . . a beautiful thing I—destroyed.

"Yes, thank you, I do need to bathe and dress. The water's hot? Excellent. Yes, I'll go up now."

* * *

The Coal Hole had been almost empty and dim as its name suggested when David pushed open the door; the only other customers were two men monopolizing the prime seats by the fire. Street ruffians, David thought at first: the big, bearish fellow with enormous, hamlike fists was certainly a type you'd want to stay clear of. But upon a moment's scrutiny he decided that the man was too heavy and clumsy to pose much threat to himself or his illustrated book. And the second man clearly wasn't dangerous in the least. Half hidden in shadow, he spoke in a thin, piercing upper-class voice pitched somewhere between a whine and a bray. Turning his back to the two men, David quietly ordered an ale and sat behind a pillar at the window table to look at his book by the fading late afternoon light.

An hour must have passed before he once again became aware of the voices by the fireplace. The upper-class gentleman, forgetting that they weren't alone, suddenly spoke out in angry, impatient tones.

"No, no Stokes, I don't want him severely beaten. Just a bit roughed up, you know. Humiliated. You might knock him into a ditch and get him all dirty if you wish. Or give him a black eye, something like that. But what I'm paying you for—and very well, I might add—is for you to follow him. Learn where he goes on these little vacations of his. For he seems to disappear into thin air. We all know he's hiding something. I want him unmasked, exposed, humiliated just as . . ."

The thin, angry voice trailed off.

"Just as wot, Baron . . . ?"

But the older man interrupted him quickly.

"Dammit, I told you to call me Mr. Bradley."

He's not about to share his humiliation with the thug he's hiring, David thought contemptuously. And he's too timid to do the dirty work of personally confronting the man who'd insulted him.

The craven scoundrel was even too low to use his own name. David tried to turn his attention back to his book. But the conversation had captured his attention.

"Aw right, then, Mr., uh, Bradley, so it's Marston I'm to go after, is it? Mr. Philip 'Phizz' Marston in Brunswick Square."

"Marston on Thursday next. Here's ten guineas now, and forty more to come when you tell me where he goes on these mysterious excursions of his."

"And I ain't to rough him up so bad, eh? Rather takes the fun out of it for a lad like meself."

"There should be enough fun in forty guineas, Stokes. And you can rough him up later, when we've got him where we want him. When he's learned not to lord it over a real gentleman."

"Like yerself, Mr. Bradley?"

"Exactly, Stokes. Like myself."

Phoebe passed an entirely unremarkable night of engagements, encountering no trace of Lord Linseley no matter how many festivities she visited or how long she stayed at them.

Are you satisfied? she asked herself with a shrug and a grimace the next afternoon. Well then, she thought wryly, you *could* try doing something useful. Time to open the mail.

Nothing special. Nothing interesting. She scrawled her replies quickly. But what was this?

The envelope was of heavy paper, like all the others. But there was no crest printed on it in raised type. She didn't recognize the handwriting either. Nor was there a discernable seal on the blob of wax that closed it.

The message, constructed of letters cut out from the newspapers and glued to a piece of flimsy paper, was simplicity itself. YOU ARE BEING WATCHED.

Unpleasant, that one.

She allowed herself a shudder, but didn't succumb to her initial temptation to toss the nasty thing into the fire.

Instead she marked it with the date, folded it, and put it into a gracefully carved box with the two dozen or so of its fellows that Marston had received over the years.

The box was of sandalwood—too fragrant, really, for the stinking missives it held; most of them reeked with hatred and cowardliness. Not a one of their authors had ever confronted Marston directly. Which was partly why she saved their letters—to remind herself how stupid and innocuous Marston's enemies really were.

Of course, most of the messages were longer and less coherent than the one she'd just opened. Scrawled and blotted, they accused Marston of a wide variety of treacheries: she'd been especially diverted by the one charging her with spying for the American Republic; she'd also enjoyed the one that had insisted she was of Negro parentage. Sexual insults abounded. It was interesting to learn the words evidently used to describe a gentleman who took other men to bed with him—from the homey *Nancy* or *Molly-boy,* to the classical *catamite* or *Ganymede,* to the puzzling *morphodite.* Marston's enemies must especially enjoy using this specialized vocabulary, she thought. Language was power, especially for those too timid to do more than fantasize about action. There were also a few gruesome specimens that threatened to "geld" or "unman" her—which would be quite an impressive feat, she thought.

Most of the letters, even if threatening, had clearly been written with the sole aim of aggrandizing their authors' self-regard or helping them recover from some passing fit of pique. Whatever Marston's enemies imagined doing to him was usually satisfied by writing it down on paper and posting it to him. Which was probably, she thought, why this last letter had given her a bit of a start. For it seemed less an end in itself than a promise of something more to come.

Still, there was certainly no cause for alarm. Nor any reason to be intimidated.

She tucked the box into its cubbyhole in her mahogany secretary and turned back to the tedious business of declining a fortnight's worth of invitations. She'd have to hurry, too, for she hadn't yet chosen everything she wanted Mr. Simms to pack for tomorrow's journey. And later this afternoon Mr. Andrewes would be arriving with a new jacket and pair of trousers. She'd wear them to Almack's tonight if the fit was good enough. If the fit was as smooth and perfect as the fine silk gowns she'd never wear again.

"No, Wolfe, no dancing or young ladies tonight. I want to be fresh for my journey back home tomorrow."

"But look here, Linseley, I thought you postponed that journey an extra day just to give yourself one more crack at the marriage mart. Isn't that what you said?"

"Hmmm, did I say that?"

I might have said that, David thought ruefully. *Who knows?* For he often made a muddle when not strictly telling the truth.

He'd sent a note to his steward telling him that he'd be back a bit later than he'd originally thought. Legal matters, he'd written. And in fact he had been terribly busy, buying up all the common lands that had suddenly gone up for auction in Lincolnshire. He'd even got a few tracts that Crashaw had had his eye on. And as soon as he'd taken full ownership, he'd proclaim to the neighborhood people that the lands were once again available for their crops and herds. He just hoped that they wouldn't lose too much work between now and then. The farming calendar wasn't a forgiving one—not that an absentee lord would know that.

He did need to get home, though; he had work of his own to do. Still, another day or two out of the way wouldn't matter. For he couldn't go home quite yet. Not when there was urgent need for his services in Brunswick Square.

"It's nine in the morning, sir. I've brought your coffee."

There was no sound from the bed except a smothered groan, as Phoebe burrowed more deeply beneath the eiderdown and embroidered coverlet.

But it's her own fault, Mr. Simms told himself. For she promised to come home early last night. Instead of waltzing and gambling into the wee hours. I wonder if she remembers that when she came home at five this morning she made me a gift of a thousand pounds?

"Sir?" Mr. Simms tried not to laugh at the absurdity of the situation. Perhaps the minx intended to bribe me, he thought, in return for another hour's sleep. And for pretending not to notice the bad language she's taken to using lately.

Well, it wouldn't work. She needed to wake up directly and to watch her manners too.

Mr. Simms had taken it upon himself to accompany Miss Vaughan back to London after she'd announced this harebrained scheme three years ago. Masquerading as a man was a risky business, he'd insisted. She'd need someone to look after her—and who better than someone who loved her and her brother like the children he and his wife had never had?

Of course, it hadn't hurt that he'd always taken a whimsical delight in masquerade and theatricals. And that he was bored and lonely living the life of a widowed, retired tutor in a Devonshire backwater. The clever, mischievous Vaughan children had been the lights of his life, especially the girl, who'd had as good a mind for Latin and mathematics as her brother. And who'd had to study in secret, away from her silly mother's prying.

He knew how to awaken her this morning, too.

He bent over the coverlet, and—softly, so that none of the other servants could hear—whispered in particularly piercing and agonized tones, "Miss Vaughan!"

"Wha . . ."

"*Phoebe!*"

"Phoebe, put away that Latin text right now! Your mother's coming!"

"What! Where?"

A tousled head emerged from under the coverlet. A pair of clear gray eyes flew open. Her face was anxious and frightened. And then her expression cleared.

"Simms, you bloody devil!"

Quite nimbly for a man his age, Mr. Simms stepped aside as she pelted him with pillows and bolsters.

"Do have some coffee, Mr. Marston. Your bath is drawn and your traveling costume is spread out there on the chaise longue. You know that you ordered the carriage for ten o'clock. And you wouldn't want to keep Lady Kate waiting, would you?"

"I should fire you, Simms."

"Indeed you should, sir, before you make me any more extravagant gifts like last night's. One might almost have thought you inebriated. And might I thank you again, sir?"

"You deserve it, Simms. And I'm never inebriated. Is it a fine morning?"

Mr. Simms opened sea-green velvet drapes to let the morning sunlight stream though the Valenciennes lace at the tall windows.

"A very fine morning for traveling, sir. Or perhaps for a little nap in the carriage."

"I never take naps. I've got the novel that Kate sent to amuse me during the journey."

"Of course, sir. But might I point out that a gentleman covers his mouth when he yawns so enormously? And certainly a gentleman ought to watch his language more carefully than you have been doing these past few days."

She got him with one last small hard bolster, aiming directly for the back of his head as he quitted her bedchamber.

Grinning at her small triumph, she stretched and strode to her bathroom. She'd miss Mr. Simms this fortnight. But it would nonetheless be refreshing to be out of Town for a while, and not constantly on the lookout for a certain gentleman she'd convinced herself she didn't want to meet.

Lord Linseley's coachman had parked in a small alley a bit before nine, affording an excellent view of Brunswick Square, though all David had seen so far were some housemaids shaking out linen from upper windows and gardeners trimming the neat yew hedges. It was far too early for any of the householders to be up and about yet.

The horses were a bit restive. The coachmen stepped down to calm them.

And I'm a bit restive too, David thought.

What a ridiculous scheme he'd concocted. It seemed sillier with every passing minute, particularly in the clear light of an unusually sunny and delightful morning. He couldn't see any sign of Stokes. And anyway, who knew what it all might mean, or whether Marston was really going anywhere today?

It would have been wiser to call on Mr. Marston and simply to tell what he'd overheard. No doubt Marston knew this Baron, and would be able realistically to assess the danger—if there were any real danger at all.

But I've been wise all my life, David thought, *wise, sensible, prudent, and responsible.*

And he was sick of it. He wanted a little adventure. He wanted—*dear Lord, this was embarrassing*—to be a hero, as in medieval legend, or like his ancestors who'd stumbled around in clanking suits of armor. He wanted to show that even at forty, and even after having failed to stop the Enclosure Act, that he could act decisively. And if that meant taking on Stokes with his own fists, in front of young Mr. Marston's admiring and grateful eyes—well, so be it.

Absurd. Embarrassing. But there it was.

And there now, farther up the alley, was Stokes, calming a large, rawboned nag. He seemed to think that he'd hidden his bulk behind the absurd slouch hat he'd worn for the occasion. David leaned back in his carriage so he wouldn't be seen.

At a quarter to ten, a coachman brought a small closed carriage around in front of a well-tended brick house with newly-painted blue shutters. Five minutes later a gray-haired valet appeared at the front door, carrying a covered wicker basket and directing a footman to load a small trunk into the boot of the carriage.

And at ten exactly, Marston himself appeared at the door, buoyant and upright as ever, with a small volume in his hand.

He spoke to the valet, who pressed the wicker basket upon him—*luncheon,* David thought ruefully, suddenly remembering that he'd forgotten to ask his cook to pack some for himself. Marston stepped lightly into the carriage.

Odd, David thought, *that he's not taking his manservant with him.* Wherever Marston was going, it wouldn't seem to matter so much that he'd be well dressed.

But there was no time for such speculation. Marston's carriage set off. Stokes waited a reasonable interval before following. And likewise the earl of Linseley.

David winced. *Ridiculous. We're like a gypsy caravan.*

Phoebe, normally sharp-eyed and alert, might have observed the same thing if she'd had a mind to. But several late nights in a row had taken their toll on her, especially last night's defiantly exuberant dancing and fierce, concentrated gambling. Buttery autumn sunlight poured deliciously through the carriage's windows. She'd soon be surrounded by the few people in the world whom she loved—excepting Mr. Simms, of course, who'd be off tomorrow on a long-awaited trout-fishing expedition with Mr. Andrewes. And warmed by the sunshine and by her affectionate thoughts, she fell happily to sleep—with her book, Miss Austen's *Persuasion,* lying unopened on the seat beside her—before the carriage had even reached the seedy outskirts of London.

A pleasant enough drive, David thought impatiently, *but it's bothersome not to know how far one is going*—especially given the unsettled state of the weather. The sun still shone brightly enough, but he'd caught a few distant rumbles of thunder. And by early afternoon his stomach had taken to rumbling as well. Finally he'd had to stop at a small inn and buy some roasted capons for himself and his coachman, and some bread, cheese, and ale to keep in reserve.

They caught up with Marston's carriage somewhere outside of Rowen-on-Close.

"Let's drive up that hill," David told his coachman. "I want to see the countryside."

Dickerson, the coachman, nodded with just a hint of skepticism in his eye. He thinks I've suddenly gone daft, David thought, like some bloody rhymester touring the Lake District. Well, perhaps I have.

The view of the countryside, however, was just what he wanted. He could see Marston's carriage, parked outside of a rambling stone house. The coachman carried the young man's trunk up the path. He's stopping here, David told himself, at least for the night. He watched while Marston leaped from the carriage, overtook the coachman, and fairly bounded through the garden and into the house. *There's someone he cares for here,* David thought, as a wave of envy flooded through him and threatened to flush out every bit of common sense he still possessed. *Someone he cares for deeply.*

But right then there were other things to worry about besides Mr. Marston's affections. For the storm had changed its mind and was blowing toward them after all.

"Should we turn back to that inn a few leagues back, my lord?" Dickerson asked after it had become clear that his master was not going to make that eminently reasonable suggestion himself. "There will be lightning, I think, and the horses . . ."

And if Marston took it upon himself to disappear during the night while nobody was watching? It was unlikely, David thought, but possible. After all, what had Baron what's-his-name said in the pub? *Seems to disappear into thin air.* Or just to disappear when his enemies were napping?

David could see Stokes down the hill as well, shivering, by the look of him, in a stand of trees.

No, I won't leave while he's down there.
But what of the horses, the lightning?

David was about to tell his coachman to leave him for the night, when he caught sight of a ruined cottage near the hilltop.

"Do you think, Dickerson, that we might be able to spend the night? We could stable the horses in that old building—the roof doesn't look too bad, at least on the west side, and I could keep watch throughout the night. You see, there's somebody in need of help below, in that house . . ."

Dickerson threw him an even more skeptical glance, but the house did seem solid enough. And they did have warm blankets and a lantern packed for emergencies—as well as some pretty decent cheese and ale from the inn.

And so they arranged themselves—Dickerson, the horses, and half the food and blankets in the abandoned building, and Lord Linseley in the carriage to keep an eye on the stone house below.

The rain began to fall sometime about midnight. It was comforting, David thought, monotonous . . .

A violent thunderclap woke him an hour later. A violent thunderclap and a thunderous knocking at the locked carriage door.

"Lemme in, dammit, afore I die out here of the cold and rain."

Stokes.

He'd probably seen the carriage on the hilltop, illuminated by a flash of lightning. The springs creaked under his knocking. In another minute he'd break the window.

David had a pistol hidden below his seat, but somehow he didn't think he'd need it. He opened the door slowly.

"Good evening, my man, and can I offer you what's left of the ale?"

Stokes hurled his big body into the carriage and immediately made for David's throat.

Just as I suspected, David thought, *too big and clumsy to be a real fighter.* He freed himself from Stokes's grasp and pushed him out of the carriage, leaping on top of him and taking out the day's tensions by giving him a good pummeling. It was absurdly satisfying, he thought with some embarrassment, even if there was no admiring Marston to watch—no one except Stokes's frightened horse, tethered to a tree.

Stokes kicked and bellowed. The two big men rolled about in the mud until David had finally subdued his opponent.

"Yer a good boxer, guv'nor," Stokes muttered—quite flatteringly, David thought, since he himself wouldn't have dignified their filthy, flailing scuffle as an instance of the sweet science of boxing.

"And you're a good loser," David returned.

"Now," he continued, "let's stable your horse with mine, over there in that tumbledown building. Would you like to come in out of the rain and have a spot of ale? We could discuss how you might improve your boxing—I'm afraid you haven't much strategy—or, more interestingly, how two fine fellows like ourselves happen to be out here on such a devil of a night."

They'd brought enough mud back into the carriage with them, David thought, to plant a few bushels of turnips. Sharing the small, enclosed space with Stokes was like sharing it with a muddy, affectionate sheepdog. David didn't find it entirely unpleasant; it was rather like a return to early, pre-civilized, childhood.

He supposed he'd have a bit of a black eye by morning, but—he allowed himself a boyish inward grin—it would be nothing compared to the colorful array of bruises that Stokes would be sporting. "Have some refreshment," he urged the man. He gave Stokes what was left of the cheese, and they passed the ale back and forth companionably.

"Can't blame a chap for trying to grab yer purse, guv'nor," Stokes confided as he chewed. "It being so dark and deserted out here, and you wi' this expensive fast coach and fancy way o' talkin'. Never expected a gen'lman like you to be a fighter."

He wiped crumbs of cheese and foam from his mouth with a bloody sleeve. "But yer right, guv'nor, I never did have the patience to learn much strategy. Usually I scares 'em enough to make 'em forget theirs. Me being so big, you know."

"Your right jab isn't bad," David conceded, "but you don't put up enough of a defense on the left. I could show you sometime, I suppose . . ."

"Ah, but I've forgotten my manners. Haven't introduced myself. David Arthur Saint George Hervey, Earl of Linseley, in Lincolnshire."

"Got a nice ring to it, guv'nor, Linseley of Lincolnshire. And I'm Archie Stokes of Soho, at yer service."

"Stokes of Soho isn't bad either."

"No, it ain't at that. Don't suppose there's another bit of that bread to be 'ad?"

"Would a leg of chicken do?"

It seemed that it would do nicely.

Stokes tossed the bones out the door and gave a contented grunt followed by an enormous belch. The rain continued to pelt the carriage, though the thunder and lightning had ceased. Too bad I didn't bring a few cigars, David thought. Nothing like a fine Havana to encourage postprandial confidences on a stormy night.

But Stokes didn't need a cigar to loosen his tongue.

"Yer a real gen'lman, guv'nor," he said, "not like some

fancy types I could name, like the Nancy-boy wot's hired me to go after this young gen'lman down there in the 'ouse."

David raised his eyebrows.

"They's high-strung, see," Stokes continued. "Scared o' their reputations and their wives finding out. Always come to me to threaten the other bloke. 'Stop wiggling that pretty arse of your'n, old chap, or Baron Bunbury promises you a bloody nose.'"

Baron Bunbury, was it? The name was dimly familiar. David might have met the gentleman some years ago. Not a very impressive specimen, he thought.

And as the implications of what Stokes was saying became clearer to him, he felt an embarrassing flush warm his cheeks. He turned his face toward the window to hide his agitation, making a show of keeping careful watch on the house. It was still pitch black outside, though the rain was beginning to slow to a drizzle.

Stokes gave a brief bark of a laugh. "Yeh, I know, guv'nor, it ain't pretty work I do."

"But are you saying," David stammered, "that there existed some sort of . . . *liaison* . . . between Baron Bunbury and Mr. Marston?"

"I'm sayin', guv'nor, that maybe there *were* a lee-ay-zone and maybe there *weren't*. But that the Baron sure *wished* there were."

David shifted uncomfortably in his seat. Stokes might be slow-witted, he thought, but eventually he'd come round to wondering what David was doing out on his own pursuit of Marston.

Stupid, he thought, *for me to give my own name. But I could never be cowardly enough to hide it.*

"O' course," Stokes continued, "I did me own research on the pretty gen'lman down there."

"Ummm?" David hoped the sound was noncommittal.

"Got other en'mies as well. 'E's quite the gambler, see."

"Oh. Oh yes."

"Ye needn't be proud wi' Archie Stokes, guv'nor. I take it that's *yer* argument with him, *you* clearly not bein' no Nancy."

David hoped the man's double negative meant what he thought it meant, rather than its strict grammatical construction. Shrugging noncommittally, he endeavored not to betray his relief.

"He's clever, that Marston," he offered weakly, "a slippery character in every particular."

"But we'll catch 'im." Stokes's big bruised face caught a few early rays from the sun coming over a distant hill. "We make a good team, you and me, guv'nor."

And like a good team, they took turns keeping watch on the stone house below, each allowing the other a nap as the rain tapered off and the sun rose through a gray, then a pinkish-yellow, and finally a clear blue sky.

"Psst, guv'nor, wake up!" Stokes's elbow in David's ribs was like a mule's kick.

"Umm, wha?"

"Somebody's coming out of the house . . ."

The two of them rushed out of the carriage to get a better look.

" . . . but what the bloody 'ell, it ain't 'im at all, just two ladies . . ."

One in yellow and one in pink, they seemed like serene spirits of the morning, strolling arm in arm to a very fine barouche—not Marston's closed carriage—that awaited them at the end of the garden path.

David couldn't see their faces from atop the hill. But the early morning sunlight illumined their costumes and postures. The lady in yellow wore a large bonnet that seemed to shadow her face, while the one in pink, the taller of the two, walked with an oddly familiar upright grace and had her hair hidden in a white turban.

He watched her in a sort of daze, immediately captivated by the set of her shoulders rising from her shawl, the bold tilt of her head under that white . . .

But of course he would wear a turban. The sudden thought seemed to explode out of nowhere, like fireworks. A turban was just the thing, David realized, to keep his cropped hair—no, he corrected himself, *her* cropped hair—from drawing unwanted attention. For it was becoming utterly, wonderfully clear to him—his body perceiving it while his mind struggled to keep up—that Marston was a woman, no matter how cleverly he (no, dammit—*she!*) managed to go about London disguised as a fashionable, elegant dandy.

A woman. A beautiful woman. The person I've been burning and aching for all this week is a woman.

Never mind why she'd chosen to masquerade as a gentleman. David was sure he'd find that out when he knew her better. For he *would* come to know her, he promised himself; he'd learn every fascinating thing there was to know about her.

He stared at the curve of her neck—how white, how beautiful without a cravat to hide it—as though he were in a dream. No: much, much better—he was waking from a dream.

And so Stokes—dear, good Stokes—was right about me after all. For I clearly ain't no Nancy-boy. He felt a sudden strong urge to hug his companion, but instantly thought the better of it.

The two ladies had arrested their walk, scanning the sky, possibly, for signs of any more storm clouds. David froze. In another moment they'd catch sight of him and Stokes up here on the hill. Could she recognize him from that distance? Especially as Stokes removed his big hat and waved it about in what seemed to be a cordial greeting and gesture of frank admiration.

Stokes! For if David could see the truth so clearly, surely Stokes . . .

He sneaked a sidelong glance at his companion. But Stokes didn't seem to see a thing.

"'E keeps gambler's hours, I expect, guv'nor, not all fresh and eager like the pretty ladies. But maybe it's time we woke 'im up."

It had been easier than he'd expected, David thought a few hours later, to send Stokes galloping off northward toward the Lake District. The elderly woman at the door of the stone house had been calm, friendly, and quite unfazed by the sight of the bruised, muddy, and altogether ruffianly pair he and Stokes made. Stokes had elected David spokesman: though abashed by his disreputable appearance, David did his polite best to inquire after their close friend Mr. Marston.

The woman had smiled warmly—beatifically, David noted with some admiration. Well, she was only the housekeeper, she said, but she was happy to help any friends of dear Mr. Marston.

Humbug, David thought. *No one could truly believe that Marston would have anything to do with us, looking as we do this morning.*

The woman prattled on blithely, her trusting manner quite disarming Stokes's intentions to burst into the house and search every nook and cranny for their prey.

Ah yes Mr. Marston, she chirped. Dear Mr. Marston, such a lovely young man, so polite, so well-mannered. And so handsome too, though she herself preferred a more manly sort of man—like her Alf, God rest his soul, gone these five years come Christmas. But the ladies of the house—the two Misses Edgertons—found him a great favorite, and had been sorry to see him leave last night, what's that sir? Ah yes, the time he left. Well, let me think—I'd put on an extra pot of tea, I did, to fortify him for his journey . . .

Strategy is everything, David told himself. *And this good woman's strategy is to talk volubly as she can, in order to give the lady in pink as long a head start as possible, while directing all comers in the opposite direction.*

Mr. Marston, the housekeeper confided, had judged that the storm would blow over, and had left directly around midnight, hoping to reach the Lake District by morning.

Stokes nodded thoughtfully. "Left while we was fighting, I expect," he muttered. "Well, we'll find 'im in the Lake District, won't we, guv'nor? For we know the look of 'is carriage, even if 'e's got a bit of a jump on us."

The woman gave another of her beatific smiles. Oh yes, she was sure that a clever pair like them could easily find their friend. But first off, mightn't they care for a spot of breakfast? For she hadn't cleared the sideboard after the ladies' early repast, and there was a bit of ham left, not to speak of some kippered herrings and a spoonful or two of clotted cream . . .

The only difficulty for David was informing Stokes that he wouldn't be accompanying him to the Lake District. He waited until they'd finished the kippers.

"Wot, a fighter like yerself, guv'nor, giving up when we've got the scent of 'im?"

But the fifty guineas helped, especially since, unlike Baron Bunbury, David was more than willing to pay up front.

"I can't take more time out from my land, Stokes. But I trust you to find him. And—er, not to mention to

Bunbury that I've taken you on as my agent as well. He might not like you doing double work, you know."

Stokes had winked broadly. "I'll catch up wi' yer in London, sometime, guv'nor, an' tell yer how it went. But I think we got 'im."

Not yet, David thought. For although his first instinct had been to follow the ladies southward, he'd thought the better of it over breakfast. *He writhes within the coils of his secrets,* Mr. Blake had said.

No, David wouldn't impose himself upon her and the pain she evidently suffered. Not until she trusted him enough to reveal those secrets to him herself. He wanted her to *want* to tell him everything. And she *would* come to trust him, he resolved, as she came to care for him as it seemed he cared for her.

"Yes, Stokes, do come to see me in London in about two weeks."

He passed the man a calling card, noting ruefully that he'd just promised to make another visit to the blighted city he hated.

Chapter 6

Phoebe smiled at Kate, seated next to her in the carriage. Her two-week-long stay in Devonshire had been restful and blissfully uneventful. It had been good to see Jonathan and his wife Emily, to accompany Jonathan on long country walks through his parish, and even to accept his parishioners' warm, innocent greetings. "Ah, it's Miss Phoebe, is it, and grown so pretty, too"—as though time had stood still and she'd never been Lady Claringworth at all. And indeed, in this sleepy, comfortable corner of the Kingdom it was possible for her to sometimes forget the years that had passed and pretend that she was still the bold, energetic girl she'd once been.

Less pleasantly, she'd shared another of Jonathan's responsibilities. Their mother, who'd always been frivolous and scatterbrained, had fallen into an anxious early dotage and needed constant attention and reassurance. "Are you my sister Betty," she'd ask Phoebe in a distracted voice several times within an hour, "or are you the other one?"

"I'm the other one, Mother," Phoebe would respond,

squeezing her hand or straightening her shawl as she led her on a slow circuit of the garden. The name "Phoebe" seemed to have no meaning to Mrs. Vaughan. Happily though, neither did "Lady Claringworth." *Which is an aid to my disguise*, Phoebe would think, *but a cruel irony for Mother:* before the onset of her dementia there'd been nothing Mrs. Vaughan had enjoyed more than prattling about "my daughter, Lady Claringworth" to anyone who'd listen.

As always, the most precious moments of Phoebe's visits were the evenings in front of the fire with Kate, at Crowden, the seat of the Beverredge family estate. Kate had never married, though many a greedy gentleman had tried to court her—for the property that had been settled upon her.

"But," as she often told Phoebe, "I've been spoiled for a marriage of convenience. I can recognize cruelty, avarice, and disgust all too well, for I've seen it all my life, since I became so disfigured. And I can recognize kindness and devotion too, because of you, dear. My only regret . . ."

Her only regret was that she'd been the unwitting cause of Phoebe's disastrous marriage. For it had been Lord Beverredge, in grateful recompense for the vicar's friendship to his daughter, who'd supplied the money for Phoebe's dowry when Mrs. Vaughan had dared to ask him for it.

"And *my* only regret," Phoebe would retort, "is that you persist in seeing yourself as disfigured. And not—as *I* see you—as a handsome woman with sparkling green eyes and glossy dark hair, whose only flaw is a complexion that's not what it might have been."

Sadly, this trip had presented Phoebe with an additional regret. For, after some years of trying, Jonathan and Emily had finally conceived a child that would be born next spring. Tactfully, they'd tried not to talk about their long-dreamed-of baby in front of Phoebe; their delicacy made her feel alternately ashamed and grateful, and she knew she wouldn't be burdening them with another visit any time soon.

Kate's closed carriage—the weather had grown too chilly for the barouche—was speeding merrily toward London. Of course they wouldn't go all the way to Town today: they'd stop the night at one of the houses they'd engaged for the purpose of Phoebe's masquerade.

And tomorrow morning, Phoebe thought, Phizz Marston would emerge from the front door, step into his own carriage, and resume his life in Brunswick Square.

To beat snobbish, selfish, fashionable London at its own game—the game that had destroyed Phoebe and Bryan.

Kate interrupted Phoebe's bitter reverie.

"And so, what did you think of Miss Austen's novel—to my mind her loveliest?"

Phoebe hadn't read many novels since she'd become Phizz Marston; it was a consequence, she supposed, of disciplining herself to think like a man. But she'd allowed herself this one as a vacation treat.

"You're right, dear, *Persuasion* is her loveliest. It's not a book of impetuous youth and innocent hope like *Pride and Prejudice*. It's something better, deeper."

"A book," Kate said softly, "about how a woman deserves to be loved, even if she's past her first youth. If she's true and honest with herself."

Phoebe shuddered. "And if she could bear the risk at this age. As I know that *I* could not."

"Are you certain of that, Phoebe? Perhaps it's only at this age that we're able to face life squarely and know what we really want, like Miss Austen's Anne Elliot."

"Perhaps. Well, I shall keep an eye out for any Captain Wentworths who sail into view. And when I find one I'll send his ship your way."

"Do that, dear, for I've decided to spend some time in London this winter. I shall move into our house in Park Lane before Christmas. It feels as though the painters, plasterers, and drapers have been there forever already. I may have to serve Mr. Marston his first cup of tea among furniture still draped in canvas—if he could be cajoled to visit me among such scandalous disarray."

Phoebe smiled.

"He'll allow himself to be cajoled. But only once." She squeezed her friend's hand. "How wonderful, Kate."

And how especially wonderful, she thought, to hear Kate taking an optimistic point of view. Perhaps there *was* a Captain Wentworth somewhere out there for Kate.

For a moment she thought of telling her about Lord Linseley. But what, really, was there to tell besides the fact that she'd met a handsome, decent man who'd attracted her admiration and her desire?

And much as she loved her friend and wanted to see her married, this was one man she wouldn't send her way.

She put her feet up on the seat in front of her. They ached after two weeks of walking without Phizz's boots. Well, she had *that* to look forward to anyway: the pleasure of being well shod and a few weeks of holiday festivities. And the joy of seeing Kate with some regularity—at least as regularly as Phizz Marston could decently visit with Lady Kate Beverredge.

She hugged her pelisse tightly about her and stared at the gray landscape outside the window. Even with the prospect of seeing Kate, the next months seemed very dreary without the hope of meeting Lord Linseley again.

* * *

David stood uncomfortably in front of the pier glass in the bedchamber of his London townhouse.

"And so you see, Mr. Marston . . ." His words trailed off awkwardly.

Damn, he thought, *it was worse than rehearsing a speech to deliver in the House of Lords.*

Because when he spoke of agricultural politics, he need only speak from the heart. He knew the facts, the people, and the land. He knew everything he needed to say and nothing more.

Unlike *this* awkward situation, where he knew much more than was good for him.

Club gossip had it that Marston was back in Town. Evidently refreshed by his journey, he'd won an impressive pile at Vivien's last night. David intended to call on him this afternoon to tell him that he was under surveillance by an enemy.

Of course, he'd reassure him that, for now at least, the enemy had been cleverly and effectively distracted. Stokes had given up the chase somewhere short of the Lake District, much—as he'd told David yesterday—to Baron Bunbury's displeasure. He'd been sure he'd sighted Marston's carriage, but there had only been two old duffers in it.

"So I believe you're safe from *that* quarter, Mr. Marston," David recited.

Yes, that sounded all right.

"But I learned as well, from your erstwhile pursuer, that you may have other enemies. And so I simply wanted to warn you of this."

Not bad.

"And to offer you my assistance, in the unlikely case that you might need it."

Well, it'll get me in the door to see her, in any case.

And after that? He shrugged his wide shoulders. After that he'd have to improvise.

Mr. Marston's household staff had kept things in splendid order during their master's absence. The tallest vases were filled with brilliant masses of chrysanthemums, all bronze and scarlet. Phizz Marston was fussy about floral arrangements; he liked to use what was seasonal whenever possible. Soon the house would be a jungle of hothouse orchids—a little private rebellion against the boring poinsettias one saw everywhere in December. But right now it was nice to have these last naturally-blooming chrysanthemums.

Mr. Simms and Mr. Andrewes had had a smashing trip. "Wonderful luck with the trout, sir, thank you very much for asking. And we were able to get a bit of a lower rate at the inn, since we shared our catch with the kitchen."

"Excellent, Simms. And the carriage was satisfactory?"

"Very generous of you, sir, to allow us the use of it while you were . . . elsewhere. We did have a bit of an unexpected encounter . . ."

"Really, Simms, tell me more."

". . . with a large, ruffianly fellow in a big slouch hat. He seemed to expect to see someone else."

"Indeed. How foolish of him. And was he unaccompanied?"

"Oh yes, sir. Quite alone."

"Ah. And you didn't see him . . . or anyone else . . . after that one meeting?"

"No, sir. Though we kept a careful eye out during the rest of our excursion."

"Thank you, Simms. And sorry for the unpleasantness."

"Happy to oblige, sir."

She remembered the fellow in the slouch hat. He'd waved to her and Kate from up the hill. She also remembered his companion: he'd had a bit of Lord Linseley in his build and posture, and for a moment she'd let herself imagine . . .

Stop it, she told herself. What was important was that once again she'd successfully thrown her pursuers off the trail. Her secret was safe and her masquerade undisturbed.

And it was high time she opened the mail that had piled up in her absence.

She'd received David politely enough, he thought, sitting across from her in her drawing room that afternoon. She seemed nervous, though he wasn't exactly sure why he thought so; if she was surprised to see him, she didn't show it. The meeting must be brief, she regretted to inform him, for she would be receiving her solicitor in an hour.

She'd ordered champagne for herself, and a pot of tea, at his request. Certainly, he thought, he didn't need any intoxicant besides the sight of her graceful, black-clad figure seated on the edge of a sky blue velvet chaise in front of a bank of flame-colored chrysanthemums.

She crossed her legs widely, as though to maximize the amount of space her body occupied and to mitigate the disparity between his muscular bulk and her own slender angularity.

She has something of a fighter in her, he thought. *Not a boxer, of course—she hasn't the weight for it. A fencer, perhaps. Yes. Feint and parry is her style.*

She'd proffered snuff from a fine enameled box and, when he'd refused, she'd taken a small pinch herself before listening carefully to the speech he prepared.

"And so, my lord, you *followed* this Stokes? And therefore followed me as well?"

It did sound a bit shabby and stupid.

Cherishing the image of the lady in pink as he had these two weeks, he hadn't thought he'd find her awfully convincing in her masculine disguise. On the contrary: upon confronting her today he'd seen that he'd underestimated the coherence of the image she'd created, the aggressive tilt of her chin, the hundred mannish gestures she employed so subtly.

Now that he knew her secret, he'd thought he'd easily penetrate her defenses, like the prince scaling the walls of Rapunzel's tower. He'd expected that it would be enough simply to gaze at her as a man gazes at a woman he desires. Surely she'd return his gaze, grant him a hint of welcome.

Not a bit of it. Her body occupied the room as though she had a gentleman's legal right to it. She straightened her back, squared her shoulders, and stared at him from alert, slightly narrowed eyes, her bearing armored with careful, outraged dignity. *As though,* David thought with some annoyance, *I were among those legions of pathetic old nances all lusting for Marston.*

"I apologize, Mr. Marston," he said quietly. "It wasn't my intent to infringe upon your privacy. Only to ensure your safety."

He's looking at me, Phoebe thought, *as I've always dreamed of being looked at.*

But was he looking at *her*? Or at Phizz Marston?

What had he seen when he'd gazed down the hill that morning at the two ladies strolling toward the carriage? For it *had* been him; she'd been right about *that* at any rate. It was disturbing, she thought, that she'd been able to recognize him so readily at that distance.

Unconsciously, it seemed, she'd memorized the lines of his body. But it was one thing to look at his silhouette on a morning hilltop; quite another to have his large physique overwhelming the neat confines of her drawing room. The newspapers were right, she thought: he brought the outdoors inside with him, as though he'd pulled aside the drapes and thrown open a window.

She shivered. The fire had burned down too low. She leaped from the chaise to add another log.

Quickly turning to face him once more, she was surprised to see a mild flush darkening his cheeks. *His summer sunburn is beginning to fade,* she thought. *But what's making him blush like that?*

Ah. She knew exactly what was making him blush like that.

He lowered his eyes, trying to compose himself. But there was no help for it now that she'd guessed the truth: that while she'd turned away he'd been staring at the curve of her derriere and thighs.

My *thighs*. Phoebe's. *He's been looking at my legs, which he can see quite perfectly in these closely-fitting trousers. And he wants* me.

She held herself at rigid attention. Three years of masculine masquerade was nothing, she thought, compared to the control it took not to betray the melting softness invading her body's center at the present moment.

Caught looking, dammit. But upon brief reflection, David decided that being caught might not be such a bad thing after all. She'd quickly regained her self-control, but he knew what he'd seen: the momentary pleasure she'd taken in his eyes' caress. David was an experienced enough fighter to press his advantage when he'd suddenly—even if accidentally—gained the upper hand.

He raised his eyes, grinned, and quickly swept his eyes over her legs.

Her mouth parted into an *O* of surprise. He could see a velvety pink tongue peeping between her white teeth.

Eyes lowered again, he sipped his tea as though nothing had happened. He'd won a small battle, but there was a whole war ahead of him. He was glad; she was too spectacular a prize to be taken easily. He leaned back in his armchair, watching appreciatively as she paced the length of the small room with her graceful, mannish stride.

She stopped now, seized by a sudden insight that lit the gold flecks in her eyes.

"You say, Lord Linseley, that your concern was my safety. And yet you clearly admit that you allowed this Stokes to pursue me into the Lake District."

"Only after I'd clearly seen that you and the other lady were headed in the opposite direction."

You and the other lady. As soon as he said it, he realized that she'd led him into a trap. *There's no going back now: I've just admitted that I know she's a woman.*

It had been clever of her, he thought, to turn the argument so deftly. But of course she was clever: from the very beginning he'd been charmed by the lively intelligence that animated her gestures and expressions.

"And how could you have known *that,* my lord?"

Caught like a clumsy bear with his leg in a trap. It was humiliating. It was delightful. And there was nothing to do but concede defeat.

"Because I saw you depart in the carriage. Southwestward. Toward Devonshire, perhaps."

Devonshire must have been a good guess, he thought, watching her eyes narrow slightly.

His grin widened, crinkling the corners of his dark blue eyes. "You were very beautiful in pink, Mr. Marston."

"And you're surprisingly insolent, Lord Linseley. Not to speak of inconsistent. You did say, after all, that it wasn't your intent to infringe upon my privacy."

"I lied. I want to know everything about you."

"But why? Not for gain, surely? Though I imagine there are those who'd pay for the information."

"I don't want that sort of money."

"For influence, then? To exchange for votes during the next session of Parliament? To sacrifice me and my petty secrets on behalf of England's deserving yeomen?"

"You're cleverer than I, Mr. Marston. I assure you I never considered such a thing. But must I continue to call you Mr. Marston?"

She laughed. "For the time being."

He'd never heard her laugh before. The sound was rich, languorous, like the murmur of spring water spilling over mossy rocks. He wanted to bathe, to luxuriate in that sound. He wanted it to last forever.

She seemed to blossom under his gaze. And then, all at once, she stifled the lovely sounds coming from her throat. Her mouth turned downward, her body stiffened—as it had, David thought, in Fountain Court, when she'd told him she couldn't stand children.

"I wish," he said sadly, "that I could make you laugh again."

"I haven't laughed like that," she said, "since . . . well, for a very long time. I don't deserve to."

"Everyone deserves to laugh."

"No, you don't know about me. You wouldn't say that if you knew."

“I’m certain that there’s nothing I could know about you that would change my feelings.”

“I’ll remember you said that, my lord. But you may come to regret it.”

She paused, crossed the room, and sat back down on the chaise. Somehow during her pause she’d decided to put a measure of faith in him.

“I’m in need of assistance, Lord Linseley. For I’ve received some rather disturbing correspondence of late. And, to be quite honest, I haven’t known where to turn. Will you help me? Or at least advise me?”

“I’ll help you.”

“You say that so readily, so . . . so innocently. As though there were nothing more natural than my soliciting aid from someone who has the power to expose and undo me.”

“It seems entirely natural to me. I want you . . . to reveal yourself to me. And that must begin with my earning your trust.”

“Trusting a man like you is a relatively simple matter. It’s trusting myself that makes me fearful. Because you—your presence, and even the thoughts I have of you when I’m *not* in your presence—could cause me to become careless, and to put me in graver danger than I may already be.”

David felt dizzy for a moment, pulled apart by this last admission. *She thinks of me. Even when I’m not present. She thinks of* me.

And if I were to kiss her right now?

No. He’d never impose himself upon a woman who’d confessed to being fearful. Right now she needed his help rather than his touch.

“Will you show me the letters?”

“I want to, but there isn’t time today. My solicitor will be here in fifteen minutes, and unfortunately he’s never late.”

"Tomorrow then?"

"Yes, tomorrow. Come back tomorrow at two."

He walked all the way to Hyde Park, surprising his groom by demanding that his stallion be saddled immediately.

"Yes, right now. Yes, I know how filthy the weather is. And no, you needn't point out that I'm not properly dressed for riding. But I need to ride. *Right now, man.*"

He needed to exhaust himself so severely that he wouldn't be able to count the hours until two, tomorrow.

He did anyway. Hours and minutes as well.

While Marston took on all comers, thrusting and parrying with unusual brilliance at Mr. McGowan's Fencing Academy for Gentlemen.

Chapter 7

Mr. Simms had to fairly shake Phoebe out of bed at noon the next day. Her limbs ached from the previous day's exertion and her eyes had deep shadows beneath them.

Mr. Simms frowned. "You're not well, sir. I think you should cancel your appointment with the Earl of Linseley. Shall I send a messenger?"

But Phoebe only shook her head and motioned him away.

I'm perfectly well, dammit. Or at least as well as can be expected, for someone resolved to risk everything she's worked to create these past three years.

Yesterday's violent activity had left her mind to its own devices. It was a good technique for coming to a decision; today her head was clear and her mind made up.

She stretched her arms high above her shoulders, savoring the well-earned stiffness of her muscles. She'd fought with rare energy yesterday, her body fueled by the new passion burning in her center. And she'd won, proving to herself that she could win any battle that presented itself. Her fencing moves had been precise, impeccable; no reason to fear that she'd become soft or careless. She could still have her freedom, still be Marston. Her encounters with the earl would simply make the masquerade that much more exciting.

The day seemed to conspire with her mood. The daylight that streamed through the windows was hard and bright, almost glaring. Good. She welcomed harsh textures, strong sensations: the coffee at her bedside was unusually bracing, almost bitter; the bath water scalding; the towels roughened by having been hung to dry in the cold air. She dried herself briskly before winding herself in the muslin bonds that secured her female body from prying eyes.

And yet he'd guessed at the body below the costume.

She armored herself in her padded male garments like a knight preparing for battle. Shirt and trousers. Waistcoat, jacket, boots. She paused, cravat in hand, staring at her slender neck in the mirror. Impossible to masquerade as a man without the indispensable yard of snowy linen wound about her throat. Deftly, she twirled it about her neck, obscuring its delicate female hollows from view.

He looked down at me from the top of the hill, when I was wearing a pink dress and white turban. With my neck bare. Naked to his gaze. Vulnerable.

She'd enjoyed hiding behind a tall cravat these past years, reveling in the freedom not to display her neck and chest to the city's thousand prying eyes. And yet she'd strode through the London streets with the outlines of her long legs entirely visible to all observers.

She shrugged. The laws of fashion were crude, barbarous: irrational and inescapable as the incessant struggles among the *Beau Monde* for social priority. All dress was masquerade, all manners a game of hide and seek. During the years of her marriage she'd labored to present herself as an elegant, expensive object, proof of Henry's wealth and position, graceful and empty as the Chinese vase she'd broken so carelessly.

And she'd succeeded. Men had wanted her and envied Henry; a nimbus of cold scrutiny and casual lust had poisoned the air she'd breathed. The lust, of course, was all the nastier for being unconsummated. Society's laws made sure of that, and she'd been a decent, law-abiding Englishwoman, promising at the altar that no man would touch her except the one with legal title to do so. The law was a pimp, she thought, a procurer like Mr. Talbot. Things were doubtless more decent and rational in Fiji or Brazil.

For an instant she imagined herself dressed in nothing but a few strips of bright cloth, a wreath of flowers around her head. No, such an innocent costume would overwhelm her. She was too tall and pale, a creature of northern chill and slanted light, of icy wit and febrile, over-civilized energy. Best to hide behind severe, tailored black and white. Best to allow Lord Linseley to find his own way to her. She was ready for him.

She stared at herself in the pier glass, watching Phoebe Vaughan's eyes burn in Phizz Marston's impassive face. She wanted to feel Lord Linseley's gaze upon her again. And not merely his gaze. Not if she could influence the course of this afternoon's encounter.

"Yes, thank you, Mr. Marston," Lord Linseley murmured. "I believe I will have some champagne this afternoon."

She looks different today, he thought. *She's pale and seems as exhausted as I am.* He yearned to kiss the dark, delicate skin below her eyes even as he sought to understand the change her looks had undergone.

Her motions were controlled, less flamboyant than

those of the day before, but still proud and angular. *She looks fearless,* he thought, *resolute.* A thrill passed through him. *She's come to a decision.* And her resolve to take the consequences had clearly eradicated all of yesterday's fears.

She led him into a small, book-lined study. There was a sandalwood box and a pile of papers on a graceful oval table at the room's center. She motioned him to one of the chairs alongside the table and then slid into the other. He picked up the first letter and began to read, trying not to be distracted by her proximity, her clean sharp smell of cucumber soap and freshly ironed linen.

He became more grateful for those smells as he read on. For reading the letters she'd received was like wallowing through mud and offal.

"Filth," he concluded half an hour later. Unconsciously, he'd balled up his fists, outraged by the fury Marston seemed to provoke.

"It's all nasty, horrible stuff," he said, "but on second thought it seems to me that there's a quite different quality about these last three." He spread the sheets of paper, their messages assembled of cut newspaper, on the polished walnut table.

"So you feel it as well," she said. "The . . . malevolence of them?"

The second letter proclaimed that: YOU SHOULD NEVER HAVE COME BACK FROM D.

And the third spat out a series of furious appellations, like curses marching crazily down the page:

HARPY
HARRIDAN
CIRCE
SHREW

"This one just arrived just a few hours ago," she said in a toneless voice. "All names for a monstrous, unnatural woman," she added, "but of course you see that."

He murmured assent.

"And does the *D,* in fact, stand for Devonshire?" he asked.

She nodded. "You're not the only person who knows where my journeys end, you see."

"It was only a lucky guess on my part."

She sighed. "It's odd, though, isn't it, that after three years of success I should be unmasked by two parties all at once. You . . ."

"Because I care for you."

"Yes well, you *want* me, in any case. Perhaps it's just as well that you don't know me well enough to care for me. And it should be clear by now that I want you as well. But we'll deal with all that in due time."

He stared at her, not quite sure what to make of the directness with which she'd addressed him. He corrected himself: his *mind* wasn't sure; his body seemed to have no problems whatsoever with her mode of address.

"But this letter-writer," she continued, "if writer he can be called . . . this *other* person hates me. I can feel it. Absolute, implacable hatred, instead of the simple pique and humiliation in the other letters, which is, on the whole, more amusing than troublesome."

"You're brave to find them amusing rather than vicious and insulting. What *have* you been doing to create such general consternation?"

She shrugged. "Beaten them at gambling. Gotten them blackballed from White's. In one way or another, I've made it clear just how cheap, petty, and ridiculous these posturing fools really are. It's not difficult and it's all quite trivial. Not at all like challenging them in Parliament as you do."

He shook his head. "It may be more trivial, but to me it seems a great deal more dangerous. Because it's still a man's game you're playing. And even if they don't suspect . . ."

His voice trailed off. Without being told, he'd grasped the unspoken decorum of her home: one might say quite erotic and provocative things to her, but one didn't ever refer to the facts of her disguise, at least in the rooms downstairs. And he wouldn't let himself think about the rooms upstairs where she dressed. Where she undressed. Where she bathed . . .

"You were saying, my lord?"

"Oh. Yes. Right. I was saying that these adversaries of yours, petty and ridiculous as they are, do sense something rather out of the ordinary. Perhaps it's simply the perfection of your masculine masquerade. You're more perfect than any real man, even the most mannered of dandies, and they sense it; they're put off balance by it even as they're humiliated by how absolutely you've captured their attention. They rather *enjoy* their humiliation, you see, and they write these letters to exaggerate the sense of titillation they feel. After all, Mr. Marston, you're a very attractive young man."

She essayed not to smile.

"You have something . . . ah, *unusual* about you. A quality. A little something extra."

"Actually, it's rather something less."

"It's not something less. At least that's not how I've ever thought about it."

"Then you're a most unusual man as well."

"Someday I hope to demonstrate that to you, Mr. Marston, at close range. But to return to the matter at hand . . ."

They must compile a list, he told her, of the gentlemen most likely to respond to Marston's having exposed their weaknesses and inadequacies to society.

This, however, turned out to be a more difficult task than he'd expected, for she seemed to have made social mincemeat of most of Polite London at one time or another. *Why?* he wondered. *Why this unceasing need to strike out at snobbery, hypocrisy, and complacency?*

Still, he had to admire the *brio* with which she'd gone about it. The energy and the sly wit. He laughed as she told him how she'd managed to blackball her victims. Clever to choose such tiny, telling details, he thought: Smythe-Cochrane's affected dinner-table manners; Raikes's idolization of Smythe-Cochrane; Crashaw's unfortunate boots.

"Drumblestone's Bargain Blacking? I shall have to ask my valet if he's ever heard of it."

"He doesn't use it, my lord. At least not on *your* boots, I can assure you of that."

"And how . . ." he'd been going to ask her how she knew what kind of blacking Crashaw's valet used. But the question faded while he became distracted by the way she'd swept her eyes down over his boots and up over his legs in imitation of his glance at her yesterday. He allowed himself a rueful shiver of appreciation: women didn't use their eyes that way. Even prostitutes were less direct, less at ease with the art of erotic scrutiny.

"You're a formidable adversary, Mr. Marston," he observed. "I must remember never to expose my own petty weaknesses and economies to you."

Whatever else, he thought, moving his chair a few inches farther away from her, *I might desire to expose.*

Her mouth had settled into the maddening curve that might or might not be a smile.

He cleared his throat. "Yes, well then. I think we can narrow the list down to three besides Bunbury."

She nodded. "Raikes and Smythe-Cochrane, certainly."

"And our mutual favorite, Lord Crashaw. Whose character is as black as his boots are not."

He frowned.

"But that brings up a serious problem. For my plan was to speak to these gentlemen directly, to see what ill will they harbor you. And whereas I can certainly approach Raikes and Smythe-Cochrane, Crashaw absolutely won't receive me. Won't even acknowledge me in a public venue."

He told her, with some pride, about the lands he'd bought up at auction, snatching them from Crashaw's greedy grasp. She listened so eagerly that he told her more than he'd intended, confiding that he was actually a bit strapped for cash these days. Not so much that he'd have to skimp on boot-blacking, but he might in fact have to practice some economies while he was in London. Still it had been worth it, to know that there would be fewer expulsions from the land in his part of the world.

"Your part of the world?"

"I suppose that's a stupid way to express it, but it's how I think of it."

"Very lordly of you."

"I rarely see it that way. Mostly I think of myself as a steward of the land. I'll be all right if the next harvest is as good as this last—but spending this winter in London is deuced expensive."

"Then why are you here?"

"You know why I'm here."

She looked down at his large hands spread out upon her table.

"I'm quite extraordinarily grateful."

"Yes, well . . ."

She reached out to begin refolding the letters. He covered her hand with one of his own. A jolt of electricity shot from his fingertips to his body's center.

"Wait," she whispered, "for just for a moment."

He lifted his hand from hers and stared as she opened

the room's double doors. He could hear her talking to a servant in the foyer.

She reentered the room, closing and locking the doors behind her.

"I told Mr. Simms that we were not to be disturbed for the next half hour."

"And after that?"

She smiled. "After that I told him that we had best be disturbed."

The doors were adorned in the French style of the preceding century, with gaily colored scrolls of fruit and flowers. They looked lighthearted, lascivious. Like the golden sparks that danced in her eyes.

"I know we still have a great deal to discuss," she said while she loosened the knot of her cravat.

"But I think that we'll be able to think more clearly after a short intermission."

Either that, he thought, or we'll be too besotted to be able to think at all.

Swiftly, she unwound the long strip of linen from around her throat.

The cloth slithered down her shirtfront to lie in a heap upon the Persian carpet at her feet. She kicked it to the side, leaned against the door, and settled back for the instant it took him to reach her.

For a moment he merely savored his body's closeness to hers. Only an inch away—he could see the pulse beating in her neck. Warmth spread outward from his center: his groin tightened, his thighs ached to press her hips between them. But he kept his legs together, his arms quietly at his sides. Gently he dipped his head toward her, tracing the curves and hollows of her flesh with his lips and tongue. He took tiny kisses, nuzzling her throat, licking the long lines of her neck, breathing her smell until it began to make him giddy.

He loosened the top button of her shirt, grasped her

shoulders, and buried his mouth in the hollow just above her clavicle. Moaning at the press of his teeth, she relaxed into his hands' grip. He tilted her head back still farther. She shivered against the roughness of his palm at the nape of her neck, the pull of his callused fingers tousling her hair. His other hand supported the back of her waist.

She staggered slightly, perhaps simply for the pleasure of feeling him tighten his hold upon her. She trembled under his mouth as he moved it upward over her neck, chin, and jaw. Steadily, deliberately, he claimed her for himself in tiny, irrevocable movements of lips and tongue, before finally forcing her lips open for a breathless kiss.

She wrenched herself away from him.

"I hadn't intended to kiss you, my lord."

"I know, Mr. Marston. But then you *didn't* kiss me—not as I imagine you're capable of kissing me. *I* kissed *you*."

"I hadn't intended to allow you to."

"You knew I'd take more than you allowed me."

She lowered her eyes, wondering if she *had* known that. "Perhaps," she murmured. "But then why not take even more? Why not take . . . everything?"

"That would be a crude pleasure. I prefer a subtler one: anticipating what you'll give me next time you're in a . . . giving mood."

"You're patient, then."

"I'm not a young man any more. There's that advantage."

"You're hardly old, Lord Linseley." She swept her eyes down over his body again.

"I'm certainly not old enough to be proof against lecherous glances like that one. I know you're a gambler, but don't overestimate your luck, Mr. Marston."

He glanced at the clock on the mantelpiece. "There are, after all, another fifteen minutes before we are—disturbed."

"Thank you. I think I shall need the time. To compose myself. And to re-knot my cravat."

"If I knot it for you, we'll have time for another kiss. A proper one this time."

"No. Not this time, for I shall also have to rearrange my hair. You've mussed it terribly. I . . . I could feel your fingers in it."

Gently, he traced the curve of her right ear with his thumb. Her neck arched, and her mouth opened slightly to let out a soft, bubbling sigh.

"I've mussed your hair wonderfully," he said. "You look like a mischievous little boy who's stolen a pie from the kitchen and knows he's in for a caning."

"It was a most delicious . . . pie." She licked her lips and grinned while he wound the cravat back around her neck.

"I feel that I'm hiding a treasure away from the common view," he sighed. "It's sad, but also lovely in its way, because only I know where to find it."

"I shall study the knot after you leave," she whispered.

He stood back to watch her comb her hair back into its accustomed waves and spit curls.

"Yes, thank you, Simms," she called when the discreet knock came at the door a few minutes later.

She opened the door to let in some air. *And perhaps,* David thought, *to signal that Mr. Marston hadn't been murdered by his still slightly wild-eyed visitor.*

She closed it again. "Now where were we?" she asked briskly. "Ah yes, we'd just agreed that it's Raikes, Smythe-Cochrane, and Crashaw. Oh, and Bunbury. But the rub is getting Crashaw to speak to you."

Surprisingly, he did feel a bit more clearheaded.

"Well, I think I've hit upon a bit of a plan. What do you think of this, Mr. Marston?"

He supposed that he had Stokes to thank for the stratagem that had just occurred to him. That and the roguish gleam in her eye just before. *I know you're a gambler, Mr. Marston.*

"After all," he said softly when they'd seated themselves back at the table. "The entire population of the Polite World knows how much I spent at the land auction. And so they'd hardly be surprised that I need money."

"And what," he added, "does a gentleman do when he wants to quickly fill his coffers?"

"He tries to borrow, I suppose," she said, "unless he's more daring, and then . . ."

He held up a hand to interrupt her. "I shall tell a few well-placed people that I tried to borrow from you and was severely rebuffed this afternoon. After which I shall . . ."

She nodded quickly. " . . . try your luck at Vivien's."

"Where I shall stupidly, recklessly, and very angrily lose an indecent amount to you this Monday next."

"And where I shall be smug, insolent, arrogant, and entirely insulting. As I have been, ah, known to be upon occasion. It won't be difficult, but you must forgive me in advance if I seem to enter too readily into the spirit of the thing."

He grinned. "Well, it won't be difficult for me to lose at cards. I've never had a head for it. And so I shall become your sworn, desperate enemy. So furious a one that all your other enemies will want to call upon me as an ally."

"Even Crashaw?"

"Crashaw might have other motivations as well.

He'll come calling on me though, to endeavor to buy back a field or two when he hears that I've ruined myself financially. And when he does I can certainly avail myself of the opportunity to sound him out about you."

"Don't worry," he said hastily, seeing the anxiety that seized her expression, "I promise that I won't displace anyone from the land. The fields I'll offer Crashaw are worthless. They're in serious need of drainage, but since he knows so little of farming, he won't know that."

He smiled at her evident relief.

"I shall have to stay in Town to effect all this business. I suppose that I shall have to stay during the holiday season."

Amazing how easily he'd proposed it, he thought. He hadn't spent a Christmas away from Linseley Manor since he'd become earl.

"Of course," he added, "we won't be able to meet after we're sworn enemies. Especially with you being under surveillance as you are."

"You're right. I hadn't thought of that."

Did that sudden darkening of her eyes signal disappointment? He hoped so.

She knit her brow. "Then how shall we communicate?"

"By the post, I suppose."

"And if we need to confer?"

"Do you have a trusted friend who can deliver messages?" he asked.

"Indeed. One whom I trust absolutely. You've already seen her, you know."

"The lady in yellow."

"Yes, Lady Kate Beverredge. But mightn't it be dangerous for her, if people of ill will are watching me?"

"We must be very public; it's sneakiness and surreptitiousness that your enemies will be looking for. Would your friend dance with me at Almack's?"

Phoebe smiled. For Kate had nervously agreed to attend the Almack's New Year's Ball, as part of her new resolve to "face life squarely."

"Yes, she'll dance with you. She waltzes beautifully."

"Good, then she can relay anything you might want to tell me. And I can send messages to you."

"So this is our last . . . real meeting for a while, I take it."

"There ought to be a way to contrive a meeting, but at the moment I'm not sure what that is. Right now, though, I want your promise that you'll be extremely careful, and take note of anything or anyone who acts in the least bit suspicious."

She shrugged. "Of course."

He should feel more disturbed, he thought, by that shrug. She was much too daring for her own good. But he couldn't quite muster the requisite concern. Not when she was so charming in her bravado.

"And this is important, Mr. Marston: you must tell me everyone who knows your secret. We shouldn't assume that they're all to be trusted."

"In theory I suppose you're right. But in this case I refuse to believe that any of my friends would betray me. Anyway, there are very few of them. Lady Kate, of course; my brother and his wife in Devonshire. Let me see . . . well, there's also the woman you met when you were pursuing me . . ."

"The garrulous one, who said you'd gone to the Lake District."

"Yes, Mrs. Grainger oversees the houses we use for my . . . transformations. Oh, and Mr. Simms and Mr. Andrewes." She explained quickly who they were.

"Well, you have kept this affair very secret. Very wise; I congratulate you."

"Thank you. So it's Monday next at Vivien's. Midnight would be dramatic, don't you think?"

"Midnight would be excellent. And now . . ." He thought he'd have something to say in conclusion, but discovered belatedly that he didn't.

She looked steadily at him through the awkward silence.

"And now it seems," she said, "that we must end this interview."

"It does seem that way. Unless you'd like to tell me your real name?"

She shook her head. "No need. I quite enjoy the way you call me *Mr. Marston.*"

"The point isn't what you enjoy. The point is that I ought to know more about you in the interest of your own safety."

She shrugged again. "After all, I didn't request your protection. Merely your help. There's a difference, you know."

We'll pay for that devil-may-care look in her eye, he thought helplessly.

She grinned, enjoying her power. "What I was about to say, my lord, is that we should end this interview properly, since we don't know when next we might meet. We should end it . . ."

"With a proper kiss?" he asked.

"I think," she returned, "that I'd prefer a highly improper one. To inspire me, you know, before Mr. Marston severely rebuffs the earl's request for a loan of ten thousand pounds."

All of Mr. Marston's servants could attest to the fearful row that put an abrupt end to Lord Linseley's visit that afternoon. A chair or two were knocked over, the two gentlemen were flushed and breathless, and

Lord Linseley stomped through the foyer and out the door in a loud, dreadful hurry as the usually unflappable Mr. Marston hurled insults after him.

And only Mr. Simms had the wit to notice what sounded suspiciously like smothered giggles on his employer's part as she shouted terrible things to the gentleman making his way out. And to wonder exactly what had transpired during the long silence that had preceded their row.

Chapter 8

Energy was high at Vivien's the next Monday. The Earl of Linseley had never been known to gamble. "Too rich, well-born, and stuffy for it," was the word among the *ton*. "Too humorless, too stiffly noble and high-minded," added his enemies in Parliament.

"Serves him right for all that tiresome prattle about the common lands and the rabble who work it. And then getting into debt, in this crusade to stifle the Progress of Industry. I hope Marston leaves him without a pair of boots to call his own."

"Indeed, let the honest yeomen he champions lend him the ten thousand he needs."

News of Linseley's disastrous confrontation with Marston had circulated about the clubs as if through the ether on Mount Olympus.

"He said that Marston promised it to him and then went back on his word."

"Marston, of course, denied the story. Said that he'd offered Linseley ten thousand for the pattern of the knot in his cravat. But then he figured it out for himself. Spent a whole night in front of his mirror working it out. Linseley flew into a rage when he realized what happened."

"Marston *would* say something like that. Well, it promises to be a diverting evening. Will you bet on it?"

"Wouldn't be gentlemanly to refuse. Five hundred on the earl. The odds on him are tantalizingly short."

Lord Linseley and Admiral Wolfe, Messrs. Marston and FitzWallace, having seated them for whist, the club's management sent over a bottle of champagne. Not unexpectedly, Marston pronounced the vintage "vulgar" and demanded the prior year. A murmur of appreciative laughter swept through the room.

Marston sipped his champagne, watching coolly as Lord Linseley quickly tossed back a glassful and immediately poured himself another. He looked flushed and rather confused, as though barely attending when Mr. Vivien announced that the pair who took the first seven tricks would be the winners, with the highest scorer getting all the money.

The admiral dealt the first hand and took the first trick. FitzWallace took the next and Marston the next three.

He was looking unusually handsome that evening. His dress was impeccable and his color was high. "I don't usually get the opportunity to ruin such a noble gentleman," he'd been heard to remark upon entering the room. "Or such a handsome one," he'd added. "Desperation quite becomes him. Rather loosens him up, eh?"

He joked between tricks and stared provocatively at his opponent. A few gentlemen with an eye for such things found his manner more than provocative.

"Indecent, I'd call it," whispered Baron Bunbury to

a young companion. "I hope the earl teaches the obnoxious Marston a lesson with those big fists of his, and I think I'll advise him to do so. About time *somebody* did, anyway."

"I think you'd be pleased to see him do anything at all with those big fists," his companion whispered back. Bunbury glared.

Linseley and Wolfe played their remaining cards capably enough but their opponents won the hand and scored the first point.

Marston dealt next, the earl seemed quite mesmerized by the sight of his slender hands on the deck.

Almost despite himself, Linseley took the first trick. Wolfe pressed their advantage and they won the hand. The score was tied.

"Marston gave them that point," someone whispered rather too loudly, "to make it more interesting for himself."

Linseley was clearly disconcerted to hear it. He played erratically, wasting some high trumps and causing even his partner to raise his eyebrows. His side lost the next hand. And the next as well. Four points to one now.

"Only one more and Phizz wins the ten thousand."

"Which will ruin utterly our fine Lord Linseley. He'll have to sell some of that land he bought so recklessly."

The admiral dealt. The gentlemen surveyed their cards.

Ten tricks played. Four for Marston, two for Fitz-Wallace. Three for the admiral, one for the earl.

Linseley's hand trembled. Another moment and it seemed he might drop his cards. A murmur accompanied his play: queen of diamonds.

Diamonds were trump.

And Marston had the ace.

"Sorry, my lord. It's all over, don't you know? And I'll take it in cash, if you don't mind."

There was a furious crash as Lord Linseley rose from his chair. "You'll take my cheque, you vile puppy. Are you insulting my word?"

"Oh no, not your word, my lord. Merely your credit. And your sobriety."

Polite Society would have a laugh over that tomorrow, as they would when they recounted how a furious and confused Lord Linseley pelted the young man with banknotes. "And he might have done a good deal more," they'd say, "if Admiral Wolfe and Baron Bunbury hadn't hustled him out of there and into his carriage."

"Fine-looking carriage. Wonder if he'll sell it."

"This is madness, David," the admiral said once the carriage had rolled away.

"I thought it went rather well." Lord Linseley fanned himself calmly with his top hat. "Stifling hot in there though. All those absurd dandies with nothing better to do of an evening."

"And *you've* involved yourself with the most absurd and scandalous of them all."

"Except that he isn't. *She* isn't. She's something special. She's something . . . extraordinary."

"Extraordinarily handsome young man is what she is, to my way of seeing. If one didn't know the truth, one wouldn't suspect it for a moment. You're quite *sure*, David?"

"*Of course* I'm sure."

Admiral Wolfe put up a conciliatory hand. "Yes, yes, don't take offense. Of course you're sure."

David hadn't told Wolfe any of the physical details

of his encounter with the lady, but he supposed his friend had guessed that *something* had transpired. Good of John Wolfe not to pry, he thought.

"The point though," the admiral continued, "is that she's putting herself into a deuced dangerous situation and has been for some time. Why? What's in it for her?"

"If I knew *that,* I might be able to play her game halfway decently—whatever *real* game it is she's playing, you know. If I even knew her *name*, for that matter . . ."

He'd already done what he could for her safety by hiring Stokes to follow her about through Town. He'd informed her of it by post, too, after a bit of deliberation, when he'd realized that she was too clever not to pick Stokes out in the shadows.

His note to her had been terse, perhaps a bit self-righteous. "For your own safety . . . I hope you understand the wisdom . . ."

She'd written back just as tersely, thanking him for his concern, protesting that she needed no protection in the streets, and adding that she'd try not to succumb to the temptation of leading Mr. Stokes through dark alleyways and losing him there. "Respectfully as always," she'd signed herself, "PM."

It was the name that rankled. He wanted to call her something besides "Mr. Marston." He wanted a woman's name he could whisper in his dreams.

But he supposed that would all have to wait. Until after next week's dinner engagement with Smythe-Cochrane. And—*ah yes, he'd forgotten the bit of paper Bunbury had—too obviously—slipped into his pocket.* Coal Hole Tavern. Fountain Court. Dusk. Tomorrow. Tell no one.

Two out of four wasn't bad, he thought. He'd inform her of his progress next week at the Almack New Year's Ball.

But it was Crashaw he was betting on. Had his performance at the gambling table been convincing enough to lure Crashaw into an alliance?

He settled back into the carriage's velvet upholstery and continued to fan himself. He was still flushed from the champagne. And from pretending to be drunker than he was. Or *had* he been pretending? His head was certainly swimming now; perhaps he truly *was* as besotted as he'd seemed. But not merely on champagne. It was *she* who'd made him so drunk. As she'd promised, she'd been "smug, insolent, arrogant, and entirely insulting." And irresistible; in David's eyes at least, her behavior had been an inducement to ravishment atop a green baize gambling table.

He relaxed into the darkness and let a slow smile steal over his face. Just wait, my young gentleman, he found himself thinking, just wait until I get you alone.

"Don't say a word." Phoebe held up a finely gloved hand. "I *know* that I was scandalously visible last Monday night and that you heartily disapprove. But do wait, Lady Kate, to hear the whole story before you pass judgement upon your humble servant."

Lady Kate Beverredge was receiving Mr. Marston in the splendidly refurbished salon of her house in Park Lane. The fresh paint and wallpaper fairly glistened, and the drop cloths had been removed from the new upholstery just the day before. Marston took an appreciative breath of the lemon oil that had been rubbed patiently into the wood of the Hepplewhite tables. "The room is exquisite, my lady. And *you* are looking equally well today."

It was true. Kate looked serene and relaxed, a lady of impeccable breeding at home in her impeccable surroundings. She inclined her head slightly to acknowledge her guest's compliment. And then shook it to signal that she was in no mood for cajolery.

"I'm delighted that we meet your standards, sir. And I hope the garden does as well. Will you take a turn with me?"

"Of course." Marston took the mink-lined pelisse from the arm of a waiting servant and swept it over his hostess's shoulders.

"I'll give you a cup of *tea* when we've finished our conversation." Lady Kate Beverredge's voice and gestures were as severe as Mr. Marston's were expansive.

Barely suppressing a grin, Marston waved a hand toward the double doors that opened onto the terrace. "After you, my lady."

The garden was bleak and wintry, its yew hedges still in need of trimming. But it was an enviably large space, set with graceful gravel paths.

"It'll be lovely in the spring, with roses all along this east walk." Phoebe took her friend's arm. "Will you be planting any of the new varieties?"

"Yes, I like the look of those new moss roses, interspersed with the big, round, old-fashioned kind. But don't you dare distract me: we're not here to discuss roses, you bad girl. We're here to assess the danger you've put yourself in by making yourself the object of all the Town gossip. Don't you remember the promise you made, when you began this mad masquerade three years ago?"

"I do indeed. I said I'd live as austerely and privately as it was possible for a gentleman of fashion to do, but Kate . . ."

"An absurdly liberal promise, I see now. We should have been stricter with you, held you to higher standards."

"Oh but Kate . . ."

"Because you simply don't understand how Jonathan and Emily and I worry over you. And poor Mr. Simms—*especially* Mr. Simms—how *could* you be so inconsiderate of someone so devoted to your welfare? He came to see me all in a dither yesterday, about a fight . . . a *physical* scuffle with Lord Linseley. In your *home,* Phoebe, what *were* you thinking?"

"I do apologize most heartily for the . . . scuffle, and for worrying dear Mr. Simms. You're right, of course; I must take him into my confidence about these matters, but . . ."

"I fail to see how your behavior is covered by *any* 'if,' 'and,' or 'but.' Or *any* exception to *any* rule of behavior, gentlemanly, ladylike, or otherwise."

It is impossible to speculate how long Lady Kate might have continued in this vein, had she not been interrupted by a most unexpected sound.

Giggles. A cascade of helpless, uncontrollable, delicious, feminine giggles.

A chagrined Mr. Marston lifted his hand to his mouth, trying to pretend that he'd been overcome by a coughing fit. But to no avail. The happy laughter wouldn't be stopped.

Kate stared in wonder. "Oh my dear."

The two friends stood face to face under a ramshackle arbor, its shaky wooden frame entwined with bare, leggy vines in winter slumber.

Phoebe gradually regained her composure, though her cheeks remained scarlet as berries.

"Unusually warm day for December," she murmured.

"Quite."

"He *knows,* Kate. He was *there,* don't you remember, atop the hilltop at Rowen-on-Close? There were two big men watching us from the hill, Mrs. Grainger told us later that she sent them off to the Lake District.

He saw us . . . he saw *me* . . . dressed as a lady. And he knew immediately. He seems to . . . to know me."

"Ah."

"He's a good man, Kate. We can trust him. And he's pledged to help."

"To help deal with the threatening letters, I take it?"

"They've gotten worse. I received one this morning, informing me that AN UNNATURAL WOMAN WILL MEET AN UNNATURAL END. I informed Lord Linseley of it by post today. But now you can see why he and I have had to pretend to be enemies; it's so that he may gain credibility with the scoundrel who wishes me ill."

"It sounds dangerous," Kate said.

"He seems quite fearless." Phoebe glanced carelessly at some shrubbery in the corner of the garden, as though the gentleman's bravery were a matter of no consequence to her.

She shrugged and turned to face Kate again.

"Well, it's all rather a bother, really. And what's particularly vexing is that he's taken all the planning upon himself. He's set a silly bodyguard on me—there, you can see him through the gate, the huge fellow lurking about in the slouch hat. And I, it seems, must simply wait like a helpless . . . *woman* to see Lord Linseley again—to . . . to learn what progress he's made, I mean."

"*Of course* that's what you mean."

Lady Kate Beverredge crooked her arm into Mr. Marston's and led the young gentleman a brisk, silent turn around the garden.

"You're laughing at me, Kate," Phoebe whispered.

"I haven't made a sound."

"You haven't needed to. Well anyway, you'll soon be able to pass judgement upon him yourself, for he'll be asking you to waltz at the Almack's New Year's Ball. At your debut into London Society."

"Ah yes, just two weeks from now. Just thinking of it makes me as nervous and flustered as you are."

"*I'm* not at all nervous or flustered. And I won't have *you* going all fluttery on me either. The Ball's not really even part of the Season, after all; it's just a small, well-bred overture for spring. So if my lady chooses to grace it with her presence, *she* will be bringing distinction to *it*. And she will be a paradigm of aristocratic serenity: calm, collected, and a great success."

"Quite right, dear. Now come inside and see my new ball gown. The modiste says it wants another flounce at the hem, but I told her that Mr. Marston must assess my costume before I agree to any changes."

Chapter

9

Kate carried off the gown with understated elegance, standing upright and serene under the Almack chandeliers a fortnight later. Mr. Marston had vetoed any possibility of an additional flounce at the hem: the modiste's creation of deep green velvet was perfect as it was, trimmed with looped ropes of woven gold and edged with tapering points of creamy Venetian lace.

The rich silk velvet draped fluidly past her back and torso, and the raised waist lent a hint of lushness to her bosom, gently rising and falling beneath a heavy gold and emerald necklace. The candlelight sought out matching emerald undertones in the gown's fabric, and Kate's green eyes sparkled as brilliantly as the gold combs in her dark hair, crowned with glossy holly leaves and one splendid ivory camellia at the peak of its bloom.

One could, of course, still discern the marks that smallpox had left on her face. But tonight it was Lady Kate's graceful bearing and not her imperfect complexion that defined her presence. She looked the very ideal of serene, aristocratic complaisance, as though attending this holiday celebration among the *Beau Monde* were but a modest family pleasure—and not, as only Phoebe knew, a wrenching challenge to her will and equanimity.

But this *time,* Phoebe resolved, *Kate will not lack for partners. Even if it's only Mr. Marston who twirls her about the room. Well, Mr. Marston and Lord Linseley,* she reminded herself, feeling her cheeks grow warm as she allowed herself to think of him for the first time that evening. For Kate had agreed to the plan: Lord Linseley would relay any messages he had for Phoebe while he danced with Lady Kate.

Phoebe had been grateful, during the first hours of the festivities, to be able to concern herself so exclusively with Kate's fortunes. Arriving twenty minutes before Lady Kate, Mr. Marston had promptly disappeared into the crowd to survey the proceedings, to wait for Kate's arrival on the arm of a distinguished, white-haired kinsman, and to watch her offer cordial, respectful greetings to the ball's patroness and the other committee women.

The exchange of compliments hadn't been audible from Marston's corner of the room, but the words didn't matter: it had been abundantly clear from the smiles, the subtle nods and glances, that Kate had found favor with the powerful women who ruled England's premier marriage mart. Even mulish Lady Claringworth had managed to bend her palsied features into the simulacrum of a smile. Marston indulged himself in a barely perceptible shrug: Phoebe hadn't received even that much warmth from her mother-in-law during all her years of marriage to Henry.

She's got them. Phizz Marston breathed a long, satisfied, and only slightly wistful sigh, much to the bewilderment of the cluster of youths who'd been studying the cut of his new jacket. He grinned at his admirers—"Andrewes, don't you know, Regent Street, devilish expensive and worth every penny,"—and drifted away into the holiday throng.

But the cocky grin faded as Marston strolled out of the youths' line of vision. Tracing a path through the crowd of high-spirited, well-dressed revelers, he seemed alternately to scan the faces about him and to withdraw into himself, as though afraid to encounter the object of his search. If any of his young imitators had seen him, they would have felt a measure of disappointment in their idol's ambiguous behavior; they might even have become troubled or confused by the occasional expression of yearning that flitted across his face. Because this evening—and for no discernable reason—this evening the normally unflappable Phizz appeared—well, there was really no other word for it—quite uncharacteristically *fluttery*.

He shook off the flutters, of course, as soon as the orchestra began to tune their instruments. Regaining his composure, he seemed to grow in poise and stature—to spread his shoulders and arch his back as though buoyed up by the waltz's soaring opening chords. Leading Lady Kate to the floor, setting his hand lightly at the small of her back, he swept her into the heart of the dance like a dolphin diving into the crest of a wave shimmering beneath a tropical sun. His rivals and admirers alike could only marvel at the alchemy he'd wrought: of skill and nerve, of muscle and control, and—they felt rather than thought this—of tenderness.

Even Lady Claringworth seemed moved by the spectacle—though it was impossible to tell from her palsied features exactly what she might be feeling. She gestured impatiently to her footman—*here, Trimble, I need a heavier cane to lean upon.* The tall man in livery handed it over while he frowned at the dancers. Absentmindedly, the dowager Lady Claringworth pounded the heavy stick in time to the music.

But if Marston's flamboyance had captured the room's attention, it was Lady Kate's comportment that kept all eyes riveted to the waltzing couple. The lady in green and gold leaned confidently into her partner's embrace and matched his steps with offhand exactitude, her evident delight in movement and music sending arcs of happiness rippling in its wake.

Of course, she's not a pretty woman, some of the gentlemen thought. But nonetheless, they observed, she definitely has something—a generosity of presence, a perfection of breeding, a finely wrought *joie de vivre* that might be appealing at breakfast or on a country drive in the early springtime. I should like to dance with her, some of the more discerning of these gentlemen thought, or perhaps simply to exchange a few compliments over a lemonade. And after all, some of the more hardheaded of them added, there's that fortune of hers to consider.

Mr. Marston steered his partner toward a sedate corner of the room. Far from the orchestra, an alcove stood like a sheltered tide pool at the edge of the sea of dancers, with only a few older couples twirling about in quiet, decorous eddies.

"You look every bit as perfect as I knew you would. Are you happy, Kate?"

"I believe I am, dear. The ladies have been extremely kind. Perhaps the Polite World is not so fearsome as I thought. And you're most . . . dashing tonight as well. Is the gentleman we were discussing in attendance yet?"

"I haven't seen him. But as we danced I thought I felt his eyes upon us."

Mr. Marston made a tiny grimace, as though embarrassed by having made such a fanciful remark. Lady Kate's green eyes shone, but her face remained discreet, noncommittal.

"Do you suppose it's possible to feel someone's eyes across a crowded ballroom, Kate?" Phoebe's anxious whisper sounded a bit hoarse.

Lady Kate Beverredge could only catch her breath and nod, having quite suddenly caught sight of two gentlemen some dozen yards away. The darker, handsomer one, whose every glance seemed to burn into Phoebe's arched back—well, there was no question who *that* was. But the gray-haired one, with the medals and the distinctly military bearing—most attractive, she found herself thinking, as she and the military man exchanged a polite nod and a tiny, private smile. But just then the music ceased and it was time to thank Mr. Marston for a most delightful turn on this most festive of occasions.

It wouldn't do, of course, for Lord Linseley to dance with Lady Kate directly after his enemy had done so. But there was no chance of that in any case, for the lady had enough partners to occupy her for the next hour.

Meanwhile, Marston, as was his custom, joked with his cronies and danced with those ladies who might otherwise have been in danger of neglect. He liked to single out a young woman possessing more wit and spirit than the more saleable endowments: money, pedigree, or unusually fine looks. And after a turn around the floor with Marston, many a young lady might find herself in surprising demand for the remainder of the evening. Gentlemen would begin to take notice of her, as though Marston's attention had shone a light on her particular charms.

"And how strange it was," the young lady might muse afterwards. "Because for all his snobbish, critical reputation, I found him quite extraordinarily sympathetic. Almost as though he understood what it's like to be a shabby bluestocking just up from the country, with the family expecting so much of me and Mamma shoving me into this horrid, uncongenial crowd."

They all appreciated his attention, and some—the more astute of them—even heeded his final, whispered words. *You're all right now, Miss So-and-so: quite ready, I think, to swim in these dangerous waters.*

But you must value yourself, my dear. I entreat you, above all things, to remember that.

"May I, Lady Kate?"

"With pleasure, Lord Linseley."

Her voice was noncommittal, her smile bland. *She doesn't trust me,* David thought, taking her hand, *and she won't until I can convince her that I care as deeply for her friend as she does.*

Decorously, they waltzed about the floor in measured circles. The sheltered alcove at the end of the hall was almost empty.

"I have a cheque for you in my reticule," Kate said, "from our mutual acquaintance."

"Your bank," she added quietly, "won't know it's drawn on her funds."

His ten thousand. A pity that he couldn't hide his relief, for he hated having to put off tradesmen and he'd been terribly short of cash this week.

"Thank you, my lady. And how shall we manage the . . . transfer?"

"You'll get me a lemonade, I suppose, and while I wait I'll bring the cheque out beneath my handkerchief. Shall we get that part of it over with now?"

"Yes, rather, while there isn't a crowd at the refreshment table. And then perhaps we could stroll down that hallway and admire the paintings."

Lady Kate nodded soberly, though her eyes twinkled at the idea of admiring the sort of painting one was likely to find in the Assembly Rooms' back hallway.

The financial transaction effected, the pair stood in rapt contemplation of a portrait of the Assembly Rooms' founder, a Scotsman who'd found it necessary to betray his family name of MacCall by twisting it into "Almack."

"You may tell our friend," Lord Linseley said, "that my meeting with Baron Bunbury was most productive."

His companion inclined her head.

"But unfortunately," he added quickly, "it only confirmed my suspicion that he had nothing to do with the problem at hand."

"Oh, he's no admirer of Mr. Marston's," the earl continued. "Quite the contrary. He wishes him only the worst, and was most voluble about the nasty letters he's sent him—in fact, he's kept copies of all of them, which he obligingly showed me. Windy, tediously labored bits of invective they were too; he's clearly not the author of the frightening threats our friend has been receiving lately."

"And the other . . . candidates?"

"Raikes has been called down to the country to attend to a family matter. He's leaving tomorrow, but promises to contact me when he returns. I dine with Smythe-Cochrane tomorrow evening. But the real progress I've made is that Crashaw is willing to speak to me. The first communications were most formal and official—through our solicitors. But I will receive the gentleman himself in Lincolnshire in a few weeks, a few days after Twelfth Night. It seems that he wants to tramp the fields with me, two country squires muddying our boots in our native English soil."

"Someone must have told him that he'd do well to acquire a veneer of your style."

Lord Linseley shrugged his shoulders. "I have no time to waste on whatever it is the *Beau Monde* likes to think of as style. But he's welcome to copy whatever he likes, as long as he helps me unravel the mystery that is plaguing us all."

"Quite so." Without meaning to do so, Kate allowed a hint of warmth to shade her voice. *For he does seem a good man,* she told herself.

"And so you must inform . . . our friend that I must defer the pleasure of another . . . personal meeting until after I have finished these interviews."

The wistfulness with which he delivered this message pierced Kate's heart. She frowned thoughtfully. There was also something about his choice of words—he wasn't using the words, she thought, that he wanted to be using.

Speaking before she'd quite got these perceptions in order, she blurted out, "Phoebe didn't tell you her name, did she?"

She saw immediately that she'd guessed correctly, for the joy that lit his dark blue eyes was like a warm harvest moon rising in an early autumn night. He laughed with the pleasure of precious new knowledge. "Phoebe, is it?"

For a moment he seemed to withdraw into a secret place. Softly and so privately that Kate felt like an intruder, he repeated the two syllables to himself, savoring them like exotic hothouse fruit. *Phoebe.*

He blinked, suddenly feeling Kate's eyes upon him, and his smile became formal, apologetic. "Phoebe, is it? Y-yes, yes of c-course it's Phoebe."

Briefly, she told him the outlines of Phoebe's story. Her marriage to Claringworth. The accident and Bryan's death. She left out the misery of the marriage; that would be for Phoebe to tell him as she would. Instead she told him a bit about herself, how much she owed her friend, and how deeply she cared for her. *Just so he understands,* she thought, *how rare a prize he's set out to win.*

But he does understand, she told herself. Of course he does.

He tried to maintain a sober, respectful demeanor, but his eyes danced with pleasure.

"My deepest thanks, Lady Kate."

"It has been my pleasure, Lord Linseley. For I think that you and I shall be friends."

"We shall indeed, it's most kind of you. And you *will* relay all this information to . . . um . . . her, won't you?"

"Of course I shall." *How beautiful the love of a good man can be,* Kate thought. *Of course,* she quickly reminded herself, *Phoebe deserves it after all she's suffered.*

But I also deserve such a love. She surprised herself by the vehemence of this next thought. And at that moment she might have experienced a rare pang of jealousy, were it not for the sound of the orchestra striking up the next dance.

Quickly, as though responding to some mysteriously foreordained signal, she glanced down the hallway. And there, quite as if it had all been planned out in advance, was the gray-haired gentleman with medals twinkling on his jacket.

She smiled and nodded, enjoying the military formality with which he advanced and extended his hand to her.

"And now, Lord Linseley," she added, turning her head slightly so that her smile might include both gentlemen, "if you could introduce me . . ."

The earl of Linseley bowed with mock solemnity.

"With pleasure. Lady Kate, may I present my oldest

friend, Rear Admiral John Wolfe? And Wolfe, allow me to introduce you at long last to the lady you've been waiting so patiently to meet, the Lady Kate Beverredge."

But what has he told her? Beneath Phizz Marston's poised exterior, Phoebe thought her heart might burst with impatience.

It was late. Lord Linseley had danced one more dance—a sedate quadrille with Lady Jersey—before bowing and making his good evenings. Most of Marston's cronies had already departed to attend rowdy holiday suppers. Attendance at the ball had thinned; the couples still on the floor were those who didn't want to part just yet.

And must Kate dance yet another *turn with the Admiral?* Phoebe knew that such a selfish thought was unworthy of her. *This evening belongs to Kate,* she reminded herself. *And just look how happy she and her partner are, gazing into each other's eyes as though they're the only people in the room.*

She usually saw nothing but scheming and corruption in these halls—young ladies brought, as she had been, like innocent lambs to the slaughter. But not tonight. Tonight it seemed like simple loveliness to meet a congenial gentleman and dance with him: to feel his hand at your waist as you matched your steps to his and gazed into his eyes, both of you sealed in a little bubble of intimacy, right under the all-seeing eyes of the Polite World.

She was glad it could be that way for Kate.

But if she didn't find out what Lord Linseley had said—*and quickly, this very instant!*—she would expire where she stood.

She claimed Kate for the next dance.

"Tell me. Tell me now."

Happily, obligingly, and in meticulous detail, Kate recounted her interview with Lord Linseley. The financial transfer—he'd been most gentlemanly about it; Bunbury's innocence—well anyway, it was a relief, was it not, to be able to check one candidate off the list. His plans seemed to be proceeding with admirable dispatch, she continued: dinner with Smythe-Cochrane tomorrow evening, and most importantly the crucial meeting with Crashaw planned in two weeks, in Lincolnshire. Of course it was a pity that he hadn't had a chance to speak to Raikes yet, but even that gentleman . . .

Phoebe's face fell.

"So he's learned *nothing* of value."

"Not exactly *nothing*, but . . ."

"And he's going down to the country in two weeks."

"For a most important meeting, after all."

"And so he won't be coming to . . . to see *me* for weeks and weeks and weeks!"

Kate had intended to tell Phoebe that she'd revealed her identity to Lord Linseley. She was a bit anxious about it, for—no matter how innocently—she had after all betrayed a confidence. Still, she'd reassured herself, Phoebe couldn't really mind. Or *wouldn't* mind, after learning how ardently he'd repeated the syllables of her name to himself.

But with her friend in such a state, Kate thought she'd better wait a bit before delivering that particular bit of information.

"Yes, the earl was most sincerely regretful to have to defer the pleasure of the next personal interview . . ."

"You know him well enough to judge his sincerity, do you?"

"Our friendship is sealed by our mutual regard for you."

Kate had almost said *our mutual love,* but decided that it wasn't her business to reveal the depths of the gentleman's affections. *He must speak for himself,* she decided, *hopefully at a moment when Phoebe isn't apt to bite his head off.*

Phoebe only nodded and attended to her feet, and they passed the rest of the dance in silence.

"Will you come see me the day after tomorrow, Mr. Marston?" Lady Kate Beverredge asked anxiously. "For tomorrow I'm driving out with Admiral Wolfe . . ."

Marston looked cold and abstracted. "I have a fencing lesson in the morning, I regret to say, and calls all afternoon, my lady. I shall send a note when I find a moment of free time."

"I shall wait patiently. *As must you.*"

He bowed and then swiveled neatly on his heel, heading for the exit and leaving Lady Kate to heave a sigh that was both loving and vexed.

She's absolutely impossible when she takes one of those impetuous turns.

Her expression softened as Admiral Wolfe approached.

Still, she'll be by in a few days to apologize—meek, contrite, and extravagantly regretful of her moment of rudeness. And in the meantime . . .

John Wolfe smiled and extended his arm. She took it easily, returning his smile as though they'd been promenading together for years.

And in the meantime, Kate assured herself, *Phoebe certainly won't do anything dangerous.*

Chapter 10

Phoebe.

So that *was her name.*

Hesitating at the door of his carriage, Lord Linseley dismissed his coachman. He needed to walk; he craved some good fresh air after the stuffy Assembly Rooms. If Dickerson would be so kind as to drive back to the stable alone . . .

Dickerson nodded respectfully, though the way he pulled down his hat and hugged his greatcoat around himself suggested that he thought his master quite daft. It was a dank, freezing night, the air saturated with poisonous fog.

But he's been suspicious of my mental state ever since the storm at Rowen-on-Close, David thought, grinning ruefully at the absurdity of choosing to walk in such weather.

He took a deep draft of the night's malodorous vapors. It did taste rather awful, he thought, trudging off into the turgid, gaslit darkness. And then he forgot the air entirely, losing himself in delicious imagining.

Odd that it mattered so much, his finally learning

her name. Just two little syllables, but the intimacy of it made him giddy.

Perhaps it was Lady Kate's evident love for her, or the sweet stories she'd told of their girlhood. Whatever had turned the trick, though, somehow she was no longer a mystery. She was his future.

Have you seen my slippers, Phoebe?

Will you ride out with me this morning, Phoebe? I have a long day in the fields planned and want you with me for at least a part of it.

No, Phoebe, there's nothing the slightest bit wrong. I'm simply staring at you, dear, because you're so lovely in the lamplight.

Yes, Phoebe, I suppose it is late. What say we go to bed, my love?

My love, my lady.

Phoebe dear.

Phoebe darling.

He walked briskly, breathing the filthy air as though it smelled like new-mown hay.

Phoebe. It chimed like soft musical accompaniment to the images wafting through his mind.

Her back and shoulders: gracefully arched and widely spread, held in perfect equipoise as she guided her friend about the dance floor.

Her neck: high and proud beneath the purity of her white cravat. Two weeks ago time had stood still while he'd watched her unwind that length of snowy linen. She'd offered him her graceful woman's neck, all vulnerable hollows and poignant shorn nape. She'd revealed herself to him in mute, eloquent prelude to the naked passion she'd shown later that afternoon.

Their last half hour together had been an astonishment; she must, he thought, have astonished herself as well. He thought of the princess in the fairy tale, the beauty trapped in hundred-year-long slumber. Cold ivory flesh turned warm and rosy, awakened by a kiss from the one man brave and steadfast enough to cut through the thorns and briars that kept her prisoner.

In his reimaginings of it these past weeks, he'd indulged himself in the fantasy that she'd been as protected, as hidden away, as the princess in the story. It was absurd, of course: no sheltered virgin would have been capable of the lascivious looks she'd directed at him, not to speak of those extravagant caresses. Still, he'd desperately wanted to believe that it had simply been her desire for him that had made her so passionate, so preternaturally knowing in the ways of the body. Of course, now that he'd learned the truth from Lady Kate, he wasn't really surprised by it. After all, she was too beautiful not to have been married before.

David hadn't known Lord Claringworth personally—certainly the man hadn't spoken very often in parliamentary debate. His voting record, as far as David could recall it, was spotty but ultimately fiercely Tory. But that wasn't something to hold against him; every gentleman had the right to an opinion, after all.

He called to mind his only clear memory of Phoebe's husband: tall and fine-boned, a handsome, laughing presence apologetically waving an expensively gloved hand to his friends when he'd arrived too late for some vote or other. He'd made David feel stodgy, older than his years. David felt a sad twinge of jealousy: Claringworth's young wife must have adored him. How tragic to be widowed as she'd been. And, dear God, to lose a child as well. His heart flooded with sympathy for her, followed by a determination to make it all right in every way he could.

Certainly to give her other children.

Phoebe, countess of Linseley. He'd fall asleep tonight

with its sound in his ears and its taste on his lips. And with his desire warming his loins and spurring him onward to success.

For if his plans went as they should—if he were as good and faithful, as clever and patient, as the princes who scaled fairy tale towers—David was sure that he'd earn his reward. The immensity of the undertaking, the richness of the outcome, made him dizzy; he staggered a bit in the yellow fog. *Hold on,* he counseled himself. *There's work to be done. There are challenges to meet, monsters and demons to vanquish before you can call her your own.*

But maybe he'd be lucky. Maybe the monster would be Smythe-Cochrane, who'd be coming to dinner tomorrow. He balled up his fists, hoping for a quick fight, a decisive victory. Unlikely, though. He was quite sure that the moment of truth would occur after Twelfth Night, at his meeting with Crashaw.

He stood still for a moment, steadying himself before he continued his swift, firm steps. His desire for her would sustain him in his battles. He'd bear it, draw nourishment from it. Having her in his bed would be a lifelong adventure—far more wondrous than the memory of one afternoon, richer and more multifaceted than any passing fantasy he could summon up. She would reveal herself to him in the fullness of time; she would open herself (but here he shuddered, almost losing control despite his best intentions) more and more deeply, as their love grew and their destinies intertwined. A lifetime of discovery awaited them. Life would unwind as inevitably and sinuously as her neck cloth, one long busy day, one gorgeous languorous night, at a time.

Well done, he congratulated himself (for he hadn't lost control after all). *Patience,* he repeated. *For now, I must content myself with the promise of spending every night with my arm around her waist, her head resting beside mine on the pillow.*

Patience! The word seemed to hiss accusingly in Phoebe's ears as she hugged her heavy woolen cloak about her and marched furiously toward Brunswick Square.

It was all very well for Kate to counsel patience, she told herself. But had Kate had to be patient this evening? No, she had merely to look up and there had been the admiral, paying her all the attention a woman might wish.

Phoebe could see quite well how unfair she was being. After all, Kate had waited many lonely years for this evening and Phoebe was happy that it had unfolded so beautifully for her. As happy, at any rate, as a woman might be who has not been able to share a glance—or a dance or even a touch of the hand!—with the only man in the world who mattered to her.

She stamped her feet against the cold. It had been foolish not to come by carriage, but the plan had been for Marston to leave the ball early for a night of gambling, gossip, and carousing with his friends. The plan had *not* been for Marston to stumble around that benighted pleasure dome while Kate and the Admiral made eyes at each other for what had seemed like bloody hours.

And the plan had *certainly* not been to haunt the crowd like a pathetic mooncalf, helplessly coveting Lord Linseley's forbidden attentions and hating every woman—even silly Lady Jersey!—with whom he danced.

She could still see his hands, gently leading a lady to the dance floor or exerting deft pressure at the small of her back. He had only danced a few times, but she felt as though he'd paid court to every simpering female in the room. Every one but herself, of course.

I shall wait patiently, Kate had said. *As must you.*

Oh indeed. Phoebe's eyes flashed in Marston's immobile face.

Women always waited, she thought angrily: they waited to be asked to dance, they waited to be asked to marry; they waited stupidly and passively at home while men went out and *did* things.

Most women waited, that was.

"But damn me if *I* will."

The half-frozen beggar standing with his hand outstretched blinked with surprise as the fancy young gentleman hurled this sudden, perhaps drunken, imprecation into the darkness.

Phoebe blinked back at him as she dug into her pocket for a coin. Two coins. The beggar hurried off to buy a bed—and a bottle—to warm himself through the remainder of the night. Despite her anger, Phoebe discovered that she was grinning. Mr. Simms was right; she did need to be more careful of her language.

And as for the sentiment she'd expressed so precipitously: crudely phrased as it was, Phoebe found herself in total accord with its substance. She wouldn't—she *couldn't*—wait passively for the earl of Linseley to rescue her from her mysterious adversary. Three years as Marston had accustomed her to doing things for herself. Three years of educating herself about her own tastes and passionate desires had made her aggressive—a taker of pleasure rather than its humble recipient.

But what to do?

For she had to admit that Lord Linseley's plan was a sound one. The only trouble with it was that it contained no role for her. She should have demanded one, she thought, rather than demanding that "highly improper kiss."

Her lips curved. No, she should have demanded both the kiss *and* an active role in the plan.

Her eyes softened at the memory of those last moments with him. For she'd risen to his challenge—to kiss him as she was capable of kissing him. ("As I imagine you're capable," he'd said; she hoped that she'd far surpassed his imaginings.)

She'd been cool, unhurried at first. She'd explored his mouth with her tongue, nibbled gently at his lips with her teeth. She'd gone as slowly as possible, tasting and sampling (oh Lord he'd tasted good—sweet as toffee, heady as tobacco, dark as earth), allowing her lust to coil within her like the muscles of a tiger before it strikes. Finally, when she could bear it no longer, she'd clasped him to herself with all her strength, breathing him in as a drowning person might inhale a deep, delicious, life-giving draft of air. She'd thrust her hands beneath his coat, tracing the lines of his powerful back and shoulders, nearly rending the linen that separated his skin from hers.

How selfish, how brazen she'd been. And he'd been man enough to delight in it. His belly had rippled with subtle inner laughter; she'd felt it against her own as he leaned into her embrace, his hands cradling her buttocks through her closely-fitting trousers.

What, she wondered, would have happened if he hadn't pushed her away from him a few delirious moments later? No wonder she'd been able to slap him so convincingly, to storm about the room shouting curses and overturning furniture. She'd been enraged when the kiss had ended, furious to find her arms bereft of him. The embrace should have continued, it should have built and crested, rising to its natural, beautiful conclusion, ebbing toward perfect satisfaction.

Of course he'd been right to put a stop to it. There had been no possibility of going any further that afternoon. But she'd been imagining it ever since. She could see it before her in the livid gaslight as though David were with her right now in her bedchamber. (She'd never called him "David" before, but daring to do so seemed in keeping with her defiant mood tonight.)

His eyes would be bright with concentration, his face intent upon the business at hand. His expression would be serious, his smile only revealing itself at the crinkled corners of those bright eyes. Smoothly, deliberately, he'd peel the trousers from her legs while she unwound his cravat and unbuttoned his shirt. She giggled, thinking of how quick, how impatient she'd be. With all her experience of men's garments, she'd have him naked in a trice. Or naked enough, anyway, to drag into bed on top of her.

Later, of course, there would be time for more leisurely, creative love play. She'd undress for him; she'd even be bold enough to demand that he undress for her, as once, a thousand years ago, she'd demanded of Billy.

Billy.

She stopped walking, the nasty chill night air entirely forgotten.

Billy was her answer—her solution to the problem of how she might participate in the plan to find and unmask her adversaries. How she might put an end to this unbearable separation and bring David back into her arms as quickly as possible.

Odd that she hadn't considered this possibility before. Or perhaps not so odd. For it wasn't easy for Phoebe to organize her thoughts about these matters. At bottom, though, she knew without quite understanding it that she kept her thoughts about Billy locked up in a separate compartment from her feelings for Lord Linseley.

But that was silly, she told herself now. There was no call to be so excessively fastidious about these things.

She hadn't made love to Billy since Lord Linseley had entered her life. She couldn't have done so even if she'd wanted to; her body wouldn't have allowed it. And surely *that* was the important thing: that she'd followed her body's honest dictates. She wanted no one but David and would do nothing to sully that desire.

But meanwhile, Billy and the other boys from Mr. Talbot's might know a great deal of useful information about the gentlemen she and David were investigating. Lord Crashaw, after all, was a regular customer. How foolish she'd been, she thought, never to have asked if Crashaw or anyone else had made any incriminating remarks about Phizz Marston.

David and I would be fools, she thought, not to avail ourselves of such valuable information.

A little creativity, she told herself, a little spontaneous improvisation was what was needed right now. And David wouldn't mind—he'd applaud her independence just as he'd gloried in her sexual forthrightness. Imbued with a new sense of purpose, she recommenced her brisk pace toward Brunswick Square.

Of course what he *might* mind, a small solemn voice at the back of her mind whispered, was that she had lied to him when recounting the short list of people who knew about her masquerade. Well, she hadn't exactly *lied*—she'd merely failed to mention Mr. Talbot. Mr. Talbot and Billy. And since neither of them knew her real identity, they didn't really count, did they?

Well, maybe they counted in a small way. For both of them certainly knew that she was a woman. To put an absolutely rigorous face on things, Phoebe supposed that one would probably have to say that she'd committed a small sin of omission by not disclosing these facts to David.

But a small sin of omission certainly didn't count as a lie, did it?

All right, so it *was* a lie. And a perilous one to boot: she'd misled David as to the danger of the situation. Phoebe knew very well how risky it had been to tell Mr. Talbot her secret. Because among the small group of people who knew that Marston was a woman, Mr. Talbot—sexual procurer to the *Beau Monde*—was the only one not committed to her by bonds of love or friendship or family.

She'd convinced herself that she was safe enough. Wasn't it true, after all, that Talbot would soon lose all his custom if he became known as a tittle-tattle? But the fear had never quite left her. Deep within herself she knew that she'd struck an expensive bargain.

She'd insisted upon living as a man instead of simply masquerading as one. She'd resolved to have a man's sexual knowledge and freedom, to exercise a man's right to sexual pleasure. She'd never regretted the devil's bargain she'd made; the excitement of living as Marston had been built on a foundation of risk.

And since she'd risked no one's safety but her own (For she'd already lost Bryan—but she wouldn't think of that now! Not now and not ever!), she'd felt herself fairly entitled to the excitement.

She wouldn't worry, she told herself. Her little lapse couldn't endanger so responsible, so invulnerable, a gentleman as the earl of Linseley. He'd taken her on just as he'd taken on the destinies of half the farm laborers of Lincolnshire. Cautious and deliberate, he was the sort of man one trusted to deal with the affairs of a nation. One would readily hand over one's fortunes for his disposing. As readily—as eagerly, as passionately—as Phoebe would hand over herself to his body's desires.

Still, Phoebe reminded herself, he'd have to remain ignorant of Billy—and of the course of sexual self-instruction she'd allowed herself. Necessary as the episode had been for *her,* there was a limit to what a decent gentleman was capable of understanding.

She'd find out whatever Billy knew about Raikes, Crashaw, and Smythe-Cochrane. She'd share the information with David and never tell him how she'd learned it. Together, they'd solve the mystery of her vicious adversary. And then they'd be free to explore life's more important mysteries—the mysteries of a man and woman who wanted each other so wholly and joyously.

He'd visit her late at night. She'd run up the stairs, flushed from winning at gambling, and there he'd be, ready to tear off her gentleman's clothes and find the woman hidden underneath. And sometimes she'd steal away from London, stop at Mrs. Grainger's to change into her pink gown, and wait at sunset for him to ride up to the gate.

You're very beautiful in pink, Mr. Marston.

Oh yes. With such a lover, her life as Marston would be beautiful indeed.

She shivered—with cold or with desire?—and hastened her steps. Billy wasn't due until Saturday. But she'd pen the note to Talbot as soon as she got home, asking if she could have Billy tomorrow instead. She'd post it first thing in the morning.

She'd been walking by fits and starts—sometimes stopping for minutes at a time to stare at nothing—and obliging a freezing, miserable Archie Stokes to blow silently into his hands and stamp his feet, hidden as he was in shadows and doorways. Didn't she notice the cold? he wondered.

He'd kept the guv'nor's card safe in his pocket after setting off after Marston in the Lake District. It would be good sport to report on finding him, he thought—

and who knew, maybe Linseley would even make good on the promise of boxing lessons. Of course, he never *had* found the man in question—not that it *had* been a man: the guv'nor had explained it all patiently when Stokes had screwed up his courage to visit him anyway. Bunbury had shouted at him and called him stupid, but the earl wasn't that sort of man. They'd had a good laugh and a mouthful of ale together over it and Stokes had been hired to follow Marston—well, to follow the young lady as it turned out—and make sure she was safe.

Not that it wasn't still a queer business, the guv'nor being so obviously smitten with her. And—Stokes shook his head—just as obviously ignorant about the pretty blond boy who came so regularly.

Of course the boy *could* just be some friend of the family. Well, there was *some* who might believe that, he supposed, but not Archie Stokes. Still, he'd never tattle and break a man's heart over it.

Maybe she'd see reason and the visits would stop of their own accord. Maybe she'd tire of the boy. Stokes hoped so. For he'd developed a strong measure of devotion to his employer: Lord Linseley had been decent with him, the work was steady, the pay excellent. And the weekly boxing lessons had been a revelation. Amazing what you could do if you had both size and strategy, he thought. And wonderful that he'd finally met someone who wasn't too intimidated by his size to take him on and teach him a thing or two.

A shame, though, that he hadn't yet been able to put the lessons to use. The guv'nor had said the lady was in danger, but Stokes hadn't noticed anybody on her trail. Maybe he'd scared them away, he comforted himself. Well, he'd just have to be patient. Certainly he'd done a professional job so far, keeping her safe in the cold, wet, dark streets she liked to frequent.

And was she finally hurrying home like a sensible girl? Yeh, it certainly seemed that way. And high time too. Still, she'd soon be tucked into her bed, and after a mouthful of hot rum and water to wash away the night's chill, so would Stokes himself.

Chapter

11

Mr. Hugh Smythe-Cochrane leaned voluptuously back in his chair, patting his bright brocaded waistcoat with a puffy, manicured hand. A few crumbs of a very fine apple tart glistened at the corner of his mouth; the wreckage of a formal dinner lay in front of him on the table.

"Snuff?" David passed him a small enameled box.

"Thanks, Linseley, don't mind if I do."

Smythe-Cochrane's teeth were large and brown, and his breath hadn't been the sweetest even before he'd tucked away the splendid meal David's cook had produced.

"A fine roast." The gentleman evidently imagined himself an authority on culinary matters. "An excellent aspic for the salmon. The sweet—what do the French call it? A *tarte . . . tart . . . tarte tartan*, isn't it? And the claret . . . One doesn't often taste such a claret nowadays."

David maintained a sober demeanor, though it was hard not to smile at the notion of an apple dessert decked out in Scottish plaid. "It's my last bottle. My circumstances, you know . . . reduced to the very devil these days."

"Marston *is* the very devil. It's a scandal that he's such a pet of the Polite World. Rather like that young Disraeli boy who's suddenly invited everywhere—the lack of standards these days is shocking. But even if Marston is no Hebrew, you were stupid to go up against him."

"Yes, rather." David inclined his head thoughtfully. Good work, the man bringing up Marston of his own accord, even as he flaunted some other unpleasant prejudices.

Smythe-Cochrane's muddy brown eyes seemed to redden, though perhaps that was just the effect of the snuff. "Young puppy ought to be horsewhipped. Publicly."

"Hmmm. I'd like to hear more of your thoughts on the matter. What would you say to our finishing the claret in the drawing room?"

"Excellent, excellent."

David led him to a large armchair and watched him spread himself in front of the fire like a spaniel. The gentleman certainly liked his creature comforts.

But one wouldn't want him dozing off. As David poked the embers and nudged the biggest log into a better position, the fire sent up a fine blaze of sparks.

"I try, you see, to maintain certain standards of hospitality, even if Marston has put rather a crimp in my style."

Smythe-Cochrane nodded, lost in private reverie.

"You proposed a public horsewhipping for him, Mr. Smythe-Cochrane?" David's voice was low, insistent.

The log caught fire. Smythe-Cochrane emitted a coarse chuckle.

"A private one would be better. Trap him when he's out on one of those mysterious jaunts of his. Surround him and drag him to some old, abandoned building. Get two big toughs to hold him down and bend him over a splintery table. Pull down those trousers and allow every gentleman he's insulted to get a whack at that pretty arse. Until he bleeds. And cries for forgiveness."

Another chuckle. Followed by what sounded like a deep sigh of contentment.

Peering over the edge of his glass, David stared pensively at the flames reflected in his guest's eyes.

"We'd make him crawl. Apologize to each of us in turn, on his knees. Lick our boot toes until his tongue is raw." These last pretty sentiments were delivered in a hoarse whisper.

"You've given the matter some thought," David said.

"Oh, I'm not the only one. Raikes and I had it all planned out. One could never organize the whole crowd scene, you know, though one likes to imagine it.

"But we could do it, just the two of us, we thought. So we hired the toughs and set out to follow him. Lovely day last spring—April, still a bit chilly, just enough to get the blood up. We'd intended to leave him in a ditch, shivering without those elegant trousers of his. We followed him to Rowen-on-Close, where he boarded for the night. And damned if he hadn't simply disappeared into thin air the next morning."

"Quite the joke on you."

"Quite."

"And are you planning to try again?"

"No, we've given up on it—no sport in being led a wild goose chase around the countryside. Anyway, the pleasure for Raikes and me turned out to be in the imagining of it. But why do you ask, my lord? Would you want to join such an expedition?"

I'd join you in hell first, David thought, balling up his fists and barely suppressing the impulse to pound this nasty-minded glutton to a soft white pudding and toss him out with the rest of the kitchen scrapings.

His fury and revulsion quickly soon gave way to a series of other emotions. Disappointment: it was clear that Smythe-Cochrane wasn't the culprit. Relief: at least, he thought, he'd eliminated two suspects and wouldn't have to bother talking to Raikes. A renewed certainty: surely it was Crashaw, just as he'd always suspected. And a renewal of his single-minded devotion to the cause he'd set himself: to rescue Phoebe from the hatred that her masquerade had inspired.

Also a measure of thanks. Because the good food, blazing fire, and fine wine he'd provided had combined with the man's over-heated fantasies to wrap Mr. Hugh Smythe-Cochrane into a warm cocoon of postprandial bliss. A happy snore rose from the deep armchair as the clock struck half past ten. Well, at least it hasn't been the longest unendurable evening I've ever spent, David thought. He offered quiet thanks for having been spared any more of the gentleman's conversation.

Staring at the fire, he came to a quick decision. Impatiently, he rang for his butler.

"Would you and a footman toss him into the guest bedroom, Grimes? And make my apologies if, as is devoutly to be hoped, I don't see him tomorrow morning. For I've decided to escape to Lincolnshire a few days early.

"Have Dickerson get the horses and carriage ready, won't you, and tell Croft to pack a small bag for me. Oh, and please ask Cook to prepare an early breakfast and pack a luncheon for me and Croft—after you deliver my congratulations on the dinner she produced this evening. We'll leave at daybreak."

He'd post letters to Wolfe, to Stokes, and to Phoebe, informing them of his altered plans. (Could he possibly write "Dear Phoebe?" No, not yet.) He hoped she'd understand how difficult it was for him to be in London and not see her. It would be better to go home. His extended stay in London had put an unfair burden on his steward, who'd had to distribute a wagonload of Christmas gifts throughout the village in his stead.

He stood up, stretching his arms and powerful shoulders, taking a few deep breaths to calm himself. His heart was beating too quickly and his stomach felt a bit off-center; one shouldn't eat good food while listening to vile conversation, he thought. But he'd feel better once he was on the move.

He'd saved the letter to Phoebe for last. Predictably, he'd blotted several sheets in his vain struggle to get it right. His first draft had been stiff and school-boyish, his second florid and word-drunk; both unfortunate attempts had been tossed in the fire. His third try was adequate, he supposed, if a bit more formal than he'd like. It would be easier, he thought, when she'd granted him the right to call her by name. And after he'd told her that he loved her.

This last thought so astonished him that he made a fair mess of sprinkling sand over the paper to dry the ink.

He loved her; the dazzling idea of it had crept unbidden into his head while he'd been forcing his emotions into acceptable shape. No wonder it had been so difficult to write the letter—he'd been telling her everything but what he'd truly felt.

He loved her. Odd, he'd thought of everything but love. Sex, marriage, even children. A lifetime together. But love? Somehow he'd thought that love wasn't meant for reasonable, responsible people. He'd done so well without it, after all.

But yes, he loved her. He didn't know where the

feelings came from or how he could be so sure of them. Still, it was true. He loved her absolutely and unrestrainedly. After a lifetime of imagining himself incapable of such a thing, there it suddenly was: effortless, natural, thrilling.

You don't know me well enough to care for me, she'd cautioned him. But she'd been quite wrong. Nothing could stop him from caring for her, from loving her. Nothing could and nothing would. He'd tell her that, he thought happily, first chance he got.

He gazed abstractedly at the fire, listening to its soft crackle and only gradually becoming aware of another sound, a loud pounding out in the street. No, it wasn't in the street; the furious banging came from right below where he was sitting. The glass panes in his study windows were shaking as though rattled by a strong gale. Someone, it seemed, was trying to break his front door down.

His butler's feet clattered down the stairs. Blast it, who could be out there at this hour?

He could hear two sets of footsteps on the stairs now, Grimes's and someone else's, both rushing up to see him. The second man had a heavier stride. He turned in his chair, rose, and hurried to open the door.

"Begging your pardon, my lord," Grimes began, "but Mr. Stokes here—well, sir, he insisted, sir . . ."

Stokes elbowed Grimes aside.

"You better come wi' me, guv'nor. The lady . . ."

Dear God.

"Is she hurt, Stokes? Did someone . . ."

"No, guv'nor, she ain't hurt. It's the . . . the boy, see."

David had never seen Stokes blush before, never heard him stumble over his words as if there were something he was embarrassed to say.

"She said I should come get you. There's a cab waiting downstairs."

It hadn't been an easy thing, Stokes reflected later, to tell Lord Linseley the story. He'd wished the streets had been empty, so that the cab could have quickly delivered them to Brunswick Square. For it had been bloody unpleasant, spending all that time in the cab with the guv'nor all pale and furious and with that dazed look on his face—like someone had finally got past his ironclad defense and fetched him a good one in the jaw.

No, he corrected himself—like someone had kicked him where a man didn't want to be kicked.

It ain't my business to say such things as I was forced to say to him, he thought indignantly. Should be the lady informing him what happened. After all, it was on her account that the boy was all hurt and bloodied.

But the cab had stood maddeningly still, mired in traffic. There'd been some kind of big reception just letting out from one of the great houses nearby. Swells and their ladies poured out of the large front doors; cabs and carriages were stacked up in the streets for block after impassable block. And the guv'nor wanted to know right now, exactly what had transpired at the lady's house. So Stokes had no choice but to spill out everything he knew.

Not that he actually knew all that much. And he wasn't exactly proud of his role in the part he did know about. He should have hung around, he supposed. But nights when the pretty blond boy made his visits—Tuesdays and Saturdays they were—he usually knocked off early. This hadn't been one of those regular nights, but Mr. Simms had been kind enough to tip him off about it.

Stokes liked the old valet. They'd become friends one stormy afternoon when Simms had invited him into the kitchen and given him a cup of tea. "No point your catching your death out there," he'd said, "when I know she's not planning to go out for a few hours."

None of the other servants had been around, so they'd been able to talk honestly, about the lady and her peculiarities, so to speak. It had been a bit of a blow to Stokes's pride to learn that both she and Simms knew he was guarding her; he'd thought he'd been wonderfully sly. But Simms had been handsome about it, and had a sense of humor as well. "If you think she leads you a merry chase in the streets, just try looking after her every day as I do."

"I'm deeply grateful to you, Mr. Stokes," he'd added, "for keeping her safe. I worry about her, you know." He sounded like a kind old uncle; it seemed that he'd known the lady since she'd been a child. Stokes would wager that the boy's visits weren't Simms's favorite events of the week either.

The boy had been due at eleven; Stokes had shoved off about nine. Had a bit of an engagement himself if truth be told. Bosomy Dolly Martin had taken rather a fancy to him since he'd had some money to throw around.

"But when I got to the Laughing Crow Tavern, there she was wi' Cummens Small's 'and round her waist. And his other 'and reaching deep down into her . . . sorry for talking out of turn, guv'nor." For Stokes had belatedly realized that his employer might not enjoy the drift his story was taking.

" 'E won't try that again, anyway, but . . . but where was I? Right, took a walk outside I did, to clear my head. And somethin' told me maybe I'd been neglecting my post back at Brunswick Square. Which I 'ad, guv'nor, no point my tryin' to deny it.

"I got back too late for the fight. The body 'ad been

dumped on 'er doorstep. Not dead, they 'adn't meant to kill 'im I don't think, but awful badly beat up—seemed like they might o' got carried away, lovin' their work as some types do. I think they worked 'im over in an alley you know, and then just 'auled 'im over."

"So you could have apprehended them if you'd been there. And we would have learned who had hired them."

Stokes nodded soberly.

"That's true, sir. Couldn't 'ave done nothing for the boy, but . . ."

"Hang the boy, I hired you to protect *her!* I told you she was in danger, didn't I?"

The outburst wasn't like the guv'nor, but Stokes took his point.

"Yer right, sir. I failed you, I did."

Still, Stokes thought, it had been the boy who'd taken the lumps. A bad beating around the face, that was for sure. And probably a broken leg, Stokes hadn't liked the look of how it had hung down all crooked. He'd appeared in awful pain: if the toughs had mashed his insides like they'd flattened his nose he might not live out the night. And if he did live he wouldn't be pretty enough to continue earning his living in his accustomed manner. Simms had told Stokes to carry him inside, lay him out on a settee. He'd sent a footman to get a doctor.

"And the lady?"

"Didn't see 'er. Simms went upstairs to inform 'er wot 'ad transpired, and I thought she'd come down directly. But Simms said she'd 'ave to dress, which always takes 'er a bit o' time, you know. Well, it makes sense, disguised as she is, so clever and natural she makes it seem, though myself I 'adn't given the matter much thought before 'e'd said it. Simms said that I wasn't to wait, but go fetch you, at 'er orders, see."

Stokes had thought that the guv'nor would like that bit, about her requesting his presence. But his face only looked paler and his eyes darker and angrier, if that were possible.

"She'd have to dress," David repeated. He spoke slowly, giving due weight to each syllable.

Disguised as she is. Stokes was precisely right. She'd have to dress, because in order to face her servants and the doctor she'd summoned, she'd have to be disguised as Marston. *So clever and natural,* as Stokes had put it.

From which it followed that while she'd been waiting upstairs for this boy—this pretty blond boy, who visited her twice a week late at night—she hadn't been Marston. She'd been Phoebe, the woman David had only asked to dream of. The woman he'd been waiting—so patiently, so politely, so idiotically, as it had turned out—to permit him to call by her proper name.

He set his mouth in a cold line. Absurdly, he'd assumed that she'd been waiting for him as well. He'd supposed that she was eager for him to finish his investigations and come back to her. A veritable princess in a tower, he'd imagined her. Had any man, he wondered, ever made such an ass of himself over a woman?

He remembered the awkward letters he'd penned tonight, his silly attempts to express his growing devotion to her. And all the while she'd been preparing for an evening of sport with her hired boy. She'd been bathing, brushing her hair, daubing scent here and there, and smiling her devastating half-smile into the mirror. She'd been doing one or all of the hundred little things he'd fantasized her doing in preparation for his own triumphant arrival at the door of her bedchamber.

She'd been Phoebe for this boy all the time that David had been obliged to address her as "Mr. Marston." Stokes had presented the state of affairs with impressive delicacy, but there was no question where things stood.

She's played me for a fool, he thought numbly. *She's used me.* In return, she'd allowed him bits and pieces of herself—a kiss, a touch, a madly provocative glance—in order to secure his assistance. And all the while she'd been paying for the regular professional ministrations of a pretty male doxy.

He became conscious of a roaring in his ears. A dull, opaque sort of sound: it was his blood, David thought, rising in jealous fury. Oddly, his blood seemed to know what he should do; it knew it better than he did himself. *Bellow with rage,* his blood insisted, *break things, wreak some fearsome damage on Stokes in return for the pain his story had caused.* He rather enjoyed the violence of the impulse, the dark brutishness rushing in and releasing him from his duties to a fellow creature.

Certainly, he thought, he was under no obligation to listen to whatever else Stokes might want to say. Not that he could have heard him even if he'd wanted to. The roar in his ears had transformed Stokes into a ha'penny dumb show, big face wagging clownishly as he continued to move his lips, with only a vain word or two—"note . . . shirt . . . swine"—penetrating the roar in David's ears.

Swine? The unexpected word almost captured David's attention, its very incongruity an appeal to his human curiosity. Almost. But words are puny things in the face of incipient violence. Why not, he thought, simply stem the flow of words issuing from Stokes's mouth? He squared his shoulders, balled up a fist, and directed all his strength toward the blow he was preparing.

Do it, the roar in his head told him. *Knock him senseless before he kills you with what he's saying.* David could almost feel the connection of fist and jaw, the sickening shatter of bone, the soft squish of what was now a human face, but which soon . . .

The face in front of him remained a human face. His fist hadn't made the connection. David blinked in confusion. He was trapped, suspended, his wrist caught in a large, meaty hand for a moment before Stokes roughly shoved him back into his corner of the cab. A perfect defensive move. Damn if the fellow hadn't learned a thing or two during those weekly boxing lessons.

"Sorry, guv'nor, but I don't think yer really want to do that. Too much blood been spilt tonight already."

He handed David a battered flask.

"'Ave a swallow, my lord. It ain't the quality yer used to, but . . ."

David obeyed. The stuff stung his mouth, burning through the haze of his fury and stilling the roar in his head. Normal sounds of civilization began to penetrate—shouts in the street, the cabbie chucking to the horses, the clatter of their hooves on the cobbles. He peered out of the window. They'd negotiated the traffic and would be in Brunswick Square in minutes.

"Thank you, Stokes."

"Thanks yerself, guv'nor, fer teachin' me 'ow to block a punch."

"Sorry for the punch, though. Or the attempt at one anyway."

"I know yer are, guv'nor. And I'm sorry I let yer down, too."

"You did your job. More than your job, really. I hadn't

required you to keep watch on the house after she'd retired for the night. And she *had* . . . retired for the night." He grimaced. "Though she evidently wasn't ready to sleep yet."

He and Stokes passed the flask between them, taking long, meditative swallows.

"Maybe there's another explanation," Stokes said soothingly. "After all, we don't really know wot all . . ."

"Do *you* think there's another explanation?"

Stokes's silence was distressingly convincing.

David nodded. "I thought not."

"But what was it you were saying, Stokes, just at the moment I tried to knock you silly? Something about pigs, was it? No, no, not pigs, *swine.* Yes, I remember now, you distinctly said something about swine."

"The note, sir. Pinned to the front o' the boy's shirt. Funny item that was, all cut o' letters from the newspapers. Lot o' work to say not very much. And the words didn't make a lot o' sense neither."

"What did it say?"

"Lemme see if I can recall 'em exactly. Yeh. Peculiar imagination behind it. Poetical like. Words said, 'AND SO WILL THE MEN SHE KEEPS LIKE SWINE.' "

The note was still crumpled in her hand as Phoebe paced the room.

Quite artful really, she thought. My vicious adversary fancies himself a poet, even as he mauls my poor, innocent Billy so savagely.

The message was obviously a continuation of the one she'd received the preceding week. They were intended to be read together. AN UNNATURAL WOMAN WILL MEET AN UNNATURAL END. AND SO WILL THE MEN SHE KEEPS LIKE SWINE.

As though the hatred inspiring them couldn't be contained in one message but must spill its venom into a second.

And why should it stop with a second letter? she thought. Why shouldn't it simply go on until I'm utterly terrorized? Or, as the letter predicted, until she had met her unnatural end. But she wouldn't think of that.

She lifted her chin. She wouldn't be terrorized. Well, she wouldn't *look* terrorized anyway: she owed that much to Mr. Simms, who stood in the shadows by the doorway, radiating quiet sympathy for her. Much as she wanted to throw the vile thing into the fire, she'd be patient, logical. A piece of paper couldn't hurt her; she'd file it away with the others, as evidence for future investigation. Forcing herself to smooth it out, she folded it and tucked it into the pocket of her black dressing gown, half expecting the thing to burn through the fabric of the robe and singe her thigh through her trousers underneath. But it didn't.

See, they are only words. Willing herself to master her panic, she took a few deep shuddering breaths and stared down at Billy.

He was too big for the settee they'd laid him on, she thought. He must be uncomfortable with his limbs all twisted like that. But perhaps Mr. Simms was right. Perhaps it was better not to carry him upstairs until they knew how badly he'd been hurt.

Where the devil was Doctor Riggs? Her lips curved in a bitter half-smile. She hadn't thought of it when she'd sent a footman to fetch him but he was probably at Lady Claringworth's reception. Odd how these things worked. Still, he'd come if summoned. In fact he'd hurry; Henry's mother's receptions were deadly dull. Riggs would be delighted: a night spent in the stifling center of Polite Society would find its perfect complement in a raffish episode at its fringe. How delightfully *recherché* for a society doctor.

Come quickly, she silently implored him. *Yes, I'll provide the entertainment. You can dine out on this evening at Marston's for weeks. Only come quickly and take care of my poor Billy.*

One of his eyes was swollen totally shut. The flesh looked like raw meat, she thought. And his nose—the elegant Grecian nose that had given his young face such purity—looked crushed, misshapen. He breathed raggedly, through bloody split lips.

She stroked his forehead with guilty, hesitant fingers. His skin was clammy. The eyelid that wasn't swollen shut had fluttered open once or twice. Possibly he'd recognized her: his lips might have tried to shape an *M* sound.

And damn me, she thought, *if I didn't feel a flash of fear when I thought he'd speak. Didn't want him calling me "Miss" while the footman was making a fire across the room.*

The abortive *M* sound had been perfectly acceptable, though. Billy could have been attempting to say "Marston," or "Mr. Marston." But how horrid that she'd had to worry about such things when Billy was in such a state. Worse that she'd had to take the painstaking time to don her masquerade this evening, instead of flying down the stairs to see him. It was hateful to have to look out for her own petty safety, when she had endangered—perhaps caused the imminent death of—an innocent creature.

Another innocent creature. *Stop it, Phoebe,* she cautioned herself, *don't think such thoughts!*

But she couldn't stop herself from thinking of the

danger to which she'd exposed Lord Linseley and Mr. Simms. Or all of her manservants, for that matter. THE MEN SHE KEEPS LIKE SWINE. How could she vouch for anyone's safety in the face of tonight's madness?

It had been Mr. Simms who'd proposed she summon Lord Linseley. Phoebe had agreed reluctantly, her native honesty ultimately winning out over her fear of disclosing this mess to him.

For he'd hate her now. Even though—she felt sure of this—he'd continue to help her. It would be a humiliation to accept his assistance, but she'd do it gladly if it meant sparing anyone else from what had happened to Billy.

And anyway, she thought, David deserved to know that she'd kept secrets from him. She feared his arrival, but she wished for it as well. The sooner she and he had it out the better, even if it meant she'd never have him in her arms again.

Suppose it had been *him* who'd been attacked tonight? The sudden thought made her dizzy. She stopped pacing, reaching out to steady herself for a moment against a length of wainscoting.

Mr. Simms reached out to her from where he stood near the fireplace. She raised a hand to reassure him. The vertigo had passed, giving way to calm and resignation. She'd simply have to accept the mayhem she'd caused. Blaming herself again and again wouldn't help anyone. Better to concentrate on whatever good she could do.

"I'll take that brandy you offered, Simms," she called, seating herself on an ottoman at Billy's side.

Sipping her drink, she held his hand. "Live, live, Billy, you must live, dear," she whispered in a voice that held not a trace of Marston's cynicism. Mr. Simms had sent all the other servants away. Good thing. She would make the most of these minutes before the doctor came. She would find her best self—she would *be* her best self—before she had to assume her mask and become Marston once more.

Chapter 12

Oh yes, the boy would certainly live, Dr. Riggs assured Mr. Marston. The toughs had done a nasty job on him, but he seemed to be a strong lad and he wasn't suffering any internal injury. The broken bones could be set, he'd be able to breathe normally through a permanently crooked nose, and the concussion would heal quickly.

"We've got a few hours of messy work ahead of us," the doctor said. "Not pleasant for the patient, either, but he'll bear up."

"You see, Mr. Marston," he added, "his eyes are starting to focus even now."

Billy stared obediently at Phoebe, to show her how well he could focus. She smiled down at him, but when he tried to return her smile he could only shudder with pain.

"What's causing most of his misery at this moment," the doctor continued, "is that dislocated shoulder. We'll need a strong man to hold him still while I push it back into place. Someone possessed of a bit more brawn than I expect you have, sir."

Phoebe nodded archly. "It's true, I suppose," she drawled, "that *my* sort of gentleman—the more ornamental sort, don't you know—isn't what's most desperately needed in the situation we find ourselves in. But there's someone quite splendidly brawny, as you put it, waiting in the library right now." She lingered on the word "brawny," rolling it about in her mouth and raising her eyebrows suggestively. "Simms, could you go fetch Mr. Stokes?"

Lord Linseley and Mr. Stokes had arrived soon after the doctor, and Simms had discreetly led them into the library to wait until after the examination.

She smiled roguishly at Dr. Riggs, who was making no secret of his curiosity about the evening's events and participants. Fine, she thought, just so long as his curiosity doesn't prevent him from doing his job. Her relief that Billy would live made it all seem unbearably trivial, but she knew that the doctor would feel cheated if he weren't presented with some sort of explanation for the odd comings and goings in Mr. Marston's home this evening.

And since she couldn't think of a reasonable explanation, the best option was probably a scandalous one. Let the good doctor surmise—as he probably had already—that Mr. Marston had intended to stage a male orgy tonight. When he got a look at Stokes, he'd probably conclude that the man had been chosen for the most decadent of reasons, his monstrous beefiness a stunning contrast to Billy's erstwhile beauty. Well, let him conclude whatever he liked. Her masquerade wouldn't be hurt by scandal. Just pray that he remained unaware that Lord Linseley was in the library as well.

The only trouble with this plan was that the man Mr. Simms ushered into the room a few minutes later wasn't Stokes, but the Earl of Linseley himself.

Phoebe watched the doctor raise a quizzical eyebrow. Well, he knew about the gambling episode at Vivien's, of course; the estimable Lord Linseley was the last person he would have expected to find here tonight.

The earl nodded. "Good evening, Doctor."

He smiled coldly at Phoebe. "I insisted on helping instead of Stokes, Mr. Marston. You and I can continue our unpleasant financial wranglings some other evening. But since our disagreements have brought me here already, please accept my services in this medical matter. I know something about dislocated shoulders, you see. Just a few months ago one of my tenants sustained a similar injury falling from the roof of a barn."

"Thank you, my lord, it's very generous of you."

Gazing keenly at him, she found that she wasn't able to decipher the expression in his eyes. He turned away from her, quickly peeling off his coat and waistcoat and draping them on the back of a chair.

Dr. Riggs shrugged, delightedly befuddled by this interesting addition to the cast of characters Marston had assembled. With some evident reluctance he turned his attention back to professional matters. The shoulder—ah yes, the shoulder. Far less interesting than the story he'd tell tomorrow at his club.

"Grateful for your assistance, Lord Linseley. Let's begin, shall we?"

Lord Linseley rolled up his sleeves.

It had taken hours, but the shoulder was back in place, the bones set, the broken rib taped up, and all the various wounds stitched up and attended to. Mr. Simms had finally escorted Dr. Riggs to the door.

Billy was asleep, worn out by the doctor's ministrations and soothed by opiates. His face was more swollen and discolored than it had been when Stokes had carried him in, a patchwork of stitches, plaster, and bandages. Still, his features had settled into some reasonable serenity; he must be plagued by a thousand pains and discomforts, Phoebe thought, but at least he was free of the agony of the dislocated shoulder.

He'd screamed when the doctor had moved the shoulder back into place. It had been no easy task for Lord Linseley to hold him still, his forearms tensed, his face utterly devoid of emotion. Phoebe had fetched and carried, helping in such small ways as she could. Mostly she had forced herself to maintain Marston's sangfroid through Billy's screams. Now that she and the earl stood facing each other across Billy's slumbering body, she had to work even harder to maintain her air of calm detachment.

Lord Linseley was more skilled at masculine inscrutability than she could ever be, she thought. His expression remained impeccably neutral as he rolled his sleeves down over his powerful forearms and buttoned them at the wrist. The only thing Phoebe could tell for certain was that he was drained of energy and spirit, his cheeks ashen beneath rough black stubble, his dark-rimmed blue eyes opaque as winter ice.

I wish he looked angrier, she thought. A visible anger would have been easier to penetrate than this frigid rage.

"Thank you, Lord Linseley. I don't know how we should have managed without you tonight."

He nodded absently. "Yes, well, I wanted to save the boy any more undeserved suffering."

She winced at the accusation implicit in the word "undeserved."

"Quite right. He's suffered enough already."

There didn't seem to be a great deal more to say.

She corrected herself. There was everything to say. If her mouth had been capable of shaping the words.

He turned to pick up the clothing he'd hung over a chair back.

She opened a pair of drapes to let in a bit more light. The gas lamps in the street were still lit; their sickly yellow mixed with the cold pre-dawn glare in the sky to illuminate his back and shoulders. His linen shirt was rumpled, sweat-stained. A bit of it had come untucked from the waistband of his trousers.

His upper body was rigid, the powerful muscles knotted from the effort he'd expended to hold Billy gently but firmly. She wanted to unbutton the rumpled shirt, pull it down over his shoulders and out of his trousers. To put her hands on his overtaxed muscles, exerting warm, healing pressure on poor, overworked, distended flesh. And then to encircle his waist with her arms while she kissed him from the nape of his neck to the small of his back. If only, she thought, he'd let her bring him back to life, to reawaken the vital breathing body hidden within the carapace of exhaustion and fury that encased him.

If only, she thought, she could touch him in any way at all.

His face was still turned away from her. His hands were busy with his clothing. Helplessly, she watched his shirt—and the muscles beneath it—disappear beneath his gray waistcoat, his dark blue coat.

He'd be leaving in a moment.

He turned back to face her. Stiffly, as though his lips were as split and bruised as Billy's, he asked, "Why did you summon me tonight?"

Here it was at last. And it would hurt, she thought, immediately loathing herself for the word "hurt." It had been Billy who'd suffered pain tonight. But the word stayed with her: for it *would* hurt to have to suffer Lord Linseley's anger and disrespect. All right then. She'd face it.

She lifted her head slightly.

"I'm not quite sure why I asked you to come," she said. "It was Mr. Simms's idea at first," she added. "He was wise enough to know that we needed you. And I knew he was right."

He grimaced. "Yes, I expect that you do need me. Your Billy being incapacitated as he is."

"I deserve that," she returned, willing herself not to flinch.

"You're quite within your rights to assume the worst about me," she added. "It was very wrong of me not to have informed you of my arrangement with him. But the situation isn't what you suppose."

He spat out a brief laugh. "I suppose you're simply helping him improve his reading every Tuesday and Saturday night."

"Actually, I am."

He blinked.

"You needn't believe me. I freely admit that I haven't been completely forthcoming with you. But I'm being quite honest with you now. The truth is that I haven't . . . I haven't taken Billy to bed since . . . well, for quite some time."

She'd supposed that she'd be able to deliver that speech with more aplomb. But her voice had faded toward the end. For it was clear that he hardly cared that she'd stopped taking Billy to bed; he wanted her somehow to assure him that she'd never made love to the boy at all.

Perhaps the whole truth would help, she thought. Well, why not? Why not tell him that ever since that first night at Almack's she couldn't possibly have made love to anyone but him? She wanted desperately to say it but she couldn't. Not yet. Not without some signal from him.

The air in the room felt heavy, freighted with any

number of things one or the other of them might have said but couldn't. Or wouldn't.

Damn his male reticence, she thought. For it was clear that she was no match for him when it came to this business of aggrieved, silent stares.

She conceded defeat and then quickly opened another line of attack. If he was too much a man to help her say what she was aching to say, he was still gentleman enough to respond to a direct question.

"Why did you come?" she asked.

He shrugged. "I'm no more sure than you were about why you summoned me. Odd, isn't it?"

"You're disappointed in me."

"I know I have no right to be."

"You thought I was something I'm not."

"As the rest of the world does. Except for a privileged few. Like Billy."

"You're very angry."

He shrugged again. As if the assertion were too simple, too obvious to warrant an answer. Or because he simply couldn't bear to admit it. She watched him carefully. He lowered his eyes for a moment, then stared truculently at her again.

"You're not safe here," he finally said.

"No," she replied. "I suppose I'm not. I think I shall take Billy to Devonshire with me in a day or two."

"I won't have you traveling without adequate protection."

Indignantly, she began, "I don't believe that it's *your* prerogative, sir, to prescribe how . . ." And then, as Billy groaned in his sleep, she stopped herself with a wry smile. "You're right, of course. It's been selfish of me, daring to be brave at others' expense. I shan't do so in the future. Perhaps Mr. Stokes would be willing to accompany me, at least as far as Rowen-on-Close."

Seeing him knit his brows, she quickly added, "Of

course in the future *I'll* pay him for his services. I shouldn't want you to think that I'd continue accepting your generosity . . ."

"I don't think anything of the sort." The vehemence of this response, she thought, seemed to surprise him as profoundly as it did her.

"Well, then . . . ?"

"I want you—and Billy too—to come with me. To Linseley Manor. In L-Lincolnshire."

Surely, she thought, *I'm not hearing him correctly. That faint stammer must be a trick of my imagination.*

But no, she'd heard him stammer once before, though she couldn't remember when. Did it matter when she'd heard it? No, of course not. What mattered was that just now he seemed to have said the most extraordinary thing. If she'd heard him correctly. Her incredulity warred with a tremulous elation, both of which she somehow managed to hide behind an air of prudent matter-of-factness.

"Is that wise?"

"A good deal wiser than your going to Devonshire. Remember, after all, that our vicious friend knows of that destination."

"Yes, but is it wise for *you?* To endanger yourself by traveling with Marston?"

"Damn it, I *said* I'd help you and I *will* help you!"

"You're still angry."

"I can't imagine what makes you think so, Mr. Marston. I'll be back for you and Billy in a few hours. At eight, does that give you enough time to prepare? Good morning, sir."

She dressed and bathed as quickly as possible, producing a reasonably convincing though rather pale and fragile version of Marston.

The important thing, she told herself, was to keep her wits about her. Not to wonder about the meaning of what she was doing, but simply to occupy herself with the details.

Clothing, first of all. Mr. Simms would help her pack—but which clothes? Marston's? Or the few gowns and pelisses she kept locked in a secret cabinet, behind a sliding wall in Marston's dressing room? She didn't have many women's garments that were suitable for winter, but she packed a few of her best. A riding costume seemed practical, she thought. The white cashmere gown with a pink satin sash, on the other hand, was doubtless absurd. Probably it was all a waste of time and effort: Lord Linseley wouldn't ever want to see her dressed as a woman. But yes, she'd take them—including the white, which was one of her favorites. Perhaps Marston would need a disguise.

The bags were finally packed. The next order of business was breakfast.

"Just coffee, Simms."

Wordlessly, he set a large bowl of porridge and several rashers of bacon on the table in front of her. She took a tentative bite—and then surprised herself by downing every bit of it, heaping marmalade onto her toast and stirring thick cream into her second cup of coffee.

Billy would also need to eat when he woke, she thought. He couldn't take more than gruel, which Mr. Simms brought to her in a pot with a tight-fitting lid on it, along with a large silver flask of strong, brandy-laced tea.

"I wish you were coming, Simms," she said. "I'm a little intimidated by the prospect of this journey, you know."

He smiled and shook his head. "You're not intimidated by anything, sir," he said.

She managed a weak facsimile of Marston's cocky grin. "Quite right," she said. "And how convenient to have a valet to remind me of it."

It was half past seven. The bags were packed. Marston's winter greatcoat was laid out on a chair. She and Mr. Simms agreed that the house should be shut down during her absence. The bloodstained rugs and furniture would have to be cleaned or replaced. The servants would be given a paid vacation, and Mr. Stokes would be hired to keep an eye on the house, reporting any strange goings-on to Mr. Simms, who would be staying with his sister and brother-in-law.

"Have the furniture covered," she told him. "Keep everything in good order. We'll have to sell some assets if my emergency account is to cover all the expediencies," she added. "Of course, you know where I keep everything. You should go see Lady Kate Beverredge about it today."

"Very good, sir. And what shall I tell her in reference to the reasons for your precipitous departure?"

Phoebe shrugged. "I expect that you'll tell her everything. In scrupulous detail and to the best of your understanding and ability. As you always do."

Mr. Simms nodded respectfully, but his eyes flooded with sudden warmth. "Very good, sir," he repeated softly, and Phoebe felt a wild urge to undermine her disguise by wrapping her arms around his neck and weeping in full sight of the footman who'd appeared at the door just a moment before. She was saved from this mortifying excess, however, by the announcement that Lord Linseley was waiting in the foyer.

"Shall I help him carry the wounded boy to the carriage, sir?"

"Yes, thank you, Woods. And then would you get my bags?"

She turned to Mr. Simms again. "I believe we've covered everything."

"I'm sure of it, Mr. Marston. Except to say that I wish you and Lord Linseley a fine, safe, and happy journey."

"Hmm. After the strife of last night, a peaceful, uneventful journey might be enough to wish for. Still, thank you, Simms. For everything. And do convey all my best regards to Mr. and Mrs. Andrewes."

Chapter

13

Somehow it all seemed a bit too familiar, David thought, watching Phoebe stride out her front door and toward his carriage. There was a disturbing sense of déjà vu about it, as though he'd taken her home with him before, sometime in the past. But that was patently impossible.

What *was* possible, he thought with a start, was that he'd dreamed it. Yes, that was it. He'd dreamed it repeatedly, most likely every night for weeks. And he would doubtless have dreamed it again last night if he'd ever gotten to bed. It was a lurid dream, all bright colors and exaggerated detail, and it had probably become more lurid every time he'd dreamed it. Rather wonderful in its way, he couldn't help thinking. He stifled a grimace. So much for those chivalrous resolutions not to indulge in erotic fantasy. The purer his waking thoughts of her, the more salacious his dream life had become.

The dream had taken place in this very carriage. In fact, she'd made her first appearance in it looking very much as she did this morning: austere, diffident, groomed to black and white perfection—almost intimidating, with Marston's voluminous caped greatcoat swinging from her shoulders.

Much as he had in the dream, he nodded cordially to her as she stepped into the carriage and took the backward-facing seat opposite him. She returned his nod, adding a solemn smile,

She had violet shadows below her eyes. Well, of course—she hadn't gotten any sleep. He wanted to kiss her there, just below her great gray eyes—to make his lips delicate enough to caress, to comfort that delicate, bruised skin. Was he capable of such subtlety? He didn't know. The light was dim in the carriage; his emotions vague and hard to get hold of. He lowered his eyes for a moment, trying to recapture some clarity.

His dream had been brightly, even garishly lit, but this morning he'd regretfully drawn the carriage's velvet curtains against intruding glances. It had seemed the prudent thing to do, though now he wished he could see her more clearly in the morning light. He felt a sudden stab of jealous anger when he realized he'd never before seen her in the early morning. He couldn't help but wonder if Billy had.

She gestured toward the curtains. "Wise of you to shield us that way," she said. "Although who knows what our enemies know by this time."

"Yes, well, we'll simply take them on if we have to." Mysteriously, his anger had subsided somewhat at the sound of her voice. Or perhaps it had simply been her choice of words: "to shield us . . . our enemies." *We. Us.* He liked the two little plural pronouns she'd used.

His feelings, he thought, seemed to ebb and flow according to their own rhythms, quite beyond his understanding or control, while his love for her seemed utterly unaffected by the emotions that roiled within him. He wondered if that was always the case when you loved someone. Were you simply bound to work backward through all the accrued hurt and misunderstanding until you found your way home to the love that made it all worthwhile? It seemed maddeningly difficult, excruciatingly unpredictable, and demanding of constant vigilance. Rather like farming in English country weather, he supposed.

He'd been supporting a half-conscious Billy against his shoulder while he'd waited for her. She nodded approvingly.

"You've done a good job, propping his leg like that," she said, "but I'd like to hold him through the journey."

"Of course," he said. "Move beside him and I'll sit opposite you."

"You don't mind facing backwards when you travel?"

"Not at all." *So long as I can look at you all along the way.*

They negotiated the change of seats carefully enough, disturbing Billy as little as possible but bumping their own knees together rather gracelessly.

In his dream, she'd also sat across from him. But no one had bumped knees. How clumsy, how tactless waking life was. This awkward jostling was the first time he'd touched her for weeks: a silly clacking of bone against bone, the rustle of fabric, shifting of feet in polished boots, as they settled into their seats for the journey.

"Sorry."

"It's nothing, my lord."

Perhaps it was nothing to *her.* He spread a large traveling rug over her and Billy and then draped another one over his own lap.

The boy settled his head on Phoebe's shoulder, sighing contentedly as she straightened the rug and smoothed his hair. David glared at him for a moment, then shrugged his shoulders and took a breath. He'd expected to hate the boy, but found himself unable to do so. Billy was too young to hate. By the look of him he'd been born a year or two after Alec, and certainly with none of Alec's expectations or prerogatives. From his own encounters, David had concluded that the vast majority of people who sold their bodies only did so to avoid far worse fates; it certainly wasn't the boy's fault that his line of work had brought him into Phoebe's bed.

Enough of that, he told himself. One could be fair-minded about it, but it still wasn't pleasant to contemplate, especially at close quarters.

Her portmanteaus were loaded into the carriage boot, the doors shut. Croft had climbed up on the coachman's box and settled himself next to Dickerson, who cracked his whip and hied to the horses. The carriage lurched forward, jolted back, and clattered over the cobbles of Brunswick Square. They'd begun their journey.

David wondered what they would find to say to each other all day.

"We won't hurry," he announced. "It wouldn't be good for Billy. This evening we'll stop at an inn I know. The beds at the Swan are quite comfortable, and the food's excellent. We'll all get a good rest."

"Good," she replied. "And I'll change my clothes there. Marston may as well effect his customary disappearance, just in case we're being followed."

"Quite so."

"And thank you for your consideration."

"Not at all."

She continued to fuss over Billy, and David couldn't think of anything else to say. It would be a long day. He leaned back, letting the carriage jostle him as it would and allowing his thoughts to wander.

In his dream, the carriage never stopped. Nor did Phoebe do something as prosaic as change her clothes. In his dream, her costume magically transformed itself from stiff male masquerade to devastatingly flimsy female attire. First the greatcoat would disappear, then the cravat. Jacket. Shirt . . . Her masculine garments would undergo a total metamorphosis, reshaping themselves into a gauzy rose-pink gown with an exceedingly low neckline and little puffed sleeves slipping down her slender shoulders to reveal her breasts.

David wondered how much time he'd devoted to guessing the exact character of her breasts. Of course, one could never know exactly what they'd be like until one saw them. Until one kissed and caressed them, squeezed and teased and tongued them. Would their texture be soft or firm, their color like cream or like bluish buttermilk, tinted by the veins close below the skin? And the nipples, the aureoles surrounding them—would they be small and discreet or wide, dark, and poetic? One could only guess. One could only hope.

Still, certain characteristics were likely. Her small breasts wouldn't be girlish—she'd borne a child, after all, and that would show somewhere. At least he hoped it would. He loved the changes pregnancy and childbirth worked upon a woman's body; until now he'd never understood the fetish for untouched virginity that animated most men of his acquaintance. Of course, he could understand *now;* it was that deuced pride of ownership: *this is mine; no one has possessed it but myself and no one ever will.* Odd how easy it was to use the pronoun "it" when employing the language of property and ownership.

Lulled by the carriage's movement and befuddled by trying to follow the winding paths of his thoughts, he felt his eyelids grow heavy. Would it be permissible to indulge in a nap? Only the most fleeting of catnaps, he assured himself, a quick visit to the colorful certainties of his dream world.

He settled back in his seat. Yes, that was better. The world beneath his eyelids was warm and rosy, soft and inviting. Raptly, his dream self watched a dream Phoebe slide slowly down onto her back, to lie upon the velvet seat. His dream self gasped softly as she parted her thighs and propped her legs on *his* seat, one narrow foot on either side of him, allowing him to lift the skirt of the pink gown and then the petticoat beneath it . . .

He fell into a blissful slumber, giving himself fully to the vision of her body so boldly splayed, so sweetly spread about him.

He woke slowly, much refreshed and happily attuned to the road running beneath the carriage wheels, the rhythmic thudding of the horses' hooves. They seemed to be making a nice pace; they must have already gained the great northern road. A margin of brightness seeped under his eyelids; she seemed to have opened the curtains a bit. He could feel the slow warmth of winter sunlight on his face. Or perhaps it was still the glow from that dream. Good thing no one could tell what went on within one's private imaginings . . .

He could hear a low murmur of voices. She and Billy were speaking softly together. He supposed he should open his eyes, just to keep clearer track of what was going on around him. No, he decided. His body still felt heavy, the muscles stiff from having held Billy down through his kicks and thrashings. What he wanted was a bit more sleep, a few more delicious dream visions. Sighing, he shifted his body into a more comfortable position under the rug. In the part of the dream that he planned to revisit, she would gaze fixedly at him while he lifted her legs over his shoulders. And then, while one of his hands undid the front of his trousers, his other hand would begin a leisurely exploration of her: sliding a finger through the slit in her drawers, allowing it to wander up inside her, watching her gray eyes grow huge and dark as he charted the wet velvet labyrinth until—all in good time—he'd find her center. Slowly, slowly, all in good time.

The dream vision was mightily seductive, but he found that his attention was nonetheless diverted from it. Now that he'd gotten some rest it seemed that he didn't need to sleep any more right now. Not while she and Billy continued to whisper so distractingly.

What were *they chattering about?*

"I expect from the look on his face that it's *you* he's been seein' in those dreams, Miss."

Phoebe's contralto voice whispered a reply that was too soft for David to hear.

"Well, he *is* the gen'lman in question, ain't he, Miss? For he does seem a good 'un, quite as I wished you."

Again, a soft, low, admonitory whisper, the words inaudible, but with a definite lilt of amusement shaping its cadence.

David sat straight up and his eyes flew open. His shoulders squared themselves; his face exhibited an icy hauteur that was quite rare for him. Well, he hated to be stuffy about it, but an eighth earl simply couldn't allow himself to be discussed in the third person, much less scrutinized so knowingly for the entertainment of his fellow travelers.

And just how *had* he looked while he was asleep? Anxiously, he peered down at the rug draped over his lap. It was heavy enough—*wasn't it?*—to have obscured any physical sign of that warm, moist, rosy dream.

The boy gave a soft, tipsy hiccup, bending his battered features into an attempt at respectful apology.

"Beggin' your pardon, guv'nor. Didn't mean to wake you. Nor to pay you no disrespect neither."

David nodded coldly as the boy drifted into sleep. What was the stuff in the flask Phoebe was holding?

She read his thoughts. "I implore your forgiveness as well, Lord Linseley. This tea's been well laced with a very old Armagnac, which goes down extremely smoothly, you know. But Billy's not used to it, and he's probably drunk more than he should."

He felt helpless against the half-smile that had returned to her face. Damn if it wasn't as provocative as anything that had transpired in his dreams.

"Well, perhaps I gave him a bit too much," she added. "To soothe him. To allow him to sleep through his discomfort—and through our conversation. For I thought you and I might want to converse."

Our conversation. It sounded very agreeable. But he wouldn't be dissuaded from his point about Billy's disrespect.

"Of course. He needs as much sleep as he can get. Still, he did speak out of turn. He shouldn't speculate about the contents of my dreams, even assuming for the moment that I *was* dreaming. Well, how could he even know for certain that I'd fallen asleep? It's all a matter of interpretation, isn't it? I was merely resting my eyes."

"Quite right, he shouldn't speculate about it. I've already chastised him for that and I assure you he won't do it again. But as for your having fallen asleep—well, *that's* hardly open to interpretation, my lord. You don't snore *loudly;* I'd call it rather a cunning, purring, comforting sort of snore that you do. A snore that might lull a bed partner back to sleep rather than waken her. But you do, nonetheless, snore, Lord Linseley."

Silently, he called upon the spirits of the seven pre-

ceding Linseley earls to help him maintain his dignity. "I didn't know. No one's ever informed me of it. You're quite sure?"

"It was, absolutely and incontrovertibly, a snore."

"Hmmph."

"I believe the inclination to snore develops when a man reaches his forties. At least, that's what Mr. Simms once told me."

"Indeed. Well, convey my gratitude to Mr. Simms for the useful information."

The embarrassment, he thought, was well worth the tantalizing sight of a grin hovering at the corners of her mouth. He opened the curtains to let in some more sunlight.

"And what did Billy mean by my being 'the gentleman in question'?"

"Ah. You heard that too, did you?"

She hesitated for a moment, shrugged, and then spoke quickly.

"He guessed that you were the gentleman I've been thinking about so continually and obsessively since first meeting you at Almack's. And . . ."

"And?"

" . . . the gentleman who has utterly monopolized all the physical desire I'm capable of . . ."

A faint blush rose in her cheeks.

"Go on."

"Well, you see, I couldn't continue to make love to Billy when he visited . . ."

He forced his features to stay grave, respectful.

" . . . with my thoughts and sensibility so entirely occupied by . . ."

"By?"

"By you, Lord Linseley."

He hadn't thought he'd be able to accept it but it

seemed that he could. Exclusive physical possession of a woman wasn't everything, he told himself. There was something equally precious about the plain honesty she'd shown and the effort it had clearly cost her.

She turned her head, affecting interest in the bleak winter landscape outside her window. And when she spoke again, her voice was light and brittle.

"We're fortunate to have such dry weather for our journey. The road is in remarkably good shape for this time of year."

"Well, it's a very good, straight road, especially the length of it from Stamford to Lincoln. Built by the Romans, you know, I'll show it to you on a map if you like." He was babbling. He must sound quite ridiculous, he thought. He felt quite ridiculously happy. "We are indeed blessed by this weather. Though I think it will storm after we reach Lincolnshire."

"You can predict the weather?"

"A farmer tries to."

She was silent for some minutes.

"Lord Linseley, I should like to explain . . ."

"You don't have to."

"I want to."

"And I'm eager to hear everything you wish to tell me. But I think we should . . . wait to make explanations."

"Wait until . . . ?"

"Until after we've deepened our acquaintance somewhat. Might we postpone all explanations until . . . tomorrow morning, Lady Claringworth? That would give us tonight in which to begin to know each other better."

The slow smile that stole across her face was all Phoebe and not a bit Marston.

"We might indeed, Lord Linseley. And may I express how profoundly I long to know you better?"

This time, the pressure of knee against knee wasn't in the least bit clumsy or tactless.

"We can sup together," David said. "The room I use at the inn has a small parlor where I sometimes take my meals."

"Yes, I should like that."

"We'll be quite private there. We can probably even find someone to sit with Billy so that we won't be disturbed."

"It sounds very pleasant indeed." *Pleasant.* The golden flecks in her eyes danced as her low voice breathed new energy into a polite, overused adjective.

Billy stirred against her shoulder, ruffling the heavy carriage rug. She smoothed it impatiently, all the while keeping her eyes locked onto David's and her knees lightly pressing against his.

"I've never journeyed to your part of the world before."

"You're not alone in that. We're not picturesque: you won't find heart-stopping crags or poetical peaks as in the Lake District. The Lincolnshire countryside is rather flat, with some good churches rising up here and there, and the low, forested, rolling hills of the wolds to add variety to the view."

"But you love it."

"It's mine. It's a large part of myself. Yes, I suppose I do love it, though that's not how I'd express it. I simply think of powerful winds blowing deep, wide swaths through thick fields of wheat that shiver under a very large, dramatic sky. Biggest sky I know. The best, most passionate thunderstorms. Blizzards too, sometimes."

"Yes, I shouldn't be surprised. You'll describe the landscape and its points of interest to me as we pass through it, won't you?"

"Would you enjoy that?"

"I believe I should, very much indeed. Of course, in that case I should have to stop gazing at you."

"And I at you. But we don't need to look out the windows quite yet; we've barely passed Cambridge. Don't worry, Lady Claringworth, you and I will have time for everything."

"Do you know, Lord Linseley, I can almost believe that's true when I hear you say it."

Chapter

14

The Swan, Phoebe thought, had proved to be as comfortable and hospitable an inn as Lord Linseley had promised. The bed in her room was large and firm, covered with a fluffy, well-aired eiderdown. There was a capacious armoire, clean hot water in a Staffordshire pitcher on a sturdy oak stand, and a merry fire in the grate. Billy was sleeping in the room next door, with a chambermaid to attend to him when he woke, and Lord Linseley was down the hall. When she'd told him she'd join him there for supper at eight, he'd said he'd come to her room to fetch her.

She'd thanked him for his courtliness, but she hadn't told him that he'd find her dressed as a woman. She'd wanted it to be a surprise. How odd it felt, she thought now, peering at herself in the room's large oval mirror. Usually, her changes of sex and costume took place overnight: she'd retire as Phizz and appear the next morning as Phoebe. But this evening she was doing something she'd never done before: removing her male garments and directly replacing them with a female costume.

The lamplight flickered for a moment; her image in the mirror seemed to shimmer as though poised on a mystical threshold. How could she recognize herself, she wondered, in this rush of precipitous change? Where was she? *Who* was she? Was she the owner of those clever, womanly hands pulling and smoothing until everything fell into harmonious order? Or was she the strange amalgam of half-forgotten gestures and facial expressions, taking female shape in the mirror as though emerging from the mists of time? The mysteries of the transformation were as confusing as they were thrilling.

She supposed that the people who kept the inn would be equally confused if they could see her—confused and most likely scandalized. Mr. and Mrs. Ernest Cockburn, proprietor and cook, had seemed like decent, friendly people. The pair of them had greeted their party effusively, welcoming Lord Linseley rather as though he were King, Lord Chancellor, and Archbishop of Canterbury all rolled into one.

She'd been gratified but a bit surprised by the warmth of the reception they'd received. After all, the Swan was just north of Stamford, not much more than halfway between London and Lincoln. She would have expected Lord Linseley to be popular within his own locality, but this wasn't his locality—not yet, not so far south. He must simply be a very pleasant and generous lodger, she supposed.

"We try to keep those rooms for him," the boy who had carried her bags had said, chatting amiably as they'd mounted the stairs. "Queer that he didn't make it home for Christmas this year, though. Well, he always does, sir. Likes to celebrate it wi' his people he does, and of course wi' the young viscount. Never known him to miss out on the joy o' the season. Must have had important business in London, but we knowed we'd be seeing him by Twelfth Night anyway."

"The viscount?"

"You haven't met the viscount, sir? But you must know about him. The earl's so proud of his son now that he's grown. Talks a blue streak about him."

A grown son. Holidays with his people. She gazed thoughtfully out the window at starry blackness behind bare trees. There was so much to learn about him, she thought. But not now. Not until after he and she had become acquainted in the way that most mattered.

And no more idle speculations until she was dressed and ready to become acquainted with him.

She surveyed herself in the mirror, as critical and meticulous in her self-scrutiny as she'd once been when she and Henry had been invited to dine at Carlton House. Turning her head slowly to the left and right, she examined the bandeau of rose colored silk she'd wrapped around it, threading it through her curls until she'd achieved the proper Grecian effect. The hair was still a bit short to look quite feminine, but she thought he'd like the curling tendrils that clustered at her nape and in front of her ears.

At least she was lucky that the silk harmonized so well with her satin sash. She adjusted the fabric at the dress's low neckline, trembling a bit as the heel of her hand brushed against the blue-white flesh of her breast. She'd always had to be careful about décolletage, for although her breasts were small the aureoles around her nipples were surprisingly dark and large.

In her days as Lady Claringworth she'd expended untold anxiety on achieving the correct swelling at the neckline without looking too extremely risqué. But this evening her anxiety was rather differently directed. Would he like her breasts? she wondered. Or would he find them laughably small, even trivial? Would he think they sagged? Well, *that* was a bit of an exaggeration, she supposed. They didn't quite *sag,* did they? Not yet, anyway. They were simply not quite . . . what they'd once been.

The more she fretted about it, though, the more her flesh ached and swelled, the nipples, so recently freed from their muslin bands, hardening against the stiffness of her corset. Finally she could only laugh at herself. *Give up the fussing, Phoebe, he'll simply have to take you as you are: small-breasted, a bit saggy, and ravenous for his touch.*

She wasn't surprised by her body's unruly behavior: she'd been tumbling in a vortex of delicious sensation since she and he had pressed their knees together in the carriage. The stirrings in her breasts, thighs, and moist, aching quim were wonderful but somehow to be expected. What was quite new and astonishing, though, was that all of her body seemed equally charged with sensation. Knees, neck, and armpits; ankles and insteps; even the delicate skin at the inside of her elbows: every inch of her seemed equally volatile. Stepping into her drawers, fastening her corset and settling her breasts into it, she'd felt as though she was handling gunpowder. *Just don't let me explode,* she thought, *at his first touch.*

Or even before he touched her. Because if she were to be completely honest she'd have to admit that she'd begun feeling so randy even before they'd settled their legs together in the carriage. She giggled, remembering how she'd stared at the stirring in his lap this morning while he'd been dozing. The growing bulge had been visible even beneath the heavy rug he'd draped over himself. Shamelessly, she'd endeavored to imagine the exact nature of the flesh that was rising up in such a lively fashion. No wonder Billy had laughed at her, to the extent that his poor bruised mouth had allowed him to laugh.

Well, she'd seen exactly two naked penises in her life—hardly a large sampling, but sufficient to have proved to her quite how individual they could be. There were so many opportunities for variation, after all. Size. Shape. Color. Texture. (Don't forget *taste* and *smell,* she reminded herself.) And of course, angle of erection. She felt herself consumed with giddy, impatient curiosity: her imagination was like a luxuriant forest of wild mushrooms sprouting after a thunderstorm.

The best, most passionate thunderstorms.

Oh yes.

Stop it, she scolded herself, *or you'll never finish dressing.*

She scanned the mirror for flaws to correct, but it seemed that she'd done what she could. Except for the shawl that hung in the armoire, she was finished dressing. Hardly a perfect toilette, she thought, but on the whole it wasn't too bad.

The dress lay in serene folds below her bosom, its puffed sleeves making her arms look delicate and rounded. A small garnet cross—a gift from Jonathan when she'd first gone to London—nestled in the hollow of her neck. Too bad the piercings in her earlobes had closed over; she would have liked to wear the tiny garnet earrings he'd given her a year later when she'd married. Henry had joked about the earrings' plainness; well, they were hardly imposing in comparison to the pirate's chest of wedding gifts his London set had contributed. But in time Phoebe had come to loathe most of her jewelry: the dazzling wedding gifts, the heavy ancestral pieces, and especially the fabulously expensive offerings the sneering footman would deliver, with appalling promptness, after Henry had acted in some particularly abusive fashion. By the end of her marriage, Jonathan's garnets were the only jewels she'd actually enjoyed wearing, and she wished she could have their warm sparkle at her ears tonight.

Far worse than her naked ears, though, were her

legs, scandalously bare beneath her petticoat. Sadly, though, there was nothing to be done about it: somehow, she'd only brought one garter along with her.

She glanced ruefully at the pink-tinted stockings on the bed, and at the single pale gray garter lying on top of them. It was a lovely piece of lingerie, trimmed with tiny gray seed pearls and buttoned by a slightly larger pearl. Absurdly pretty and extravagant and all the more so for being hidden—from the eyes of everyone except the person who'd be privileged to slide it down its wearer's leg. It was just the thing to make a woman feel completely and elegantly dressed. But it was entirely useless without its mate.

She wished she could blame the missing garter on Mr. Simms. But he'd never been comfortable with women's clothes—especially not women's underclothes. Phoebe hadn't felt that it was fair to require him to become so, and had always packed the women's costumes she chose for her little vacations. Unfortunately, she'd been so exhausted and distracted this morning that she must simply have left the garter out of her bags.

Of course, it would be impossible to allow Lord Linseley to see her with one stocking smartly clinging to her right leg and the other sagging on her left. And so, as much as she hated the idea, her only choice was to go without. And to stop fussing about it, she told herself. But it infuriated her: she'd wanted to be perfectly, exquisitely clothed in anticipation of the moment when the clothes would be coming off again.

There was a polite knock on her door. Was it so late already? How much time *had* she wasted on all that fuss and fantasy?

No, it wasn't late. The clock on the mantel said seven twenty-five.

"Lord Linseley?" she called.

"It's not Lord Linseley, sir," came a voice through

the door. "It's just Mrs. Cockburn, hoping you've found everything comfortable and convenient. Is there anything else you need, Mr. Marston?"

Mr. Marston. How astonishing. For in the complexities of feminine dressing Phoebe had all but forgotten the existence of Phizz Marston.

Yes, quite, quite comfortable, she imagined herself calling back through the door. *No, I don't need a thing. Everything is perfectly as it should be, thank you for asking, Mrs. Cockburn,* she'd say in Phizz's cold, polite voice.

But everything wasn't perfect, she did need something, and right now she didn't want to be Phizz Marston. Right now what she wanted, more than anything in the world, was a garter. And Mrs. Cockburn would have one.

I'm quite mad, she told herself. No matter. Slowly, she opened the door and motioned the woman in.

The stately auburn-haired innkeeper had maintained her composure exceedingly well, Phoebe thought, upon discovering that Mr. Marston was really a woman. She listened slowly as Phoebe apologized for what might be a bit of a shock, and nodded sympathetically when she learned what her surprising lodger required.

"I'll pay you for your garters," Phoebe said hastily, "and I'll give you this single one if you want it, too." She pointed to the one on the bed.

"It's a lovely one, Miss . . . ?"

"Miss Browne." It was the name on the birth certificate of the woman who'd been buried in her place. "Thank you, but you can see where it doesn't do me much good by itself. And of course I'm rather in a hurry."

"Yes, dear, I suppose you are, and we'll be bringing your supper to the earl's rooms soon enough."

Mrs. Cockburn's eyes betrayed her amusement at the situation. They were large, a warm, reddish brown, with thick lashes and friendly crinkles at their corners. She's really very pretty, Phoebe thought, and surprisingly elegant for a provincial innkeeper. Her dress was dark and serviceable below a big white apron showing a few inevitable kitchen stains, but she'd gracefully draped a pale green silk kerchief around her lightly freckled neck, and her earrings were of fine gold filigree.

Quickly, she lifted her dark skirt, revealing long legs encased in neat black stockings held up with matching garters.

"Well, these may show a bit through your dress's fine weave, but with your Grecian hairstyle—very nicely done, by the way—you can pretend you meant it like that: ladylike, but just the slightest bit daring, a hint of the look of the old French empress Josephine. That style is lovely on your figure, by the way; you're wise not to insist upon those new longer waists that are coming in."

Wise, or simply pleased not to have to change my style at every whim of the fashion magazines, Phoebe thought. Especially since she only wore her three-year-old gowns to visit family in Devonshire. But if an innkeeper could see that her costume wasn't quite au courant . . .

"You don't think I look dowdy, do you?"

Mrs. Cockburn spoke purposefully. "No, never dowdy, dear, you wear your clothes too well, like a regular member of the *ton,* you look. But no use my pretending not to notice that it's not this season's. Still, I never really liked a gentleman who cared more for the gown than for the body within it, did you?"

Truly and plainly stated: her language and bearing were wonderfully urban and ironical. She comes from

London, Phoebe thought. I wonder how she came to be in her current situation.

"Here you are, dear." The garters were of plain black grosgrain ribbon, but fresh and in good condition. Phoebe handed Mrs. Cockburn the single pearl-trimmed garter in return and sat down on the bed to put on her stockings.

"How much do I owe you?"

"Just let me help you with the button. Yes, they'll do nicely. A sweet pair of slippers, too. And no, you don't owe me anything; the pearls on this pretty thing are quite enough payment. I'll have the big one set on a chain and work the little ones into some embroidery I'm doing for Ernest's mother's birthday. She's a good sort, you see, and never holds my past against me. 'As long as you and Ernest understand each other, Alison,' she says to me, 'I'm quite content with it.' "

Phoebe wondered if she was supposed to understand what all that was about. She might have asked, she supposed, if she'd had the time. For she quite liked Mrs. Cockburn. But it was growing late and Lord Linseley would soon be knocking on her door. She took the shawl from the armoire and wrapped it around her shoulders.

"I say, what a fine India paisley. I do like the gold thread running through it. Subtle, not too gaudy, not like you had anything to prove. You must have done very well for yourself."

And what could that *mean?*

"Of course," Mrs. Cockburn continued, "when I was working in London I didn't actually know anybody who went after that trade, but I've heard that the gentlemen who like it will pay monstrous sums for girls pretending to be men. And with you so convincing in your cravat and trousers, well, it must have been quite a fancy custom you pulled in. Still, you're well out of it.

A husband or a respectable business, that's what you want. Or both, if you should chance to be as lucky as I've been."

"Oh," Phoebe murmured, as the import of Mrs. Cockburn's remarks finally became clear to her.

Stupid, she scolded herself. After all, what *else* could the woman possibly have been talking about all this time? She supposed that she should feel insulted by what Mrs. Cockburn had so readily assumed about her. But in truth her interpretation of Phoebe's male costume was as reasonable as any other—probably more reasonable than the truth of the matter. It was all really rather humorous.

"Well, you're right about a great many things," she replied brightly, "but right now, well, you see, I can't converse with you as long as I'd like because I expect Lord Linseley directly."

Mrs. Cockburn nodded. "Helping you find a better life, I expect he is, just like he did me. Found me this situation, introduced me to Ernest too. Well, he's a kind man and I'll always be grateful to him."

She turned to go.

Phoebe smiled at her. It was pleasant to dream of a better life, unlikely as that was. "Thank you. I've enjoyed our conversation. It was good of you to tell me about Lord Linseley."

She'd always admired his concern for the farm laborers of his district, but one could, after all, ascribe it to the enlightened self-interest of an intelligent landowner. But what Mrs. Cockburn had just described was an act of the purest charity, a generous effort to help make better lives for women that very few people tried to help—and one, she suspected, that he'd be too modest to tell her about himself. How fine and selfless he was.

Mrs. Cockburn paused at the door. "A very good and kind man he is indeed, and I saw few enough of *them* in my old life, that's for certain." The corners of her eyes crinkled. "*And,* goes without saying, one of the best that a girl could hope for in bed, eh, dear?"

Or perhaps not quite so selfless.

At a loss for any other response, Phoebe nodded dumbly.

Mrs. Cockburn grinned. "Yeh, he's a rare one, ain't he? So modest with his clothes on, and such a . . . what-do-you-call-'em . . . a satyr without them. In my time all the girls were mad for him, each and every one hoping he'd want her for a regular arrangement, but he liked variety, see, a different one every night. I expect he's still like that, a man of his energies, after all. We used to comfort ourselves by saying that when all's said and done it would be a shame not to share him around, the creator having made so few like him."

She winked. "Of course, what's most important is how a man uses what he's given. But still and all, it's always a pleasure simply to *look* upon the fancy work when it's of such a size and elegance as what our gentleman's got. Don't you agree, dear?

"And I'll just let my household girls know about your costume, so they'll be comfortable with it. They're from the country and brought up sheltered, not like us . . ."

Flashing a last sly, conspiratorial smile over her shoulder, she quitted the room, shutting the door behind her and leaving a meticulously dressed and utterly befuddled Phoebe to blink in astonishment.

A good man. A selfless man. A paradigm of charity.

Charity, my arse, Phoebe muttered.

Well, she'd certainly become better acquainted with him, she thought—though rather precipitously, and not at all as planned. Mrs. Cockburn had shown her quite another side of the earl of Linseley, whose reputation among the *Beau Monde* ranged from the noble to the estimable to the rather stuffy. But then, the *Beau Monde* did tend to take a shortsighted view of things. Best to consult a sharper-eyed segment of the population for a better, clearer view of reality. Reality from the other side—the underside, if one liked.

He liked variety, see, a different one every night.

Yes, she supposed that *a man of his energies* might well find variety congenial. She couldn't help but wonder about the extent of those vaunted and much-discussed energies.

And there was *the size of the fancy work* to be considered as well. Not to speak of the elegance—whatever *that* might mean.

She laughed dryly. No point pretending that a small, disreputable part of her hadn't found all this information rather thrilling. A very small part of herself was wildly curious to get a look for herself—the part of her that wasn't seething with rage.

How *dared* he be so furious about her adventure with Billy? He'd made her single, prudent foray into the world of bought pleasure seem so bold, so far beyond what the very proper Lord Linseley could be expected to assimilate to his understanding. She'd wanted to explain it to him, to make it clear how stunted her marriage had been and how profoundly she'd needed to acquaint herself with the desires at her body's center.

Explain it? Clarify it? Bloody hell, she would probably have apologized to him for it. Humbly, she would have begged his pardon for not twiddling her thumbs until that oh-so-romantic moment when *he'd* come galloping over the horizon, a knight errant come to claim her.

While *he* had bedded a different dolly every night, with no explanations necessary.

She remembered the scene in her parlor after the

doctor had left. How angry he'd been; how meekly she'd accepted his right to be angry. What a pathetically passive face she'd shown. And if it hadn't been for the silly business with the garter—if Mrs. Cockburn hadn't been given an opportunity to share her confidences—she would at this moment be waiting, breathlessly, passively and pathetically, for his knock at the door. Aching and quivering for his touch, just another stupid, simpering, overdressed, pretty *woman.*

She stole a glance at herself in the mirror. Oh yes, very pretty indeed. Though it was perhaps inaccurate to say overdressed—"overdressed" hardly seemed the right word for the exposed, vulnerable expanse of bosom and neck she'd taken such pains to display. Too bad there wasn't enough time to become Marston again; she would have preferred to confront the earl of Linseley from behind a buttoned shirtfront and high cravat. In truth, she would have preferred her padded fencer's tunic and screened face mask.

Nonsense. Best to confront him as she was.

A soft, stacatto knock at the door. Soft, and yet—was she imagining it?—peremptory, somehow. An impatient knock. A man's knock.

She hadn't drawn the latch after Mrs. Cockburn had left.

"Yes, come in," she called. She was surprised at how natural her voice sounded.

She took a step forward toward the door, stopping in a pool of lamplight that that her heightened senses told her was the most flattering spot in the room. The light glowed on her face and bosom, while her anger lent an unaccustomed flush to her cheeks. Good, let him think she was blushing. She licked her lips quickly and parted them in a small, soft *O.*

He opened the door and stepped across the room's threshold. And then he stopped abruptly.

"Ah."

She felt the heat in his glance as his smile widened.

"My word," he murmured, "you're . . . you're a revelation."

How can it be, she thought, that wherever he goes he seems to stir the air like a fresh breeze? She felt her anger waver, like a flickering candle flame. He advanced slowly toward her. In another moment he'd take her hand. He'd bow at a precise, gentlemanly angle, raise her fingers to his lips, and she'd be lost.

A mere eighteen inches away now. Half the length of a fencing foil.

A swordsman's best defense, she told herself, was a good offence; she slapped him hard across the cheek.

"You hypocrite," she said. "You self-righteous prig."

He staggered back a step or two, though it was with surprise rather than with the force of the blow. She was gratified, however, to see that she had left a mark on his face.

"But . . . but what?" he stammered. "What the devil have I done? Wh-why, Phoebe?"

"I haven't given you leave to call me by my Christian name, Lord Linseley."

"No, and I most heartily apologize for taking the liberty. But you must tell me how I've offended you."

She turned toward the window. The stars were so infernally bright in this part of the world, she thought.

"I had a little talk with Mrs. Cockburn. While I was dressing."

"I'm surprised. I shouldn't have thought you'd want to expose your double identity to anyone here. You're usually so careful."

She turned back to him with a low laugh.

"Well, we should have had to tell her something tomorrow morning anyway, when I appeared for breakfast dressed as a woman."

"You're right. I hadn't been thinking ahead. I hadn't been thinking of anything except tonight."

He frowned. "But you haven't told me how you'd come to be conversing with her, or what she said that's upset you so terribly. She's a very good person, after all, though she might seem a bit crude."

"I wouldn't say crude. I'd say rather, direct. She said several *direct* things about you."

"Hmmm."

She supposed that he took her meaning.

"You two must have hit it off rather well," he offered. "It sounds as though your conversation touched on some rather intimate matters."

Ungracefully, she raised her skirt above her knees for a moment, smiling coldly as she watched him endeavor not to stare at her legs. She let the fabric drop. "I needed a garter. I wanted to be as perfectly dressed as I could. For you."

"I see."

"Yes, I expect that you do see that. Well, two women can become quite close when they're sharing intimate garments. Especially when they've shared a lover as well. Or so she assumed."

He nodded warily.

"Well, not a lover, perhaps. A customer, rather. For she also assumed that we'd shared a profession."

"Dear me." He looked angry and yet somehow relieved. "Well, *that* must have been distressing for you. I can see how you would find *that* most unpleasant. I'm awfully sorry about it. *That* was quite my fault, not to have explained your situation to the Cockburns."

He smiled so charmingly and apologetically that she wanted to slap him again.

"Oh, no you don't. I *won't* have you thinking that I'm offended by what she thought about me."

"But . . ."

"In some ways she was quite right. My miserable marriage was no more than a form of prostitution; it was simply the form that the church and crown have chosen to sanction as legitimate. I got a lot of clothes and jewels out of it though, so Mrs. Cockburn was quite correct, from a certain point of view, to say that I'd done very well for myself."

"I didn't know. I'm sorry." He nodded soberly, moving forward to take her hand.

"Don't touch me."

"But . . ."

"You really don't understand what's making me so angry, do you?"

Shrugging uncertainly, he opened his mouth to speak.

"No, you don't see it at all. You think it's perfectly all right if *you* fuck half the prostitutes of London—"

He raised an ineffectual hand.

"Yes, I know, not really half. You didn't bother with the poor old diseased ones we see cowering in doorways. Well, neither should I have, though I do try to give them a coin when I pass.

"But among the young and pretty ones, the ones specially chosen to service members of your class—well, *there* you did pretty well, didn't you, Lord Linseley?"

"I tried to help them."

"Don't change the subject. In fact, you did *so* well with them that according to Mrs. Cockburn you gained a certain celebrity in her circles."

Try as he might, he couldn't quite hide the flash of gratified surprise that lit his eyes.

"Lord, you're insufferable. Oh yes, they found you quite the *satyr,* as she put it, didn't you know? You had every high-class dolly in London twittering over your capacities, over the size of the, the . . ."

She found she couldn't quite complete the sentence. He smiled at that.

"But it's nothing," he said. "After all, that was all in the past, before I'd met you."

"Indeed. And let me remind you of one little episode in *my* past. Because when you learned that before I met you *I'd* wanted a little pleasure, a little bit of human warmth, or even, perish the thought, a little bit of *fun* . . . Bloody hell, Linseley, when you discovered that *I'd* had needs and desires and the sense and wit to figure out how to satisfy them . . ."

"But that was different."

"Exactly *how,* pray tell, was it different?"

"It was different because . . ."

A shadow of doubt passed quickly over his features, to be replaced by a stubborn certainty.

"Because I'm a man, dammit. And you are not."

This time she would have done more than strike him. Rake her fingernails across his face, perhaps, or do something considerably ruder with her knee. But he caught her wrist before she was able to do any damage. He held her immobile for a long moment, peering curiously down at her.

I could kiss her right now, he thought, just to prove to her how different a man is, how implacable his desires. She was remarkably strong for a woman; under her dainty puffed sleeve he could see a slender muscle flexed in her arm, tensed to resist him. But would she resist a kiss? Perhaps a kiss would be the best way to resolve all this foolishness.

He looked into her eyes, searching for a signal to continue. He knew she wanted him; after the air had cleared she'd probably thank him for cutting through all these clumsy recriminations. Anger was a strong passion, after all. And all the passions were finally rooted in desire.

But it wasn't anger he saw in her eyes. It was profound disappointment.

He dropped her arm. "I implore your pardon, but I'd better go."

"Yes, I think you'd better."

She turned again to stare at the piercing stars in the black sky outside her window. Dully, she heard him shut the door behind him.

And that's the end of it, she thought.

She'd feared losing him the previous night when he'd found out about Billy. And she supposed that, in fact, she had lost him then, no matter how aroused they'd both become by their enticing proximity in the carriage all day.

The strength of their mutual desiring was simply not enough, she thought sadly. No point beginning an affair if she were to be held to some stifling standard of feminine sexual conduct. Better to continue to be Marston, even if Marston were in danger. She'd stay in Lincolnshire for a week or two as she'd intended anyway, care for Billy, and plan the safest and most prudent way to bring him back to London. For she couldn't depend on Lord Linseley's protection forever. It wouldn't be fair.

In the long run, she told herself, it didn't really matter. She and he could have no future together anyway. It's just that she'd been so happy with him in the carriage today that she'd let herself forget that.

Meanwhile, there was this silly costume to take off. Surprisingly, she discovered that she didn't want to. Not quite yet. Perhaps it was all the labor that had gone into dressing up for him, but she rather liked the way she looked. Perhaps, before she changed her clothes, she'd see how Billy was doing.

He'd woken just a quarter of an hour ago, the chambermaid told her quietly. His wounds pained him considerably, the girl added, trying hard not to stare at Phoebe's costume; he'd refused to take any gruel. But he had allowed the girl to change his bandages. It seemed to Phoebe that she'd done an excellent job.

"I'll try to feed him," Phoebe said. And indeed, he brightened at the sight of her pretty dress and bright shawl, and did take a few spoonfuls from her. She sat with him until he fell back to sleep, and then, regretfully, returned to her room, which seemed rather lonelier and drearier than it had a few hours earlier.

She supposed she could go downstairs and get some supper. But Mrs. Cockburn would be surprised to see her, she'd have to explain why she wasn't with Lord Linseley, and anyway, she wasn't hungry.

I might as well go to bed, she told herself. Best if we make an early start tomorrow.

Chapter 15

She'd folded the shawl away in the armoire, and was standing before the mirror, arms raised to unfasten her necklace, when she heard yet another knock at the door.

Her heart leapt. *Three's a magic number,* she thought. *Don't be ridiculous,* she scolded herself a moment later. It was probably only the chambermaid, come to report on Billy's condition. Phoebe hoped he wasn't developing a fever, for if he were they'd have to remain inconveniently stranded at the Swan for quite some time.

"Yes, yes, just a moment. Thank you, I'll be right there."

But it wasn't the chambermaid.

The earl of Linseley stood in the doorway holding a covered basket. He looked truculent, ill at ease; she hoped he wouldn't want to continue their earlier set-to. But his voice, when he spoke, was warm and quiet.

"You must be hungry," he said. "They said you hadn't come down for supper, so I packed what they'd brought up to my room. I'll leave it with you, if that's all right."

She nodded. Perhaps she was just a bit hungry after all. "Yes, thank you. That's very kind. You can put it on this little table."

"Of course. On the little table."

But he didn't put it down; he simply stood in place, looking profoundly uncomfortable. His ears and hands were red and chapped, she thought, as though he'd been out in the cold without hat or gloves. Finally, he took a breath and began to speak.

"I took a walk," he said. "I needed to think about what you'd said to me. I found it . . . confusing, you see."

"I expect that you did."

"In truth, I found it deuced disagreeable."

She frowned and he continued quickly. "Well, it's always disagreeable to discover that one has been in the wrong. But it seems that I can't avoid the unpleasant truth. Please accept my apology for having acted so possessively, and for holding you to different standards than myself. It was unworthy of us both. I was wrong and you were right."

She stared at him in amazement. Clearly this little speech hadn't come easily to him.

She wanted to throw herself into his arms, to laugh with joy, weep with relief, and praise heaven for his stubborn integrity. But instead she only smiled. "You truly are a most unusual gentleman."

"You forgive me then?"

"You know that I forgive you, David." Gently, she took the basket from him and put it on the table.

"In fact," she continued, "I might have acted a bit possessively myself. Every dolly in London is rather a lot of competition for a lady no longer in her first bloom of youth. Especially one whose dress is so utterly passé."

He grinned. "Do you really feel possessive of me? I shall enjoy knowing that. And could so perfect a gown truly be out of fashion?" he asked.

She nodded. "It's three seasons old."

He took a step across the room's threshold.

"Of course," he said softly, "it's the *fit* of a garment that matters and not its newness, isn't that so?"

She smiled to think that he remembered their first conversation so exactly. *She* remembered every word, but she wouldn't have thought that he . . .

He kicked the door shut behind him. "Isn't that so, Phoebe?" he said.

They stared at each other over what seemed an insurmountable gulf of space, but which was, in fact, only about a yard of empty air between their bodies. As if to test the distance, he raised his arm and reached out to trace the tops of her breasts with his index finger. She gasped, perhaps at the coldness of his hand. Or perhaps, she thought a moment later, she'd gasped to hear her name pronounced with such hot, slow passion.

She felt a wave of dizziness. Quickly, she took a deep, shuddering breath to steady herself as he caught hold of her shoulders with rough, icy hands and pulled her toward him. His face was cold from the outdoors, his lips and tongue almost unbearably warm in contrast. He tasted faintly of brandy. *Fire and ice:* the words echoed in some distant reach of her mind. She held him tightly, slipping her bare arms beneath his coat. She could feel the muscles girding his torso; damn those stern, proper layers of wool and linen that prevented her from touching him directly. She wanted to touch, to smell, to taste his skin.

To taste him . . . quite as he was tasting her mouth at

the moment. His kiss was deep but leisurely; she arched her neck and threw back her head, opening herself to his explorations of her. His lips slid down her neck, and for a moment his tongue filled the tremulous hollow of her throat.

She felt a sudden loosening, a short, sudden rush of cool air into the warm space between her breasts. He'd undone the top few hooks of her dress and had pulled it a few inches down her shoulders. Impatiently, he pushed her chemise down below her breasts; the fabric strained but didn't tear: a moment later he'd buried his face in the space he'd freed. His tongue—it felt rough now, like a cat's—flicked against one of her nipples. A clever tongue, she thought: what tiny circles he made with it; a mischievous tongue, darting and weaving, teasing and tormenting her. Sensation radiated from the little knob of flesh he seemed content to pleasure so exclusively; warm, undulating waves of feeling cascaded downward to her knees. She pressed her thighs into his. Wantonly, she rubbed her belly and pelvis against him, murmuring her low laugh as she felt his erection press and swell in response.

Good, she thought, absurdly proud of this evidence of his arousal. Good, I'm not the only one feeling such transports.

Ah, but he'd been waiting for exactly such an unguarded moment, she realized an instant later. Her self-satisfaction had made her careless. She'd been caught.

Quickly, he'd drawn her nipple between his lips—oh Lord, he had it between his teeth now. It was too late for retreat—if she'd truly wanted to retreat. She breathed out a long *ohhh* while fear and trust waged delicious warfare within her. He bit down, not hard enough to hurt her, but hard enough to show her that he could—and would, if she dared back away from him. His grasp on her shoulders tightened as she cried and groaned and shuddered through the waves of orgasm that racked her. He raised his head, and, still holding her (for at that moment she would have found it difficult to hold herself upright), he watched with interest as she struggled to regain her composure. His pupils were distended, deep black pools surrounded by rings of blue.

"You need a lot of lovemaking, don't you?" he whispered.

Well, it's a bit humiliating, isn't it, she thought, to have one's measure taken so quickly and accurately. Still, there was no disputing it: she might feel quite glorious, but she was hardly satiated. He'd merely taken the edge off her desire. She wanted a great, great deal more from him.

"A lot of lovemaking," he repeated. "Don't you, Phoebe?" He spoke the words aloud this time.

"Yes," her voice was hoarse, and seemed to have come from a long distance away. She cleared her throat. She raised her head proudly. "Yes, I expect that I do."

"Good. You're in the right hands, then."

Wonderful hands, she thought. As though leading her through a dance, he guided her with gentle pressure at the back of her waist, maneuvering her and himself to an armchair in a window alcove. He sat down; she stood before him, trapped within the embrace of his thighs. He nuzzled her bosom. "You smell sweet," he murmured as he lifted his head. She stared down into his eyes.

"I would have undressed you by now," he said, "if my hands weren't so confoundedly stiff from the cold. And rough, too—I've almost given myself chilblains—we're lucky that I haven't pulled the fabric of your dress.

"But instead, I want you to undress for me. I'll help with the occasional hook or lace, of course."

"Yes, but what of *your* clothes?" she asked. "You're to remain all laced and shod and buttoned up while I take off my clothes for you? How very unfair to me. I want to see you."

"We're not discussing what's fair and what is not. You'll undress *me* after you undress yourself."

She laughed. "How *exquisitely* unfair. And very lordly of you, too, I must say."

He slapped her rump lightly and kissed her breast.

"Well, I am a lord, don't forget. I try to be a good, honest, and decent one, but the fact of the matter is that I own rather a lot of land. And I'm afraid that the habit of being lord over all that I survey is a hard one to break.

"Now go stand there by the fireplace." This time his slap on her rump carried a little more force with it. "You know the spot. It's where the lamplight meets the light from the flames and makes you look so bewitching."

He loosened his legs from around her hips. Slowly, she backed away from him toward the warm pool of golden light. One walked backwards, she thought, after having made one's curtsies at court. In respect, in humility . . . but hardly with the slow, lustful, provocative movements she felt herself employing. *Lord of all that you survey, are you, sir? Well, we shall have to see about that.*

The light flowed over her as she reached the spot he'd described. She remembered Billy, his first night with her, when she'd commanded him to undress. His gestures had been meek, his posture compliant, but there'd been a boldness, a daring, to how he'd bent and turned for her. He'd felt his own beauty in the heat of her eyes. He'd basked in her desire, glorying in his power to arouse it.

Well, it *was* delicious, she thought, to be the object of such imperious desire. And yet not *purely* an object: surely an object couldn't be as suffused with feeling as she was at this moment. But she'd untangle those paradoxes some other time. Right now she'd simply absorb it all. Her skirt blew softly about her legs, even as her naked breasts lifted and her nipples tightened under his gaze. He was staring at her breasts with—*oh thank heaven!*—delight.

His gaze traveled slowly downward. She raised her chin, preening for him, slowly arching her back as a cat might do. Peering at him through her eyelashes, she watched the corners of his mouth twitch as he took note of the black garters just visible through the white skirt of her dress. His smile widened as his eyes descended to the dark red ribbons that crisscrossed her ankles.

"I wondered about those narrow, graceful ankles when I watched you waltzing at Almack's, Mr. Marston," he said. "They were remarkably neat for a gentleman. But I simply thought them an aspect of your sublime elegance."

"I'm less sublime this evening," she murmured. "But that's because I'm not Marston." She cupped her breasts in her hands. "Or hadn't you noticed?"

"Well, you don't seem to be. But perhaps you're simply an unusually . . . fleshy young gentleman."

He swept his eyes over her thighs and belly, focusing his gaze upon the spot where her legs met. "If you're not Marston you should present me with irrevocable proof of it."

"That's easily done." She reached behind her to undo the hooks at the back of her dress. She put it aside, quickly drew off her chemise, and stepped out of her petticoat. More slowly now, she began to loosen her drawers. His eyes hadn't moved from her center. Fumbling with strings and buttons, she stared at his large hands spread out on top of his knees. He flexed his fingers: she hoped the warmth had returned to them and that he was feeling less stiff now. Well, his hands didn't look stiff. They were large and strong, and looked capable of just about anything. *Why, just the thickness of his thumb,* she thought dreamily, *would be enough to . . .*

Her drawers slid down her legs to the floor. "I believe that's the proof you required, my lord," she announced, stepping out of them and kicking them aside with a shameless giggle. She hadn't expected to flaunt her naked quim quite as readily as it seemed she was doing. Perhaps she'd taken encouragement from the involuntary sigh that had forced his mouth open as he stared at the triangle of chestnut curls on the plump mound rising below her belly.

Oh yes, she'd enjoyed both the sigh and the intensity of his eyes upon her. She rubbed her thighs together to try to control her excitement.

"Keep them parted," he growled. He winced immediately after, embarrassed at having revealed the extent of his impatient desire.

But she was beginning to feel rather impatient herself. Although this game of displaying herself for his pleasure was a most provocative one, perhaps it was time to move on.

Well, she had only the corset and the shoes and stockings to remove now. Frowning, she tugged at the laces at her back.

"My lord."

"Ummm."

"There seems to be a knot that I can't untie. Would you help me . . ."

"Well, hurry on over here, then."

But now he was becoming careless, too. For if he'd really wanted to continue with this game, she thought, he would have turned her around and concentrated upon the corset laces, instead of fumbling absently with them while he nuzzled her breasts.

It didn't matter. There hadn't been a knot. The corset fell to the floor at his first tug on the strings, as she took advantage of his momentary surprise to unknot his cravat.

He shook his head. "You're headstrong, disobedient."

"I've been a man for three years. It engenders habits that are hard to break."

His hand moved downward, tracing the cleft between her buttocks, his finger stopping for a moment to probe her. She closed her eyes and stiffened, only relaxing a moment later, when his finger crept forward between her legs and into the very wet opening there.

"All right, undress me then, if that's what you're so keen to do."

"I—I don't know if I can undress you, David, wh-while you're doing *that* to me."

He'd found her clitoris easily. She let out a long, whistling breath as he moved his finger against it.

"Of course you can undress me."

And so she did, clumsily pulling away his garments and flinging them every which way, while he moved his finger within her and she gasped and groaned in the throes of helpless, brutish pleasure.

Coat, waistcoat, shirt and cravat finally gone, she kissed her way down his naked chest, dragging her lips along the ridges of muscle, rolling his nipples between her fingertips, rubbing her cheeks and chin along the line of thick black hair that bisected his belly and disappeared at the waistband of his trousers. She teased him a few times, reaching his waist and then moving upward again, rubbing her breasts against him before kissing her way back down. She wouldn't simply give him what she knew he wanted next; he'd have to show her that he wanted it.

He groaned, took his finger out of her, and gently pushed her shoulders downward. She moved down to her knees to unbutton him, to open his trousers—he groaned again, happily this time—and to kiss and stroke and run her tongue along the length of his erect penis.

The fancy work—ah yes, it was fully as impressive as Alison had said. A pleasure to look upon—for those who might be satisfied by looking. Phoebe wanted more than that. She touched him every way she could think of, transported by avid curiosity and delight. Her hands spanned the thickness of his penis and cupped the weight of his balls; her tongue explored the sculptured contours of head and shaft, the elegant tracery of distended veins, the taut bow of his erection. She pressed her breasts together, caressing him between them while she kissed and tongued him at the tip. Finally she drew him into her mouth, arching her neck to accept him as he lengthened still more, past her cheeks and toward her throat.

His belly trembled under her lips. One of his hands grasped her hair to guide her head, occasionally slowing or speeding the movement of her lips over him. She was beginning to understand which rhythms he preferred when he pulled himself out of her mouth and nudged her head away. "My boots, my trousers," he whispered, and she removed them quite as deftly as she had once imagined.

"Come here," he said. She straddled his lap, holding herself up for a moment while he moved into place beneath her. Slowly, she lowered herself onto him, feeling a marvelous ache and opening as the walls of her quim opened to reshape themselves around him.

Quickly, abruptly, he thrust himself upward a few times, and then, when he felt himself comfortably within her, he lifted both himself and her out of the chair and walked to the bed. She could see them, so joined, in the mirror as he carried her past it. She was still wearing her stockings, though one of her shoes had fallen off and the other was just about to. Pink stockings, black garters, long crimson ribbons dangling from her shoe—how oddly, ineffectually civilized it all looked in contrast to his dark, animal body, legs thickly muscled and covered with just a bit too much wiry black hair. She hugged his waist more tightly with her legs.

"Satyr," she whispered, twisting the thick locks of hair on his head until they stood up like goat horns.

He'd whispered something back, but she couldn't hear it over the creak of bedsprings. She was on her back now; he smiled down at her as he lifted her legs over his shoulders—was he really going to drive even more deeply into her? It seemed that he was. Throwing her hands back, she grasped the bed's headboard; thus anchored, she moved her hips in vigorous harmony with his.

They each came quickly—merrily, even—like an orchestra hurrying through the final chords of an overture. They lay next to one another for some minutes, looking, resting, considering. Slowly, they stretched their hands toward each other as the curtain rose on a slower, more passionate drama.

Laughing with delight or groaning with passion, they moved together through the portals of a world that seemed to create itself at their touch. Each of them dared the other to go further—with eyes wide and shining, bodies taut, and senses ready to be astonished, they coaxed each other into new positions, each with its profound or novel sensations, its possibilities for new and daring intimacies to be stolen or granted. He nibbled her ears, stroked her eyelids, kissed her slowly and lusciously on the insides of her thighs until she moaned and whimpered. She tickled him under his balls, sucked his nipples, licked the sweat that pooled in the center of his chest, took his testicles into her mouth, rolling her tongue around them as though they were a ripe, double fig.

He sank back on the pillows; she straddled him, leaning over him while he tongued her breasts and squeezed her buttocks in his hands. He guided her onto himself, his hands cupping her while she rode the shaft of his penis. Until finally, spent beyond the limits of her endurance, she shuddered and collapsed on top of him, falling into his arms while he climaxed mightily below her.

And just as she'd told him it would—had it just that morning or had it been several lifetimes ago?—his purring, comforting snore lulled her into delicious, refreshing sleep, her head atop his chest.

She might have slept all night if her empty stomach hadn't awakened her, perhaps an hour later. She stretched her muscles, trying not to disturb him. He was curled around her, arms around her breasts, belly sweetly curved around her buttocks.

"You're up, are you, Phoebe?"

"Ummm, yes. And I'm absolutely starving."

He laughed, and padded out of bed to light a lamp—a satyr still, she thought, but perhaps a domesticated one. Or perhaps not.

"Stay there," he called. "Now where did we put that basket?"

"Oh, thank heaven, the basket. Is there anything good to eat in there?"

"A cold veal roll in aspic. A Stilton. Bread, oranges, and a bottle of excellent ale. Wait. I'll bring it to you."

He joined her against the pillows where she sat, among the twisted disarray of sheets and quilts that were strewn about them like spent ammunition after a battle. Her stockings were bunched around her ankles. She pulled them off, smoothed them, and put them on the bed table, along with a garter that had somehow lodged itself under a pillow.

Her muscles ached as thoroughly as if she'd been fencing. Well, it *had* been rather a battle, she thought. A delicious, mock-heroic epic. She was ravenous.

"Here, try some of this." He popped a bite of Stilton into her mouth, following it with a slice of veal; she sucked his fingers between the morsels of food he fed her. Another slice of meat now, this time with its rich jelly folded within it. A bite of crusty bread.

"My goodness, what lovely food. There isn't a cook in London who could do a better job with this veal."

"It is good, isn't it? Alison's father was French. He'd had a good job as chef for an aristocrat who'd emigrated during the Terror. Her favorite childhood memories are from when he'd bring her down to the kitchen with him. His only legacy to her was a precious portfolio of recipes; both parents died when she was twelve, you see, leaving her to the care of her father's employer, who promptly tossed her out onto the street. Luckily, she was pretty, which allowed her to survive. And unluckily, she was pretty, which rather determined how she would survive out there."

"She praises your kindness to her."

"When she's not praising me in other ways."

"Perhaps it was just as well that she'd prepared me for you." Her hand had crept under the sheet and into his lap. He slapped it away.

"Not until after I've fed you properly. You need to eat, to keep your strength up. Otherwise I'm in danger of wearing you out, tempted as I am to fuck you until you're but a pale shadow of yourself."

"How awful. Why don't I find it a fearful prospect?"

"I expect that you're too brave for your own good."

He took an orange from the basket and peeled it, feeding it to her a section at a time. She chewed slowly, letting the sweet juice slide down her throat.

"Not too brave, really," she said. "When I took risks as Marston, I thought that I was only endangering myself. Which didn't matter, you see. I'd already lost every that mattered."

"You mustn't think that way. You matter to *me.* You matter terribly." He ran the tip of his thumb around the outside of her lips, watching intently as her eyes and mouth softened.

"But you must try the ale," he added quickly. "Ernest Cockburn's brother brews it. Here, I'll pour you a glass."

She took a long, thirsty draught. "I don't usually drink ale, you know. Hmmm, it's sweet . . ."

"That's the malt."

"And bitter, too, in a rather haunting way."

"Yes, those are the hops. Sweet and bitter in a rather haunting way. You're exactly right, James Cockburn's as much a poet as a brewer. His ale is as subtle as the best champagne."

He laughed. "Enough about poetry. I fear I've given the ale rather too foamy a head. Come here, let me lick off that bit from the corner of your mouth."

Which led to a kiss and another bout of lovemaking.

("I've lost count," she whispered afterwards. "Good," he whispered back, "I don't like counting in bed.")

"Mr. Cockburn's brother brews a marvelous ale."

"Yes, I think so too."

"We spilled a little of it on the sheets, though. We should have taken care to finish it up before we became otherwise engaged."

"It's your fault, you know, for being so irresistible."

"And not yours, for being so . . . at the ready?"

"Oh well, maybe a little." He blew out the light and gathered her to him under the chaotic tangle of bed linens.

She sighed contentedly as he rested his lips on the back of her neck.

"But do you think, David, that we shall ever make love in a way that is not quite so . . . combative?"

"I think that we shall make love in every conceivable way in the lifetime we'll spend together. Now go to sleep. I don't want you dozing through your first view of my countryside."

A lifetime. The word drifted through her head as his purring snore started up. Pretty word, *lifetime,* she thought. *Well, I'll simply have to make do with as much of a lifetime as we can cram into a week in the country.* She nestled into him, cradling her buttocks against his belly. His hands were tight around her breasts. His penis—lively even in sleep—quivered softly in the cleft of her arse.

A real lifetime together—the sort of happy, productive married life he had in mind, anyway—simply wasn't possible. But she wouldn't let regrets spoil their first night together. And anyway, she thought, it was impossible to feel anything but profound happiness—the sweet and bitter of it simultaneously—while his big body enveloped hers. They'd have a week together. Two weeks, perhaps. She'd live every moment as fully as she could. And then she'd state her terms. They wouldn't be what he wanted; she'd understand if he found them impossible. And if he couldn't comply, well then, the memory of these weeks would have to suffice.

Chapter

16

"I see." Lady Kate Beverredge raised a graceful fluted teacup to her lips as she endeavored to understand everything Mr. Simms had told her.

As Phoebe had known he would, he'd had taken the earliest possible opportunity to inform Kate of the previous night's events, begging leave to see her just hours after Phoebe's departure. As Phoebe had predicted, he'd told the story in meticulous and scrupulous detail. But what Phoebe wouldn't have imagined was the extremity of the anxiety with which he'd recounted what had happened. His face seemed somehow caved in; for the first time in Kate's memory he looked old. She was startled by how the violent events had taken their toll on him; his teacup rattled in its saucer.

Poor dear man, Kate thought. Well, of course the blood and screaming must have been most harrowing, not to speak of the pain and terror the boy had had to endure. "But we mustn't worry about our beloved friend," she told him. "She'll be absolutely safe with Lord Linseley. He's a good man, Mr. Simms."

Mr. Simms sighed. "He seems so. But I'm afraid it's

going to be difficult for me to cease worrying about her, your ladyship. Worry has become rather a way of life with me, you see. Somehow, no matter how outrageously she acts when I'm under the same roof with her, I feel that I can protect her. But with her gone so far away . . ."

"Yes. Well, she's led us all a merry chase these past few years. But perhaps she's finally found what she's been looking for."

His eyes looked skeptical.

Kate smiled apologetically. "Of course, she did choose rather an eccentric manner of searching for her heart's desire. But I expect that in our secret souls we're all eccentrics."

She paused. "And then again, there's the fact that she's kept our lives from being as tedious as they might have been these few past years."

He nodded. "Well said, Lady Kate. I've certainly been grateful for the excitement. But lately I've come to think that a tedious patch or two might not be such a bad thing at my age. Of course, not at *your* age, obviously. For may I tell you how very well you are looking this morning?"

She smiled. "You may, Mr. Simms, and thank you. No, life isn't at all tedious, these days." She sneaked a quick, tactful glance at her pocket watch, for she had an appointment at half past eleven.

"Well, I won't be keeping you, but I brought you these for safekeeping." He handed her a small black velvet pouch. "And to enable us to pay for the repairs to the Brunswick Square carpets and furniture."

"Quite right." Carefully, she spilled a few gems into her hand.

After Phoebe's "funeral," all the ancestral jewelry had gone back to Henry's mother. But a few of the gifts that Lord Claringworth had made his young wife couldn't be accounted for and had had to be reported stolen. Over the past few years, however, one or another flawless stone would make its occasional way out of the velvet bag, journeying to a narrow building beside a canal in Amsterdam, where objects of dazzling beauty were handled with solid, unimpeachable, and untraceable rectitude.

"My blood money," Phoebe would say, whenever the fee for one of those stones had made its way back to her. "The only money I've ever truly earned." And in fact, Kate thought now, the rubies she held in her palm did look like drops of blood.

"Yes, I'll take care of it," she murmured.

"And these." He gestured toward sandalwood box. "The poison pen letters, my lady. She said they were important evidence, and must be kept safe."

"Indeed." What sad objects he'd brought for safekeeping: the spoils of a dead husband's abusive behavior and the ravings of a vicious, anonymous madman. "Well, I'll protect them, but I certainly shan't read them."

She reached across the table and took the old tutor's brown-spotted hand into her own soft white one.

"And do try not to worry, dear Mr. Simms." she added. "I know how much you love Phoebe. But if we are very lucky, from now on we will be forced to share her with someone else."

"I don't want to let you out of bed." Lord Linseley tightened his arms around her as the first morning light peeped under the curtains.

"I need a wash," Phoebe protested. "You've made me quite wonderfully sticky all over." She kissed his cheek and pressed her body into his, belly against belly, the mound of her quim against his spent penis. "Sticky and still wet, some places."

"Umm, yes, that was nice just now, wasn't it? But as soon as you get out of bed, you see, our first night together will be officially over."

"What a romantic creature you are," she murmured. "Fascinated by symbol and ritual and using silly words like 'official' to mask your fascination. I'll wager that you loved reading the Arthurian legends as a boy. And volume after volume of fairy tales as well."

He laughed. "People don't generally describe me as a romantic."

She slid out of his grasp.

"But yes, you're right, I've read them all," he added. "Numerous times. Especially the tales where the hero wins his princess."

She dipped a sponge into the hot water that a servant had brought up to her room a little while earlier. How clever of her to have guessed what sort of child he'd once been, he thought as he watched her soap her arms and neck.

Gracefully, she raised an arm and began to scrub herself in the slender hollow underneath it. How miraculous it was, he thought, that someone could know such private, personal things about you without having been told. And how provocative those moist tendrils of pale brown hair were, how tenderly they outlined the swooping curve below her arm. They were a shade fairer than the bright chestnut bush between her legs. Marston's Byronic dark locks were dyed, then—he wouldn't have guessed.

"If anyone should inquire, I'll tell the Cockburns to say that Mr. Marston left quite early for Scotland," he said. "And that Lord Linseley spent the night with a mysterious lady of great beauty and charm."

He smiled as he said it, for in fact she looked entirely *un*-mysterious this morning. She simply looked very pretty, energetic, and unselfconscious, flushed pink and white in the cold morning air. Her nipples, with their devastatingly large aureoles, were puckered to a dark, pinkish brown. A small, secretive, satisfied smile played about her lips as she spread her legs to sponge the insides of her thighs.

The smile became wistful, troubled.

"I find it difficult," she said, "to keep in mind the hatred that's been directed at me—and at Billy, and probably at you as well, in consequence. We're really *not* safe, are we? And yet everything *feels* so sweet and safe this morning."

"It doesn't matter. I'll handle Crashaw when he comes, and then we'll be done with the problem. We can be done with Marston, too."

She turned her face away, reaching for one of the towels that the servant had hung by the fire to warm. "I do hope Billy spent a comfortable night. I must go see to him before breakfast."

He rolled over on his front, resting his chin on his hands as he watched her step into her drawers and slide her legs into her stockings. She knit her brow; he tossed her a garter that he'd retrieved from among the bedclothes. She smiled, caught it neatly, and then immediately lost herself once again in the serious business of dressing.

He liked to watch a woman costuming herself in the morning. Especially after a long, languorous night of lovemaking, he found himself oddly touched by the quick movements, the brisk, everyday deftness and self-absorbed concentration women seemed inevitably to adopt as they donned their clothes in preparation for reentry into the everyday world.

You'd never know from looking, he thought, that

Phoebe didn't dress every morning in dainty lawn drawers and pink-tinted stockings. Her quick tugs at buttons and laces, little frowns of annoyance or nods of satisfaction were deliciously spontaneous. He felt as moved by the sight of her nakedness disappearing behind her clothes—well, *almost* as moved—as he had by the revelation of her nakedness last night.

But what was she doing now, over there near the window? Ah yes, searching for the corset that had got flung somewhere or another. She laughed, waving it like a pennant as she rose to her feet.

"Will you help me with this, David? But I mean really help me with it. No sly stratagems to pull me back into bed."

"Yes, come here. It's all right, I must begin dressing as well. And so I hereby declare our first night together officially over and our life together officially begun."

Billy was much better this morning, almost managing to grin from out the carriage door, where Phoebe and David found him waiting. He'd slept most of the night, the chambermaid reported rather prissily, which was a mercy . . .

Since he'd had to sleep through all the commotion David and I were making, Phoebe finished silently on the disapproving chambermaid's behalf. In any case, his eye was no longer swollen shut and his complexion looked healthy under the bruises.

"G'bye Rosie. Thanks for ev'rything, luv," he called to the chambermaid, who waved and blew him a kiss in return. *He won't absolutely lose his looks,* Phoebe thought, *he simply won't be as breathtaking as he used to be.* Dr. Riggs thought he'd probably walk with a slight limp; he certainly wouldn't be making any more monstrous profits for Mr. Talbot. As the carriage rolled out of the Swan's courtyard and into Ermine Street, she wondered what Billy could do now to earn his living, for he wouldn't be picking any more pockets if she had any say in the matter.

Perhaps she could ask David about it this evening, she thought, if he wasn't still feeling offended by the disrespect Billy had shown him yesterday. She looked up, realizing with a start that while she'd been wool-gathering, he and Billy had struck up a lively conversation.

About horses, it seemed. More specifically, about the four horses pulling the carriage, whose names and vital statistics Billy seemed to have learned from Mr. Dickerson early this morning. It wasn't the sort of discussion Henry and his friends had when considering the purchase of a new team or saddle horse: gentlemen of their set had been interested in a horse's price, pedigree, and elegance of proportion. This morning's conversation, in contrast, was quite a bit messier: David and Billy, it seemed, shared a lively fascination with the diseases that horses were prey to and the possible remedies for them, in all their infinite variations.

Phoebe found the substance of the discussion less diverting than the look of deep concentration animating the faces of its participants. And when the conversation turned to the fine points of draining pus from an infected hoof, she decided that perhaps she didn't have to listen at all. She nestled into the sealskin lining of her pelisse, ignoring the sense of the words while she enjoyed the good-humored cadence of the voices speaking them. Billy had clearly quite forgotten about his disrespectful behavior yesterday. And David, just as clearly, had decided not to dwell on the offense.

Ah, but now they *were* talking of something interesting.

"Yessir, I learnt *that* one from an animal surgeon

when I were a little nipper, no higher than yer waist. A good man he was, the surgeon, old and wise and the animals knew it too. Well, when I weren't helpin' me dad on the land—Yorkshire it were, thanks for askin' sir—I come and watched the surgeon, and helped him too, when he'd let me, for he knew everything and I wanted to know it too.

"That was before we had to leave. Killed me dad, leavin' the land. So I never learnt as much as I'd wanted to."

Billy had told her a great deal about being a prostitute, and something about picking pockets as well. But he'd never told her anything about earlier, happier times, the times he was so readily sharing with David now. She hadn't even known he'd been a farm boy.

"So you like animals and the people who take care of them, do you."

"Yessir, I does, a lot, sir."

"I ask, you see, because I thought you might pass your convalescence at the home of a Mr. Goulding, who helps care for the livestock at Linseley Manor. He's a nice old fellow, talks a blue streak about animals—loves any creature lucky enough to have been born with a tail, wings, or even fins. Mrs. Goulding is very nice too—and a good cook, we wouldn't put you with somebody who wasn't a good cook. Their children have grown up and gone off on their separate ways; all well employed and starting families of their own. And not a bad one in the bunch, as Mrs. Goulding enjoys telling me—she'll tell you that too, every chance she gets. Anyway, they've got a spare bed and lots of affection going begging. Does that sound like it might suit you, Billy?"

She saw from Billy's hesitant new smile how much it did suit him.

* * *

"But it's not just what *he* needs," David whispered to her later after Billy had dozed off. "Or what Mr. and Mrs. Goulding need, though they *will* be quite delighted to have him to talk to and fuss over. It's what *I* need. For you don't mind, do you, that I don't want him under my roof? I mean, he's a good young fellow, but having him too close to us—I find it distracting, in the light of . . . recent history, you know. Somehow it all feels too liberal for me, rather too much like one of those cultish erotic experiments Mr. Blake might favor."

"No, I don't mind." She smiled. It was interesting to discover the multiple, contradictory facets of his personality. A satyr, a dreamy romantic—and also a stuffy, conventional country gentleman with a horror of "cultishness" and "erotic experiments."

"Oh no, by all means let us stay clear of 'erotic experiments,'" she said.

"You're mocking me, you know what I really mean . . . oh but look, straight to your right. Do you see that church spire?"

For they were entering "his countryside." He became boyish, eager to point out every village and steeple. And in fact some of the churches were quite fine, many of the ancient villages comfortable and prosperous. But it was the huge sky that captured Phoebe's imagination. Fully three quarters of the view that presented itself through the carriage window seemed to be moody, poetic, passionate sky.

Of course, she thought, it would be prettier in summer, with the beech trees all green atop the wolds, those low, rolling, forested hills that softened the sweep of the landscape. But in bleak winter the sweep of it was exciting just by itself. "From those wolds over there to the east," he told her, "you can see clear to the spires of Lincoln cathedral. And you can see my lands as well."

"Will you take me riding over wolds like that?"

"Of course I shall. I want you to see it from alongside me. I want you to feel as proprietary about it as I do."

"I do like your countryside, David. I feel safe here."

"You *are* safe here."

At least so long as I stay. It would be a beautiful stay, she thought. And for now she simply wouldn't think about its inevitable ending.

The Gouldings had been delighted to take Billy. And to entertain the earl and his party at a gracious, if simple, impromptu supper. It was dark outside when Phoebe and David left the cottage; Billy was still seated at the kitchen table, with three spaniels and two terriers dozing beneath his propped-up leg. A second helping of leek and potato soup sat steaming in front of him; Saint George, the big, imperious ginger cat, had taken possession of his lap; and Mr. Goulding was deep into a disquisition on how to cure a bull of sunstroke. David had been right about Mrs. Goulding's cooking, Phoebe thought. The soup had been delicious.

It was pleasant finally having the carriage to themselves. A few lascivious fantasies flitted through Phoebe's head as David handed her in. After he'd climbed in beside her and shut the door behind him she turned toward him for a kiss, but stopped herself abruptly.

Because once we begin making love, she thought, we won't want to stop. She giggled softly at the thought of the carriage rolling to a stop in front of his house and some very proper butler opening the door to find the earl and herself in flagrante delicto.

"What are you laughing at?" he asked.

"Oh nothing, just how nice it is to be alone together. And how difficult I find it not to fling myself at you."

"I was thinking of doing some flinging of my own, but it's only two miles to the house itself, and . . ."

"Quite."

They moved decorously apart on the velvet seat. A few stars shone through the coach window.

"And so I shall introduce you around as Miss Browne, if that's all right," he said.

"Yes, I rather like the name. I have some papers, you see, that belonged to the girl who was buried in my stead. Oddly, she was also a Phoebe. So to the extent that I have a legal identity, I expect that I'm Phoebe Browne."

"I love you, Phoebe Browne."

It suddenly became a lot more difficult not to fling herself at him.

"And I love you, David Hervey."

She paused, as though still tasting the sweetness of the words in her mouth.

"But," she added now, "'David Hervey' is far too short a name for a nobleman. What long procession of ancestral and geographical appellations come marching in between the 'David' and the 'Hervey'?"

"Not so many as all that. Just 'Arthur' and 'Saint George.' David Arthur Saint George Hervey."

"The same Saint George as Mr. Goulding's cat?"

"The very same. Saint George is a folk hero here in Lincolnshire. He figures prominently in the Plough play we'll be seeing the Monday after next."

"Plough play?"

"Ah, I see that I shall have to educate you on some of our customs. The Plough plays used to be performed to herald the beginning of planting season after the Christmas holidays; at one time, you see, we didn't begin planting the winter wheat until the Monday after

Twelfth Night. Nowadays we plant earlier: the seeds have been in the ground since before Christmas, but we still have the play and a celebration on Plough Monday.

"The play's performed at my house. The local troupe has been practicing it for weeks. It's great fun, lots of clowning and morris dancing too. We crowd the entire village into the Great Hall and there's a banquet afterwards."

"Is that customary?"

"Well, in most parishes it's a simpler affair: the mummers simply go from kitchen to village kitchen. But it's how *we* do it—couldn't do without it.

"I feel quite guilty already, you see, for having spent Christmas in London rather than at home. It would be utterly unthinkable for me to miss a Plough Monday."

"And will your son be there too?"

"Yes, of course. You'll like him, Phoebe. Well, I'm rather proud of him, actually. You'll see why when you meet him. And I know that he'll like you."

"Yes, I hope so." She also hoped that her voice was calm enough to mask her sudden discomfiture.

An entire village gaping at her while they should be watching the morris dancing. And they *would* gape, she was sure of it, because any lady the earl brought home with him was bound to arouse their curiosity.

Foolishly, she'd imagined something rather more intimate: a simple series of brisk quiet days on the wolds and long hot nights of lovemaking. What a goose you are, Phoebe, she scolded herself silently, you probably also imagined that the meals would be served by elves and the fires lit by invisible hands.

The prospect of meeting David's son was hardly a comfortable one either. Suppose he disapproved of her or was in some way jealous of his father's affections? Suppose he was greedy, worried about new half-siblings who might diminish his inheritance? Her mouth took a wry turn here. The young gentleman needn't concern himself about *that* eventuality, she thought sadly.

Luckily, David hadn't seemed to notice her sudden attack of nerves. He was peering through the carriage windows into the black starry night as though he could see every detail of the landscape.

"We're in the park now," he told her excitedly. "If it were light you could see the lake to the left, the hermit's hut down there to the right in that little declivity . . ."

He stopped himself. "I must sound awfully silly to you."

"No," she said, "you sound lovely."

Their hands had crept together across the space that separated them. She linked her fingers tightly within his. Perhaps just one kiss? But her natural competitiveness forbade it; if he could discipline himself, so could she. She scoured her mind for more questions to ask about the local customs.

"When did you change your planting schedule to get the wheat in before Christmas?" It sounded rather forced to her, but he seemed to find it a quite reasonable and interesting query.

"I'm not quite sure," he answered slowly. "Two hundred years ago, perhaps? I think it was under the Tudors, but I'm not absolutely . . ."

"*Two hundred years* ago?"

"Well, or thereabout."

"But when you said, '*we* didn't plant our winter wheat until after the Christmas holidays,' I thought you'd meant that you, personally . . ."

"Lord, no, Phoebe, that was an ancient way of farming." He chuckled.

"You said *we*."

"I simply meant my family, the people of this district, *whoever* was doing the farming then."

"You feel a part of them."

"Shouldn't I?"

"Yes, you should."

And it was a lesson for her, she thought. A fine example of how there could never be an intimate, "private" visit to him here at Linseley Manor. Not only was the entire village population utterly and irrevocably present in his consciousness, but so were all the generations who'd worked the land before him.

He squeezed her hand, still chuckling at the notion of himself farming according to that ancient calendar.

"Yes, I think introducing you as Miss Browne will be the right thing. You'll like Mrs. Oughton, my housekeeper. And you'll meet my steward, Mr. Neville, tomorrow. One of the first things I'll have to do, of course, is have a long talk with the cook about the banquet . . ."

Of course.

Well, I am a lord, don't forget, he'd said when he'd told her to undress for him. Oh yes, he'd been utterly, marvelously lordly about taking what he wanted in bed.

But, as she was beginning to realize, there was a great deal more to him than the easy sense of entitlement that made him so irresistible. His being Lord Linseley didn't just mean he owned a lot of land; it meant he'd made certain promises to the land and its people.

She'd forgotten—as he never would—the weight of duty that he carried. It probably wasn't very exciting on a daily basis: his days must be crowded with nagging petty responsibilities, stupid trivial obligations. But he stood faithful to them; she knew that what was best in him was his sense of obligation, his heroic willingness to accept the challenges good fortune had thrust upon him. It was, she supposed, what she most loved in him.

"I want to share it with you, Phoebe."

Had he read her thoughts? No, that was impossible, thank heaven.

She felt ashamed, choked by the emotions coursing through her. *Tell him now. It's cruel to let him go on thinking that I can give him what he wants.*

Anyway—*she* didn't want it. She wanted her London life: smooth, stylish, and elegant; unencumbered by responsibility or obligation; answerable to no one but herself.

Then tell him. Tell him that.

Too late. Here they were. She could see the lights of the house from the carriage window. The butler who handed her out was as proper as Phoebe had imagined; a good thing, she thought, that they'd managed to maintain such rectitude on this last few miles of their journey.

"And may I bid you welcome to Linseley Manor, Miss Browne, and wish you a pleasant stay?"

"Thank you, Stevens, I'm sure it will be."

They climbed the wide steps to double doors that opened to embrace them. Stevens's lantern threw soft light on mellow, honey-colored stone, on well-trimmed ivy climbing to generous curtained windows.

A pleasant stay and nothing else. No matter if, in an unguarded moment, I may wish for more.

Chapter

17

Ninety-eight. Ninety-nine. One hundred.

Kate put down her silver hairbrush and prepared to plait her hair for the night. The new hairstyle—a knot of curls ringed by small, looped braids—had been a success. If the success of a hairstyle, she thought, blushing happily, might be measured by how sweetly disordered it could become—and simply from an evening spent kissing John in front of the fire. Imagine, she thought, what might happen to one's coiffure after an evening of doing . . . well, rather more.

She smiled at herself in the mirror. It was easier, she'd learned, to discipline one's hair than one's body. A host of delightfully anarchic sensations coursed through her: throbs, stirrings, and tingles, all new and unpredictable. It was as though she'd somehow been given a new body, open, alive, achingly ripe and ready. Of course, one might also call what she was feeling "frustration"—yes, there was certainly something of *that* too, she thought—because kissing, delightful as it was, clearly wasn't all that she wanted from John. But a better word might be "anticipation." Happiness could be gulped or it could be savored; having waited so long for hers, Kate was happy to savor it.

Unlike Phoebe, who'd always wanted to swallow her happiness in one immense, glorious, unseemly gulp—*as perhaps she's doing at this moment,* Kate found herself thinking quite suddenly. She smiled in mock consternation at the double entendre that had wafted, unbidden, into her consciousness. Wherever had the very proper Lady Kate Beverredge gotten such ideas? No matter, Kate intended to have a great many more such ideas, to think a great many more such thoughts. And not merely to *think* about such things either, she resolved.

She loosened her silk peignoir and smoothed her muslin nightgown over her body. Ummm, that felt lovely; she cupped her breasts, feeling their weight, as she hummed a happy private tune to herself. Vague plans and gauzy fantasies filled her head. There were decisions to make: she and John had begun a delightful debate about how and when to announce their engagement. And when to marry: they both rather liked the idea of spring, but could all the arrangements really be made in such a short time? A pity that Phoebe wasn't here to advise her. Or perhaps not, Kate thought; a married couple ought to get into the habit of making their own decisions.

They might even resolve it at luncheon tomorrow, before setting off together to visit the gentleman with connections in Amsterdam. The black pouch was locked in the drawer of her dressing table, while the sandalwood box sat next to the brush she'd just put down. Pretty box, she thought, fragrant, too. And yet somehow malevolent: having placed it among her things, she'd taken rather extreme pains not to touch it again. The panels of smooth sandalwood at its top and sides seemed to contain a universe of perverse, buzzing human evils. Pandora's box.

Well, there's a foolish fancy, she thought. *I must stop wondering about those letters,* she scolded herself. Tomorrow, first thing, I'll lock them up in the safe, along with the remainder of the jewels—the ones I'm not sending to Amsterdam this time. I won't read a word of the letters; I won't even open the box, no matter how curious I am. She shook her head, sighed, and blew out the candle, surrendering herself to joyful thoughts and sweet dreams, and hoping that Phoebe, in her own impatient, impetuous manner, was spending an equally happy evening.

But Phoebe, wearing her pale pink dressing gown and pacing in front of the fire in her bedchamber, wasn't acting at all impetuously at the moment. She'd been obliged, on the contrary, to exercise quite extraordinary and uncharacteristic forbearance since arriving at Linseley Manor.

She was waiting. She hated waiting.

Though she had to admit it was a lovely room in which to wait. The green bedchamber, they called it.

Yes, you did understand me correctly, Mrs. Oughton, David had said. *No, you weren't mistaken,* Miss Browne *will* be staying in the green bedchamber. Have Harper bring her luggage there, and ring for Lissie to help her unpack her things.

He'd sounded a bit peremptory, Phoebe thought. Well, perhaps "peremptory" was too strong a word. Still, there'd been a stubborn edge to his voice, in sudden contrast to the warmth of his conversation with the servants gathered in the entrance hall to greet him—Stevens the butler, Mrs. Oughton the housekeeper, and Mrs. Yonge the cook. While she'd been waiting for the chambermaid to take her to her room, Phoebe had seen quite clearly how pleased his employees were to have him home.

And how suspicious they were of the lady he'd brought with him from London.

Smiling stiffly, nodding as gracefully as she could in response to their veiled, skeptical glances, she'd drifted up and down the entrance hall, pretending to be interested in the equally stiff—sometimes embalmed-looking—oil portraits of former earls and countesses of Linseley. Occasionally a familiar smile or pair of dark blue eyes lit one of the faces staring back at her from across the generations, making her feel a bit less like an intruder.

Suits of armor stood guard at the corners of the room, old swords—quite interesting, some of them—were mounted on the walls. The hall was a long, barrel-ceilinged chamber; she could just make out a series of paintings on the curved panels above her head—Saint George again, it seemed, in various stages of victory over a scaly, fire-breathing, and highly vexed dragon. All the while, bits and pieces of David's conversation drifted up to the curved ceiling vaults and echoed back down to her.

"So the village children liked that new style of holiday cracker I sent from London, did they? Oh good, what a relief—nothing worse than a cracker that doesn't crack, don't you agree, Stevens?

"No more trouble with your sciatica, Mrs. Oughton? Well, heaven be praised for *that*, eh? It's true, it has been a dry winter, though that storm coming down from the north may well . . .

"No doubt about it, Mrs. O., you did exactly the right thing, getting the roof repaired. Nasty spot, the tiles always blow off there in a storm, but we'll be snug and ready this time.

"And Mrs. Yonge's cousin seems to have done a tip-top job with it, though I'll just climb up on the ladder to have a little peek myself tomorrow. Oh I'm sure I'll find his bill eminently reasonable. Thank you, Mrs. Yonge, for recommending him, and I'm delighted that your granddaughter liked the doll. Well, she should have a splendid present. After all, three years old is a very important birthday.

"No, no supper at all. Quite full, I assure you, but could you promise to save the ham for our breakfast?"

She'd left him conversing on these and many other equally fascinating matters when the maid came to fetch her.

The rooms on the way to her bedchamber had looked large, square, a bit old-fashioned, by the light of the chambermaid's lamp. Though it was clearly a rather grand house, comfortable and well cared for, Linseley Manor wasn't in the least showy, she thought. She liked that. But why were they stopping here, in front of those tall double doors, finished in light oak?

"Is this it, Lissie?" Phoebe had expected her room to be upstairs. Weekend country house parties were all the rage among the *ton:* and so all the fashionable people of her acquaintance had moved their bedchambers to the upper floors, reserving the space below for parlors, saloons, and galleries through which their guests might circulate. Well, but David wasn't a very fashionable person, was he?

"This is it exactly, miss." The chambermaid nodded vigorously, surprised in her turn that this ninny of a London lady could have had any doubt of it. She opened the doors, and Phoebe followed her into the room, staring about her with increasing wonder.

Oh, I see, she thought slowly. *Oh dear.* No wonder Mrs. Oughton had been surprised that he'd wanted to put her here.

The room was large and beautifully proportioned; French doors led to what she suspected had been a lady's garden. The rug was a delicate Aubusson worked in a rose design; the damasks that covered the wall were pale gray-green, the upholstery just a shade brighter; the graceful moldings were painted a rich cream color. The generous hearth, with a good fire in it, was done in creamy enameled Belgian tile; some of the tiles had elaborate lacy bas-relief designs molded into them. There were portraits on the walls here too, but these were much more intimate and pleasant than the ones in the entrance hall: paintings of smiling family groups, featuring dogs, picnic baskets, children and their toys.

She could have done without the children and their toys.

A luxurious dressing room, where Lissie had hung Phoebe's clothes, led off to the right, next to a glorious marble bathroom and water closet. To the left, there was another door. Well, she knew whose bedchamber *that* one led to. For this gorgeous green room, where David had insisted she stay, was manifestly *not* a guest room. It was the room where the countesses of Linseley had slept.

By putting her here, he'd made a clear statement of his intentions—both to her and perforce to his servants. The statement demanded a response. She shook her head sadly. However could she respond?

The door to his room rattled, opened. He wore a dark blue velvet dressing gown and slippers.

She looked up anxiously. *Please,* she thought, *don't ask me how I like the room.* He didn't. Obviously, there were more pressing issues to be dealt with at the moment. Tonight the distance between their bodies dissolved without either of them even knowing how.

"Lord," he sighed, after some long, urgent kisses, "what a chaste and dutiful day we've spent."

She laughed. "You must make it up to me. Immediately."

"But not in here," he murmured. "It's too ladylike a venue for what I have in mind."

He took her hand and led her back through the door.

Yes, she thought, *this is better.* Dark heavy old furniture, chairs upholstered in leather with bright brass studs. The walls were covered with framed maps, architectural drawings, mechanical diagrams.

He lifted her onto a massive bed with a high, carved headboard. Somehow, both their dressing gowns had slipped to the floor since they'd entered the room. They ran their hands over one another's bodies, staring into each other's eyes, taking their signals from the gasps and moans they coaxed from one another's lips. There hardly seemed a need for all this play, she thought; his penis was hard, beautifully velvety beneath her fingertips. He could enter her right now: she could feel the heat, the wetness, the luxuriant easing between her legs.

And yet he didn't enter her. Patiently, delicately, he caressed her, his fingers so light against the slit of her quim that she thought she would expire. He wanted her to ask for what she wanted.

She wouldn't. She couldn't. She was comfortable with touch, but timid with words. Words were too . . . intimate.

Oh, but he'd moved his hand: now it was only his thumb that rested along the damp line bisecting the mound of her vulva. The rest of his hand simply cupped her, there between her legs—as though she were a goblet resting in his palm—his fingertips moving softly along the bottom curve of her arse. As though he were pausing in thought before making a toast at a banquet.

"Such a beautiful bum," he murmured. "Its curve, its lineaments so visible through Marston's trousers. You should have been arrested for incitement to riot."

He seemed content simply to trace the shape of her bottom, perfectly pleased by such a gentle, meditative caress. As though it didn't matter in the slightest how much time passed before his body's evident desires were finally satisfied. As though it were of no importance whatsoever what *she* might want, or whether she wanted anything at all.

Or course, she thought, she could always *ask* for what she wanted.

His touch became softer. More diffident, if possible. In a moment he might remove his hand altogether.

Ask for it? Bloody hell, she thought, she'd *beg* for it.

Her voice trembled. It sounded high and thin in her ears, as though she'd lost her rich lower register.

"*Please,* David."

"Please what?"

"P-please, David, I want you inside of me."

"Hmmm, which part of me do you want?"

"I want your . . . ah, finger."

"Ah, well here it is then. Are you satisfied?"

"Yes, it's very . . . hmmm . . . *nice.*" Damn him, it was hard to speak between gasps.

"Just nice, eh?"

"No, it's . . . wonderful . . . but . . ."

"But?"

"But it's not enough. Oh God, David . . ."

"Another finger perhaps?"

"All your fingers, add them one at a time, oh but . . . please, David . . ."

"But what?"

"But *nothing,* damn your eyes," she bellowed. *"Yes, all of them. Now!"*

She lay back upon the pillows, throwing her arms over her head to grasp the bed's headboard. Digging her toes into the velvet coverlet, she lifted her hips into the air to follow the vigorous, sweeping arcs he made with his forearm. He knelt beside her, smiling to see her so helpless and yet so greedy. He threw a leg over her, straddling her belly and then inching himself forward; his knees were around her shoulders now, though it seemed he could still reach behind him with his arm, because his fingers—his fist, his *knuckles,* Dear Lord—were still within her. She tilted her pelvis a bit, so he wouldn't have to reach so far back. Quickly he slipped a bolster behind her neck, to angle her head closer to him.

He probed at her mouth with the head of his penis. Quickly, she licked the pearl of moisture from its tip. She widened her lips to take him in, to feel him lengthen and—was it possible?—harden even more as he pushed toward her throat. She sucked, pulled at him, arching her neck and spine to allow him to enter as deeply as possible into the back of her mouth. When he pulled back, so that she might caress the tip with her tongue and lips, she felt the weight of his balls, the wiry hair beneath them tickling the tops of her breasts. His hand, though still in her, was quieter. He wanted his own pleasure first, she thought.

Well, all right then, my lord, you shall have it.

She moved down on the bolster, burrowing her face between his legs, flattening her mouth against his belly. She pulled with the muscles of her cheeks, harder and yet not so hard as to distract him from the lascivious flicking and stroking of her tongue. He moved his hips, answering her mouth's caresses with his own short, hard thrusts.

She heard him groan. She saw the muscles of his belly tighten. Tighten and tremble now as well. She breathed his dark earth smell. The salts and vapors of him seemed to seep through her pores; she feasted on his private, pungent flavors: sour, salt, bitter; yeasty, like good bread rising. She opened, loosened, lost herself; she needn't, she couldn't, caress him any longer, she had only to contain him now, to absorb him, to receive what issued from him. To drink him.

Or, as she thought a moment later, to drink as much

of him as she'd been capable. Because try as she might, she simply hadn't been able to swallow it all. *But there was so much of it,* she told herself ruefully, *what was a lady to do under the circumstances?* A thin stream of his semen dribbled gracelessly from the corner of her mouth. She tried to chase it with her tongue; she didn't get all of it. There was nothing to do but wipe her cheek with her thumb, smiling wryly up at him still kneeling above her. She tried to pull him down on top of her.

Ah, but he was a man of honor, a gentleman with a debt to pay. Ceasing to straddle her now, he kneeled next to her again; his forearm had resumed its vigorous arcs, the fingers even spreading a little, rekindling the all-but-forgotten fires he'd lit earlier. For an instant she wondered how close, how high his hand was . . . .

But no more questions, no more thoughts—no more *thinking*—for now she was falling from a very high place, and drifting, drifting downward through the softest, darkest, starry velvet night.

Space and time seemed to swirl about her. Had it been minutes? Hours?

The air was chilly where his arms and legs weren't entwined with hers. She reached for the velvet coverlet, hoping to drape it around him and herself without effecting any major changes in position. He coiled himself more tightly around her.

"Don't move yet," he whispered.

"It's all right," she whispered back. "I'm not sure that I *can* move quite yet."

"Perhaps," she added, "we should simply freeze in place here. We should have died happy, in any case."

"You're happy, then, Phoebe?"

"I am when you make love to me."

His body stiffened. It wasn't the answer he wanted.

"You said that in Marston's voice."

"It was my own voice."

"No, I can tell the difference."

"You're simply embarrassed by the image of yourself in bed with Marston."

He rolled away from her.

"Forgive me. That was frivolous, cruel of me. Shallow. I—I don't even know why I said it."

Were those tears starting up in her eyes?

"I'm sorry. I can't imagine what's gotten into me. I never cry."

But now *she* could hear it, too. She *was* speaking in Marston's voice.

She sat up against the pillows, knees against her breasts, arms hugging her shins. As though to hide herself from him, as she'd tried to hide her feelings behind Marston's light, mocking phrases. She wouldn't let herself cry: a stray tear or two didn't count, she told herself.

He'd moved up beside her, wrapping the coverlet and then his arms around her.

"It's all right, Phoebe."

She leaned into his embrace. But her eyes were dry now. Her mouth was dry too. And her throat was so tight that she thought she'd never be able to speak again. They sat silently for a few minutes.

"Was your marriage really as bad as that, Phoebe?"

She stared at him.

"Last night, at the inn, you said . . ."

It was true. She'd called it "miserable," and a "form of prostitution." But her mouth was still too dry to speak.

"Look," he said. "I'm freezing. Let's take some pillows and blankets and sit next to the fire."

He led her to the hearthside, to the edge of the thick

Persian rug, where he quickly built a nest for her of bedclothes and bolsters.

"Wait," he said, "I'll get you something to drink."

An old, smooth brandy. He joined her under the blankets, his arms around her again.

She took a small swallow of brandy and stared into the flames.

Little by little, in a low monotone, she began to shape hesitant phrases, lonely little islands of sound in a vast ocean of shamed silence.

"It wasn't the pain or the violence, you know, for really he wasn't very violent with me . . . physically, anyway . . . well, only for the last few months . . .

"It was the *humiliation*. There always seemed to be some dreadful sneering footman lingering about—well, there were more than one, but one was worse than the others: there was something . . . carnal about how he'd feast his eyes upon me groveling to the master. I don't think it would have been real to Henry without his little audience of household acolytes. And it made it very real to me, too; it showed me how much of myself I'd abdicated . . . to someone so, so *small*. And for so little, really.

"Glamour. Compliments, God help me. Exclusivity and distinction. The heady sense that when you ascended the staircase at Carlton House you were at the absolute center of the world. Well, I was very young. Devonshire had been very boring. London was thrilling.

"And having achieved it, having woken up one morning and understood how much I'd given away to get it, I was resolved to keep the devil's bargain I'd made. I thought I deserved the fine mess I'd found myself in.

"And you must believe me, David. I never once complained."

He did believe her. And he didn't ask any questions.

She was grateful for that, for she couldn't have explained it to him any better than in the few halting phrases she'd offered.

For truly, she could hardly understand it herself. As thrilling as the public part of it had been, she didn't really see how her headstrong, harum-scarum younger self could have tolerated such contemptuous treatment, such petty, self-serving disrespect. Of course, it hadn't happened all at once. It had happened gradually. Moment by moment, it had been easy to fool herself, to pretend that it wasn't really happening at all. To devote all her attention to the child she'd adored . . .

But she wouldn't think about that part of it.

"So now you see what a fraud I am. Pretending to be brave and devil-may-care when instead . . ."

"You're not a fraud. You *are* brave."

What could he do, he wondered, to make her understand how touching he found her—in her honesty, her confusion, her stubborn insistence upon the complexity of things. He probably couldn't do anything except wait for her, with all the love and patience he could muster. Stay by her side while she relived the painful past. For she clearly wasn't ready for the future yet.

Her head nestled in the hollow just below his collarbone. Softly, he kissed her brow.

"And I said something to you last night, too," he whispered, "after you called me a satyr. Do you remember?"

"No, I think I became distracted. Well," she laughed nervously, "I don't usually have a satyr in bed with me."

He took her hand.

"I said that I should love you all my life. And so I shall."

She squeezed his hand back.

"I shall love you exactly as you are," he said.

She smiled and shrugged, almost imperceptibly. His lips moved down to kiss her eyelids. Her cheeks. The tip of her nose. Finally, lingeringly, her lips. He held her more tightly; she curled her body into his embrace. Until suddenly, simultaneously, they both drew back, staring at one other in surprise.

"You must believe me . . . I hadn't thought I'd become aroused again so quickly. I beg your . . ."

"Don't apologize. Do you know that I also feel quite . . ."

"Not really. You too?"

How sweet to have been taken unaware—each of them and both of them—by their bodies' brusque, untactful demands.

Slowly, he laid her down on the rug, stroking her from her shoulders to her knees. It was true: he could see, touch, smell the desire coursing through her. Hard as cherry stones, her nipples grazed the work-hardened palms of his hands. Her eyes shone, tiny beads of perspiration gathered in the hollow of her throat, a pulse beat quickly in her neck. He kissed her there; she quivered under him like a captured bird.

He parted her legs, opening her with gentle fingers. She was like a flower: he loved to peel back the layers, to probe the mysterious inner parts. How flushed, how swollen and sensitive she was between her legs. When his finger slid between those hungry lower lips, her mouth parted in a deep, involuntary sigh.

She smiled up at him, arching her limbs, moaning sweetly under his hand. Her fingers played with his hair where it grew a bit long at the nape of his neck. She was so ripe, the mound of her quim so plump between those long, slender white thighs. Like a shameless bright red poppy, he thought—burst wide open during the long days of spring suddenly turned to summer.

And yet so young, so untouched in other places. That tiny, frightened knot of flesh in the cleft of her beautiful arse—untouched, he was sure of it. Virginal. Waiting for him, though she didn't know it yet. *Not now, David. Another time, when she's ready.* Another time, another mood, another season.

For she needed him right now. Just as she was, and just as *he* was, too. Well, how he'd been a minute ago, anyway. Her mouth had pursed itself into an insulted little pout—she could tell that his attention had wandered.

He laughed and kissed the pout away. *Begging your pardon, my lady. Here I am, entirely at your service.*

He raised himself above her, on his hands and knees. She lifted her hips, wrapped her legs about his waist, and pulled him close. Ah, she'd taken him a bit unaware there. She was stronger than he'd expected—it was rather thrilling, that unanticipated tug of muscle and sinew in her back and limbs. His hips, thighs, and belly tightened and tingled with the uncomplicated pleasures of taking and being taken. He sank into her; he let her draw him into the depths of her body.

The last thoughts he had, before losing all thoughts, was of how natural and joyful this was. Challenges lay ahead, of course: vanquishing her agonized memories would be a daunting, difficult task. But all in good time. Everything in its season.

Chapter 18

She woke up alone the next morning. Confused and disoriented, it took her some minutes to realize that she was back in the green bedchamber. Her pink dressing gown, she noted vaguely, lay on a chaise longue near the bed. Turning to look for David, she found a note on the pillow next to her.

My love,

You were sleeping so soundly (and beautifully), that I was able to carry you here quite early and barely wake you. Do you remember? You fell back to sleep in the middle of a kiss. I brought you back into this room because I think the household staff would prefer it if we tried to keep up appearances.

But I can't stay abed mornings when I'm home. I want to get a good start on the day, so I'm off for a few hours. I'll be back for breakfast at nine.

I'll bring my accounts and correspondence into the breakfast room, so that I can wait for you there if you insist on keeping a London dandy's hours.

But don't keep me waiting too long, sleepyhead. Come, let's ride on the wolds today, shall we?

With all my heart,

D.

P.S. I miss you already.

Sweet, hazy memories passed through her head: warm, fragmentary sensations of lolling back in his arms and clinging to his neck, of being gently set down and neatly tucked between cool, silky sheets. But it all must have happened in the very early hours, she thought, for according to the clock on the tiled mantelpiece it was only nine now.

She yawned, stretched, considered sleeping some more, and gave it up. She felt glorious, energetic, and madly curious about her surroundings. The room was warm; a servant must have rebuilt the fire while she'd slept. She threw off the covers: sweet-scented currents of air (for there were large silver bowls of pot-pourri on the mantel) drifted across the room, mingling with the sharp, briny smells that wafted from the hollows of her body. She spread her arms and legs, breathing deeply, trying to absorb every atom of him that still clung to her skin.

Pale winter sunlight shone through the French doors; she wondered what was growing in the garden outside—evergreens of some sort, holly or ivy. She wanted to explore the rest of the house, too. To try the marble bathtub. To see the countryside. To spur a horse over the wolds.

Where *was* the breakfast room anyway? She'd have to ring for Lissie to bring her there. She was starving; hadn't Mrs. Yonge promised that there would be ham for breakfast?

She'd wash and dress quickly. She missed him too.

* * *

The bathtub was a marvel—hot and cold water thrummed merrily through the spigots; the tub, big enough for two, was made of a delicate, pale pink, blue-veined marble. Like flesh: a warmth, a softness seemed to inhere in the stone. Whoever had built this wonder of modern sanitation, she thought, was as much a sensualist as the house's current owner. The countesses of Linseley must have been happy women.

But she wouldn't linger. For it was really rather lonely, washing herself in a tub that was big enough for two.

Humming to herself as she dried her damp hair, she wrapped herself in her dressing gown and went to find the bell pull. Ah yes, there it was, near the door that led to the corridor. She'd just given it a sharp tug when she'd stopped suddenly to listen to an odd, unexpected little sound.

A mouse? No, it didn't sound like a mouse. Her senses had always been acute, and three years of cautious, deliberate masquerade had only heightened her receptiveness to small signals from her surroundings. The sound in the hall had been soft, subtle—and unmistakable. There was someone outside her door. Watching and waiting. Listening. Peering through the keyhole at her.

"Stop! Who's there?" she called. She could feel, rather than hear, a sharp intake of breath on the other side of the door. *Surprised you, did I, you rascal?*

There was a bump now, and a rustle. But no footsteps. The villain was frozen in place, waiting for her next move, hoping she'd decide she'd been mistaken and turn away.

A good swordsman could exploit an enemy's misapprehensions, she thought. She took a step backward, exaggerating her motions, trying to make some slight noise that would strengthen the illusion that she was moving away from the door. She almost thought she saw an eye blink on the other side of the keyhole.

"No, it's nothing," she murmured.

Had she murmured it too loudly? Had her ruse been too crude, too obvious? No: she could feel the relief from the other side of the door. Now, she thought, now while I've got him unaware . . . swiftly, in a neat continuous arc of motion, she stepped forward, grasped the doorknob, and thrust the door open.

A gasp, a clatter, and the sound of quick footsteps pattering down the corridor's waxed parquet floor. She caught a glimpse of bright, unruly red hair, of bunched-up, itchy-looking winter wool stockings, and of the torn edge of a flannel petticoat fluttering over worn-down little (unbelievably little) boots. And then nothing. Her mysterious three-foot-tall adversary had skidded round a corner and disappeared.

But she (*She!* How typical, Phoebe thought, that one would naturally and stupidly assume one's adversary to be a *he*) had left some evidence behind. A doll. A large, beautiful wax doll, dressed for a round of London calls in a red velvet afternoon dress and matching bonnet and pelisse—and fully half as tall as the meddlesome little girl had been.

She heard a half-stern, half-amused voice, echoing somewhere within the maze of corridors. "Well, don't *cry,* you silly thing. *I'll* get your doll. Just you run down to the kitchen where you oughter be anyway and I'll bring it to you directly, after I help the lady. Well, off with you then, what are you waiting for? No, no, you little goose, I won't tell your granny."

Lissie.

"I'm here, Lissie," Phoebe called. "In the dressing

room. Will you help me with my corset?" She needed the help; her hands were trembling. She turned away to allow Lissie to tug at the strings and tie them smartly.

"There, that should do you, Miss Browne."

"Excellent. Yes, thank you."

"And I hope the little girl didn't startle you too bad. She shouldna been spyin' like that, but she meant no harm. 'Twere my fault, I let her come wi' me early when I lit the fire. Her ma's in bed wi' a new one, see, and her granny's off her head preparin' for the feast come Plough Monday. So we all takes a turn wi' her now and again. 'Come wi' me, Susan,' I says to her, 'and I'll show you a lady even prettier than yer new dolly.'

"And she did think you was pretty, miss. Right fell in love with you while you was sleepin' she did. Beggin' your pardon for the trouble it caused, though."

"Oh, no trouble at all, Lissie. It's just that I'm a bit high-strung. Easily surprised, you see. And a child makes sudden noises . . ."

Lissie promised her that it wouldn't happen again and Phoebe promised herself that she wouldn't continue to fuss over it.

But how very tiny those worn-down boots were. One forgot, living in a world of only adults . . .

Enough. Calm down, you silly thing. David is waiting.

He looked up eagerly from his coffee as she hurried into the room.

"Oh good, dressed for riding. We shall have a sunny day, I think, before the storm blows in this evening."

"But what's troubling you, David?" For something was clearly amiss, though she wasn't sure how she'd discerned it.

"Nothing."

"Come," she coaxed him as she filled her plate from the sideboard, "you can tell me."

"I didn't want to bother you. Anyway, I thought I was being bluff and hearty about it."

"You needn't be bluff and hearty with me."

He smiled.

"Oh, well it's nothing really. Only my disappointment that Alec won't be here for Twelfth Night after all. Seems he's been in London these past few weeks. Makes excuses in this letter, says when he came round to see me I'd already gone. He didn't come before because he's been staying with a friend from university, who, it seems, has a . . ."

"A sister?"

"Exactly, how did you know?"

"I simply thought it likely that a young man, making excuses to his father in such circumstances, might have such a motivation."

"Yes, I expect so. Well, it's not the worse thing, I expect. And he *does* sound awfully happy. Makes her sound quite nice—here, you can read the paragraph where he describes her. And he adds a page of greetings to Stevens, Mrs. Oughton, Mrs. Yonge, et cetera, et cetera, et cetera. Even to Mr. and Mrs. Goulding—well, he was always fond of the Gouldings.

"Still, I did want you to meet him. And of course you will. Just not this week."

He shrugged and turned back to his correspondence, after passing her the newspaper. "Not much real news, since Parliament's in holiday recess. But there's an essay on the struggle for Greek emancipation that will interest you."

She stared at him. No, he wasn't mocking her. He'd known that the essay would interest her just as she'd known that something was troubling him. They'd begun to know each other. It was as ordinary—and as miraculous—as that.

In London, Lady Kate Beverredge had also received a disturbing communication in the post. Worse than disturbing: unlike Alec Hervey's letter to his father, this one had no redeeming virtues. Nor did it wish anybody well. Her hand trembled as she passed it to Admiral Wolfe over the luncheon table. INFORM P. THAT ESCAPE IS IMPOSSIBLE.

"I know it's silly of me to be so agitated. But there's something dreadful about these messages."

She'd read the rest of them this morning.

"Do you think the two of them are really safe, up there in Lincolnshire?"

"I do, Kate. David's extraordinarily capable and I've never known a gentleman whose household people are more deeply devoted to him."

"Still," the admiral continued, "I'll pen him a note, telling him to be on the lookout for strange characters. There will be a crowd in his house next week for the Plough play. Supposed to guarantee fertility to the land, you know. Tedious thing—local folk culture and all that—but he swears by it. He dragged me to it one year and I've been sure to have a ready-made excuse every year since then."

"Hmmm, I wonder how Phoebe will like it. She's developed very sophisticated, Londoner's tastes—dandy's tastes, you know. Still, she's in love . . ."

"I hope you're right about that, Kate. I wouldn't want to have her hurting my friend."

"I *know* I'm right."

The admiral shrugged. For such a proper lady, she

could be awfully stubborn sometimes. Just as well; he'd never want to sail with a meek, quiescent ship's mate.

"And just how do you know that?"

"I know a great deal about Phoebe. And a little bit about love as well."

He put his hand upon hers. If she could be stubborn, so could he.

"I defer to your opinion. But only because I've one of my own, and on a matter of some importance, as it happens. I've decided that we're going to be married in the spring and not the summer. And I shall brook no counterargument."

"Let's make it the *early* spring, shall we? I'm very happy, John."

The ride over the wolds would have been perfect, Phoebe thought, if she hadn't had to sit sidesaddle. She'd loved the silent expansiveness of the land, its vast horizon punctuated by austere, iron-studded church steeples, its gentle curves embracing rare, thousand-year-old Saxon chapels. But she wished that she could have galloped full out, propelling Oberon—the big black gelding David had chosen for her—forward with her hips and thighs rather than merely sitting atop his back.

"Well, you needn't ride sidesaddle if you don't want to," David said, as they wandered hand-in-hand among the ruins of an ancient monastery. "I'll have Mrs. O. hunt up an old pair of Alec's breeches—from when he'd gotten some height but was still a skinny boy. You can wear them with Marston's boots and the coat you're wearing today."

She laughed.

"Quite the costume. Phizz would never stand for it. I'll look a fright."

"You'll look like Miss Browne, wholly herself and wholly adorable. Here, have an apple, I brought a few from the cellar."

She munched it appreciatively. "I'll look like one of the mummers from your Plough play, all ill-assorted bits and tatters. When I was a girl I made my mother quite furious, you know, for I never could be bothered to mind whether my clothes matched."

"Which reminds me of something Alec said when he was little . . . well, you know he's always had this rather formidable intelligence, and he said . . ."

They strolled on, crunching on their crisp apples and savoring this or that serendipitous bit from his or her past. Amazing, Phoebe thought, how much there was to learn about a person. And what precious, silly—sometimes even embarrassing—memories one wanted to share in return. Their conversation meandered like a rivulet through hilly countryside, flowing, swirling, bubbling and eddying in cheerful disorder. And yet a pattern seemed to emerge, glorious as a cathedral window.

They leaned their elbows against a fence, peering down from the hilltop to the gentle patchwork of his fields, some planted with winter wheat, some lying fallow until spring. His cheeks were ruddy from the cold air, his thick hair unruly. A ray of slanted afternoon sunlight illuminated a ridge of stubble on the edge of his jaw. She put up a hand to stroke it.

"I'm afraid I did a poor job of shaving this morning. I was preoccupied, and too impatient to wait for Croft to do it."

"I like it."

He leaned back to let her nuzzle him, to rub her

smooth cheeks against his rough ones, to tease his lips into a kiss.

"You'll get a chill," he murmured. "Do you feel the sharp edge to the wind?"

"The storm you predicted?"

"Exactly. Come on, let's go back, the wind will be making our horses skittish."

It was dark after they'd stabled the horses. They ransacked the cellar for more apples, and begged some toasted bread and wedges of Cheshire cheese from a very busy Mrs. Yonge.

"A simple late supper," Phoebe thought she heard David tell the cook, her own attention having been mildly distracted by some suspicious movement under a deal table in the corner. *But perhaps it's nothing. And even if it* is . . . *something—or somebody—I won't fuss about it.*

"You're still cold," he said as they entered the green bedchamber. "Shall we sit by the fire?"

"Or," he added quickly, the sudden deep vibrato of his voice leaving no doubt as to his preference, "shall I draw us a hot bath?"

There was a bench, or a sort of shelf, carved all around the sides of the tall marble tub, so that two people might sit next to each other, the water reaching to their chins. Or, if they were tall, long-legged people, they might sit facing each other, their legs intertwined.

"This is paradise," Phoebe murmured, stroking her foot along David's shin. He grunted some contented syllables of agreement, his eyes half closed, mouth curved into a drowsy, satisfied grin. She wondered, if she slid down just a bit, how far her leg would reach—ah, yes, just to the bottom curve of his scrotum. She prodded him suddenly with her big toe, giggling to see his eyes fly wide open, his mouth shape itself into an *O* around a sharp intake of breath. It took him a moment to recover his equanimity.

"If you've got enough energy to make mischief," he growled softly, "I shall have to put you to work."

He paused, as though trying to choose a task onerous enough to constitute suitable punishment.

After some exaggerated deliberation, he announced, "Wash me."

"Must I? It's so delightful simply to soak oneself . . ."

Rising like Neptune from the tide, he towered over her, sending buckets of water slopping over the rim and splashing onto the marble floor. Gathering up the soap, sponge, and loofah, he waded across the water to where she sat.

"Take these and wash me."

The water came to his waist. She could see his penis floating—no, not just floating now, it was rising, stiffening—just below the surface, not far from her chin. The black hair along the flat line of his abdomen curled against him like coiled baby ferns. Shorter hairs made little black pothooks around his nipples.

"Come on." Miming impatience, he tapped the tip of her nose with the sponge.

"Umm, if you insist. But shall I wash you from the top down, my lord? Or from the . . . bottom up?"

"Work your way down."

She knelt up on the bench to reach his neck and shoulders, so elegantly interwoven of muscle and sinew. She reached her sponge into the deep pits under his arms, moving outward along his arms, reaching to each of his hands in turn. Hmmm, how lovely: both hands were carefully manicured, each fingernail trimmed extremely short and perfectly filed. This was something new, she thought. And a bit surprising in a man so lacking in vanity.

"I cut them this morning."

"Very pretty." She kissed the tip of each finger.

"Now turn around," she told him. She pressed her breasts against his back for a moment, wrapping her arms around him where he tapered from shoulders to waist. He untangled himself from her embrace—*enough self-indulgent dawdling, Phoebe*—and she ran the sponge down the diagonal ridges of muscle, soaping and rinsing him in circles along the surprising whiteness and roundness of his arse, the deep dents in its sides. But she would tumble off the bench and into the water, she thought, if she reached down any farther in that mysterious direction.

"Is that all?" he asked. "Nothing more in that area?"

"Turn around again," she said.

All right, now to work downward from his chest to his belly. And below his belly, where the tip of his penis had risen like a droll sea lion surfacing for a breath of air. She bent to kiss him there, and then sat back down on the bench to sponge him gently, rinse him lovingly, and to do the same for his balls and inner thighs.

"Not bad, but you missed some spots. I'll have to show you how to do this properly." He tried to frown as he lifted her to her feet and sat down in her place.

His style was to wash her briskly—she felt almost like a child being given a weekly businesslike scrub in an iron tub in the kitchen. Lots of soap, lots of splashing—but, as she sputtered and giggled under his hard, slippery hands, she knew that this was no childish pleasure. And when he used the sponge to wash the tips of her breasts, she thought she might simply dissolve into the suds.

"Kneel up on the bench," he told her now. "No, face the other way. Well, I've already done your front, haven't I?"

"Arch your back. Part your legs. Wider, Phoebe, that's a good girl."

No sponge or loofah: simply his hands. He pushed upon the small of her back; her belly tightened against the marble side of the tub and her legs had no choice but to spread themselves for him. Gently, slowly, he touched and teased her with his beautifully manicured fingers, exploring and caressing until her breath came raggedly.

New sensations rippled through her—highly improper ones, illicit and irresistible. Bending and stretching beneath his hands, spine arched, nerves thrumming, she imagined herself feasting greedily upon some exotic perfumed fruit whose name she didn't know and whose wholesomeness she doubted. Sinuous, iridescent shapes drifted before her eyes. The heat from his fingertips flickered up from her belly to her breasts, to her throat and armpits and the palms of her hands.

Her mouth opened in a delicious, shuddering sigh as he bent to kiss her nape.

"That's enough for now," he murmured. "Come, I'll dry you."

The towels were soft, thick; the almond oil he rubbed into her skin smelled light and delicate. His skin gleamed beneath the black hair on his chest and legs; she watched greedily as he stretched his spine and briskly toweled himself.

"I think," she said as they walked arm-in-arm to his bedchamber, "that I've left a layer of myself behind me in the bath."

A dead, constricting layer. Of used-up skin and useless, needless proprieties. She felt light, shameless and almost giddy, buoyed by the currents of warm air rising from the fire in the hearth and lapping at their naked bodies.

"But what's that noise?" she asked. For there was a howling somewhere.

"You've forgotten." He drew back the red velvet curtains from the tall window to reveal the storm raging outside.

She nodded. "I *had* forgotten." Indeed, it felt as if she'd lost touch with everything beyond the confines of the steamy perfumed bathroom. But there it was: the natural world gone mad. Ferocious, heedless of human consequence, the gray-white snow whipping by in violent diagonals against a frozen black sky. Beholding it, she was seized by a wave of pity for the lost and unprotected. Pity—and yet exhilaration as well. Because for all the storm's brutality, she recognized something of herself in it, the force of desire coursing through her flesh.

"A passionate storm," she whispered.

"The *most* passionate of storms."

She could hear, in the slight thickening of his voice, that he recognized it too.

He pressed behind her, the front of his body warm and solid against her back as they gazed together at the havoc raging on the other side of the window pane. Standing firmly, she traced tiny arcs of movement with her pelvis, each movement a caress when she rubbed against him. He wrapped his arms around her, taking hold of her breasts; she parted her legs to allow him to lengthen into the cleft of her bottom.

The window glass—with black sky behind it—was like an old silver mirror. She held her breath as she watched the pale reflection of his hand move slowly down her front, to cup, to cover the dark triangle between her legs. And then to open her, to touch her, there at the triangle's apex.

"Ah." The quick rush of warm air from her mouth

clouded the glass and dissipated the images reflected there. It was startling, she thought, suddenly to lose those shimmery mirror doubles. She and David were alone now. Alone together in the eye of the storm, sheltered from its violence and yet as one with its passion.

She gave a low laugh and tuned to him, putting her arms around him and (after hesitating for just a moment) letting one of her hands slide down his back, down below his waist. Softly, delicately (for she needed to be careful, at least until after she had trimmed her own nails), she allowed her fingertips to caress, to fondle and explore him in the cleft of his buttocks, to make him moan and shudder and harden against her belly.

His eyes were black, the pupils distended by sensation. He'd thrown his head back; his mouth was parted, the breath came roughly. She'd taken him further than either of them had expected.

Taken him: the syllables echoed in her consciousness.

Taken him: her fingers loosened as she absorbed the meaning of the word.

Taken.

He'd recovered his self-possession now; with some effort, his mouth had reshaped itself into a jaunty grin. Still, she thought, he looked a bit abashed to have found himself so absolutely at her mercy. Abashed, and yet (how she loved him for it) eager, surprised, and wildly aroused.

"We had better get to bed immediately," he whispered.

Immediately. Oh yes, immediately. She let him lead her across the room and pull her onto the bed.

"Ride me," he told her, lifting her astride him and lying back upon the pillows.

"But *not* side-saddle," she'd intended to reply. Lightly, vivaciously. But she lost the last syllable of her phrase, her voice catching in her throat as she slid down upon him.

For although he might pretend to be lying at his ease below her, he was no docile mount. He lifted her with his hips, bucking beneath her, his muscles demanding that she use her thighs and back to guide, to control, to master him.

They would gallop, she thought, they would race and jump, prance and play and cavort. They would ride as one—centaur in an ancient forest, beast with two backs. The years and miles would disappear below their feet: they would move together (just for tonight she'd allow herself to believe it) through a world they'd build and own, discover and dwell in. Tightening her thighs about his hips, she laughed with joy at the expression on his face beneath her, his gaze a caress, his eyes lit with pride and admiration.

He pulsed within her. One last, high—oh very high—hedge to jump. They took it perfectly, together even as they lost their individual selves in orgasm. And together, still together, for the descent into inevitable sadness, the recognition that (as all things must—as life itself must) it had come to an end. He pulled her down to him and they lay very still, hearts beating so loudly that they could barely hear the blizzard raging and howling outside.

Chapter

19

They found themselves a bit shy with each other at supper later, and hesitant—even befuddled—the next morning. Everything seemed new, heightened, shining and delicate as the tree branches that were edged with ice from the storm. An accidental touch of a hand—when she gave him his coffee or he passed her the newspaper at breakfast—seemed freighted with confused, dreamy intimacy.

They laughed stupidly at nothing, lost the thread of the simplest conversations, stumbling together through mazy crystal palaces built of their shared thoughts and entwined gazes.

They fell silent for long, meditative stretches but when they did speak they were able to communicate volumes. Slowly and haltingly, Phoebe managed to describe her most nightmarish memories.

The moment when she'd known for certain that the phaeton would overturn.

The sickening feeling of losing her hold on Bryan's little body.

The sight—blessedly brief, for she'd been thrown out of the carriage herself the next moment—of him lying, still and broken (and oh, so tiny!) on the gravel path.

"It's as though someone had made pictures of those moments—not paintings, more like horribly precise engravings, drained of color, etched by a flash of light—and affixed them eternally in my thoughts. Thank heaven there's no machine that can create such pictures—only my accursed guilty memory. I've never tried to describe this to anyone before, David."

"Mr. Blake once told me that you suffered the torments of hell."

She shrugged. "Yes, I suppose Mr. Blake would be able to recognize that. And it didn't frighten you away?"

He shook his head and put his arm around her.

She didn't say anything for perhaps an hour afterward and neither did he. The skies were heavy, uncertain; Phoebe and David trudged across snowy pastures as though in a dream—until finally the sun made its way through the clouds and they somehow woke from their dark reverie to find themselves in the midst of a raucous snowball fight.

"You started it," she gasped, almost overcome with manic laughter, "but I got you a good one there at the back of your neck, didn't I?"

"*I* started it? You lying little witch, you know quite well that this titanic battle is all your doing. Ah, but look out, I've got you now . . . No, wait, hello, who's there?"

The young cowherd was clearly discomfited by having to deliver a message to the earl when that gentleman had just finished rubbing a lady's face with a handful of snow.

He begged Lord Linseley's pardon, and the lady's too, for disturbing them, but it looked like the red cow with the straight hocks was going to have her calf. Way too early, of course, but Mr. Goulding had resolved to get the little creature out alive. They were there in the barn now, Mr. Goulding and that new fellow that's staying with him. It looks like it's going to take some time, too, sir.

"Blast it, I knew we should have trouble there. No slope to the pelvis on that cow at all. And she'll be in extraordinary pain, too, poor thing," David said. "But you can find your own way back to the house, can't you, Phoebe? For I expect this will take quite a while."

"Of course I can find my way. But must I? Can't I come with you?" She didn't want to leave him yet, no matter where he was going. And anyway, it would be a chance to see how Billy was faring.

"A difficult, premature calving is a nasty business. The herd isn't due to give birth for more than a month, you see. But of course you can come if you want to. This boy will bring us all some hot cider from the house, won't you, lad? It could be a long wait."

It was a nasty business. Bloody too. And loud—horrible how the cow was suffering.

"It's all turned round in there, poor little thing," Mr. Goulding told them from the stool where he sat. For it wasn't he, as Phoebe had expected, who lay on bloody, filthy straw with his arm plunged up inside the terrified, suffering cow. It was Billy, his broken leg stretched out alongside of him in what surely couldn't have been a comfortable position.

"The lad knows what he's doing," Mr. Goulding explained proudly. "Begged me to let him have a try at it. Well, why not? I quizzed him on the best way to pull the little creature out. *He* knowed it all quite exactly."

"Got clever hands, too," he added.

Clever enough to have kept him alive on the London streets during five years of pickpocketing, Phoebe thought. But Mr. Goulding wouldn't have to know that unless Billy wanted him to.

She shuddered for the poor cow, but it was Billy she was watching. Even in his bruised and broken condition, he was clearly the calmest person in the barn. She marveled at how adult he looked, how skillful, throughout his repeated, frustrating, failed attempts to maneuver the calf's nose into the birth canal so that he could pull the poor little thing out.

He kept missing. He kept trying. An hour passed. It was growing dark outside. The young cowherd lit the lanterns; Mr. Goulding puffed on his pipe. The hot fermented cider helped keep everybody warm, but the situation was beginning to look quite hopeless. There were ways to kill the calf and save the cow; David and Mr. Goulding had begun considering them.

"Just one more try," Billy said.

He knit his brow and rotated his arm. Phoebe could tell from the sudden spark that lit his eyes that he'd finally made a connection.

"And it's alive," he called. "Here it comes."

She wanted to hug him afterward, but merely smiled and congratulated him. David shook his hand, Mr. Goulding clapped him on the shoulder, and everyone toasted him with what was left of the cider. And now, they all agreed, it was best that that he go warm himself and get some rest. After a good wash, of course.

"I'll discuss it with Mr. Goulding first, of course, but I want to offer Billy a position here," David told her as they walked back to the house. "He's extraordinarily skillful. Cool headed, too—well, that's a big part of the job, confidence, patience. He'd be an immense help to Mr. Goulding, who's getting on in years, much as hates to admit it. What luck to have brought him here."

What luck for Billy to be able to stay here.

Even after she'd returned to London.

"But you're pale," he exclaimed. "You look exhausted. I shouldn't have let you stay through all that nasty business. Lord, what was I thinking?"

"No, I'm glad I stayed. It was wonderful, to . . . to see Billy succeed so brilliantly. I had no idea that he could do such a thing. I simply need a little rest . . . the cold air, you know. But do come wake me for supper, won't you?"

As though, she thought, staring at the flames leaping in the green bedchamber's tiled fireplace, there existed the slightest chance that she'd be able to sleep. As though she could shut out the thoughts that plagued her. Or the images—even the pretty ones. Even—or especially—the lovely sight of the cow nudging and prodding her baby, licking off the birth mess with her strong, rough tongue until the calf blinked its eyes, stumbled to its feet, and began nosing the swollen udder, rooting about for a teat to suckle at.

She and David, the cowherd and Mr. Goulding, and a rapt, prideful Billy had all watched, quietly spellbound by the spectacle of new life. It was hardly something special here on a farm, of course, but one couldn't help be thrilled and fascinated by it all the same.

In a month's time, she thought, all the cows would have calved. And soon afterward David and his crew would begin plowing and planting the corn—and the hemp, woad, oilseed, turnips, and sugar beets as well. They'd shear the sheep and cut the hay in the spring, while the days grew longer and the rest of the crops ripened.

And in late summer they'd begin the harvest. Skin burnt brown by the sun, sleeves rolled up and collar unbuttoned, David would be out abroad in his fields from morning till night.

She'd give anything to be there beside him, to be part of the cycle of unfolding life, the turn of the rough wheel that fed and clothed the people of Britain. But it was impossible. She needed to return to the city as soon as she could. To take up Marston's endless, futile round of calls and dinners, balls and appointments. To pronounce the subtlest, cleverest judgements upon those matters of style that constituted the Polite World's raison d'être. To participate in the Season—as if the word "season" could mean anything at all when abstracted from the earth's cycles of dark and light, heat and cold, sun and rain. As though there could be any "world" except the natural one, turning on its axis in the heavens.

She had to return to sooty, poisoned London, and absolutely as soon as she was able. She'd stay for the Plough play, of course; she couldn't leave David to celebrate his cherished ritual without a companion. But she'd take herself away soon afterwards, after having made it absolutely clear to him why this course of action was the best thing—the only thing really—for them both.

Oddly, she began to feel a bit better for having reaffirmed her resolution. Having faced it squarely, she could take comfort from the knowledge that she wouldn't be leaving as precipitously as all that. There remained a full week between today and Plough Monday. And Lord

Crashaw would be arriving two days after that; best to stay until *that* business had been resolved. Not that she felt in any danger from the author of the hate letters; it didn't seem that anything bad could happen here in the country. But one never knew, and Billy's wounds were a reminder that it was best to be careful. It was only responsible to let David speak to Crashaw and put an end to the threats and intimidation, as she was quite sure he would.

And so, adding it up, she had nine more days here. Nine days in which to live so deeply and happily and consciously—at his side and in this place—that she'd be able to remember it forever, every moment engraved upon her memory and her heart. For after all, she thought, she deserved a few *good* memories, too.

"I sent the letter off to Linseley." Admiral Wolfe handed Lady Kate into his carriage and sat down beside her, closing the door behind him. The opera had been delightful, he thought, but rather *long,* especially since it wouldn't have done to sit as closely beside her in the box as he'd longed to. He moved a bit closer to her now. Ah yes, much better.

She smiled up at him as the carriage started up. "I'm glad, John. Because even though I know I shouldn't worry, I do anyway."

"You worry far too much about your friend Phoebe."

"Perhaps because I haven't had anyone else to worry about."

"But now you do. You should worry about me."

"It's difficult to worry about someone who came through the Battle of Trafalgar so heroically, but I shall try if you'd like. I *think* about you constantly, though. Isn't that sufficient?"

"It will suffice quite nicely. Because I take your

point: I'm really not the sort of person one worries about. But how about children, then? I'm told that children are life's biggest worries, and the best as well. You would like to have children, wouldn't you, Kate?"

"Indeed I would, John."

"Good. I want them too. I've always envied Linseley that son he adores so exceedingly. Nice young chap, by the way; I've invited him to dine with me tomorrow. And I'll bring him around to call sometime as well; you'll like him too. All the same, Linseley probably can't wait to start a household full of new ones now that he's found someone to give them to him. But what's wrong, dear?"

Lady Kate's lighthearted smile had faded.

"He wants more children, John?"

"He's mad about them. I think the desire for more children was probably what brought him to Almack's in the first place."

"Oh dear. Yes, I can see that now. He's just the sort of gentleman . . . oh, but I should have realized."

"Kate, will you please explain what's upsetting you so."

"It's Phoebe. Forgive me, John, but this time I truly can't stop myself. Because it will be so difficult . . . so painful, for her, and for the earl too, to resolve this . . . disappointment. Well, maybe she's told him about it already. At least I hope she has.

"You see, she lost a baby when they had that accident in the phaeton. And the doctor . . . well, after the accident the doctor said . . ."

"Ah, I do see. Hard on her, that."

"Yes, he said she'd never be able to bear another child."

* * *

"The door's unlocked, David. Please come in."

He breathed a sigh of relief when he saw her, tall and serene, and smiling at a small painting on the wall.

"Do you know," he told her, "I was quite worried about you. You looked so fragile two hours ago."

Still smiling, she turned her graceful neck to look at him. "Yes, I'm much better now."

"I expect you were right about the cold air. Anyway, your little rest seems to have set you up wonderfully."

"That and the entertainment of this picture gallery. I take it that the truculent little fellow in curls and petticoats, gripping his pail and shovel so determinedly, is you?"

Absurd picture, he thought, the sort of thing only a woman could enjoy. His mother had loved it too. He nodded, trying not to wince.

"Are you hungry for supper?" he asked.

"No, not quite yet."

"Oh well, supper can wait then. A brandy, perhaps?"

"Umm, yes, that would be nice."

Nice. Astonishing what an erotic undertone a simple word could have, when she spoke it with her eyes veiled and her mouth curved like that. Her low voice was as mellow as the brandy he poured.

"Oh yes." She sipped it slowly, looking up at him over the rim of the heavy glass. He looked back steadily.

"You're trying to seduce me, Miss Browne."

"I haven't touched you, my lord."

"Not directly, no. No more so than the sun touches the budding corn."

"Wonderful the images you use to express things."

But they weren't merely images, he thought. They were the deepest truths he knew. The attraction he felt for her was entirely of a piece with the tropism of growing things to sun and soil and pure water.

"Well, here are some other images, if you prefer. Ruder ways to express the same thing. For I might also say that you're making me randy as a drover's dog. That you're making me primed, proud, prickstruck. Raking, rammed, rigid. Goatish."

"Goatish, eh?"

"No, I take that back, goats are too small. More like a bull."

"Yes, that's more you, I think. A longhorn, naturally."

"Come here, let me unbutton that. And you must unbutton me, too. Ah yes, good. You see, you've awakened the whole barnyard now."

"Ummm, I do see. Barnyard . . . yard—no, that's a nautical word. Yard . . . spar . . . mast. Still, it does seem quite a yard long, doesn't it?"

"You're seeing it from a flattering angle, but, certainly, if you wish. But not *yard*—I'm a man of the land, not the sea. What about *horn*? There's a word for you. Horn, staff, dragon. Prick, pike, stiff, and lance."

"Lance, I like that one. Very chivalric."

"Manhood."

"No, I don't care for it. Your manhood is all of you, not just *that* part."

"Indeed. Well then, my lady, where should your liege knight put this . . . this *lance* of mine?"

"Oh dear, must we speak of my body too? You know it's difficult for me. Well then, in my . . . pussy. In my quim."

"Yes, go on." Wonderful, he thought, that he could still make her blush.

"In my . . . oh dear, in my cunt."

"You're doing very well. Give me a few more words and you shall receive your reward."

"I was a proper young lady once."

"Nonsense. You were a schoolgirl once, making jokes with the other schoolgirls."

"Oh well, then. In my kettle. Kitchen. Oven. My penwiper. Pitcher. Pin-cushion. Needlecase. Spleuchan."

"*Spleuchan*??"

"There was a Scottish girl who came visiting our village for a few months. It's some sort of a . . . pouch, I think."

Pouch, pitcher, or oven, she could feel that he'd slid two—no, three—of his fingers inside of it. And moved another finger into the cleft of her buttocks, while his other hand curved around the bottom of her bum.

Her dress was in wild disarray; the bodice had slid down her shoulders and he'd lifted up the skirt around her hips. She glanced quickly over her shoulder, checking the pale green damask wall for a space where there were no paintings to disturb. Leaning against the silky fabric, she pulled him toward her, holding her arms around his neck. He lifted her up, propping a hand against the wall to steady himself. She raised herself a bit higher and then fiercely, suddenly, lowered herself onto . . . onto *whatever* one wanted to call it. Even—if one insisted upon it—his manhood.

He groaned and pressed his mouth into the hollow of her neck as she raised and lowered herself onto him. He could feel the muscles of . . . *what had she called it?* He found that he'd forgotten every word and that he didn't care in the slightest. What he cared about was how tightly, how intensely, he felt himself caressed and embraced. She was so fierce, so hungry, and so strong, that he felt free simply to be made love to—to let go, if just for a moment, his constant burdens of obligation and duty. And so he merely held her, crying out repeatedly and letting her fuck him with her entire body—perhaps one could call it her *womanhood*—

until she screamed her orgasm and he could hold his no longer.

They slid to the floor together then, helpless, spent, and all in a laughing, gasping, disordered heap, under the watchful protection of a never-slumbering household deity—the little boy still tightly holding his pail and shovel.

Chapter 20

The only problem, Phoebe was to think from time to time during the coming days, was how quickly time passed when life was as busy and agreeable as she found it at Linseley Manor. David didn't spend as much time with her as he had at first, but this seemed somehow natural and reasonable. She was glad that things had become so relaxed and workaday: he had his tasks and obligations to attend to, while she rather enjoyed poking around the house and grounds by herself. She read in the library, wandered about the farm and fields, and galloped over the wolds, absurdly but comfortably dressed in the ill-assorted costume David had suggested, his son's old breeches allowing her to sit properly astride her horse.

He joined her whenever he could, and of course they ate together and made love as often—and as variously—as possible. *We shall make love in every conceivable way,* he'd told her. Well, they wouldn't accomplish *that* in the brief time left to them, she thought, but they'd make quite a respectable beginning.

It would be better, she thought, if she could only

stop counting the days. But that was impossible in a household so occupied with preparations for the Plough Monday festivities.

"Only six days left, my lord," Mrs. Oughton announced after breakfast on Tuesday. "And the gentry will be arriving the day before, of course, so I shall have to have all the floors scrubbed and all the linens in the guest bedrooms laundered before then. Not to speak of seeing to the damask tablecloths and velvet runners for the banquet itself. I want to hire some girls from the village to help, if that's all right with you. Mr. Neville says we can afford the extra fees, even with what we're paying the gang of fellows cleaning the chandeliers in the Great Hall."

"Well, if Mr. Neville says we can afford it, then we can." David grinned. "And I'm glad we decided to clean the chandeliers; last time I looked, they had about a century of hardened tallow stuck onto them."

The chandeliers were large rough wheels of wrought iron, each a yard across and suspended by chains from the Hall's high, vaulted ceiling. They were a practical design, as David pointed out to Phoebe. "You see how those iron cups are affixed to catch the dripping wax from the candles. Well, at least they *would* catch the wax if they weren't full to overflowing. Wonderful that they'll be clean for this year's celebration."

Of course, the extra help—maids and mechanics both—needed to be fed. Which led to some consternation on the part of Mrs. Yonge, who had quite enough to do in preparation for the banquet. There would be roasts and hams, stews and stuffed poultry, pies and puddings. And overflowing pitchers of cider, ale, and mead.

"Could you use a bit of help preparing the pies?" Phoebe asked shyly. "I always enjoyed making pie crust when I was a girl."

She hadn't donned an apron for years. It would have

caused a scandal among the *ton* if Lord Claringworth's exquisitely dressed wife had been caught anywhere near an oven or pantry; Phoebe had never even entered the kitchen of their Mayfair establishment. But the rules of the Polite World weren't observed so strictly at Linseley Manor. And anyway Mrs. Yonge was desperate for the help.

The crust of her first pie was a bit tough, her second a little overcooked, but her third was quite creditable. And by the end of the afternoon she'd actually produced enough nicely browned meat and mince pies to earn some sincere, although rather astonished, commendation from Mrs. Yonge.

"She obviously didn't believe I had it in me," she told David that night in bed, "but I knew I'd finally get my knack for it back. I enjoyed it so thoroughly, you know, that I hardly noticed the bothersome little girl with red hair—the one who insists upon staring at me from under the table."

"I wish she wouldn't," she added quietly.

"But it's only because Susan admires you so much," he said. "She told me that you're the prettiest lady she's ever seen, and that it's her dearest wish to receive a kiss from you."

She could feel her body go tense within his embrace.

"Yes, yes," he said softly, "I understand, don't worry. I told her she was right: you're the prettiest lady *I've* ever seen as well. But then I made it very clear that you've been ill and couldn't kiss her yet. And that she mustn't bother you until you were absolutely well."

"Thank you," she said. He'd probably done the best anyone could do without making a fuss about it. For it wouldn't be fair to expect a three-year-old to understand that the long, wistful, meltingly sad glances she directed in Phoebe's direction might constitute a bother.

And since Phoebe would be gone so soon, she supposed that it didn't really matter that David had tacitly encouraged the little girl to hope for a kiss she'd never receive.

"There will be a lot of children at the play on Monday," he said. "I hope it won't be too difficult for you."

She kissed his shoulder. "It won't be easy, but I think it's best that I do see them. I can't avoid them forever, you know."

He laughed, stroking her flat belly as though he hoped to find a bulge starting up there. "Well, no. I should hope not."

Only five days, she thought, staring into the darkness as he drifted into sleep. Five days until she had to tell him the truth, blasting his hopes every bit as completely as she would have to disappoint little Susan's desire for a kiss.

Oddly, though, as the weekend drew near, she found herself less distressed by the sight of her small admirer than she had been at first. In fact, when she went to the kitchen—the pies were done now, but she was helping chop the ingredients that Mrs. Yonge would stuff into three dozen fat geese—she found herself mildly disappointed if the child wasn't there. When she *was* around—usually playing under the table with her doll—Phoebe would nod formally to her, and Susan would nod back quite solemnly, as though to signal that she understood that the pretty lady had been sick and was not, on any account, to be disquieted.

"What's this?" David looked up from his mail on Saturday morning. "A letter from Wolfe, how nice."

"Lady Kate's exceedingly well, he says . . . that's

good . . . plans for dinner with Alec . . . that's good too . . . and—ah, splendid—he and his lady will be announcing their engagement shortly. They plan to marry in April."

"How wonderful, David."

He looked a bit abashed for a moment. "Listen, Phoebe, you haven't minded that I haven't moved to . . . to *formalize* things between us yet, have you?"

"Of course not." Actually, she thanked heaven for it every evening. She looked at him warily now.

"I simply thought," he continued, "that we'd wait until the business with Crashaw was cleared up, if that's all right with you."

"Oh yes. Perfect. Rather what I had in mind as well."

"Good. Well then, let's see—what else does Wolfe write? Oh blast it, the scoundrel . . ."

"What is it?"

"Dammit, Crashaw couldn't resist sending one more of those infernal notes—this time to Kate. INFORM P. THAT ESCAPE IS IMPOSSIBLE. Bloody hell . . . excuse me, my love, but I'm going to find it deuced difficult not to punch him in the jaw when I see him."

"Bloody hell indeed. It's one thing for him to torment *me,* but quite another when he takes it out on someone completely innocent."

And it would be even worse, she thought, if it *weren't* Lord Crashaw who was responsible, but someone they hadn't even considered. But no, she assured herself immediately, it had to be Crashaw.

"Anyway, Wolfe warns me to be on the lookout for any suspicious characters lurking about during the celebration."

"That's wise of him."

"Wise but unnecessary. I know everyone in the village and countryside. In fact, I've been at the christening of everyone younger than myself—and everybody who's older than I am came to mine. But yes, of course we should all stay on the alert. A pity to have to be suspicious during a celebration, though, don't you think?"

He tossed his napkin down. "Finished your coffee? Good. I'll see if they've brought the sleigh around yet."

The two of them were off to cut boughs of evergreen to decorate the Great Hall. No, David had told Mr. Neville, he didn't need any farmhands coming to help: Miss Browne had the strength of ten; he was lucky to have engaged her assistance for this year's harvest. And quite cheaply too, he'd added, winking. She'd pretended to smile.

But it was delightful to be alone with him, out in the cold, bright sunlight.

Cutting and sawing, they worked quickly and well together, tossing the fragrant boughs into the back of the sleigh until Scots pine and yew, holly, ivy, mistletoe, juniper, and box were heaped several feet deep.

"My goodness, smell them, David," Phoebe called. "They're so strong and tarry. Gorgeous."

She threw herself on top of the pile of greenery and buried her face in the soft yew needles.

He lay next to her and nudged her around until they were kissing each other's cold cheeks. "Well, it's rather the opposite of kissing under the mistletoe, isn't it?" he murmured.

"I'm cold," she said. "Cover me up."

"With branches?"

"With yourself. Cover me and fill me too. You know what I mean."

"Out here? In the cold?"

But she was already lifting her skirts and undoing his buttons. "I don't mind."

He fumbled with his leather gloves but they fit tightly around his big hands. "Here," she said. She bit the very tip of the middle finger, neatly pulling the glove off his hand with her teeth. He slid the other one off. His hands were warm; he lifted her buttocks to him, holding her tight and open as he entered her.

"Your belly's cold. But not your prick."

"Not now. Well, you're so hot inside. I shall never want to leave."

Stray bits of clothing threatened to get in the way—buttons and buckles dug into their flesh and a few of the branches were rather spikier than they'd seemed at first. None of that mattered.

The deep thrusts of their joined bodies rocked the heavy sleigh on its runners, causing the horses to turn their heads in mild curiosity. The scent of the needles rose around them, the sweet potent oils mingling with their bodies' saltier smells. They came quickly, basking in each other's hot breath and then, as their energy subsided, groaning with the effort of drawing their wet, sticky clothing back on in the cold air.

"Well, *that* was absurd," he whispered. "*Perfectly* absurd."

"Perfectly absurdly lovely," she whispered back.

"Exactly, but, oof, move a little to the right, will you darling, so I can get that button. Yes, that's better . . . well, it's all very well for *you,* you know—it mostly happens *inside* your body, where everything's so nice and warm."

"You don't regret it, do you?"

"Not for a moment. And you?"

She began to tell him that she'd cherish the memory of it forever. But no—she stopped herself quickly; there had been something discordant, she thought, about that solemn, valedictory declaration. His eyes had begun to widen in confusion, so she only laughed and told him that no, she didn't regret it either, but that she *was* looking forward to her bath.

"We must hang these first."

"If we haven't crushed them too horribly."

"Come on, let's see how quickly we can get home."

What a pretty word home *was.*

The Great Hall did look lovely all festooned in green and finished off with bare hawthorn branches laden with red berries. David and Phoebe worked by the light of large torches ensconced in the stone walls: the eight hundred and thirty-six candles in their freshly cleaned chandeliers wouldn't be lit until tomorrow. Ancient tapestries hung between the torches: their faded reds and blues told the stories of unicorns captured and dragons slain, of Noah and the flood, Abraham and Isaac, and the flight into Egypt. The high table rested on its platform along one of the short ends of the hall; set perpendicular to it were four rows of trestle tables, each of which would seat thirty people. The players and dancers would have plenty of space at the end of the hall opposite the high table.

"And will you—or we, I expect—sit in the center of the high table surrounded by the local gentry?" Phoebe asked.

David laughed. "Not a bit of it. The gentry will sit at the high table, but you and I will be at the foot of one of the trestle tables. It's an ancient tradition here; everybody expects the earl to sit among his people on Plough Monday. Nature's democracy or some such thing, I imagine. It's a reasonable enough idea but what I really like about it is that we'll be able to see the entertainment so well from close by."

"This is an extraordinary chamber," she said. "It seems to ring with centuries of past festivities and ceremonies."

"It will look very bright," he told her, "with all the

candles lit and reflected in the plate. Not to speak of the white damask tablecloths and red velvet runners. You'll look quite of a piece with it in your white dress and red shawl."

"Yes, I suppose I shall."

"It's more than a celebration, Phoebe. It's quite magical. You'll see."

She'd smiled and turned to examine the crossed Saracen swords that hung above one of the big fireplaces. Walking slowly around the hall, craning her slender neck to peer up at the old ironwork and the woven hangings, she looked as delicate as the lady in the unicorn tapestries. But she wasn't delicate, he thought happily; she was wonderfully strong and lusty.

He remembered the feel of her body underneath him in the sleigh. How cold her cheeks had been; how hot, how voracious, she'd been in other places. It was glorious, he thought, that she seemed as hungry for his touch as he was for hers. And even, perhaps—his eyes lit hopefully—as eager to start a baby. At least he liked to imagine so; how wonderful if she was beginning to get beyond the terrible pain and loss she'd suffered.

But he mustn't hurry, he reminded himself; he must be cautious. The way he'd stroked her belly the other night, for example—it had been childish, and impatient. He'd be more tactful from now on— especially in those times when he couldn't entirely read her emotions. Her odd solemnity after their coupling in the sleigh today—what had *that* been about, he wondered.

Their week together had been as magical, mysterious. But perhaps love simply *was* this mysterious. Perhaps it took a lifetime to learn everything about someone you loved: well, that would be the commonsense explanation, anyway.

Still, it *felt* magical. *It's the time of year,* he thought, *the old rituals.* Or simply the depth of his emotions—sometimes he felt so overwhelmed by his feelings for her that he'd accept any assistance that presented itself, natural or supernatural.

Not that he really believed that the Plough play had magical properties. Well, he was as modern as the next gentleman, wasn't he, adopting up-to-date farming methods and machinery and even subscribing to scientific papers from the Royal Society. When he'd told Phoebe that the ceremony was magical, he'd merely meant that it felt that way to him. That when he watched the play—which he supposed might seem a bit simple-minded to someone who hadn't loved it all his life—he became a child again, filled with as much joy and wonder as any child sitting on the benches alongside him.

Of course he didn't believe in any of that claptrap about how the play guaranteed fertility to the land. It was simply a useful custom, a time-honored way to ease the people's painful entry into a new planting season after weeks of holiday carousing. And any fool would agree that the land would yield better crops if it was worked willingly by laborers who'd put some good food in their bellies.

And as for the legend that a woman in love would soon conceive a son after having watched the Plough play—well, *that* was nothing but the rankest medieval nonsense.

And yet . . .

Completing her circuit of the Great Hall, she came and stood next to him. Enough of his silly speculations, he thought. What *was* clearly magical was her smile. Her hand slipping into his. Her eyes half closed as she asked in her low voice whether he might like to join her in the bathtub now. And his own immediate physical response. Which perhaps was not precisely magical—he'd always been a ready sort, he supposed, or so women had told him—but certainly a *bit* readier than he remembered being in the past.

A bath would be very nice indeed, he told her. A long one, for this would be their last night alone without guests in the house.

Chapter 21

"And your dinner with Viscount Granthorpe, John?"
The admiral looked surprised for a moment. "Ah right, young Alec Hervey, you mean."

He smiled. "You know, sometimes I can hardly believe that he's not still the little chap who sailed his toy boats with me on the lake at Linseley Manor.

"Dinner was very nice indeed. Conversation very pleasant, very amiable, though from time to time the boy would become a bit scattered: he supposes himself in love, you see, and I'm afraid that his young lady is leading him a merry chase. Not only that, but her brother likes to gamble at Vivien's and has been taking Alec along with him.

"He'd have been better off in Lincolnshire. He'd have had to sit through the Plough play, of course, but he might have done well to signal the lady that he had more to do than dance attendance on her."

"He has a romantic nature, then, like his father."

"Very like him, though Alec's a bit of a scholar as well. But just as bad at gambling, I suspect."

Kate shook her head in mock solemnity. "Of course,

it's a simple matter for such wise and temperate types as ourselves to pass judgement upon the rest of the world's folly."

He lifted her hand to his lips and kissed it. "Our behavior was *anything* but temperate two nights ago, my lady."

"No, I suppose it wasn't. It was very . . . agreeable, though."

"*I* thought so."

"But John . . ."

"Why did I suspect that there would be a *but* somewhere?"

"I have no *buts* about *us,* John. But I have been thinking."

"Not about the hate letters again."

"I'm afraid so, dear."

"And . . ."

"Well, I've read all of them now. And I don't believe it's Lord Crashaw who's been sending the pasted-together ones. I don't think our culprit is any of the gentlemen who felt wronged by Phizz Marston—wronged by him and attracted to him at the same time. The tone is entirely different. There's no sport in the pasted-together ones. No sense of guilty pleasure. There's simply hatred."

She bit her lip and looked away.

"You have something else to say, Kate. What is it?"

"I think it's someone who hates Phoebe and not Phizz."

"But who then?"

"I don't know, John. I wish I did."

The gentry of David's neighborhood were no better and no worse than the usual run of such characters, Phoebe thought as she went down to breakfast on

Plough Monday. In fact they'd turned out to be remarkably like the people she'd grown up with: sedate, country gentlemen and ladies whose staid behavior and predictable conversation she'd been mad to escape from as a girl but now found rather comforting. During the introductions David had made the preceding afternoon, she'd been a bit relieved but not terribly surprised to see that the ladies were obviously less aware of the three-seasons-old cut of her dress than Alison Cockburn had been.

Fat old squires had tried to flirt with the pretty Miss Browne, while disapproving ladies and their disappointed daughters had nodded stiffly; even after so many years, the Earl of Linseley was clearly the prize catch of the neighborhood. People had inquired politely about her connections: luckily, no one seemed to know much about Devonshire so she'd been able to use the real name of her tiny village as well as some details from her childhood.

As Phizz, she'd learned how useful it was to salt one's deceptions with an occasional carefully selected truth. A little veracity went a long way; she was a bit disconcerted to see how easily it came it her now, and a bit chagrined when she noticed that David was listening in.

"Never been married, eh, Miss Browne? But what a misfortune for the male sex. And where has such a pretty woman been hiding herself?"

The obvious best thing to do in such a case was simply to sigh and roll her eyes a bit, hinting at a sadness too deep for polite conversation.

Well, she tried to signal to David, *what* would *you have me do in such a situation?* He nodded and looked away, the corners of his mouth twitching.

Her one misstep had been to confide to a Miss Finchley that it was she who'd baked the delicious pie they were eating, horrifying that young lady as thoroughly as she would have done any member of the Claringworths' London set. In order to atone for her lapse, Phoebe had forced herself to lose repeatedly at casino after dinner.

"You showed great restraint," David had whispered to her in bed later, "not to have fleeced Miss Finchley at least."

She'd laughed. "I don't beat people at cards unless I need the money or they need to be taken down a peg. Your neighbors are all right. Even Miss Finchley."

"But," she'd arched her back as he'd moved his mouth down between her breasts and nuzzled her belly, "if you'd like to make me a bit of a prize, by way of . . . of . . . *consolation* . . . yes, David, don't stop. But a bit more slowly, darling . . . yes, like that, *exactly like that* . . ."

How delightful to say *exactly* what it was she wanted in bed, she thought now as she paused at the door of the breakfast room. And how compliant David had been: what a patient, obedient mouth he had; what a light, delicate tongue. Of course—her face and neck flushed a bit—the rest of him had been gratifyingly *impatient* afterwards, which had also been quite nice in its way . . .

"Ah, how do you do, Miss Browne, and a very good Plough Monday morning to you."

"Quite well, thank you, Colonel Colton, and a good Plough Monday to you as well. But you must excuse me. It seems you caught me wool-gathering."

"Hmm, wool-gathering seems to agree with you—either that or you've slept wonderfully well in our fresh country air. Here, allow me to open the door.

"Of course, we must eat sparingly this morning, to leave room for the feast. Lord Linseley promises that it will be the best banquet ever, due to some unusually fine kitchen help this year."

* * *

The villagers and farmhands, as they began to arrive sometime after noon, were a more varied and interesting group. Each person was dressed in some sort of pieced-together finery, and everyone seemed quite at home milling about the Great Hall and greeting the earl. David, devastatingly handsome in formal black and white, shook hands, clapped people on the shoulder, and accepted hugs and kisses from old ladies.

The cloths had been laid with fine pieces of plate and goblets, and a boy on a tall ladder had almost finished lighting the eight hundred and thirty-six candles, whose reflections twinkled in the silver. Stevens led a small army of footmen from table to table, setting out the pitchers of drinks.

"How pretty you look, dear, all in your red and white." Mrs. Goulding was resplendent in a bonnet with a slightly battered peacock plume crowning its brim. "And aren't you proud of our Billy and his new position?"

She was indeed, and delighted to see how well he could walk on one crutch; he'd tossed the other away, he told her, and was getting around the barns perfectly well on only one. His bruises were beginning to fade and Phoebe thought he looked as lovely as before, the color of his eyes exactly that of his new, sky blue neckcloth. He seemed to have made some friends, too, particularly among the village girls.

Children darted about everywhere, bright-eyed and mischievous, daring each other to peek down the hallway where the actors and dancers were having their last rehearsals. A small gang of boys chased each other through the crowd. "Beggin' your pardon, Miss," one called as he careened against her legs and ran on. She saw David knit his brow and prepare to chastise the child. *Let him be,* she signaled him with a shrug. It was a holiday, and anyway, the boy was just about the size that Bryan would have been. Let him be and let him enjoy his day.

It took some time for everybody to find a seat at the tables. She sat at the very edge of one of the long benches, closest to where the players would be, with David at her side.

The maids and footmen began bringing out the roasts and pies, stews and stuffed geese. A general sigh of pleasure and anticipation arose, to be followed by vigorous eating, prodigious drinking, and contented murmurs and belches afterward. David told everyone at their end of the table about Miss Browne's pies and—not a bit horrified by the information—everyone complimented her upon the fine texture of the crust.

There had been toasts before dinner. They were repeated now, sometimes a bit more slowly and drunkenly but just as heartily. To the cook. To the earl. To the land. To the harvest, and speed-the-plow.

And finally to the players, who marched in now and made a little procession about the hall, accompanied by drums, horns, and the beating of kettles.

Phoebe was suddenly aware of a small shadow at her elbow. It was little Susan, who seemed to have forgotten where it was she'd been sitting. She'd wandered over to Phoebe's place, evidently enthralled by Phoebe's red shawl, its gold thread glittering in the candlelight. And now, Phoebe thought, she stood directly in the path the actors would have to traverse in order to finish up their parade.

"Move down a bit, please," Phoebe said to David, who stared with surprise as she reached out to the little girl, drew her to herself, and quickly lifted her onto the end of the bench.

Well, she thought sternly—as though someone had challenged her—*someone* had to take care of a child who'd wandered from her place. Susan's granny had probably been called back to the kitchen to deal with some minor mishap. It wouldn't do for the little girl to be trampled, would it?

"Now let's see what this play is all about," she whispered. Susan nodded with wide eyes as she watched the actors circle round to their end of the Great Hall.

Of course it was hardly Covent Garden or Drury Lane, Phoebe decided quickly enough. Still, the actors, dressed in top hats and smocks decorated with ribbons and other shreds of colored cloth, recited their rhymed couplets with a vigor and directness that made up for their lack of subtlety.

The announcer, Tom Fool, introduced each stock character: the Farmer, the Farmer's Man and his Lady (played by a young man who'd let his golden curly hair grow long for the occasion), a Recruiting Sergeant, Saint George, Old Dame Jane, Beelzebub, and—oddly, Phoebe thought—a quack Doctor. It was the Doctor who drew the most applause and the loudest catcalls; he was clearly a gifted actor, though in an ancient, naïve style that a London audience might have found a bit embarrassing.

He was also clearly the leader of the troupe: inspired by his aplomb, the rest of the actors threw themselves into their simple roles with added vivacity. Not that they had to worry about missing a line, for if one of them hesitated, the audience would supply the necessary words quickly enough. The audience supplied the stage directions, too, along with running commentary. Everyone yelled encouragement when Beelzebub and Dame Jane battled each other with frying pans and everyone booed when the Recruiting Sergeant marched the Farmer's Man off to the wars. Many people warned

Tom Fool not to threaten Saint George, and a few called "I told you so" when the Saint ran Tom through, leaving the golden-haired Lady desolate and despairing.

Serves her right, Phoebe thought, for being so fickle. After the Farmer's Man had been dragged off by the Recruiting Sergeant, the Lady had quickly given her heart to reckless Tom Fool, who now lay supine on the stone floor—though occasionally winking at the audience, who had begun to call for his resurrection.

"Don't worry," Susan whispered. "The Doctor will help."

He did, too, though only upon having exacted an enormous fee for his services, the Lady fairly staggering under the weight of the bag of coins she gave him. Still, here was Tom Fool, jumping to his feet and hugging and pinching his sweetheart. Cured, quite cured of everything, including death. No wonder the Doctor was the favorite character in this play, Phoebe thought—for an instant it had seemed to her that he *could* cure death.

For an instant it had seemed that way to everyone in the audience, she realized, though of course everybody knew better, especially those among them who'd lived the hardest, poorest lives. Perhaps because of their own experiences, they were grateful for the momentary illusion. And now, as the actors smiled and took their bows, the audience leaped to their feet, yelling and stamping their approval.

"He could help *you* not be sick anymore, too," Susan whispered, as Phoebe tried not to shudder.

But what was that?—a quick shadow, a rush of air as a candle blew out, a sudden slight change in the light . . . she'd suddenly become aware of a set of signs that were too subtle to be interpreted, but that somehow had caught her fencer's reflexes and signaled danger.

"Out of the way," she yelled, grabbing up Susan into

her arms and somehow managing to move a few crucial feet to the left—just before the chandelier that had been swaying above their heads came crashing down, right onto the bench where she and the little girl had been sitting.

There were screams, jostling, and absolute chaos for some minutes. Miraculously, no one was hurt in the brief melee that ensued and then died down, everybody becoming quite silent and serious as they began to realize what had happened.

"Everybody out of this hall," David yelled. "Go *now, right now!* We don't know if the rest of the chandeliers are safe."

The panicky hubbub started up again. Numbly, with the little girl still tightly clasped in her arms, Phoebe joined the crowd rushing toward the doors. David had reached her side. His face was white and his lips were pinched.

"My God, you could have been killed." His voice was harsh, awestruck. "You and Susan both. All that sharp, heavy iron, falling straight down atop your heads."

"It's . . . it's all right," she kept repeating in a toneless voice. "It's all right. No death. I've got her."

Gently, he attempted to pry Susan from her arms to give to her frantic grandmother. But Phoebe didn't seem quite able to let the little girl go. *What a sharp clean smell a child had,* she thought, *there was really nothing like it on earth.*

What was upsetting everyone so much anyway? she wondered. *Everything was all right, wasn't it? And why had they taken the child from her?*

There was a gap then, an emptiness, and a darkness.

Her reason and senses returned slowly over the next half hour. She found herself in a big armchair, at the fireside of the green bedchamber, with her dress unhooked and her stays loosened. She felt cold, though the fire was quite indisputably hot and she was swaddled in soft blankets. David was at her side, on a footstool. He held a mug of something to her lips. She took a sip; it was hot, spicy, and alcoholic.

"Phoebe?" he whispered.

"I . . . I think I'm a bit better," she said.

"You had me frightened, though. I think you were in some sort of shock."

"Yes, I think I was."

"You're a heroine, you know, saving the child's life like that. Not to speak of your own."

"I felt very strong for a moment. Strong and quick and invulnerable. I've had the feeling before, sometimes when I've been fencing. Even gambling."

"Yes, I know, it happens, sometimes, in the midst of a fight. I love the fighter in you, Phoebe."

He kissed her forehead. She took hold of his hand.

"I want to go to bed, David."

"Of course. You need your sleep. I'll finish undressing you."

"No, I mean I want to go to bed with you."

"Do you think that's wise?"

"No, probably not. But then, it wasn't very wise of Lord Linseley to follow Mr. Marston to Rowen-on-Close, was it?"

"I expect not."

"Or to offer his services when Marston announced he was in trouble?"

"No, but . . ."

She put his hand to her lips and kissed the palm. "Or to take Phizz home with him to Lincolnshire, giving their enemies in London plenty to gossip about, you know."

"You have a point."

She held his hand against her cheek.

"It wasn't an accident, David. Somebody wanted to kill us. If I hadn't brought Susan over to sit by me, the chandelier would have been suspended directly over me and you."

"I know. You saved us."

"Maybe the play saved us. The moment of exhilaration when that ridiculous Doctor makes everything all right. Maybe *that's* what gave me the eyes to see what was coming, and the energy to move away quickly enough."

He smiled at her and shrugged his shoulders.

"It's fading, David, that moment of exhilaration."

"I don't think it fades. It sinks in, rather."

"Perhaps. I don't know if I believe that. But while I can still remember how it felt, I want you inside me."

He tilted his head to the side. "You want what? Where?"

"Oh all right." She laughed. "I want your cock inside my cunt, if you insist upon a specific request. Deep inside, my lord. Yes, I'm sure of it."

He'd been extraordinarily gentle at first; she'd had to encourage him, to persuade him that she wouldn't break. She stroked the upward curve of his erection, caressing him with long, light, adoring fingers. He lengthened and hardened at her touch, and when she cupped his scrotum, she could feel it grow dense with seed.

He moved his hands up and down her body, watching her arch her back and stretch her limbs. He breathed sharply, touched her more deeply, and felt her open and soften under his caresses. Smiling, she bent her knees and tilted herself upward, moist and shining along the furrow between her legs. "Now," she whispered, "yes now, please."

His cock entered her easily, like a plow in rich, rain-soaked earth. She wrapped her legs around his waist. He rose to his knees and thrust from his hips. He lifted her, cradling and rocking her, sweetly and strongly, beyond will or consciousness or fear or regret. Until his thrusts became shorter, harder, deeper; until he had to let go, to pour, to spurt and spew, to spend himself within her while she still bucked and bounced and vaulted underneath him, still riding him, her legs tightly wrapped around his waist. They both cried out, their throaty, inchoate shouts of pleasure and release mingling in unembarrassed barnyard cacophony.

He allowed himself to fall on top of her then, his cock still buried deep, his semen seeped into her. In her mind, Phoebe saw the fields of Linseley Manor, winter wheat sprouting in the earth below its heavy blanket of snow. They lay for some time as she slowly let him go from between her legs. And when he drew himself out of her he did it so slowly that she cried out afterward—surprised to find herself emptied of him.

Empty and so soon to be alone.

But she wouldn't allow herself to weep, she told herself, stretching her body gently while he slumbered in her arms and the moon rose high in the sky. Taking extreme care not to disturb him, she gradually untangled herself from him and extricated herself from his grasp.

She didn't need to sleep. In the cold white flash of consciousness that seemed to be the consequence of the shock she'd suffered, she felt that she'd never sleep again. Crouching by the fireplace, she scribbled the letter that told him everything she couldn't say out loud. Her mouth had learned to shape the words for love-making, she thought sadly, but she still didn't know how to say good-bye.

Wraithlike, she walked quickly across the carpet to the dressing room. One of the portmanteaux was still strapped shut; she'd told Lissie not to bother with that one. She unstrapped it now: Marston's suit was a bit wrinkled, though his shirt and cravat remained reasonably fresh. She shrugged her shoulders: it wouldn't be Phizz's most elegant night.

In the unpredictable way of these things, though, her hair—Marston's hair—fell easily into place, its unaccustomed length seeming to lend itself to a dashing, Byronic look. She'd have to dye it immediately upon returning to London, though: there was a definite pale cast to it at the roots now.

She'd overdone the eyebrows a bit, but she left them alone. For if she didn't keep moving, she might never leave this place.

The French doors that led to the garden closed softly behind her. What a solid house this was, she thought: no telltale squeaking of hinges or creaking of floorboards to wake him and bring him running after her. Nothing to stop her in her flight, no one to throw his arms tightly around her, carry her back to bed, swear he'd never let her go.

Only silence. She walked quickly, noting that her limbs had taken on Marston's stride as soon as she'd slipped through the yew hedge and turned in the direction of the stables.

She could see from her shadow against a snowbank that her top hat was tilted at exactly the correct, fashionable angle.

Oberon knew her well now, and the moonlight was so bright that she was quickly able to saddle and bridle him. It might snow tomorrow or the next day, she thought—David had taught her some of the signs—but she'd be safe tonight. It would be a clear quick ride due east over the wolds to Lincoln, whose spires would soon become visible in the gray light preceding the dawn. And where Phizz Marston would be boarding the early morning coach to London.

She allowed herself one glance back over her shoulder. At the slumbering house, with its mellow stone and well-trimmed ivy, its stately architecture affectionately enfolded in the curve of the land. A sense of loss threatened to overwhelm her. Phoebe might have wept at this moment, she thought. But Phizz Marston never wept.

A gloved hand flicked the riding crop smartly at the big black horse's flank. A moonbeam briefly illumined a slice of white cravat, an angular plane of pale cheek, the curve of a cynical, downturned mouth.

Hooves thundered. The young man on the large black horse disappeared beyond the rise of a hill.

Chapter

22

Stupid, stupid. How *could* he have been so stupid? Stupid and callous, he added, grasping the pages of her letter while his face burned with shame. *And while we're at it, David, let's not forget crude and ill bred.* Because for the entirety of their week together—or so it seemed to him now—he'd done nothing but drop broad hints about how he wanted to make her pregnant. Perhaps the only way he *hadn't* announced it was to engage a crier to shout it out in the village square.

While she'd been agonizing about how to tell him the painful truth, he'd been mugging and grinning like an ape. Not to speak of capering like a goat and strutting like a turkey-cock. Of course he hadn't known what she'd been feeling—after all, he comforted himself, how *could* he have known?

But he might have noticed something, he thought now, if he hadn't been so intoxicated by the pleasures they'd shared. He might have discerned the hurt he was causing, if he hadn't been transfixed by thoughts of the fine new life they'd be embarking upon together. Or if he'd been able to cease congratulating himself ahead of time for rescuing her from Crashaw's vile threats.

Who could say what he might have understood if he'd been paying attention? If he hadn't been so overwhelmed by her beauty and thrilled by her desire for him. Or so absurdly gratified by the potency and frequency of his own performances.

But he hadn't known, seen, understood, discerned, or divined a blessed thing. Her letter had come as a total surprise. An absolute embarrassment. As difficult for him to read as it must have been for her to write.

You see (she'd written), *I can't have children. It was a terrible blow to me when the doctor told me this after the accident. It's why I became Phizz Marston—if I couldn't have a woman's greatest happiness, I told myself, I would bloody well enjoy a man's privileges and prerogatives.*

But now I wonder if I was correct to assume that children are a woman's greatest happiness. Loving you has made me wonder. This week has been the happiest I've ever spent.

And at the same time, I've learned how important children can be to a man—a certain sort of man, anyway. I've seen how deeply you wanted us to have them. Every word, every gesture of yours (he shuddered) *has proclaimed it.*

Well, you should have them. We should have them. But we won't. Because I can't.

I should have told you all this in my own voice, but I couldn't. I was too cowardly. I've adored being with you at Linseley Manor, but everything I've seen and touched here has seemed to reproach me for my sterility.

I still want you, David. But I want us to be to-

gether in London, not Lincolnshire. I can't remain at Linseley Manor any longer.

I shall love you forever, but I shall understand if you decide that I'm not what you want after all. I'm certainly not what you thought—somehow you keep discovering one or another scandalous truth about me, don't you?

She'd signed it with a *P*. The initial made him sad and even a little angry, for it clearly indicated Phizz as well as Phoebe. In fact—her letter had spelled this out on its last page—she did intend to become Phizz again. What she wanted, though, was for Phizz to have a secret lover—one who'd come down from the country for occasional trysts, brief sweet erotic interludes, during which she'd unknot her neck cloth and drop her mask for a precious hour or day at a time.

He thought of her in her slim trousers, high cravat, and veiled, ambiguous smile. Very elegant and very arousing; any number of London gentlemen would agree with him there. She was offering him something those gentlemen would probably kill for—a crack at the real, naked Marston.

No, he howled. No, he didn't want her that way.

Yes, he whispered. He wanted her any way she'd allow.

Absurd. This wasn't a dalliance he was considering. There was real substance between the two of them: they *loved* each other, dammit. One couldn't, one *shouldn't* limit it to what she was proposing. It would be a sort of blasphemy, he thought, to reduce what they'd had together to a series of provocative intrigues. He didn't want an affair. He wanted a *life* together.

Even if that life together didn't include children? *Be honest, David. Your dearest hopes have been dashed. Will you be able to give that up?*

* * *

He sent Mr. Dickerson to retrieve the horse. Phoebe had written that she'd stable it in Lincoln near the inn where she intended to pick up the London coach.

He wanted to follow her himself; certainly his own fast carriage could catch up with a lumbering public coach. He imagined himself heading them off, highwayman-style. In his mind's eye he'd throw open the coach door, pluck her from her seat, and carry her off.

"Come home with me. Now. I love you. It doesn't matter . . ."

Did it really not matter?

The truth was that it *did* matter. He didn't love her a whit less but—*be honest, David*—he *had* cherished the image of her with his child in her arms. He'd delighted in fancies of his seed taking root within her after he'd plowed the earth of her body.

For a moment he thought he could almost feel what she'd suffered—the pain of knowing she was going to disappoint him.

And for the next moment he could only taste the bitterness of his own disappointment.

Perhaps—there was a measure of shame in admitting this to himself—perhaps it was just as well that he *couldn't* follow her today.

Well, of course he couldn't, he reminded himself. Murder had been attempted yesterday in the Great Hall of Linseley Manor. The earl's guests had been threatened; his people had been threatened. And *he* had been threatened himself. The Earl of Linseley couldn't leave at a time like this. He had to stay and investigate. To find the culprit and bring him to justice. The Earl of Linseley was obliged to make things right with the land and the people before he could think of himself.

He summoned Mr. Neville and a few very agile young men to help him. Together they inspected the chandeliers, each in its turn. The thirty-seven iron hoops that still hung from the ceilings were solidly in place, suspended from strong chains and sturdy hooks. Their very stability made the single fallen chandelier look even more ominous and malevolent.

"But here's yer culprit, my lord." A sharp-eyed young fellow had retrieved something from under a bench. A chain link that *looked* like all the others—for it was painted a dark, rusty gray-brown—but wasn't at all like the others. For instead of iron, it was made of thin, soft copper, which had bent and opened, melted by several hours of the heat from the candles. A brief search yielded several of its fellows. While the crew of chandelier-cleaners had been busily scraping away at a century of tallow, someone among them had substituted these weak links.

"Clever," David muttered. "Well planned." The culprit would be miles away by now.

"Do you know the names of the men in the gang, Mr. Neville?" he asked.

Well, not all of them, the steward admitted. Of course most of them were local lads. The chief of the gang, Jeremy Paternoster, had played the Farmer's Lady in the entertainment. It was he who would have hired any outsiders. Perhaps *he* might know.

But Paternoster—his blond locks closely trimmed now and a handsome new beard starting up—didn't know. There *had* been a few outsiders, he said, but he'd been so intent upon rehearsing for his part in the play . . .

Well, wait a minute now, my lord. For Jeremy did remember something after all. Yes, there'd been a tall fellow, with a London accent . . . London with a strong undertone of Derbyshire. The man had mentioned that he'd had enough of the city; he'd been making his way home when he'd run out of money. Well, of course Jeremy had wanted to help him get home. His name?

Hmmm, let's see. William Smith? William Jones? William Byrd, perhaps. Anyway, something like that, my lord.

The stranger had been good with his hands. Had a good reach, too, and some skill with metals, so he'd been set among the men patching the chains. He could easily have been the culprit, Jeremy thought.

No, my lord, he answered David's next breathless question. Jeremy hadn't seen Smith-or-Jones around here since he'd paid the fellow. Said he wanted to get home for his own local village's Plough Play, you see, though of course it would be small beer compared to how we do it.

"And we hadn't thought of looking for suspicious characters who'd been here *before* Plough Monday, had we, Mr. Neville?" David scowled and Mr. Neville agreed sorrowfully.

"He's given us the slip," David concluded. "We *could* send someone to sniff out every Smith, Jones, and Byrd in Derbyshire, but I rather think that's what the blackguard wants us to do—he and whoever has engaged him to do this mischief. I rather suspect that our Smith-or-Jones is back with his employer. He'd probably lain low somewhere, waiting for the chandelier to fall. But when he learned that we'd survived, he needed to relay the news to whoever had wanted the deed done in the first place."

To Crashaw? Had Smith-or-Jones been waiting at some inn to relay his progress to Crashaw?

David smiled grimly, taking some small consolation in imagining Crashaw's anger and chagrin upon learning that his plot had failed. The gentleman would be off his game tomorrow, David thought, when he came to visit. And with any luck David would be able to learn the truth from him.

But could Crashaw really be so evil? David pondered the possibilities as he took his lonely cold supper in the echoing dining room. He and Phoebe had certainly picked an unsavory suspect: a man who cared more for money than he did for the common well-being, and who valued a club membership above the humanity of the boys who serviced his erratic lusts. An unsavory specimen certainly, a vile and vicious man absolutely. But a murderer?

Somewhere within himself, he felt a stirring of doubt. There were plenty of men like Crashaw and they surely weren't all murderers. Quickly, he suppressed this inconvenient thought.

Somehow, the man would expose his character and motivations. If not, David would simply have to beat it out of him, which would hardly be difficult. What would be difficult was restraining himself from using his fists.

He briefly allowed himself to imagine what would have happened if Phoebe hadn't been so quick, so preternaturally aware of the chandelier lurching downward toward her. He imagined her body crushed and broken, her long white neck torn and bloodied by heavy, rusted iron.

He put his napkin to his mouth and pushed his plate away while he endeavored to stifle the retching at his throat. He swallowed back the bile, but he couldn't stop his head from swimming. Resting it in his hands, he pressed his palms against his closed eyelids until he could erase the hideous vision from his inner eye.

The black emptiness that followed was almost worse. For the first time, he tried to imagine living the rest of his life without her.

He sat that way for some time until a footman nudged him timidly, thinking that he might have fallen asleep over his ale.

"Thank you, Harper," he heard himself say. "No, it's all right, I'm not asleep, thanks. Not quite yet. But I think I'll finish the ale in front of the fireplace in my bedchamber. Yes, and a good night to you too."

I'm all right, he told himself as he settled into his armchair, as long as I don't imagine her being hurt or killed.

Better to concentrate on Crashaw, to plan for his visit tomorrow.

Better to assume that he was indeed the culprit, and had contrived this fiendishly clever and coherent plan.

First, contrive to cause an accident that would kill both Linseley and Marston—or the troublesome young lady who wore Marston's trousers.

Then arrive innocently in Lincolnshire just in time for the funerals.

And *finally,* take advantage of the situation to get control of all the lands he wanted.

Who would suspect? Crashaw would exhibit shock, surprise, even a measure of grief for a noble parliamentarian struck down in his prime. He'd be properly sympathetic about the loss of Miss Browne as well—such a shame, and was it really true that so little was known about her? How perfectly dreadful.

But perhaps, he'd suggest delicately, there might be a way that he could be of service at this tragic juncture. Because inheriting the whole of the estate without preparation might be more than the ninth earl of Linseley was ready for. The young gentleman, grief-stricken over the sudden death of his father, might prefer it if someone took a few fields off his hands and injected some always-needed cash into the running of the estate. David grimaced: more than a few fields, probably. Crashaw would exploit Alec's grief and inexperience as fully as possible.

How dare he take advantage of David's beloved son like that?

If he dared at all. David shrugged and tossed back the rest of the ale. Amazing how one could be carried away on the wings of fancy. He didn't usually think of himself as an imaginative sort; but if he didn't watch himself he'd be spouting verses next. For this entire intricate hypothesis was nothing more than rank speculation—a story he himself had woven out of whole cloth in order to try to convince himself he knew who had tried to kill Phoebe.

Love and suspicion had turned him into a sort of poet, and a rather bad one at that. He grinned. He and Phoebe weren't dead; Alec hadn't accepted money for the fields. And Crashaw hadn't yet proved himself to be the culprit. Only the prime suspect.

But I'll find out tomorrow, he promised himself. The constable would be waiting in the next room while he spoke to Crashaw and got the truth out of that unsavory gentleman.

And then—*whatever* the truth might be—he'd head straight for London and demand that Phoebe come home with him. Just exactly as she was.

He didn't need more children. He already had a perfectly good son just entering manhood—a son who might, in fact, stand to receive a little guidance from his father at this trying and critical time in his life.

And if Alec needed David, David absolutely needed Phoebe. He needed her exactly as she was.

And if she refused to come home with him?

He yawned. Enough hypothesizing for one night.

He stretched his arms and stood up from his armchair. He needed his sleep. Or at least some rest. For he doubted that he'd be able to sleep without her in his arms.

The moon was just past full and very bright. He kept

the curtain open so that he could look at it. He finally drifted to sleep by forcing himself to imagine her staring up at the same moon, as it sailed through the swiftly moving clouds.

In his imagination, her face was white and drawn.

I'm coming, Phoebe, he tried to call to her over the wolds that separated them. *Forgive me. I love you.*

He'd imagined her quite accurately: she *was* staring up at the same moon, from her room at the inn where the London coach passengers were staying the night. An inn at Stamford, but not the Swan.

A far inferior hostelry, she'd adjudged it, much as Marston would have done. The bed was lumpy and the sheets clumsily darned. Thank heaven, she thought. She was grateful to be staying anywhere but the Swan.

Her face *was* white and drawn. Perhaps with the day-long effort of keeping up those unaccustomed masculine gestures and expressions. Perhaps it was because she hadn't slept the night before. Or because she had discovered how much she disliked sleeping alone.

In truth, she thought, she was furious at herself for having stared out of the coach window all day, imagining his carriage in pursuit of them, imagining . . . but she'd have to cease these stupid imaginings immediately.

She knew that he couldn't have come even if he'd wanted to. There was, after all, the little matter of an attempted murder to investigate. Not to speak of Lord Crashaw's visit tomorrow.

But he probably didn't want to anyway. He had probably spent the day wrestling with his anger and disappointment. She'd always known that she shouldn't have kept that secret from him. Well, now he knew. And by now he'd probably given her up.

She could hear a sharp wind somewhere. She wondered if their coach would get to London before the snow blew in.

But the sharp wind's howl was all that she could hear.

Grimly, she forced herself to sleep. Tomorrow, she promised herself, I'll wake up as Marston and I'll bloody well take up where I left off. It's over, dammit. And it was only a dream anyway. Tomorrow I'll believe that. Tomorrow, I'll wake up from my wonderful dream.

Chapter 23

"Lord Crashaw," Harper announced at precisely two minutes after eleven the next morning, ushering the gentleman into the library.

Well, he's prompt anyway, David thought. Prompt, carrying his legal papers in a portfolio, and wearing a not-unpleasant look on his face—modest, not too ingratiating. Soberly dressed, too, in a well-tailored jacket that minimized his paunch. Even his boots didn't look too bad this morning, the spurs glittering as well.

Crashaw shook hands, took the chair David offered him, and refused a cup of coffee. He'd take as little of Lord Linseley's time as possible with business matters, he said; a pity to have to deal with them at all, so soon after that nasty accident with the fallen chandelier. Shocking, shocking. Why, someone could have been killed.

He'd been glad to hear that no one *had* been killed, though. Well, *that* was the important thing, of course.

David nodded darkly. *The gall of the man, to bring it up like that.* So casually. So . . . innocently. As though they both didn't know who'd caused the mischief.

"It wasn't an accident," he replied. "But of course you know that."

"I beg your pardon, Lord Linseley," Crashaw said. "I *didn't* know that. No one told me. How dreadful."

He's a good actor, David thought, *and he doesn't seem at all discomfited by our survival.*

"Ah yes, how silly of me," he replied, trying to mask his anger with sarcasm. "You know *nothing* about it. Other than what you've *heard,* of course."

Crashaw nodded, clearly a bit befuddled but otherwise unscathed by the blunt barrage of irony directed at him. "Right. All I know is what everyone in the street is saying. Well, people are curious, Linseley. Chandeliers don't fall down every day, you know, and people *will* chatter."

A surprisingly *good actor. Quite unforthcoming. Not at all like Bunbury or Smythe-Cochrane.* Of course, what had inspired those gentlemen to reveal themselves had been the opportunity to talk about Marston. David decided to try that.

"I had a guest with me, you know," he said.

Crashaw's cheeks reddened a bit.

Now we're getting somewhere.

"Really, Lord Linseley? But I'd heard *he'd* gone on to Scotland, though none of my informants knew his exact whereabouts after he'd left Stamford . . ."

"You have informants, do you?"

Crashaw shifted his bulk in his chair. "Well, he's so awfully elusive, you know."

"So you admit that you spied on Mr. Marston."

"It's not something I tell everyone, Linseley." Lord Crashaw's jowls trembled. "But I thought *you* would understand."

"*I* would understand!"

"Well, we're rather birds of a feather, aren't we?"

"Ah yes, enemies of Marston and all that."

Crashaw raised his eyebrows.

Time to deliver the body blow, David thought. "We *do* have something in common, sir, but . . ." he said. He paused, to put his opponent off his guard. "*I* hadn't been planning to murder Phizz Marston," he concluded. *Well delivered,* he congratulated himself.

Or perhaps the blow hadn't been so well delivered after all. Perhaps it had missed its mark entirely. For David's guest had burst into hearty laughter.

"Come, come, Linseley, no need for conundrums. You're in your own house now, and anyway your secret's quite safe with me."

"M-my *secret?*"

Crashaw seemed to have entirely recovered his self-possession. David remembered, rather ruefully, that when challenged, his parliamentary opponent enjoyed the opportunity to deliver a full rebuttal. Crashaw launched into his exposition with relish.

"Well, you're quite obviously besotted with Marston, and he with you as well. No hard feelings, old man. It's not so surprising when one thinks about it: after all, you're one of those rugged, handsome sorts. Vigorous, not at all nancy on the outside: you're the type no one suspects, but who manages to do quite well with the young gentlemen.

"And of course you're young, rich, got that title that goes back to the Stone Age—I shouldn't have expected Marston to enjoy that 'noble, traditional old England' stuff you prattle on about, but one never knows, does one?"

David decided to ignore these compliments, such as they were. "But *you* were at Vivien's. *You* saw me try to throttle him."

"Yes, quite the public exhibition you two put on. I

expect you fooled a good many of the crowd in attendance, at least those who didn't have the eyes to see . . .

"Well, of course you probably have some stiff old relatives who'd die of apoplexy if they knew. Don't worry, man. I understand completely; I'll never breathe a word."

"Th-thanks," David found himself saying.

"You *did* put on a good show," Crashaw assured him. "Very few people credit Dr. Riggs's gossip, even if he *did* find you there in the middle of the night. *Linseley's simply not the sort,* is what people instinctively think—though they *do* wonder why you two went off together the next morning. Of course, it was all quite clear to me, but then, I've been nursing my secret passion for Marston for so long that I feel myself rather an authority on our young gentleman."

David blinked. "People are *talking* about . . . me and Marston?"

Crashaw shrugged. "Not many people. As I said . . . it takes a constant observer, a devotee, if you will, like myself . . ."

David collected himself. There would be time later to worry about what people might be saying. Right now he needed to untangle the nonsense Crashaw was spouting at him. Not that the man wasn't expressing himself clearly. On the contrary. But it was always difficult, he reflected, to credit something quite opposite from what was expected.

"And this . . . this . . . *passion* of yours, sir?"

Crashaw looked away. "I'd have thought you'd be able to tell, somehow. Instinctively, you know, just as I'd recognized the truth about you. A bit embarrassing to have to spell it out, but since you will insist . . . I'm in love with him. Have been for years, I expect. Oh, don't worry. I wouldn't burden Marston with my attentions; I've never approached him and I never shall. I can't even imagine touching him."

He paused for a moment before continuing. "Well, *that's* a lie, of course. I've imagined any number of things. But you know what I mean: he's a sort of cherished dream to me. An ideal, I suppose one might say. And anyway, he'd never *look* at an old walrus like me."

A cherished dream. An ideal. Crashaw had so idealized Marston, David thought, that he'd rather neglected one important dimension of reality.

"You've never sent him any sort of note, then?" he asked.

"Oh, I've *written* a great deal of romantic twaddle to him. But always tossed it in the fire, you know."

"Yes, I should imagine. And you weren't angry when you were blackballed from White's?"

"Embarrassed, rather. Yes, the story made its way back to me. I do know it was Marston who turned the vote the way it went, and I'm glad you know about it too. Well, it's why I came to see you, after all."

David supposed he must be being very dense. But he needed to be clear about a thing or two.

"And so it wasn't you who hired a Mr. Byrd to set the chandelier crashing down upon us?"

Lord Crashaw allowed himself to take umbrage at that. As well he might, David thought.

"Really, Linseley. That last question was rather out of bounds . . ."

"Sorry, but I had to know."

"I'm not a murderer, sir."

"No, of course you're not. I heartily apologize."

"Not even in passion. *Of course* I'm madly envious of you, well, what would you expect, dammit? But envy doesn't imply murder, after all . . ."

For the first time, David looked closely at his guest.

He still didn't like what he saw: a crude, selfish gentleman willing to sell England's soul in order to subsidize his own under-funded estates. But he felt a surprising measure of sympathy as well. Crude or not, the man had loved and suffered, burdened with a passion that would never be requited—for all the reasons Crashaw would have expected, and for those he'd never know.

At least, David thought, he'll never know the truth about Marston if *I* have anything to say about it. Let him keep his ideal, he thought. Well, wasn't that what Marston really was? Nothing more than an ideal, an illusion.

Let Crashaw have his illusion, David told himself, surprising himself even further by his sudden protectiveness toward a man who envied him so deeply—for all the wrong reasons. Or perhaps for the right reasons, just turned topsy-turvy. He peered curiously at the man in the armchair opposite his own: it felt rather like examining one's reflection in a warped, tarnished old mirror.

Unfortunately, he still had not an inkling of what Lord Crashaw wanted from *him*. Just as well; he was going to embarrass his guest if he continued gaping at him.

He roused himself, affecting a businesslike demeanor.

"Perhaps, Lord Crashaw, we should proceed to the matter you came to transact."

Crashaw relaxed.

"Still," he said briskly, "I should have had to explain a good deal of this in any case. I contacted you because I thought you could influence Marston on my behalf. And in return, I'm quite willing to pay a good price for whatever bad pieces of property you might want to fob off on me."

"Influence him on your . . . behalf?"

"Well, not regarding . . . matters of the heart, of course. I simply mean that, if I were to reapply for membership in White's, could Mr. Marston be prevailed upon to vote for me this time?"

"You see," Crashaw added quickly, "my boots are quite presentable now."

His boots. The poor man still thought this was about his boots.

David took a deep breath. There were so many truths, whole and partial, woven into the gauzy web of desire that Crashaw cherished. How to pick and choose? Which of those truths could safely be revealed and which of them must, at all costs, remain hidden?

Crashaw was becoming impatient. "I can pay very well. My investments have done wondrously since the Enclosure Act passed."

Ah yes, and there was that, *as well.*

"You've lost on that one, Linseley. And you'll continue to lose. England's common lands *will* be enclosed, will be developed, and in time will turn a handsome profit. The country will be modernized. Industrialized. No matter if a few headstrong, sentimental traditionalists like yourself resist it."

David could feel his hands balling themselves into fists. "I shall continue to fight you, every step of the way."

Crashaw laughed happily. "Indeed you shall. We need you, after all—you and your yeomen happily tilling your soil in East Anglian Eden out here in the middle of nowhere. A man like you makes such a splendid, chivalrous, knightly sort of . . . of *image* for England, don't you know. Helps us keep up appearances, makes us look less like those money-loving Yanks across the ocean. Oh yes, man, fight your fight by all means—while grubbier, less noble-spirited types like myself turn our shoulders to the wheel of history, enclosing fields and building factories."

David could feel his muscles straining. If not to break the jawbone that must lie somewhere beneath those quivering jowls, then at least to shoulder the man out the room and kick him out of his house.

His head ached. How could everything have gotten muddled together like this? Style and substance, illusion and reality, desire and self-regard. While the common welfare—such a simple, decent concept—became trampled under the boots of selfishness, blackened by the soot of industrial progress.

Still, he thought, there was one decent card left to play. One so obvious that even a bad gambler could see it there at the bottom of the deck.

"I *could* prevail upon Phizz to help you . . ." he murmured the words thoughtfully, allowing his mouth to shape the name *Phizz* as sensuously as it might say *Phoebe.*

Crashaw maintained his equanimity, though his voice had lowered to a jealous growl. "Need the money, do you?"

"A farmer always needs money. Yes, and I've also been thinking of adding a new classroom to the village school. If we did that, the children could spend another year there; well, that's the sort of progress *I* prefer. So I shall have to sell you a rather smaller plot of land than I originally offered. Of course, this one needs drainage too, not that *you'd* see that . . ."

"Get to the point, Linseley."

"Gently, gently, Crashaw. Allow me to have my sentimental, knightly, leisurely way with it, won't you? You see, there will be an additional term to our bargain."

"Eh?"

"You shall have to promise faithfully not to inflict physical pain upon your . . . ah, partners. Unless you're able to find one who's willing—one who enjoys it as much as you do, you know. Otherwise just let your boys give your boots a good polish. I see you've already given up on Drumblestone's. That's a good start. Leave off the spurs, though, will you? Phizz finds them absurd on a man who never sits a horse. But most important of all is a lighter hand with the riding crop."

Actually, Phoebe had never expressed an opinion on men wearing spurs even if they didn't ride; *that* particular modish affectation was David's own bête noire. But why not slip it in, he thought: Crashaw's look of chagrin when he'd mentioned it had made it worth the effort.

And it had made the business about the riding crop easier for him to say without blushing. Awful business, knowing about a man's secret pleasures. Still, one *shouldn't* impose one's tastes on anyone else, especially on those like Billy, who lacked the power to refuse. Pleasure should be a matter of choice for everyone, though Crashaw was obviously having some difficulty accepting this lesson.

"Ah. So it wasn't the boot polish after all."

"Not the boot polish really, no. Though, as you can see, he had informants set on you, the boot-polishers, shall we say, the boys who are the recipients of your other favors."

"I shouldn't have thought he'd care how a gentleman took his sport."

"He's an unusual . . . personage once you get to know him. Believes in fair play, respect—chivalrous notions like that."

"Hmmpf. And if I agree to lighten up a bit?"

"Of course, I can't promise anything. Well, it's not as though he were answerable to my will. He's not m-my *wife,* after all. A gentleman makes his own decisions.

But I think he'll come round in the end. At least I *hope* so."

"Leads you a merry chase, does he?"

"Yes, rather."

"Just as well for me, perhaps, that I continue to cherish him as an ideal, rather than a reality."

"Perhaps."

They finished their business quickly, for Crashaw wanted to try to get back to London before the next storm blew in. The final signatures would be affixed after Marston recommended that Crashaw be reconsidered for membership in White's.

They shook hands on it, rather stiffly, and then David rang for Harper to see his guest out. And after that, he added, do bring in the mail, will you, Harper? Not that he really expected to hear from her yet. But one never knew. David didn't like to think about how often he'd been proven wrong in the past few days. At this point he was ready to be surprised by all events.

But there was no letter from Phoebe. And no surprises in the letter from Admiral Wolfe. Only a communication that Lady Kate didn't believe Crashaw was the culprit; she was sure it was someone who wished ill to Phoebe, rather than Phizz. Wolfe had recorded this speculation with some embarrassment—woman's intuition, what was one to do?—and then had added that for *his* part he heartily hoped that it *was* Crashaw and that they'd straightened everything out by now.

Thank you, Wolfe, David murmured, *for the hearty, manly, entirely useless expression of support.* And thank *you,* Lady Kate, for the womanly intuition, which, though probably true, wasn't a great deal more useful at this moment. His head ached. He poured himself a cup of coffee from the silver service at his elbow and stared into the fire.

His mind began to wander. Still, it was good to have friends who were at least trying to help. And it was good that they were so manifestly happy together. He remembered the spark of recognition that had passed between Wolfe and Lady Kate when he'd introduced them . . . Almack's . . . New Years Eve . . .

Pleasant images flickered before his eyes . . . the admiral twirling Lady Kate about the floor as though he'd been waltzing all his life . . . And before that, when he'd first entered the ballroom . . .

For a moment he allowed himself to savor the memory of Phoebe and Lady Kate waltzing together. Everyone—himself especially—had watched them with rapt delight.

But he remembered something else now. For—responsible as always—he hadn't allowed himself to watch them with as full attention as he would have wished because he'd also been scanning the crowd for possible enemies. And in fact he had noticed something rather odd—a discordant note, though he'd dismissed it at the time. It still seemed hard to credit, but perhaps it deserved a bit of investigation.

This time, however, he'd make no assumptions. This time he would base no hopes upon unfounded theories. He wouldn't even share his suspicions. Not until he got to London.

He scrawled a note to Phoebe. By God, they were running through paper and ink as though they were the protagonists of some sentimental novel from the prior century—those boring wordy ones done all in correspondence. Still, it was important to send a warning. The mail coach would arrive in London before he did, for he'd need to sleep from time to time along his journey. He'd catch a bit of a nap when he had to stop to change horses: at Coleby, perhaps, or Navenby—no, he'd try to make it all the way to Welbourn tonight if he could.

He wasn't absolutely confident that the incipient blizzard would allow either him or the mail coach to get all the way to London—or even to Welbourn, for that matter. But he wouldn't think of those eventualities. His letters *would* reach the people he loved in London. And so, a day later, would he.

He needed to inform Phoebe that Crashaw wasn't the culprit and that the enemy was still at large. He implored her to be careful, and—because he didn't have time to think how to phrase it more elegantly—he told her the barest truth he knew, which was that he loved her more than his life and that nothing else mattered in the slightest.

Upon reflection, he decided that he couldn't be absolutely sure that Phoebe *would* be careful. So he wrote another letter, to Wolfe this time, beseeching him to keep watch over her.

He had Croft lay out his warmest clothes, and ignoring his stableman's warnings, demanded that Lucifer be saddled, bridled, fed, and watered for a long trip. He asked Mrs. Yonge to pack as much food as he could carry: plenty of sliced cold goose and beef from the banquet, cheese, apples, and one of Phoebe's pies. He filled his flask with brandy, the same brandy he and she had drunk some of the times they'd made love. He stopped what he was doing for a moment; no point trying to suppress the delightful ache, the hardening and tightening, he felt every time he thought of their lovemaking. He let it pass over him like a warm ocean wave. Another wave of emotion followed: this time an icy one. Fear. *She was in danger and he was too far away to help her.*

He stood his ground, refusing to let himself drown. *He was coming. She'd be safe.*

The sky was a cold, turbulent gray. A few flakes of snow were beginning to fall already. He needed to start immediately if he was to get to London at all. He swung himself into his saddle and was on his way.

Chapter

24

London, five days later

Having returned to Town with no warning, Phizz Marston had decided to stay with Mr. Andrewes until Mr. Simms could reassemble his household staff and properly reopen the house in Brunswick Square. He didn't mind; it entertained him to accept his tailor's hospitality. Mr. and Mrs. Andrewes were open-hearted, grateful people; after all, Mr. Andrewes owed his startling latter-day prosperity to Phizz Marston's patronage. Mr. Simms was staying there too. Everyone was pleasant, and no one asked too many questions about the sojourn in Lincolnshire.

Anyway, it was a good way to refresh his wardrobe. And to practice wearing it again. A new suit of clothing awaited him at Mr. Andrewes's shop in Regent Street—he'd completely forgotten that he'd ordered it.

He quite liked the look of the jacket, though: it was something new, the sleeves a bit puffed at the top, *en gigot* was the term for it, Mr. Andrewes had told him. It had taken some craft, the tailor added, to make the sleeves and shoulders meet in a sober, harmonious line. Marston admired the subtly curved side seams and the neat darts at the back; he nodded appreciatively as Mr. Andrewes pointed out how perfectly flat the collar lay—the result of much laborious rolling, steaming, and pressing.

"Well done," Phizz said, gazing into the fitting room's three-sided mirror. "And it also gives me a bit more breadth of shoulder, without the need for additional padding."

"In truth, sir"—Mr. Andrewes never could help grinning when he had to call Phoebe *"Sir"*—*"your* particular deficiencies of physique are easier to correct than a lot of what I put up with from my other clients. 'Your waist's too wide for this dandified style, my lord, and your belly's too tubby' I tell 'em. 'Go home, and don't come back until you're wearing a decent corset.' "

"I take your point." Marston smiled. "Well, what's needed is a strong diagonal line—from broad shoulder to narrow waist—for a gentleman to wear a tight, high-waisted coat correctly. One sees that diagonal on the marvelous statues they're carting back from Greece, don't you know. I shouldn't wonder if half the attendees at the sculpture exhibitions aren't makers of gentleman's corsets, looking for a perfect torso as a model."

Of course, one wouldn't have to look at sculpture if one had already learned the lineaments of the perfect male torso. From putting one's arms around it, kissing one's way along the ridges of muscle . . .

Stop it, Phoebe! Remember, *that* was only a dream.

Marston turned to Mr. Andrewes. "Now about this waistcoat I ordered. I don't usually wear color, you know, except perhaps a dull snuff hue once in a while. This gray violet I chose, though . . . I must have been uncharacteristically giddy—perhaps it was during the New Year holiday. Mr. Andrewes, do you really think . . ."

The tailor insisted that the subdued violet was a splendid choice. Colors were coming back into style for gentlemen. Of course, black would never be incorrect—not to imply that Mr. Marston need follow anyone's dictates as to matters of fashion correctness. But this gray violet, now—if Mr. Andrewes might be permitted an opinion—well after all, it was hardly a frivolous color, and it made a very striking effect against the young gentleman's ivory pallor and lustrous dark hair.

Newly dyed dark hair. Marston glanced in the mirror with satisfaction. A good job, that.

And besides, Mr. Andrewes added, the unaccustomed color was rather a novelty. A bit of a conversation piece. He wouldn't suggest it for gloves or a cravat, of course . . .

Phizz Marston shuddered delicately at the notion of violet gloves.

But for a waistcoat, Mr. Andrewes concluded triumphantly, this particular color was quite acceptable, and even a bit of a welcome change.

Marston nodded, mind made up at last. "Of course you're right, Mr. Andrewes; you're always right on such matters, heaven knows why I argue with you, though I probably shall continue to do so into perpetuity."

He peered into the mirror for a last time—as much to adjust the cynical expression on his face as to certify the waistcoat's propriety.

And then, Mr. Andrewes added, there was the fact that Mr. Marston was looking so well; his winter vacation had done him a great deal of good.

Mr. Marston shrugged his perfectly tailored shoulders. He supposed it must have been the clean country air that had set him up, he replied languidly. Or the boredom, he added: all that sleep one got in the country, don't you know; well, sleeping is the most interesting amusement to be had at a country house party.

"Yes, I think the waistcoat will do very well after all. For conversation value alone, the new color is worth whatever it is you're charging me. No, don't tell me. I prefer to fortify myself with half a bottle of champagne before opening a bill from your establishment."

"I shall wear it now—well, why not? My first night out, you know—White's and then Vivien's. But first I must pay my belated respects to Lady Kate Beverredge—I'm due there directly.

"Good afternoon, Mr. Andrewes. Yes, I shall be home quite late. I've got a key, though, so please tell Mrs. Andrewes not to worry, won't you?"

He put on his top hat, allowed the tailor to help him on with his heavy winter greatcoat, and sailed out into Regent Street, drawing on fur-lined gloves.

At White's, the new violet waistcoat would constitute an event of first rank. Marston yawned, politely covering his mouth with a dove-gray glove. The thought of wreaking consternation by means of a waistcoat constituted proof—if proof were needed—of exactly how uneventful the day-to-day life of the Polite World really was.

Every dandy would have to decide whether he wanted a colored waistcoat for himself. Well, it would distract attention, anyway, from the inevitable inquiries about where Phizz had been these two weeks.

Not that he wasn't prepared for such inquiries. He'd rehearsed his selection of uninformative and entertaining *bon mots* in front of the mirror this morning until he was perfect. He'd befuddle and amuse everyone he met tonight—as coldly and skillfully as he'd ever done. He'd end the evening at Vivien's, where he'd make a nice pile at the gaming tables.

The only person it might not be so easy to talk his way around was Lady Kate. A bother, he thought, to have agreed to go visit her today. He wasn't sure he was ready for her keen-eyed concern. But perhaps it was best to get it over with.

Nodding to acquaintances, he trod lightly upon the wooden walkways that had been erected over the streets of the West End, at least those parts of it whose pedestrians were deemed too good to muddy their feet. It would have been more than he could bear, he thought, to ruin his boots in the particularly disgusting yellowish muck clogging the gutters since all that snow had blown in from the north. The walkways were a bit slippery. He was glad of the skinny little sweeps pushing with their brooms against the ice that gathered so perilously in the lengthening afternoon shadows.

He gave out pennies, noting, as he did, that none of these children were wearing gloves against the cold. One of them, perhaps a bit less starved than his fellows, smiled up at him in thanks. He almost returned the smile, but thought better of it. Better to keep his attention on the slippery walkway. It was difficult enough simply to maintain one's balance.

Tilting his hat brim a bit further forward against the chilly wind, he hurried westward to Park Lane.

How terribly unhappy she looks, Kate thought, as her footman ushered Mr. Marston into the salon.

But it's not from lack of physical attention, she thought. She felt her cheeks flush slightly. She wasn't at all sure how she could discern this, but in the past few weeks Kate had learned something about how a woman looked when certain desires had been satisfied.

Phoebe's physical needs had been quite well taken care of. This was something worse.

They chatted about inconsequential things while Lady Kate gave Mr. Marston his tea.

"And now," Kate murmured to her footman, "will

you leave us for a while, Matthews? I shall ring when I need you."

The footman bowed and shut the double doors behind him.

Kate's eyes were soft. "The roads are so bad, you know, that the mail coaches cannot get through from the north. It's rumored that one of the coaches turned over on the highway."

Her guest returned a brittle laugh. "I returned just in time then. Lord Crashaw is probably stuck in that dull Lincolnshire backwater until spring. Serves him right."

"If it is indeed he who's been causing all the consternation."

"Of *course* it's Crashaw. By now, Lord Linseley will have gotten him to stop, though. I'm sure I'm not in danger any more."

Lady Kate raised a hand in protest.

"Oh, don't worry, Kate. I've still got Mr. Stokes following me about. Poor man, he's probably freezing."

"No, I told my household staff to let him into the kitchen whenever he comes by—some nonsense about him being related to my childhood nurse."

"You think of everything. Thank you, dear."

"I try to, but I've probably forgotten something terribly important. Still, you must promise not to go out without Mr. Stokes's protection. Not until we hear from Lord Linseley that this business of the hate letters has been entirely laid to rest. Do you promise?"

"I do promise. I don't want to endanger anyone. I worry about you, after all, since you received that note. And of course I worry about poor Mr. Simms. He's so busy reassembling my household staff—I returned without warning, you know."

"You could have stayed here."

"Thank you, no. It's easier to become Marston again

where I'm surrounded by talk of seams and piping and the various grades of worsted fabric."

Her facial expression—Marston's veiled eyes and downturned mouth—was severe, discouraging further questions and shunning confidences of any sort.

Perhaps I shouldn't burden her any further, Kate thought. But she found it impossible not to try to offer a few words of encouragement.

"Lord Linseley will certainly contact us as soon as he can with the news. Of course it's only the dreadful condition of the roads that has prevented him from doing so already."

"Yes, I'm sure he will," was all that Phoebe seemed able to say. "Well, he's the perfect gentleman, isn't he?"

Kate reached for her friend's hand, but Phoebe shook it off. Her eyebrows rose above cold eyes, and her lips made the curve that Marston would typically affect, before launching into a critique of someone's new overcoat.

She spoke softly, in a passionless monotone.

"He's kind, well-bred, adored by tenants and servants, employees and neighbors alike. Oh yes, and he fucks like an angel. Well, you *were* curious about that, weren't you, though you were too proper to ask about it directly."

She stood up, staring into the middle distance and still speaking in the soft, dead voice that was neither Phizz nor Phoebe.

"I expect that he *will* contact Admiral Wolfe. But you see, I'm not at all sure that he'll ever speak to me again."

She swallowed and closed her eyes for a moment. When she opened them her face seemed carved of impenetrable marble, and her voice was that of Marston at his gayest and most trivial.

"*So* sorry to have to run away like this, Lady Kate. We shall have to chat again soon, though. Yes, thank you, *do* ring for Matthews to let me out.

"And be assured that I can see how well and happy you are, and although an old cynic like myself isn't good at expressing such a thing . . . please know that I do feel it. I *do* rejoice for you, with what's left of my heart.

"I know you'll forgive me any liberties I've taken this afternoon. Well, I *will* have my witticisms, you know. Of course, if a lady like you dares befriend a raffish type like myself she must bear the consequences . . ."

Her voice crescendoed as she made her way toward the door, becoming more resolutely cheerful with every graceful step she took. A smart bow from the hips now, a last wave of a long, elegant hand—and she was gone, leaving Kate to stare sadly after her.

The muck from the streets seemed to have distilled into a nasty, choking fog. Phoebe could hardly bear to breathe it as she traced her way along the walkway to St. James's Street, her boots perfectly invisible beneath her. Her stomach churned unpleasantly. Of course, she thought, it might have been her own ill-bred behavior just now that had brought on the queasy fit. I deserve it, she told herself.

She fought off the accompanying vertigo. The important thing was to keep her balance on the wooden plank. She thought suddenly of a tightrope walker, at a traveling circus she'd seen when she was a little girl. After the performance she'd hurried over to the field where the players were encamped, demanding to be taught how to balance on the rope. The lithe young man—Phoebe still remembered the sweat stains on his spangled tights—had laughed, lifted her up onto a practice rope, and had begun to teach her.

She'd loved it; for an instant she'd almost gotten the knack of it, too. But just then her mother had come running, screaming that she'd have the entire circus troupe arrested for kidnapping. Still, Phoebe had never forgotten the young man's instructions.

Choose a spot in front of you and look at that, she repeated to herself now. *Don't look down and don't look back.* Defiantly she turned her attention away from the horrors that plagued her imagination. On the one hand, there was the constant, gnawing fear that David had given her up entirely, infuriated by the secret she'd kept and by her betrayal of his hopes. And on the other, a still more terrible possibility: one she hadn't even wanted to speak of in Kate's salon. She swayed for a moment before regaining her equilibrium. Suppose he'd tried to follow her to London, and had been injured or even killed somewhere on the treacherous road between there and here?

A vision of a broken body on a lonely country road took shape somewhere beneath her, shimmering balefully in the yellow gaslit haze.

She wouldn't look down at it. Or *Marston* wouldn't, anyway.

Marston would think instead of the figure he'd cut at White's this evening, resplendent in his new waistcoat. He'd wonder if the oysters would be good; if so, he'd order them for supper, with caviar. Yes, a shining mound of black caviar in a massive silver goblet, served with a very dry iced champagne—the whole meal so expensive that he'd have to win hugely at Vivien's later in the evening not to feel bankrupted.

Marston would maintain his balance—just as Phoebe

was regaining hers now—by dancing exquisitely, at the very brink of a bad reputation.

And if, tonight, anyone asked Marston about how he'd happened to be traveling north with his enemy Lord Linseley, his answer would be, "But, my dear, dear chap, don't you know *already?* Ah, but I thought . . . well, everybody who's anybody *does* know, you see. After all, it's *last* week's scandal. *I'd* sooner dine on stale oysters than chew *that* old story over one more time."

Gossip, style, and gambling, she thought—in the end they were all a matter of standing firm behind a good bluff.

She walked quickly, on light, sure feet, to St. James's Street. She gazed straight ahead of her, staring at a fixed point in the distance: the amber glow of White's bow window, where, in her imagination, she'd already regained Marston's seat.

Chapter 25

Alec Hervey, the young Viscount Granthorpe, had never understood what his friends found so intriguing about gambling. He supposed that it had something to do with the speed of it—the breathtaking rapidity with which a vast sum of money could leave your pocket, as quickly as you could lay a few bits of pasteboard down upon a green baize table.

Or perhaps it was the dizzying abstractness of the concepts: what *was* five thousand pounds, anyway—and *where* was it?—if it could change hands so quickly, so meaninglessly, so utterly randomly?

But then, Alec found everything rather an abstract concept when he was under the influence of strong drink. The world began to resemble the neat, Newtonian patterns that fascinated him at school—though he knew it wasn't quite gentlemanly to enjoy his books as much as he did. He found it relaxing, nonetheless, to reduce things to mass and energy, velocity and acceleration. More pleasant than some of the human attractions and interactions he'd witnessed lately. Absently, he nodded his thanks as his companion poured more hock into his glass.

Of course, he thought, the motion of money in and out of a gentleman's pocket wasn't always a random matter. The notorious Mr. Marston, seated diagonally across the room from him, evidently had been winning steadily since he'd sat down to play an hour ago.

He looked down at his own hand. Nothing decent at all there; he'd lose the hundred pounds he'd just put down, as certainly as his father had lost ten thousand to Marston, in a game that Alec had been hearing about until he was ruddy sick of it.

What *had* all that been about, anyway? He'd resolved to ask Admiral Wolfe at dinner the other evening but had lost his nerve at the last moment. Of course, Alec could understand how Papa might have been rather desperate for cash after buying back all those enclosed lands. What made it all so strange—and rather embarrassing as well—was the other, whispered story, the one about him turning up at Marston's in the middle of the night and going off with him the next morning. Most people simply discounted it, but the story kept cropping up here and there, like a rank, unkillable weed.

He supposed he might have gone home and asked the old man directly. He'd rather wanted to go anyway, after having concluded that a certain young lady didn't care a fig about him. After a week or two it had become distressingly clear that she'd had her brother bring him home for Christmas simply to make her *real* suitor jealous.

But in truth he'd been rather timid about going to Linseley Manor. Not that he'd expected to find Marston there; everyone had said he'd gone on to Scotland, and anyway, he wasn't the sort of person one invited to a

Plough Monday festival. It was just that there was something unsettling about one's solid, responsible father having such a surprising connection.

The whole thing was probably just a rumor, Alec told himself. After all, Papa was hardly the type to . . . well, Alec wasn't exactly sure what he was defending his father against. Of course, his father wouldn't have minded if he'd asked directly. Alec couldn't remember ever having asked the earl a question that his father hadn't replied to honestly—even those difficult queries about one's body and its unruly desires. Perhaps, he thought now, this was why he *hadn't* wanted to ask about Marston. Perhaps he'd feared what he might find out if he had.

A house footman brought over a fresh deck of cards. Alec nodded to the dealer: yes, he supposed he would play another hand. What was another hundred pounds, after all? And thank you, another drink would be topping.

The cards from the used deck fluttered about his ankles. His head felt light. He saw immediately that his new cards were just as bad as his old ones. But this seemed to matter less with each hand he was dealt. Gratefully, he erased his troublesome thoughts from his mind and returned to his comforting private world of speed and motion.

If she weren't careful, Phoebe thought, the sight of David's son was going to ruin her concentration entirely. She'd been watching the young man since she'd come in an hour ago. Well, any woman would, she thought upon first seeing him. Impossible to refrain from looking at him, he was so young and ripe, his new adulthood sitting so lightly on him, like the blush upon an apricot. He seemed shy, a bit introverted and out of his depth; one wanted to protect him. It would be another year until one could feel entirely comfortable simply desiring him. She'd hoped he'd be ready for *that* when it happened: next year at this time he wouldn't be able to enter a room without raising a storm of lust.

Passing by his table, she hadn't known who he was. She'd been able to gull herself so thoroughly, she thought now, because his obvious resemblance to his father was altogether *too* obvious. She saw David's image wherever she went anyway; his face and body superimposed themselves over every passably attractive man who came her way. So she hadn't been surprised to see him in this radiant young man with the large, light eyes. She'd quickly discounted the evidence of her senses: *eyes light green instead of dark blue—there, you see, Phoebe, not the same thing at all.* She'd joined a table and turned her attention to her cards, taking ten tricks out of the next twelve.

"Are you in for the next game, Granthorpe?" she'd heard someone ask—perhaps after her sixth or seventh winning trick.

Granthorpe. Of course, she'd thought; how absurd not to have seen it immediately. Astonishing how one could will oneself not to know what one didn't wish to.

Raising her eyes now and calling for a new bottle of champagne, she could see that he looked drunk, bewildered. He's too young to be here, she thought. Someone should take him home.

She peered steadily at him until he flinched under her gaze and she had to lower her eyes. I mustn't discomfit him like this, she thought—after all, he's heard the gossip about Marston and his father. He'd be mortified to speak to me.

But *someone* ought to see to him. He was close to passing out.

It was her turn to deal.

A dreadful hand. No way to play it. She lost it gracefully.

There seemed to be some sort of altercation at his table. Someone had accused someone else of some misconduct. She could tell from the set of his shoulders that he intended to join the fight. Fight? He'd barely be able to stand up, she thought.

And if no one else in this room full of absurd, affected, posturing *men* was prepared to do anything about it—well, then the most absurd and affected of them would have to do so.

She made her apologies to the players at her table and strode quickly across the room.

"Get up. You need to go home."

He could barely focus his eyes upon her face.

Still, he wasn't too drunk to insist upon the proprieties. "Have we met, sir?"

"Allow me to introduce myself, Lord Granthorpe. Philip Marston. Luck all run out for the evening, don't you know. I wonder if you might like to share a cab. I'll drop you wherever you say."

A low laugh rumbled in a distant corner of the room. "Like father, like son." Hell, she thought, someone *would* have to say that right now, wouldn't they?

But perhaps it was an opportunity.

"And you may ask me anything you like—about recent events, you know."

She'd dared him to confront the truth, whatever it might be. Even as befuddled as he was, he couldn't refuse the challenge.

"All right, Marston. You may drop me at . . . Upper Brook Street. At my father's."

She slipped a hand under his elbow to help him to his unsteady feet.

Quickly collecting her winnings and their coats, she led him from the room. The amused murmur that had accompanied their encounter gave way to the usual busy, ambient hum at Vivien's. There were cards to be cut, fortunes to be lost. Weary gentlemen turned their attention back to the hands they'd been dealt.

Alec had surrendered himself to her firm grasp upon his arm. Of course, she thought, she wouldn't have to tell him anything about herself and his father; he'd pass out as soon as they got into a cab.

A footman opened the door. She led him out, into a swirl of gaslit yellow fog.

"That's Alec," Admiral Wolfe said, peering into the fog from the window of his carriage. "Rather the worse for wear, too. Got a cab quickly, though. Well, not too many people are leaving so early, the cabman's eager for the custom on such a filthy night. Who's the chap helping him, I wonder? Well, I'll just go lend a hand. He can come with us if he likes, of course. Good job, Kate, your suggesting we come here after the opera."

"The chap helping him is Phoebe," Lady Kate murmured to herself as she looked out the carriage door after John had stepped down. How strange to see Mr. Marston arm-in-arm with Lord Granthorpe. Or not so strange, she supposed on second thought.

She watched John make his way toward the two young men. Phoebe was intent upon holding Granthorpe steady; she hadn't yet noticed John approaching her. Kate glimpsed Mr. Stokes's reassuring bulk, lurking in the shadows. Good. She nodded approvingly: things were as they should be. When suddenly—she couldn't see very well in the fog, but suddenly things weren't at all as they should have been.

While the cabman was opening the door for Phoebe and Granthorpe, a man had suddenly run up behind John Wolfe. The man's silhouette obscured Kate's view of John; all she could see was his back and raised arm. Was he holding some sort of club? Kate heard a sharp, frightening, cracking sound. The man disappeared into an alley, and for a moment Kate thought that John had disappeared as well.

But of course he hadn't, for now she could see him lying sprawled upon on the cobbles. She heard a shout.

It must have been me who shouted, she thought; I must have called out when I jumped from the carriage. She had no memory of any of this, but there she was, kneeling beside John in a puddle of dirty slush.

But it hadn't been Lady Kate who'd shouted.

Let me out! She heard this second shout; with a start, Kate realized that the voice came from Phoebe's cab. Phoebe must have seen the attack, she thought vaguely; she'll help me, perhaps she'll call the police.

Right you are, guv'nor, the cabman replied cordially. Good, Kate thought, she'll be with me in a moment. Turning her attention back to John, she whispered a prayer of thanks. For although there was a cut on his head, he was breathing and his eyes were open. Ah, and here was Mr. Stokes, kneeling beside her.

"He'll be all right, my lady," he said. "A nasty cut is all he's got."

"Kate?" John's voice was weak, but he seemed to be trying to sit up.

"It's all right, dear. You weren't badly hurt, but lie back for a moment."

But where was Phoebe? "Mr. Stokes," Kate began, "would you please make sure . . ."

"I said *to let me out!"*

"*Gee-up,*" the cabman called, cracking his whip.

"Stop, you idiot!" Phoebe yelled. Kate turned, just in time to see Phoebe's pale face at the cab window. And to hear Phoebe's fist, banging at a door that must

have been locked from the outside. The cab jolted into motion and turned the corner sharply.

Mr. Stokes gasped.

"Go!" Kate whispered harshly, "Right now, Mr. Stokes. Take the admiral's carriage, we'll be all right."

He rose, hesitated at the carriage door, and instead, heaved his big body up beside the coachman. Bouncing on its springs, the carriage moved off in pursuit of the cab.

"If you scream once more, *Mister* Marston, I'll put a bullet through the boy's head right now."

She hadn't even realized that there was anyone sitting across from them. But it seemed that there was: a tall man holding a pistol pointed squarely at young Alec. He wore a dark, heavy cloak, his face muffled in a high collar. She couldn't see much of him, but she could easily make out the dull shine of metal in his hand.

His voice was distantly familiar. There was a nasty, cringing quality to it that chilled her.

"Who the hell are you?" she asked quietly.

He laughed, showing large, grayish teeth. "You don't recognize me without my livery, do you?"

He leaned a bit forward. Holding the pistol steady with one hand, he unbuttoned his cloak to reveal a footman's humiliating comic-opera costume: white ruffled jabot, velvet coat and breeches, in powder blue, the color worn by those in the service of the Dowager Lady Claringworth. The footmen had worn a brighter blue in the younger Claringworths' household, but the effect was very similar.

"Trimble?"

"At your service, my lady," he sneered, laying his hat on the seat next to him. His powdered wig caught the light from a lamp as the coach hurtled forward.

"But I don't have to call you 'my lady' anymore," Trimble added. "I can call you what you deserve to be called. Harpy, harridan, Circe, shrew. Well, I've already called you all those things, haven't I? Of course the word *I* wanted to use was the one the Dowager Lady Claringworth was too refined for. Bitch. Oh yes, I like the sound of that one. Bitch."

"*You* sent those letters?"

"I cut out the letters for my lady, at her request. Her hand can't manage the scissors these days, you see. And as to the content—well, that was her choice, though I made a few suggestions."

"Was it you who beat Billy so savagely?"

"A pack of amateurs did that. Misunderstood my instructions entirely. *We* had much more interesting plans for you and your dolly boy."

He laughed.

"Good for you, bringing a fresh new one with you tonight."

She glanced at Alec, seated beside her. Too bad, she thought, that he hadn't fallen asleep as she'd expected—at least he'd be saved the insulting filth issuing from the madman opposite them. Instead, he'd recovered from his drunkenness and seemed intent on understanding what had happened. Well, David *had* said he was quite formidably intelligent. Good luck to him, she thought, if he expected to make sense of *this* mess.

In any case, he wasn't about to make any misplaced heroic gestures or remarks. He was intelligent enough—and sober enough—to see that there was a pistol pointed at him.

"Just be kind enough to let Lord Granthorpe off at

his father's house in Upper Brook Street. You can do anything you like with me after that."

"Granthorpe, is it? Convenient, that. Missed the father with the chandelier, but we'll get the son instead. *She'll* enjoy that, I think."

You can't, Phoebe was about to scream. *He's innocent.* And then, for the first time, she began to wonder. *Innocent of what, exactly?*

"And just *what* was my crime, Trimble?"

"*Mr.* Trimble."

"Mr. Trimble, then. Just what have I done to make you and the Duchess hate me so?"

"You had no respect."

"No respect?"

"None at all. Well, who *were* you, anyway? While *our* household was among the highest of the *ton*—still is, of course, well, my Lady Claringworth's a patroness of Almack's, can't get much higher in the world than that, you know.

"And my young gentleman . . . the very image of a gentleman he was, made me feel important to be in his service.

"You could have been the image of a lady, too. Well, you had the looks for it. And he spent more to dress you than he did to stable his horses. And yet, day in and day out, *you* managed to make him feel stupid. 'But Henry,' you'd say, in that high-minded way of yours. 'But Henry, don't you think . . . ?' 'But Henry, consider the plight of the Red Indians . . .'

"It was the happiest day of my life—and his mother's too, because of course I brought the news home to her—when he finally took a hand to you.

"But you wouldn't be stopped. I don't know how you did it, but you made him feel worse and worse, even those times he'd use his cane . . . I watched through the keyhole, I did, wish it had happened more often. *Finally,* I'd think, he'll show her what's what. But you'd just take it. Couldn't you have pled for his mercy? Couldn't you have asked for forgiveness? Couldn't you have let him win one, just once? Not you. You'd just pick yourself up and walk out of the room."

There was nothing she could say. For she *couldn't* have asked for forgiveness—not when she'd known that she had done nothing wrong.

Poor Henry. Trimble was right, he'd been the very image of a gentleman. All image and no substance whatsoever.

And although *she* remembered their last months together as an endless humiliation, evidently it hadn't seemed that way to him. Somehow he'd never been able to degrade her as he'd wanted. As badly as he'd treated her, it had never been enough to elevate himself.

Of course, she reminded herself, mistreatment of others rarely did much for a person's sense of self-worth. Most people simply knew this fact—from a quick look at the pitying expression on Alec's face, she suspected that he'd known it from babyhood. How sad that Henry had never learned it.

"We thought that you'd died. But when we discovered that you'd survived and were disguising yourself as a gentleman . . . and taking pretty boys to bed . . ."

"*One* pretty boy." Somehow she wanted to make that distinction very clear to Alec.

"One pretty boy and one meddlesome earl," Trimble corrected her.

Alec nodded slightly, having finally worked his way through the plot. Quaint young man, she thought—he looked so satisfied to have understood the situation that he didn't seem worried about the danger he was in.

"What do you intend to do with me? And with Lord Granthorpe?"

"Well, you'll just have to wait and see, won't you? Won't be long now. Sit tight, we're almost there."

It was one thing, Archie Stokes thought, to have followed Marston's carriage almost to Devonshire, in daylight and over open country roads. But quite another to figure out which of the identical black cabs traversing a crowded midnight Piccadilly was the one he wanted.

He supposed that was what they'd intended. Clever buggers. He hated it when his adversary was clever; seemed like cheating, somehow. They could have taken her anywhere—her and Lord Linseley's son. Stokes shuddered, imagining having to confront his employer with *that* failure.

He couldn't imagine it—which meant that he couldn't let it happen. *Think, Archie, where would they take her?* For there was no point pretending that he hadn't utterly lost sight of her cab. He'd simply have to go where he was sure they were going.

For he *was* sure. That was the odd part of it. He had no idea who the villains were, but after all this time he'd learned a little about how they saw things. And what he knew was that, in all the foggy vastness of midnight London, with its countless filthy alleys and dens of iniquity, there was only one place they wanted to do their mischief. Same place they'd dumped Billy. Same place they sent their hateful letters. They could *hurt* her anywhere. They wanted to despoil her home as well.

"Turn right," he told the coachman. "We're going to Brunswick Square."

"Dash it, if only I'd brought the pistol that I keep under the seat of my carriage," Admiral Wolfe muttered. "It's useless to Stokes, since he doesn't know where it is."

He'd insisted, over Kate's objections, on getting up and walking around. But he'd been right, she thought. He was quickly becoming steadier on his feet, and the blood no longer flowed from that ugly cut. Still, he did look rather dreadful, livid from the shock of the blow, crusted with dried blood, and soaked in the muck of the streets. Rather as she must look, she suspected.

She reached for her bonnet, but she seemed to have lost it somewhere. He smiled. "You're beautiful tonight."

They could be arrested for making a spectacle of themselves, she thought, two filthy, disheveled, no-longer-young people, kissing passionately beneath a street lamp.

"I have enough money in my pocket for a cab," he said. "But in which direction do we sail, mate? Where do you suppose they've taken their hostages?"

She squeezed his hand. "I should have mutinied, you know," she said, "if you hadn't asked 'where do *we* sail?'"

"I know."

"It could be anywhere, I suppose." She frowned. "I can't imagine what's in their minds, even though I'm pretty sure I know who's behind this. We could go to the . . . culprit's house, perhaps. But her servants would simply tell us she was asleep.

"No, there's only one place to go, John. I don't know if it's wise or stupid, but please tell the cabman we want to go to Brunswick Square."

"There's nothing for it, Elizabeth," Mr. Andrewes lit the bedside lamp. "I can't sleep not knowing where Simms is: I'm going to Brunswick Square to look for him. Of course I don't expect Miss Phoebe home yet, but your brother likes his sleep. If he didn't come home tonight, there's something amiss, you can count on it."

"Quite right, dear," his wife replied. "He *should* be home by now. But he's so conscientious, wanted everything to be perfect when she moves back in tomorrow, you know. You must be very careful, though."

"Hmm, wish I had some weapon more prepossessing than a tailor's rule. Ah, I'll take the poker from the fireplace."

The last soldier in this gathering ragtag army had only now reached the outskirts of London. Chilled, exhausted, muscles sore from riding over miles of icy road, he tried to encourage his horse onward, but the poor mare was just as tired as he was. He'd have to feed and water her before he proceeded. Perhaps he should simply tether her somewhere, risk having her stolen, and take a cab. Well, at least he still had food for the horse. He'd finished up *his* provisions—the pie and cold goose—many miles ago.

Still, Lord Linseley thought, the accident and injury had been worth it. He'd passed over impassable roads. He was here, just as he'd promised himself. Well, almost here. Just a little more to go, David, he told himself, and you'll sleep in Brunswick Square tonight.

Chapter

26

The cab did, in fact, soon make its way to Marston's house in Brunswick Square. Trimble hustled Phoebe and Alec out of the vehicle and up the front steps, warning them that if either of them made a sound the boy got it then in the head.

How strange, Phoebe thought: the house was all lit up, as though Marston was giving one of his intimate late night parties. Four large, strapping footmen stood at attention in the front hall, quite ready, from the look of them, to usher guests into the salon or dining room. But the only guests were she and Alec; the tall, smirking men in velvet breeches were here to keep everyone else away.

"Up the stairs," Trimble said now, half-dragging, half-shoving them to her bedchamber.

This room was particularly bright; the flame in every gas lamp, it seemed, had had been turned as high as possible. It took a minute to adjust her eyes after the dimness of the cab. And so Phoebe heard her enemy's voice while her enemy's face was still taking blurry shape before her eyes: Fanny Euston, Lady Claringworth, a feeble old woman grasping a heavy cane in shaking hands. Solicitously, Trimble took his place beside her chair.

"Good evening, Phoebe." The old lady's voice was harsher and weaker than Phoebe remembered, but it still carried considerable authority. Out of habit, she almost began the little bobbing nod of respect that her mother-in-law had liked, almost a curtsey. She stopped herself—to hell with curtseys—and stood very tall in front of the armchair, with Alec at her side.

"Good evening, Fanny." Before this moment, she'd never called her mother-in-law anything but "Your Grace."

"Show a little respect," Trimble hissed.

The old lady laughed, if the harsh sounds accompanying the rictus seizing her face could be called a laugh.

"She's always been arrogant." Her voice came out a wheeze. "You could fairly taste her rudeness, even when she was pretending to be otherwise. Why should tonight be any different? The only difference is that tonight she'll die for it. As she should have done before she ever got her hands on my poor Henry."

"Found her with a boy, did you?" She seemed to be speaking to Trimble now, though it was difficult to follow the movement of her eyes. "Splendid."

Trimble nodded proudly. "Lord Linseley's son, my lady. Of course, I haven't yet told them what's in store for them. I thought you might like to, my lady."

"Well, it's simple enough," Lady Claringworth seemed impatient. "We shoot both of you—you in the heart, him in the side of the head, as though he'd taken his own life after taking yours. We'll arrange the tableau after you're dead, of course."

Of course. Phoebe wasn't surprised. What was surprising was how calm she felt. There could be a way out of this, she thought, if I can think this out very clearly.

Ask them some questions, she told herself. *After all, they're proud of themselves, and it's not as though they're going to be able to dine out on it. Give them a chance to boast.*

"But why should he shoot me?"

"How silly of me to forget to tell you that part. But my mouth is dry. You tell her, Trimble, while I drink some water."

"He kills you, the police will surmise, because he's just discovered that Phizz Marston is a woman. It shocks him, you see—just as the scandal sheets will shock everyone with the news."

"And how will it be apparent that he's discovered I'm a woman?"

"Well, what do you think? When the police come to investigate, they'll find you half naked. Take off your coat; it'll save us the trouble. Yes, that's good. And the cravat now, too."

She shuddered to lose the protection of those garments, but she complied. Nasty, she thought, looking at the white linen at her feet, to end up as an item for a scandal sheet.

The old lady had laid down her cane while she picked up a glass of water from a table beside her. The cane would make a formidable weapon, Phoebe thought, if she or Alec get hold of it. If they just were a little closer to it. If the plan she was quickly conceiving could be put into action.

"It's a terrible thing you're doing," she said slowly.

Trimble sneered. "You deserve it."

"I suppose I do," she answered. "Because you're quite right. I had no respect at all. I still don't. But I'll get down on my knees and beg you for Lord Grant-horpe's life if you wish. And so will he."

He *was* an intelligent boy, she thought. For he'd quickly fallen to his knees beside her—a few inches closer to Lady Claringworth's cane. But he'd need to be a few inches closer still, which meant that she'd have to put on a very good show, in order to distract attention from him.

Well, actually there *were* a few things she wanted to say.

"It's a tragedy to lose a son," she began softly. "You know it is, Fanny, though you often forget that I lost one too, that terrible day.

"A terrible tragedy. *Two* terrible tragedies in one moment. But there was a *third* tragedy as well, Fanny. Think of it. Two women lost beloved sons and couldn't comfort each other. Couldn't help, couldn't even share a kind word. Things might have been different, you know, if we could have." She was astonished to feel a tear trickling down her face.

Phizz Marston never cried. And, except for a very few tears a week ago, Phoebe hadn't cried since the accident. But she was weeping now. Not for Bryan, or even for herself exactly. In some odd way she was crying for an officious old woman she'd always loathed.

"And now you want to cause another tragedy. You want Lord Linseley to lose his son, who he loves as much as we loved ours. When will it stop, Fanny? When will you understand that you can't cure loss with loss?"

Lady Claringworth stared ahead blankly: it was impossible to know what she was thinking. Trimble, of course, had quite enjoyed the spectacle—the tears especially. But Phoebe had meant every word. She'd almost forgotten that she'd had any ulterior motive for getting down on her knees.

But Alec hadn't forgotten. While Phoebe had monopolized the attention of their captors, he'd quietly laid hold of Lady Claringworth's cane. And now, in a quick, elegant arc, he moved its tip directly against her windpipe.

Trimble blinked.

"If you shoot me," Alec told him calmly, "the bullet's pressure will probably cause a spasm of my arm, pushing it upward in the direction of her cane, and strangling her as I die. You see, the velocity of the spasm of a dying man's muscle . . ."

"Oh do shut up," Trimble groaned.

"I beg your pardon, Your Grace." Alec gazed solemnly up at her with wide green eyes. "I wasn't brought up to treat the old and infirm with anything but respect. But I'm afraid that my current situation makes that rather impossible."

"What a lovely job of raising you your parents did, Alec," Phoebe murmured. "However this all ends, I'll be happy to have met you."

For it wasn't over. After all, Trimble still had a gun. And she recognized the expression on his face; she'd seen it often, across the gambling tables. It was how a man looked when he couldn't decide if he was facing a bluff.

He *might* still shoot Alec, she thought, if he decided that the boy had been bluffing. And for all she knew it *was* only a bluff, this business of a spasm of velocity, or the velocity of a spasm, or whatever it was he'd said.

The ill-assorted quartet in Phizz Marston's bedchamber stared at each other, frozen in their perilous tableau like courtiers in Sleeping Beauty's castle. Phoebe wondered what could break the spell.

She hadn't expected the fearful row that suddenly broke out downstairs. Mr. Stokes must have followed me here, she thought. Mr. Stokes or . . . someone. She heard a woman shouting. Kate. And now she could hear Admiral Wolfe as well.

Furniture was being smashed, vases were crashing. It was impossible to know who was winning.

Not that it would have mattered to the quartet in the bedchamber. Trimble still pointed his gun at Alec, and Alec still held the cane pressed against Lady Claringworth's throat.

The noise was abating somewhat downstairs. One side or another must have prevailed.

Lady Claringworth spoke in a shaking voice. "Put down the gun, Trimble. She's right. It can't go on forever."

"Sorry, my lady, but I can't agree. The boy's bluffing." He began to squeeze the trigger, when a shot rang out from the doorway. Trimble's gun fell to the floor, and bright red blood—like a Christmas poinsettia, Phoebe thought wildly, how tasteless—spouted from his shoulder.

Phoebe looked up in amazement. "Mr. Simms?"

He looked equally surprised, staring at the pistol in his hand as though he didn't know how it had gotten there. "I've never shot one before. It's the admiral's . . . I was hiding in the wine cellar, you see, until our friends arrived. And I knew the back way here, through the passageway that leads to the partition in your dressing room."

He leaned against the wall, his eyes rolling a bit. She ran to embrace him, to hold him steady. "I've been so frightened for you, Phoebe," he whispered.

And now here were John and Kate, Mr. Stokes and Mr. Andrewes. Evidently their side had won the battle—"Well, we had a hero of Trafalgar directing our strategy," a very disheveled, very exhilarated Lady Kate Beverredge explained. "Those footmen will never escape from the nautical knots the admiral made in your new curtain ropes, Phoebe."

"Here, Alec," the Admiral Wolfe called, "let's see how you've done tying up this fellow in Phoebe's curtains. And let's bandage his shoulder, too, with some of that lace."

The house would have to be redone again, Phoebe thought.

"But won't the police be coming?" she asked. "To investigate all this ruckus coming from my house?"

"They won't." Everyone turned to stare at Lady Claringworth in her armchair. Her voice trembled, but she spoke loudly enough. "I bribed the constabulary to ignore the sound of shots coming from this house tonight. Much as Lady Kate bribed the authorities a few years ago, to fabricate Henry's wife's death."

Kate cleared her throat. "There are a few irregularities about this case that I think we shall want to keep a secret amongst ourselves."

"But did you always know the truth then, Fanny?" Phoebe asked.

"Indeed I didn't. It was only after I'd hired a detective to try to trace the stolen jewels. I wanted them, you see, because Henry had bought them."

She loved him, Phoebe thought. Fanny hadn't loved her son very wisely, but Phoebe knew she couldn't hate the old lady for that.

"I'll give you some of the jewels that are left," she said, "to remember him by."

"Well," she corrected herself, "those of them that I won't be selling in order to renovate this house once more."

"If I stay," she added wistfully.

She stared with wonder at the collection of people crowded pell-mell into what had recently been a dandy's exquisite bedchamber. What an ill-assorted group we are, she thought, as motley a collection as the characters in the Plough play—and just as deeply engaged in the struggle of life against death.

It was late; they were tired. If only, Phoebe and her friends agreed, they could just take their bows and go home. If only there weren't the nasty fact that murder had been attempted tonight—and had been attempted last week in Lincolnshire as well.

Yet even fastidious Mr. Simms had to agree that—given the unorthodoxy of the situation—it might not be the wisest course of action to inform the police of tonight's events. There was, for example, the matter of Mr. Marston not legally existing—which might prove rather a disadvantage, Alec speculated, when calling upon the law. The circumstances of Phoebe's death might also be questioned.

They debated the situation's legality and morality, wondering just what *was* the proper punishment for an infirm old woman who'd been maddened by grief? And if none of them felt quite right about punishing Lady Claringworth, what did that mean about the servant who'd never learned to live except as a tool of his masters' warped desires? It looked rather as though Trimble might lose the use of that pistol hand anyway, the admiral observed. In the end, after freeing the men tied up downstairs, they sent the old lady and her head footman home together, to take care of each other—and perhaps to serve as each other's punishments.

It was almost four in the morning by then.

"We'd serve you breakfast," Phoebe said, "if there were any food in the kitchen."

Kate shook her head. "I want to go home and go to bed."

"Right you are, my lady," Mr. Stokes's yawn could have served as a landmark for travelers, so awesomely cavernous was it.

"You'll come back with Mr. Andrewes and me, won't you, Phoebe?" Mr. Simms said.

She smiled as she retied her cravat. "Well, it is where most of Mr. Marston's clothes are. And Marston's most at home where his clothes are."

If Marston was really what she wanted anymore.

"And will you go back to your hosts, Alec?" she asked.

"I'd rather not," he said. "I said I'd be going to my father's. They'd be surprised to see me turn up, and anyway, the young lady of the family . . ."

His boyish face so obviously bore the wounded look of "rejected suitor" that everyone tried to look quite solemn on his behalf.

"I'll walk to Upper Brook Street with you," Phoebe said, "and then I'll go to the Mr. Andrewes's."

Perhaps she wanted to stay with him a bit longer because they had risked their lives together. Or perhaps it made her feel a little closer to David. In any case, she didn't want to bid him farewell just yet.

They were the last people to leave the house in Brunswick Square. Phoebe locked the door behind her.

"It's hard to know what I'm locking in except a lot of broken pottery and torn upholstery," she said. "Or what I'm locking out, given what we've been through tonight."

He laughed, and his laugh turned into a massive yawn.

"Poor boy," she said, "you're more tired than you thought. Shall we hail that cab that's just come around the corner? It looks like it's going to stop nearby."

The cab stopped right in front of them, to let out a tall, weary-looking gentleman, who stared with astonishment at the two of them standing in the light of a street lamp. And then, as he registered Phoebe and Alec's equally incredulous stares, he began to laugh until his dark blue eyes grew moist.

"Is this some sort of dream?" he asked. "The two people I most love in the world together like this? I haven't somehow died on the road and gone to heaven, have I?"

David and his son exchanged a hug disguised as an awkward, half-embarrassed clap on the shoulder. Phoebe was amused by their mutual masculine reticence, and jealous as well. For *she*—who would have given him a proper hug—couldn't touch him at all, except for a handshake.

"And good morning to you, Mr. Marston."

He put enough warmth into the handshake to make her forget her jealousy. She forgot to take her hand out of his; both of them forgot that Alec was watching. For a timeless instant they simply clasped hands and gazed at each other in a most ungentlemanly fashion.

"Marry me," he said.

"With all my heart," she replied.

Laughing, they shook hands on it, in a completely gentleman-like manner now. Each of them shook hands with Alec as well, receiving his congratulations.

"But what on earth has brought you two together like this?" David asked.

"Gambling." Alec said quickly. David raised his eyebrows.

"It's true," Phoebe said. "We became friends while playing for high stakes. Alec is a wonderful bluffer, you know." Which remark quite convulsed Alec with laughter, all the more to see his father so befuddled.

He turned now, in the direction of Upper Brook Street. "I'll just hurry on," he called, "and let the older generation follow."

How naturally tactful he was, Phoebe thought.

"He's a lovely young man, David," she said as they set off behind him. "You're right to be proud of him."

"We actually were just on our way back to your

house," she added. "There's rather more to the story, of course. But it can wait until later."

"Well, I have a story, too," David said. "Rather an amusing one, about Lord Crashaw."

"It wasn't Crashaw," she said softly. "I learned that tonight."

He shrugged. "No, it wasn't. But it seems that my story can wait too. What's important is that you're safe."

She smiled up at him. There would be time for all the stories, but no story could be as important as the happiness she felt walking alongside him this morning, this first in a lifetime of mornings together.

The stories they'd tell each other would be complicated, ironic, compounded of the oddities of human nature in all its surprising twists of thwarted or satisfied desire. But what she felt right now was much simpler, and only needed the simplest of words to express it.

"I wasn't safe, but I am now. Let's go on home to bed, shall we, David?"

Epilogue

Lincolnshire, 1824

Admiral and Mrs. Wolfe had had glorious weather for their drive up from London. They weren't expected at Linseley Manor until tomorrow, but Phoebe had said that it wouldn't matter exactly when they arrived. "We're so occupied with the haying that the days are rather a blur," she'd written in her last letter, "but we shall adore seeing you whenever you turn up."

"And she also said that when she and the earl were busy, little Kathy would have to entertain her godparents," Kate added. "Which will be both useful and agreeable, since we need practice with children anyway."

Complacently, she surveyed the slope of her own rounded belly. "Kathy will be a year old soon. Just about when this one arrives, John. Fancy that."

He smiled. "And I always pooh-poohed the healing powers of David's Plough play."

"We're almost there now," he added. "Shall I drive up the wold? We can get a good view of David's lands from there."

"Do, the sunset is delicious."

The wide sky above the wolds was most beautiful, perhaps, during the gold and purple evenings of harvest time. The admiral stopped the horses on the top of a gentle rise. From their barouche, he and Kate could see miles of countryside framing the harvest scene spread below them.

Haycocks, their shadows growing long, dotted the golden field. Workers were making their way home, waving their good-nights to the tall gentleman who stood holding a wide straw hat in his hand. As the last of them disappeared over a rise, he turned now, toward the hay wagon, atop which a slender figure in overalls stood leaning on a rake.

The person in overalls pulled a scarf from her hair, letting the breeze blow pale chestnut curls around her shoulders. Laying down her rake, she seemed to be calling something to the gentleman in the field.

From their barouche atop the hill, of course, Kate hadn't been able to hear what Phoebe had said. Nor what David had replied, when he's strode to the wagon and lightly swung her down. He still held her now, but lightly, gazing into her upturned face and taking her right hand in his left.

But Kate didn't need to hear the words. For both she and John could easily discern the language of trust and love and ever-renewed desire engraved in the long curve of Phoebe's torso. How elegant she is, Kate thought, even in those clothes—and how eloquently she leans into the strong hand at the small of her back.

A stronger breeze had started up now, bending the high grasses in its long wake. Moving into the curve of her husband's arm, Kate smiled up at him, both of them stirred by the wind's rippling caress of the hills sprawling around them.

And both of them watched silently as Lord and Lady Linseley, alone in the field now, began to dance: a slow waltz, under a darkening purple sky, to a tune that only the pair of them could hear.